W9-AUB-407

SEBRING

Orland Park Public Library
14921 Ravinia Avenue
Orland Park, Illinois 60462
708-428-5100

JAN – – 2016

SEBRING

Kristen Ashley

ORLAND PARK PUBLIC LIBRARY

Ashley,
Kristen

4/19
LAD 7/31/17
rc—11

License Notes

All rights reserved. In accordance with the U.S. Copyright Act of 1976, the scanning, uploading, and electronic sharing of any part of this book without the permission of the publisher is unlawful piracy and theft of the author's intellectual property. Thank you for your support of the author's rights.

This book is a work of fiction. Names, characters, places, and incidents are the product of the author's imagination or are used fictitiously. Any resemblance to actual events, locales, or persons, living or dead, is coincidental.

Copyright ©2016 by Kristen Ashley

First ebook edition: January 11, 2016
First print edition: January 11, 2016

ISBN-10: 0692573763
ISBN-13: 9780692573761

Discover other titles by Kristen Ashley at:
www.kristenashley.net

Commune with Kristen at:
www.facebook.com/kristenashleybooks
Twitter: KristenAshley68
Instagram: KristenAshleyBooks
Pinterest: kashley0155

WARNING

THIS BOOK IS an ADULT EROTIC romance featuring an anti-hero. This novel contains explicit scenes of pain play, domination (control) and bondage. The hero in this novel lives a life by his own code with no apologies. In an effort not to spoil it for you, I will not explain further about the hero, but he is most definitely not your (or my, in my other books) "normal" hero. If you do not enjoy the above, I would suggest that this novel is not for you.

AUTHOR'S NOTE

With *Sebring*, I complete my Unfinished Heroes Series.

Though, as you'll find, nothing is ever complete in the worlds that live in my head. I can't say good-bye, so I don't ask my readers to.

What I will ask of you is to find the song "Stay Alive" by José Gonzalez. If you're not already familiar with this extraordinary song, I make the request that you wait until you've hit Chapter Twenty-Five before you cue it up in order to experience its beauty along with the scene I wish for it to accompany.

I often offer soundtracks to play with my books because, as I type them to give to you, they play like movies in my head. And everyone knows, the soundtrack is essential to the experience.

But "Stay Alive," along with every song I've ever heard by the masterful Gonzalez, is essential to life.

I took chances with this series, starting with *Knight* and onward through the tortuous beauty that followed with *Creed, Raid* and *Deacon*. As ever and always, I thank my readers, my fabulous Rock Chicks, those who had a direct cheerleading hand in the birth of this series (and you know who you are) to those who championed it simply by buying the books.

I love it that you love my worlds.

As much as I may try to explain how much, no words can express it.

I'm blessed by legions of champions.

How do you express gratitude for that?

The only way I know how is to give you the best story I can.

To that end, I hope with all my heart you fall in love with *Sebring*.

You're here forever and you're by my side.

Prologue

FOR HER

Nick

"Nick."

He was sweating. His wrists torn raw. His muscles strained well beyond pain. The gag in his mouth filthy, and not just with his blood and saliva.

His eyes were locked to hers.

"Nick."

As the asshole made his approach, his gun aimed to her head, he didn't speak. Didn't touch her. Didn't take off her gag and let her say a thing.

She was speaking, though.

To Nick.

Her eyes were filled.

With love, as usual.

And fear.

"Nick!"

He jolted awake.

Instantly gripping the wrist at his shoulder, his body knifed up and twisted off the couch. Yanking the wrist up a man's back, Nick forced him forward with the intent of shoving him against the wall.

"Nick," the voice was soft now. "Brother."

That voice hit him, the fact the man wasn't struggling hit him, he let him go and stepped back.

His brother, Knight, turned to face him.

Bending slightly, Knight switched on a light by the couch. Through the now-illuminated room, he caught Nick's eyes.

"You're not sleeping well," Knight told him quietly. "Heard you all the way down the hall."

This wasn't good. He was sleeping on his brother's and his woman, Anya's couch. They had two little girls. Little girls needed their sleep. What they never needed was their uncle losing it down the hall and waking them.

Nick tore his hand through his hair and turned his head away, muttering, "Sorry."

He felt something and twisted his neck, looking to the doorway where Anya was standing, wearing a long, gray cashmere robe, her beautiful face troubled but her eyes were warm on him.

Knight saw her too.

"Go back to bed, baby," he called gently.

She didn't look from Nick. "You need anything, Nick?"

"I'm good, Anya," he lied. "Sorry I woke you."

"It's okay," she whispered, her face no less troubled, her eyes still warm but also concerned and moving to her man.

"I got him," Knight told her.

She studied his brother, nodded, threw a small smile Nick's way and disappeared out of the doorframe.

Nick walked to the big windows that were two sides of the corner room of Knight's and Anya's high-rise condo. Windows that now showed the lights of a nighttime Denver.

He glanced at his brother before looking at the city. "You can go to bed too, Knight. I'm okay. It'll be good. And tomorrow, I'll find somewhere else to crash."

"I think right now you need to be with family."

At Knight's words, Nick's mouth got tight.

He didn't deserve that. He knew it.

But Knight was giving it to him. So was Anya. Both of them having reason to spit right in his face.

He felt Knight draw nearer and stop.

"We haven't been close," Knight told him something he knew. "But what you were doin'. Why you were doin' it. What you lost—"

Oh no.

As much as he owed his brother in a lot of ways, they were not going there.

Nick cut his gaze to Knight and bit out the question, "Can we not do this now?"

Knight looked into Nick's eyes a beat before he answered, "Yeah. We can not do this now." He moved closer and dropped his voice low. "But, Nick, we gotta do it. You gotta talk that shit outta you, brother. What they did to your wo—"

"Can we...not...talk about this now?" Nick repeated through clenched teeth.

Knight nodded. "It's too soon."

It fucking was.

They blew a hole in her head right in front of him two fucking days ago.

So yeah.

It was way too fucking soon.

"You're here," Knight decreed like his big brother was prone to decreeing, this happening Nick's whole life. "You're here with your family until you can sleep easy. I'll give you time. We'll talk it through later." He held Nick's eyes as he lifted a hand and curled it around the side of Nick's neck, squeezing firmly. "But just gonna say, fuckin' proud of you. I'm sorry for you. I hurt for you. But I'm fuckin' proud of you."

Nick didn't want that to feel good.

He'd spent his whole life wanting that from his brother. His father. Fuck, even his mother, who loved him like crazy, had spoiled him, but he knew she didn't think he'd amount to much. Not like her glory boy. Not like she knew her Knight would do.

And she was right, everything Knight touched turned to gold.

Nick had also spent a lot of time and energy trying to beat the need out of himself to make his family proud.

Then he'd spent a lot of time doing whatever he wanted to do to feel good despite knowing they wouldn't, chase whatever highs life offered to drown out that need, convince himself he didn't give a fuck what they thought.

And when his brother took what Nick wanted, namely Anya, Nick had pulled some lame-ass bullshit in order to try to tear them apart. Bullshit that, if it was Knight who did it to him, he wouldn't give a fuck two days ago the woman Knight loved had a hole blown into her head. He would not be standing in his sweet crib telling Knight he was proud of him.

But the fact remained it felt good, his brother giving him that. It felt good because it was from Knight.

And it felt good because he knew Knight was right to be proud.

Last, it felt good because he knew *she* died proud of her man.

Even with all that, he just muttered, "Thanks."

Knight took his hand away. "Watch a movie. Read a book. Try to get some rest."

He wouldn't be doing any of that. He still nodded.

Knight studied him a second then nodded too and walked out of the room, saying before closing the door behind him, "See you in the morning."

Nick turned his attention back to the lights of Denver.

Within moments, the city went out of focus and all Nick could see was his reflection in the glass. He could also feel the sweat trickling down his spine, pooling around his balls, the agony radiating through his muscles as he struggled against the restraints.

He lifted his hands and looked down, seeing at his wrists the scabs, deep scratches and pus-colored broken skin of cuts so deep they had not yet begun to heal.

He'd used those hands. For once in his life, he'd used those hands and his head and his gut and his strength and his courage and everything he had in him to do right.

Not for himself.

Not for his dad.

Not for his mom.

Not for Knight.

For her.

The mission had only marginally succeeded.

But she was gone.

Three Weeks Later

"I'M OUT."

Nick said this firmly, looking right into FBI Special Agent Eric Turner's eyes.

"I get that," Turner replied quietly.

Nick didn't want to give him what he had to give to him next. He didn't used to be that guy. He didn't used to be the guy who found it in him to do the right thing.

But the man he was now, the man she taught him to be, he gave it to him.

"You were right. I shouldn't have gotten involved with her."

"Shit happens, Nick," Turner responded. "It was really her as an agent who shouldn't have blurred those lines but that can happen to anyone. I had a job once. A job that involved a girl and it happened to me. I fell for her. It wasn't right but I couldn't stop it. I lost her too." His gaze grew intense as he hid a flinch. Knowing he'd said the wrong thing, he finished quickly, "Not like you lost Hettie. But I fell hard for her and she's still not mine."

Nick didn't want to sit around listening to Turner telling tales he hoped would help Nick feel better. Turner knew no words would make that happen.

There was only one thing that would make Nick feel better.

Turner knew that too.

Which was why he asked, "You gonna stay in town?"

Fuck yes, he was gonna stay in town.

"Yeah," Nick answered.

At that, Turner did what a lot of people were doing these days.

He studied Nick closely before he said, "Doesn't feel like it, but with time, it'll hurt less. It just will, Nick. Give it time and then get on with your life."

Turner had no fucking clue what he was talking about. He didn't know what girl Turner fell for but if she wasn't dead, never to see her again, never to smell her hair, taste her pussy, listen to her laugh, eat the fried eggs she always broke the yolk when she flipped them over, knowing she wouldn't give that to him or to *anyone*...

If he didn't survive that then he had not one *fucking* clue what he was talking about.

Nick did not share this.

He just repeated, "Yeah." Then, to turn the subject, he said, "Talked to Knight, Raid, Sylvie, Marcus, all of 'em. Had to, Eric. Their women and families were targeted. They had to know what we were doin', why we were doin' it and how they were gonna use anyone that was close to me or Knight in order to use him to get to me to stop us from doin' what we were doin'. My brother and his crew also dragged my ass out of that hellhole so they had to know why I was there in the first place."

"Not thinkin' any of those folks will talk," Turner muttered in reply.

He was absolutely right.

Nick nodded.

His gaze still intense, Turner stated, "We were planning an extraction, Nick."

Nick nodded again, this time sharply.

He didn't want to go there.

"I know you were," he said in an effort to stop Turner from talking about it.

He did know that. Turner wouldn't leave Nick hanging. He definitely wouldn't leave Hettie that way.

"Your brother and his crew, they don't have to worry about the rules like my crew does," Turner explained. "They could go in hot. They could take those risks, no plan, flyin' by the seat of their pants."

"I know," Nick replied.

"We were comin' for you," Turner went on. "You and Hettie."

Nick didn't repeat himself.

They were. It was still too late. When Knight and his crew tore in there to save his ass, they were too late too.

Too fucking late.

"Coupla weeks, we'll go for a beer," Turner suggested.

It was Nick's turn to study him.

"You do that a lot with your ex-CI's?"

Turner suddenly looked pissed. "Jesus, Sebring, the shit we been through the last coupla years, you seriously think you're still just a confidential informant to me?"

Now that...

That felt good.

Nick had not had a habit of surrounding himself with good people.

And Turner was definitely a good man.

"Fucked thing to say," Nick muttered.

Turner's face again changed. He might not have any clue how bad it was but he still got where Nick's head was at.

"Coupla weeks, buddy," he said quietly.

Nick nodded.

Unexpectedly, Turner was whispering, "Be smart, Nick."

Yeah. He knew.

But Special Agent Eric Turner had taught him a lot.

So he also knew Nick had some of the skills he needed to get the job done.

And she'd taught him patience.

He'd acquire the skills he didn't have. If it took him a decade, he'd do it.

Then he'd get the job done.

Five Months Later

NICK STOOD BY the river, its banks covered in tiny but bright bursts of wildflowers, the spring thaw of the mountains having subsided, the rush of water still heavy but also soothing.

He felt him coming before he came to a stop at Nick's side.

"Me and Cassie are glad you showed," Deacon Gates said to him.

"You put a pink bow on your dog," Nick replied.

"I didn't," Deacon returned.

"Your woman put a pink bow on your dog," Nick said then turned to look at the man at his side. "And that dog is a German shepherd. It's a wonder every shepherd breeder in North America isn't rushin' this location to put a gun to your head to demand payback for that dog's dignity."

Deacon grinned at him, shrugging one shoulder. "It's a wedding."

It was.

That day, in a gazebo by a river in the middle of fucking nowhere in the Colorado Mountains, the man known throughout the dark, harsh, fetid, hostile underbelly of this great United States as Ghost got married to one of the most beautiful women Nick had ever laid eyes on.

She was also one of the most down-to-earth.

Nick had been around Cassidy Swallow-now-Gates a number of times since it all went down and that day was the first he'd seen her wear makeup.

Even made up, her hair done in big, soft curls, pulled back at the top and sides, pins hidden with fixed daisies, she still got married in a long white cotton dress that had a two foot deep hem of lace at the bottom but other than that it just looked like a seriously fucking pretty sundress.

"Happy for you," Nick muttered, looking back to the water.

"Worried about you," Deacon responded.

Nick returned his attention to Deacon.

"See it in your eyes," Deacon went on quietly.

He would. Deacon had seen the same in the mirror for years.

Nick knew Deacon's story. Nick knew Deacon descended into that foul underbelly to find his missing wife. Nick knew Deacon stayed there after what he did but especially after what he found when he located his wife. Nick knew this not because Deacon shared this information liberally to anyone who might listen. Deacon didn't say much to anyone, except the woman he loved, the woman an hour ago he'd made his wife.

But in the past months Knight had rallied the troops to try to pull his brother's shit together. To yank him out of his grief. To steer him from the path he was determined to tread, even if Nick had not shared that shit with anyone either.

But Knight knew.

Deacon knew.

Rhash, Raid, Marcus, Sylvie and Creed—Knight's closest friends and strongest allies, now Nick's friends—they all knew too.

If the same happened to them, this was the path they'd be on.

With no chance of veering off.

"I need you to teach me," Nick said straight out.

A muscle jumped in Deacon's cheek.

"You know I need you to teach me," Nick pushed. "You know if you don't, I'll get someone else to do it. You know, Deacon."

"Your brother wants—"

Nick shook his head. "Love my brother, means everything to me how he's kicked in. How he's given me his family to help me get through. But sometimes Knight can't get what he wants. You know this is one of those times. Fuck, *he* knows this is one of those times."

Nick looked beyond Deacon to the wedding-goers milling about the wild-flowers, the streamers, the balloons, the tables laden with food and booze, to a band setting up well beyond the gazebo.

He looked back at Deacon.

"Enjoy your wedding. You deserve it, man. Enjoy your honeymoon. You're in, we talk when you get back. You're not, no hard feelings."

Deacon moved closer.

Nick braced.

"You just looked at what I got," Deacon's voice rumbled low. "I thought I lost it all and you just saw all that behind me. Streamers. Balloons. A fucking German shepherd with a pink bow around her neck. And a woman tied to me I couldn't even build in a dream. You can move on. You do not need to do what you think you gotta do."

His voice suddenly raw, Nick whispered, "I had my woman I couldn't build in a dream. And I sat, tied to a chair, powerless to do anything, looking right into her eyes when they blew a hole through her head. That mission is not complete. Our mission. The one I had with her, *our fucking mission*. It isn't complete. There's work to be done. For her."

They locked eyes.

They didn't move.

Deacon broke it.

"I'll teach you."

Nick nodded.

Deacon drew breath into his nose.

Then he lifted a hand and slapped Nick on the arm before he turned and walked to the woman that was now his wife, a woman who was beyond even a dream.

1

HIS GIRLS

Olivia

Four Years Later

"Liv, you need to come...*now.*"

I lifted my gaze from the electronic ledgers I was entering numbers into in my computer to see Tommy, his scarred but still handsome face tight, standing in the door to my office.

I knew that look so I didn't delay in rolling my chair back, pushing to my feet and moving swiftly across the floor his way.

I didn't give anything away in any way, not ever. I didn't raise my voice. I only allowed the minutest reactions to show on my face, to leak from my eyes, to set in my frame.

So my voice was soft because it was always soft, and without inflection because it was always without inflection, when I asked, "Who does he have?"

"Green," Tommy answered as we moved quickly down the hall.

Green.

One of my men.

My soldier.

Green was not his real name. It was a nickname my older sister, Georgia, had given to him. It had been Georgia who had used her special skills to recruit him years ago. He was so eager, and so stupid, fresh, naïve…*green.*

And that was who he became.

He was no longer stupid, fresh or naïve.

But he was still Green.

I walked down the hall, my strides fast but restricted due to the tight skirt I wore.

As I did, my mind was moving from annoyance at what I was certain was happening in my father's office to wondering for perhaps the thousandth time why he insisted we continue to do business in this foul, possibly rat-infested warehouse.

It was the middle of a sunny day and the hall was ill-lit and murky, the floors filthy, the walls grubby.

Even in my office, which I'd insisted—like Georgia had with hers, like my father had always had with his—was clean and decorated (mine with a classic elegance; Georgia's a modern sharpness; Dad's a lavish obnoxiousness)—the windows were grimy (on the outside).

But my father's father started the business there. Now Dad felt it sent a message. He was convinced in its top-to-bottom filth that it terrified anyone who might think they shouldn't take us seriously.

He also felt it said we were one with our roots.

He was right.

My grandfather had been a lowlife thug who was willing to do anything for money and power.

And he did.

He'd done very well. He'd built an empire.

My father was also a lowlife thug with the same mission.

He wasn't as successful.

I saw the double doors at the end of the hall, Gill standing outside them.

But I heard my father shouting.

"Is Georgia around?" I asked, eyes to Gill, my question aimed at Tommy who was at my heels.

"Nope," Tommy answered.

That was not good.

I had very little hope of calming my father down. There was a slim chance, but it wasn't much. I had more chance of earning his ire. His temper was quick, unpredictable and volatile. Although he seemed more in control of it around Georgia, otherwise, he didn't discriminate.

But without Georgia at my side, or better, taking the lead, the highest likelihood was that whatever this was was not going to go well.

We got close to the door and Gill turned to it, knocked twice, loudly, put his hand to the handle and pushed it open.

My father's shouting didn't cease throughout all this.

Gill got out of our way and Tommy and I moved into the room. A room that was ridiculous. It had been ridiculous when my grandfather sat behind the massive, ostentatious desk. My father had just made it more ridiculous.

I had no time to ponder this oft-pondered thought.

Dad was shouting.

And he had a gun. A gun he was aiming at Green.

In other words, the situation was critical.

"Dad——" I called, moving into the room, but abruptly stopping and unable to fight back the wince and twist of my head when the gun went off, the loud sound cracking through the room.

Green shouted in agony and dropped to one knee.

Dad rounded the desk and advanced on his soldier, gun still raised.

"*You tell me that shit?*" he screamed. "*You talk to your king that way?*"

God, I hated that *king* business.

My grandfather started that too.

"Jesus, fuck, Jesus, *fuck*," Green chanted, still down on a knee, one hand to his wound, blood oozing between his fingers. He tilted his head back and scowled at my father. "What the fuck's the matter with you? You shot me!"

"You fuckin' *turd*! You do!" Dad shouted. "You talk to your king that way!"

I turned to Gill who was standing in the door.

"Call Dr. Baldwin," I ordered.

"Liv, Baldy's not our biggest fan," Tommy muttered under his breath behind me.

I nodded slightly, eyes still on Gill, knowing that but forgetting at this dramatic juncture that my father had alienated Baldwin some months ago. "Tell him I requested his attention personally."

Gill nodded back and disappeared.

I cast my gaze over my shoulder to Tommy. "Get some towels."

"Olivia, you do not need to be here," Dad stated, and I looked to him.

"Dad—" I started.

He swung the gun my way.

Tommy, who had been moving toward my father's bathroom, stopped and moved back, positioning in front of me so I still could see my father but Tommy's body was mostly shielding mine.

God. Tommy.

I watched Dad's eyes shift to Tommy before I watched his mouth curl.

"Take a bullet for her, yeah?" Dad asked derisively.

Tommy had been playing the game a long time. But he'd also been taught a lesson he had no choice but to learn.

He knew the right answer.

"She's yours, so yeah."

Dad stuck his nose up in the air, sniffed his approval at that response, then lowered the gun.

He glared at Tommy. He glared at me. Finally, he turned to Green.

I tensed.

"I fuckin' see you again and you still aren't doin' your job, I won't aim at your leg. You hear me?"

I fought a sigh.

I saw Green's teeth go to his lip and I knew exactly what he intended to say. I was pleased he managed to beat back the urge and instead fell to his hip and put both hands to his wound.

Dad stalked my way. "Get his ass outta here, Olivia. Get him producing." He indicated Green behind him with a swing of his gun. "And clean this shit up."

With that, he walked out the door.

"Towels, Tommy," I reminded him quietly.

He jerked his head and moved to Dad's bathroom.

I moved quickly to Green, crouched and dropped forward on my knees.

"We'll get you to Dr. Baldwin. He'll sort you out," I murmured.

"I'm done, Liv," Green clipped.

I drew in a careful breath and looked in his eyes.

"Fuckin' asshole's lost his goddamned mind," Green went on. "Knew it already. He didn't have to shoot me in the fuckin' leg to know it. But definitely know it now."

"Eli," I called him the name only I called him occasionally after Georgia christened him Green.

"Stuck it out for you, babe. Did what I could. But I gotta fuckin' eat," he bit out.

"Georgia is working on——" I started, knowing it was a waste of breath.

Green was done and I didn't blame him and not simply because my father had shot him in the leg.

"*He* calls *me* here to kneel before him and explain why I'm not moving product?" he cut me off to ask incredulously. "Then *he* loses *his* mind when I remind him I got no product to move because all his shit has dried up because he's a fuckin' lunatic and no one wants to do business with him? And Liv, you gotta be a *serious fuckin' lunatic* for the lunatics in this business not to want to do business with you."

"He's under a lot of pressure," I stated as Tommy approached, squatted close and pressed a clean towel to Green's leg.

"Yeah, Liv, he is. That is not lost on me. That isn't lost on any of the fuckin' minions he treats like minions even though nearly two fuckin' *decades* ago, Leon Jackson cut off his balls and served them up. Vincent Shade ate his own balls and he did not grow those balls back. Leon bit it, his wife ruled his roost and dug your dad's hole deeper. She got outta the game, Valenzuela stepped in. He never got his shit together to win his patch back."

He shook his head impatiently but gave me no chance to reply. He kept talking.

"I am not tellin' you shit you don't know. Shit like the fact that Denver's only got two real players left. Marcus Sloan, who acts like your dad doesn't even exist, and Benito Valenzuela, who doesn't bother fuckin' with your dad because he knows he's a fuckin' joke. Hell, Seth Townsend's still in prison and he's got more pull on the street than your dad."

"You are, of course, telling me something I know," I confirmed, about to go on, but Green continued explaining a situation I knew all too well considering the fact I lived and breathed it.

"Sloan's got the guns because he wants to control who's usin' 'em on the streets. Other than that, he's gone legit. Valenzuela has the rest, Liv, and there's no gettin' it back from him. Only outfit who might have the power to see that through is that crazy MC and only because the brothers of the Chaos Motorcycle Club are fuckin' *crazy* and they got bigger balls than practically anybody."

"Green—" I tried but got no further.

"Pot went legal, we got even more fucked, 'cause that's all Valenzuela let us have. He's got the rest of the dope. He's got the whores. He's got the film sets. He's got the protection racket. He's got state senators eatin' at his table. He's got that prosecutor bitch lubed and beggin' to take more of him up her ass. He's got *it all*. Your soldiers been existing on dregs for you, whatever Georgia can drum up for us to put on the street, which isn't much and it sure as fuck ain't quality, and I'm not the only one who's done."

This didn't surprise me.

It concerned me, but it didn't surprise me.

I was, of course, their team leader, as it were. They were all my soldiers. They answered to me. They also communicated with me. So I knew this all too well.

"Eli, Georgia has had a series of meetings with Valenzuela in an effort to—"

"He wants her to suck his cock," Green declared. "After she gets on her knees, he wants her bent over his desk. He does not take her seriously, Liv, and please God, tell me one of you Shades are smart enough to know that's the mother-fuckin' truth."

I made no reply because I was the one Shade who *did* know that.

"You know," Green whispered, eyeing me closely. "Only one with a god-damned brain in your head, *you* fuckin' know. Your dad is done, Liv. He's so fucked in the head, it's not fuckin' funny. Livin' in the past, thinkin' he's still coastin' on the legacy his father left him. This shit…" He indicated his leg. "Him still thinkin' he's king of the scene when no player acknowledges him, suppliers from here to Colombia to fuckin' Afghanistan knowin' he's a joke, that shit he pulled four—"

All of a sudden his eyes jerked to Tommy's hands on his wound then to Tommy's face.

"*Fuck, man, what the fuck?*" he clipped.

"We need to get you to Baldy," Tommy stated.

"Yeah, only reason Baldy will look at me is 'cause he's sweet on Liv, but you get that, don't you, Tom?" Green asked.

Tommy's eyes flashed.

I quickly shifted closer to Green.

"How about we focus on sorting out your injury?" I suggested.

Green turned his attention back to me and the look in his eyes held pain but also intensity.

"Get out, Liv," he urged, his tone intense too. "Get the fuck out, gorgeous. He will drag you down. Georgia's blinded by bullshit, thinkin' she can resurrect her legacy. She'll go down with him and she don't fuckin' care, so loyal to a whackjob, she's totally fuckin' lost. But you know better. So get...*the fuck*...out."

I held his gaze before I rolled back to my feet and straightened to standing.

I looked to Tommy. "Let's get those towels tied tight and then get him up. I'll find something to use as ties and call Gill to bring a car around."

Tommy nodded.

I moved to my father's desk.

"Man, you give even a minuscule shit about her, and I know you do, *you* get her out and far away from him." I heard Green advise Tommy as I moved.

It didn't come as a surprise that Tommy didn't answer.

I found nothing at Dad's desk that we could use for Green's wound and was headed to the bathroom as Tommy called, "Bring another coupla towels, Liv. I'll rip one, use the strips. But need another clean one. This one's soaked."

I nodded to him, got the towels and brought them to Tommy.

He took them and started ripping strips immediately, doing this with his bare hands.

I didn't watch Tommy's strong hands tear the towels to shreds. Strong hands I knew could be gentle and sweet.

Tommy was off-limits to me. We'd both learned that the hard way.

I looked to Green.

"Done, Liv. You won't see me again," he said when I caught his eyes.

That hurt. I liked Green.

No.

Loved him.

I loved all my boys.

I never told them this. That wouldn't do. I was a Shade, but that wasn't all there was to it.

I'd learned. I didn't allow myself to show emotion.

Ever.

I still knew my boys knew it. I went to bat for them. I protected them. I did the best I could for them. And I didn't hide it.

So they knew and the look in Green's eyes, his concern, wasn't the first time he didn't hide he felt that back.

"But I gotta eat, babe," he repeated as explanation.

"I understand, Eli," I replied.

Green stared at me a moment before he shook his head.

"That…that right there states plain this is not the business you're meant to be in," he declared.

I drew in a breath to speak but Green kept talking.

"Your sister's not as dumb as your old man. She knows, you lead their soldiers, we'd all march over a cliff for you. She's got a pussy tastes like sugar and acid in her veins. Men'd do a lot for sugar but they eventually learn to steer clear of acid since that shit burns and leaves scars that never go away."

Again, on Green's comment, I avoided Tommy's eyes.

This time, Green did too.

He also kept speaking.

"So she gave you to us. You give a shit. You let that show. You treat us like family. Keeps us motivated. Keeps us devoted. But not a single general in an outfit like this should let a soldier go with an, 'I understand, Eli.'"

I knew that too.

"You want her to put a bullet in your brain?" Tommy asked and Eli looked to him.

"She couldn't do it. But you'd do it for her, all she had to do was ask."

"You're right," Tommy replied.

"And she'd never ask," Green returned. "And that's why we're all totally fuckin' devoted. Just like you," Green said to Tommy and looked to me. "But we're not dumb, Liv. All a' us gotta eat."

I said nothing.

"You should put a bullet in my brain," Green whispered.

That was a warning.

I felt Tommy's eyes come to me.

But I held Green's.

"I'll never do that," I whispered back, hoping he'd take my meaning that he shouldn't burn any bridges. Instead, he should disappear.

"That means you need to get far away, Liv. This life's gonna eat you alive."

I felt Tommy's intensity.

But I had only one answer for Eli.

"It already has."

I watched anger flare in Green's eyes as his mouth went hard.

Tommy tied the bloody towel to Green's thigh before he shifted, shoving a broad shoulder under Green's arm to heft him up.

Green grunted.

I took them in, giving them both a nod before I moved quickly to Dad's desk and grabbed the receiver from the phone.

I hit a button and turned to watch Tommy and Eli make their slow way to the door.

Gill answered on the second ring.

"Bring the car around, will you, Gill?" I requested. "Tommy and Green are on their way."

"You got it, Liv," Gill replied and disconnected.

I put the phone back in the cradle and saw the boys had disappeared out the door.

I took a moment to look around my father's office, not knowing why because I'd memorized every inch of purple damask-papered wall, every etch in the heavy, dark wood, every swirl in the silk rugs that cost so much entire villages in developing countries could live on it for years.

I did this thinking Green was gone in more ways than one. If he was stupid, which I hoped he wasn't, he'd go to Valenzuela or Sloan. He'd offer his services. He'd offer information.

If that happened, Dad would make the order.

Georgia would have it carried out.

Gill would do the deed.

If he was smart, he'd get out of Denver and find work elsewhere.

Then Dad would forget him and my sister would offer her sugar pussy to whatever green recruit she'd make promises of living large, drowning in Cristal, fucking on soft beds covered in greenbacks.

It wouldn't take long before the fresh one would learn.

We had very few soldiers left and all of them were uneasy.

Except Tommy.

Because of me.

And Gill.

Because of Georgia.

Green was right.

I should get out. I should get away. I should go to Thailand. Bali. Any end to this earth where he wouldn't find me.

I didn't because I knew that place didn't exist.

Vincent Shade had lost nearly everything his father stole, dealt, stabbed, lied, tortured and killed to get.

But there were two pieces in the chess game he played very poorly, a game that just happened to be our livelihoods, pieces I'd learned without a doubt he'd never lose.

Not ever.

His girls.

2

SHE'LL HAVE COMPANY

Olivia

My phone was ringing as I drove into my garage.

After I turned off the car, I grabbed it and looked at the screen.

I took the call before I shifted out of my white Range Rover Evoque.

"Hello, Pam," I greeted my real estate agent, moving to the door that led to the house, clutch under my phone arm, my other hand out to hit the button to close the garage door.

"Hey there, Olivia," Pam replied. "Listen, that couple that looked at your house on Monday, they wanna come back tomorrow."

I walked to my marble kitchen counter and dropped my clutch to it, responding, "Excellent."

"They have to come in the evening. Around five thirty. Can you do something after work so they can see the house?"

Could I do something after my work of managing drug dealers—who these days had no drugs to deal—and keeping a variety of books for really *not* legitimate enterprises my father ran very poorly, considering we barely had any money—as well as laundering said money, how little of it there was?

"Yes," I answered.

"Great!" she cried. "I'll let them know and set it up. This is looking good. We haven't had a second visit since we put your place on the market."

That day was apparently my day for people to tell me things I already knew.

Because I already knew this, I had no reply.

"I'll keep my fingers crossed we'll have an offer by Friday," Pam carried on.

"I will too," I said. "And if you can have their agent tell you when they're done, I'd appreciate it if you'd text me when I'm good to come home."

"Of course," she stated.

"Wonderful. Thank you, Pam. Have a good evening."

"You too, Olivia."

I took the phone from my ear and disconnected.

Then I looked around my house.

From my position standing in the acres of extraordinary ivory, russet and bronze-veined marble countertops and custom-made cream cupboards, I could also see the kitchen seating area (which was not a place to eat…it was a place to sit on couches by a fireplace and converse). I could also see the great room, the formal dining room and vast expanses of wood-that-was-imported-from-Europe floors.

It looked fabulous, as it would. I was responsible for every inch of fabric, every stick of furniture, down to the ribbed silver or mirrored Kleenex box holders.

It was like my office. Classic elegance, except more refined.

I did not hesitate to congratulate myself on wringing a miracle, because even with its extreme beauty, it was also welcoming and comfortable.

I loved it.

But it had to go.

It had to go because, along with all I'd mentioned, there were also four bedrooms, a casual family room, a game room, a study, a "mom's room" (that looked like a place set up to make crafts or wrap packages, as everyone knew it was *mom's* job to be craftsy and wrap presents), a laundry room that was as big as a bedroom, a larder that was as big as most full baths and a master suite that the Queen of England would feel comfortable in.

This didn't count the mini-me-mansion guest house with its own sitting room, small kitchen, bedroom and bath at the back of the property.

All of this (save the guest house, of course) was in a u-shape flanking an in-ground, heated swimming pool with a massive mosaic-tiled deck. This situated on a huge lot situated in Governor's Park, in other words, smack in the middle of the city proper of Denver.

It cost millions of dollars.

It was too much for me.

When viewing it, as gorgeous as it was, I'd wanted nothing to do with it.

But when I moved out of my father's home, he would not hear of me living in one of the lovely high-rises that straddled the south side of the city that offered two- to three-bedroom condominiums.

A Shade lived like a Shade.

Not a *real* Shade, those being degenerate criminals, two of whom hid this behind Christian Louboutin shoes and Givenchy blouses.

But the Shades we showed the world. Those of us left who had not escaped my grandfather's need to perpetuate a massive, grisly, scheming, brutal *Fuck You!* to those many who thought (rightly) they were better than him as well as to those who didn't care either way.

Namely my father, because even if Georgia lived in a fabulous penthouse apartment, she thought her place was too much too.

Therefore, since my father wanted me to have that house, I had no choice but to have it.

Now, it wasn't only too big for me—a single woman rambling around what could be described as nothing other than a mini-five-thousand-square-foot-mansion—we couldn't afford it.

Dad's rambling manse would never go. He'd die in there in a shootout rivaling the Alamo before he'd let anyone take it from him.

And Georgia was turning a semi-blind eye to the money situation, aware of it but certain she could do something to turn it around while breaking her neck to do just that.

But I kept the books. I knew.

So my house was on the market and neither of them was stupid enough to say a word, because even if neither of them would admit it out loud, both of them knew why.

I walked the warm-colored wood floors of my hall, past the informal family room, the study, these separated by a powder room, both to my left. To my right was a series of arched windows and French doors that led to the deck and pool.

I arrived at the end of the hall where my bedroom suite was. This included a comfortable sitting room, his- and hers-walk-in closets and a colossal bathroom that had a dressing area at the back with a built-in dressing table that any fabulously wealthy housewife would give her eyeteeth for.

Alas, none of them were in the market for a house. I knew this since mine had been available for four months with only one second viewing that hadn't even happened yet.

I sat on the side of my bed and was toeing off my pumps when my phone in my hand rang again.

I looked at the screen and wished I didn't have to take the call.

But she'd called yesterday and I hadn't called her back. I knew the headache I'd catch when I stopped avoiding her was not worth the peace of mind avoiding her afforded me.

So I took the call.

"Hello, Mom," I greeted, leaning back into a hand in the bed.

"I called you yesterday, Olivia."

More of someone telling me something I already knew.

"I'm sorry. Something came up and took my attention," I lied.

She let my lie go and decreed, "We're having dinner. I've had my assistant make a booking for us at Beatrice and Woodsley next Wednesday evening."

Why my mother needed an assistant, I had no idea. She didn't work. She'd never worked.

But why she called her assistant "my assistant" I did know. Because they were slaves to her.

Since slavery was abolished in the United States some time ago and most people didn't like to be worked like one, they told my mother how they felt about it. Therefore she had on average six "assistants" each year. In other words, they weren't around long enough so she didn't bother with their names.

I wanted to go to Beatrice and Woodsley. It was a fabulous restaurant.

I did not want to spend two hours with my mother frowning at every morsel I put in my mouth (even though she'd dragged me out to dinner in the first place), nonverbally (and sometimes verbally) sharing she thought I needed to watch what I ate even if I was smack in the middle of the healthy weight range for my height.

I also did not want her (contradictorily) to encourage me to drink my weight in vodka, something she would do while she pushed her food around on her plate.

Nor did I want to listen to her telling me what a reprobate my father was, even though I personally arranged the monthly kickback my father gave to Mom's second husband, the president of a local shipping company. I did this at my father's command in order for my stepfather to offer his services should Georgia's machinations bear fruit and we needed something illegal shipped in or out of Denver and we couldn't use our own legitimate shipping company as that would be stupider than my father's usual stupid.

A kickback my mother was highly likely aware of because my stepfather might run a large, successful shipping company but she had his testicles in a vice and he barely took a breath without her permission.

No, I did not want any of this.

"I'll be certain I'm free," I told her.

"Excellent," she replied crisply.

I knew it would be a wasted effort, but I did my next anyway because I was me.

"Would you like me to see if Georgia's free?"

This was a wasted effort because Mom and Georgia had not spoken in three years. This began after Georgia lost her temper at Bistro Vendôme and let her mouth loose when Mom had a variety of things to say about Dad, much of this centering on the swelling and cut at my upper lip.

Swelling and a cut my mother knew who delivered on me.

My sister was her father's daughter.

But she was *my sister*.

She might have always been and continued to be the golden child (when I was never anything close, though it must be said, I never actually wanted to be), but we'd been through a lot together. She was loyal to our father and she was loyal to me. She loved us both. This to the point I honestly didn't know if Dad and I were both drowning, which one of us she'd save.

Anyone who knew us would say Georgia wouldn't hesitate. She'd dive in and drag Vincent Shade to safety.

But I knew there was a fifty percent chance she'd grab hold of me.

And this was why she lost it with Mom, not because she was loyal to Dad and Mom was saying ugly things about him.

Because when Mom got fed up with Father making her life a misery, she took off.

And she left her girls behind.

But she fought tooth and nail for alimony.

Georgia knew I bore the brunt of Mom's leaving. She knew I continued to bear the brunt of our father's disposition.

She knew Mom knew it too and did nothing about it, not then, not ever.

So now they didn't talk. I suggested opportunities to both of them to heal the breach, but three years had passed and I suspected thirty more would before Georgia would show at Mom's grave and spit on it.

"No. I. Would. Not," Mom answered my question.

Obviously, she felt the same way.

I sighed.

"Would you like me to have my driver come to get you?" Mom asked frostily.

Her driver was also her "driver" seeing as he or she too would likely be replaced in a few months (or weeks).

"I can get there myself, Mom. Thanks," I replied.

"Good. Then see you at seven o'clock Wednesday at the restaurant. Good-bye, Olivia."

There was no, "In the meantime, how are you?" Or, "What's my girl doing for fun these days?" Or, "Are you, by chance, seeing someone?" Or, "My darling girl, I'm worried about you. You're thirty-one years old and you haven't had a steady boyfriend since your father tortured that handsome blonde man and did what he did to you when you were twenty-five. I'm aware you can be alone, but I don't want my daughter to be lonely."

No, none of that.

Mom just disconnected.

I felt no loss that my mother didn't care even a little bit about me, taking me to dinner because it was her duty, something she'd tell her friends about, woe-is-me'ing about my weight, my hairstyle, my manicure or whatever she found fault in.

I was just grateful the call was over.

I was in the kitchen looking into the refrigerator and considering calling Bistro Vendôme to see if they had a table for one open when my phone rang again.

I moved to the counter to look at it.

The screen said GEORGIE CALLING.

Normally, I did not avoid my sister's calls.

That day, however, my father had shot Green. Green had then been transported to Dr. Baldwin who took care of his wound for ten thousand dollars in cash. After that, Green had either disappeared or begun to make overtures to Marcus Sloan or Benito Valenzuela.

None of this would please my sister Georgie.

"Hey," I greeted quietly.

"Are you fucking kidding me?" she replied.

I leaned into a hand on the counter. "I walked in, Dad shot him. There was nothing I could do."

Even with my life as it was from the minute I could cogitate, it still was not lost on me how completely insane it was that anyone would utter those two sentences, including me.

"Your boys get an order from Dad, they tell you. They don't just show up at Dad's office and tell him shit he already knows, pissing him off enough to grab his fucking gun and take a shot at one of his own men."

"They have that instruction, Georgie, but I talked to Tommy after he got back from dealing with Green and Dr. Baldwin. Tommy told me that Gill picked up Green. He took his phone. Dad still has it. And I've no doubt he did that because he wants money coming in and he knows I've given that instruction to my boys. So he's not getting straight answers because they come to their meets with me in tow and we feed him information everyone knows is bogus so he won't lose his mind and, say, shoot one of his own men."

"*Fuck*," she hissed.

I said nothing. I wasn't the kind of woman who rubbed it in when I was right.

"Green is gonna bail," she declared.

I said nothing to that either because this time, she was right (except about the "gonna" part) and I wasn't about to confirm that just in case she was in a *seriously* bad mood and decided to do something about it. If Green intended to disappear, I wanted him to have as big a head start as he could get.

"He sniffs around Sloan or Benito, Liv..." She made the statement and trailed off so she didn't have to make her threat verbal.

"You need to have a word with Gill," I advised. "He can't do that again. He has to work with us to keep Dad from tying our hands."

"I'll talk with him," Georgia muttered.

She would. She'd do this before and/or after she fucked him.

Gill would come to heel.

I wondered if I should monitor the rats in the warehouse since, if they abandoned a sinking ship, perhaps, even in a warehouse, they'd do the same and this would provide forewarning when the house that Clive Shade built was going to come crashing down.

I again knew it served no purpose to say what I was next going to say considering I'd mentioned this to my sister repeatedly and she'd ignored it repeatedly.

I didn't give up.

"We need to focus on the legitimate businesses, Georgia."

"Facilitating the export of dart guns is not going to keep you in your house, Olivia," she retorted.

"Perhaps not, but that's not all we have and we don't pay enough attention to any of it, including the man Dad has handling it."

Now it was me saying something she knew, mostly because I'd been sharing my concerns about this now for years.

But David Littleton was Dad's man. A friend from back in the day. They'd met in grade school.

So David got to do what he wanted.

"David is good," Georgia decreed.

"David has too much power and not enough oversight."

"Then oversee him."

My back shot straight. "Is that permission?"

"Fuck yeah," Georgia said. "What do I care?"

Georgia was my big sister.

Georgia was also heir to the throne.

Therefore, Georgia was higher up on the hierarchy. I had autonomy to manage our soldiers and keep the books, but I deferred to her in all other matters.

"You didn't want me interfering before," I pointed out.

"My baby sister wasn't selling her house so we could inject that cash into our operation before. Deal with David. I don't get what you get from him so you don't have to bother telling me I'm right if you find out I am. But I also don't do our books. Goes without saying, if I'm wrong, I want to know."

"Okay, Georgie."

"And I've got some stuff I've been working on for a while. Things are looking good with it. Once I know it's solid, we'll make a meet. Okay?" she asked.

"Yes," I answered.

I wanted this to be promising.

As hard as my sister worked and had done it for years, with the results of that so far I was not holding too much hope.

"Great, sis. Go out tonight. Have fun," she ordered. "See you tomorrow."

"All right. See you."

She disconnected.

I dropped my phone hand to the counter but just stared at it.

I looked behind me to the fridge.

There wasn't much in it.

I should go to the grocery store. Or I should call Bistro Vendôme and see if they had an opening. Or perhaps even find a nice, trendy bar with good lighting and expensive cocktails and go there, people watch, find someone to fuck then come home.

I looked from the fridge to my house which needed to be sold. I only had a few hundred thousand dollars-worth of equity in it, but with Dad shooting soldiers and ten thousand dollars in cash going out to doctors, not to mention other bills, salaries to pay—we needed every penny we could get.

I had a dinner appointment with my mother in a week.

I had a father who was out of his mind and no matter how much Georgie worked and I schemed and scrimped, he was going to bury us. I knew it.

I'd never see Green again and I'd miss him. He'd always been sweet and respectful to me. Also, I worried there was a good possibility I wouldn't see Green again because Dad or Georgia would make it so no one would see him again... ever.

And I knew the last load of product Georgia had managed to get her hands on was of inferior quality, but more importantly, it was running out. If Georgia didn't get the boys something, Green wouldn't be the only one to go in one way or another.

I just knew the only two who couldn't go were Georgia and me and I was probably the one who wanted to go most of all.

With all this on my mind, I didn't go to the grocery store or call Bistro Vendôme. I also didn't go for a drink at a nice bar.

I went to the closet in my bedroom and direct to the wall safe installed there. I opened it and grabbed one of the four burner phones I kept in it.

I engaged the phone, went to contacts, scrolled down to B. Ross and hit her number.

I put the phone to my ear.

"Ms. Lincoln," a woman answered. "It's been some time."

Now even Ross was telling me something I knew.

"Yes," I agreed. "I know it's late notice but do you have any openings tonight?" I asked.

"In the private salons, I'm afraid not."

I drew breath in my nose.

That was disappointing.

"However, we've had no one book in the social viewing chamber," she went on. "And it's late in the day and quite rare for anyone to call at this time. Although if another booking comes in, I must accept, at this moment, you would have the social chamber to yourself."

I looked to my watch. It was well after six. Normally when I went to the club I would call days in advance to be certain to have a private salon.

But what did it matter? I'd go. I'd enjoy a drink. I'd enjoy the performances, perhaps in the company of someone else, but who cared?

After that, I'd come home and take care of myself, making myself come hard. And maybe I'd sleep without everything weighing down on me, making that sleep restless and inadequate, which meant I'd wake up exhausted with puffy eyes and no motivation to take on the day. But rather, I'd sleep well and get up with some infinitesimal motivation to take on the day.

"I'll book the social chamber," I told her.

"We'll see to that," she replied. "When can we have your drink waiting for you?"

"I'll be arriving at ten thirty."

"We'll see you then, Ms. Lincoln."

"Thank you, Ms. Ross."

"My pleasure," she said then disconnected.

I took the phone from my ear, called Harry and set him up to pick me up to take me to the club.

That settled, I moved to my fridge in order to make a salad.

———

Alias B. Ross

B. ROSS PUT the phone down on Ms. Lincoln and moved to her purse in the back room. She took out her personal cell and scrolled down the contacts. She found his name and engaged.

She felt her heart beating hard. Since she first saw him, he'd always made her heart beat hard. He also made her pussy get wet. Not to mention a variety of other things.

"In the middle of something, babe," he said as greeting, sounding distracted.

She hated it when he was busy (or distracted), which was often. Before she'd had him, when she made excuses to contact him, and especially after she'd had him.

"She's coming," B. replied on a whisper, head bowed.

She didn't want any staff to hear. When at work, they were banned from making personal calls.

Though, since this was an order from her boss, it wasn't exactly personal.

Still, he'd made it clear he wanted this matter treated with the utmost confidentiality.

And she was a girl who lived to serve.

"What?" he asked, now sounding a lot less distracted.

"She's coming. Tonight. Ten thirty. I told her all the salons were booked. She's in social, where you asked me to put her."

"Do not put anyone else in there," he ordered. "And cameras off the minute you leave her in there."

"Okay," she agreed. "Does that mean you're coming?"

"Yeah."

Her heart skipped.

"Just so you know, I'd tell another client who shows that someone else is expected in the chamber," she told him. "She's never gone social as far as I know but she'll know to expect that. You can't just show. She'll know that's fishy."

"Then share she'll have company," he allowed.

"Okay. See you later, Nick."

"Later," he grunted perfunctorily then disengaged.

But she was going to see him later so she didn't mind his abruptness.

She smiled, stowed her cell and walked back to reception, anticipating Nick Sebring's arrival and hoping, after he did whatever he did with Olivia Shade, a.k.a. Ms. Lincoln, he'd have time for her.

3

DAWN COMING

Olivia

I LEANED TOWARD THE front seat of the car, the folded bills between my fingers, my eyes on Harry's profile.

"As usual, I'll probably be a few hours, Harry," I told him, extending my hand over the seat.

He turned to catch my eyes. "Walk you to the door."

I allowed my lips to curl up and my eyes to get moderately soft.

Harry was a leftover from a different time. A time long ago when I'd slept easier. When I believed my daydreams could come true. When a look or a stolen touch was a promise. When plans were whispered and my stomach flip-flopped or my heart skipped with excitement at the mere thought of carrying them out. When I faced the dawn every day joyful because one day I *knew* it would be over. I would be free. We would be free. We'd be normal. We'd be together. We'd make babies. We'd grow old together. We'd be happy.

We'd die clean.

He'd helped us, Harry had. He'd helped me and Tommy.

Because my sister loved me and because Harry was a leftover from my grandfather, out of respect for me (from Georgia) and for my dead grandfather (from Dad), they'd let Harry live. They'd made him unemployable and taken nearly everything he had so he lived in a tiny house in a terrible neighborhood taking jobs at odd hours, all of them for cash, all of them, except mine, for a lot less cash than he should considering many of them were dangerous.

Sixty-eight-years-old, scrimping, saving and destined to work until the day he died or was killed because he was at the wrong place at the wrong time with the wrong people.

This was why the bill in my hand was a hundred dollars and the bill I'd hand him when he took me home in a few hours would be the same.

This was also why he had no choice but to accept it.

I used him only for the club.

My car had a tracker on it and my home randomly had someone watching it.

Dad had a long memory.

Harry knew how to spot surveillance. He also knew how to avoid it. He'd taught me both and utilized both for me.

We were good at our game. We'd had practice.

In the end, when it mattered most, not good enough.

But good enough to get me to the club.

"Harry," I said in my soft voice. "They have cameras in this alley and Mr. Revere is right there to open the door for me." I didn't move my head to indicate the big man standing under the lone light in the alley, his eyes on Harry's shiny, well-kept but not-near-new black Lincoln Town Car. I didn't have to. Harry knew he was there. "You don't have to walk me to the door."

Harry continued to look at me for half a second before he turned and opened his door.

I sat back on a sigh.

He came around and opened my door. He shut it after I climbed out.

His hand to my elbow, his head turning this way and that to scan the empty alley, he walked me to Mr. Revere.

"Ms. Lincoln," Mr. Revere greeted as we got close.

I nodded to him.

Mr. Revere jerked his chin up to Harry and moved to open the door of the club.

I turned to Harry, his hand dropped from my arm and I grabbed it. Pressing the bill into his palm, I gave him a squeeze and let him go.

"I'll text you when I'm ready for a pickup," I told him what I always told him.

Like much of what I said, these were wasted words.

Harry jerked his head to the side. "I'll be parked down the way."

He didn't need to be close. He didn't need to have my back. No one was going to charge into the building with tommy guns and shoot the place up, whereupon Harry had to be close in order to rescue me and/or provide a quick getaway.

"You can go have a drink," I said. "Something to eat. Go home and catch a program. You don't have to—"

He interrupted me. "I'll be down the way, Olivia."

Wasted words.

I didn't know why I bothered.

I needed to learn to stop doing that.

I nodded. "Thank you, Harry."

He nodded back, jerked his chin to Mr. Revere and didn't move until I was through the door Mr. Revere was holding open for me.

I walked through the narrow, dark vestibule of the private VIP entrance to the club where Mr. Paine was lurking in the shadows.

They were very good at security here.

Security and, for VIPs, anonymity.

Everyone's name was an alias, including staff.

I tipped my head to the side as I passed Mr. Paine and moved into the reception area which was lined with deep-seated, comfortable, curved couches with plenty of tables around for easy access to lay drinks, although it was infrequent people lingered in reception. That said, the club was available for private parties and this area was used for that when the club was closed down to accommodate such an event.

There were large and small bouquets of extraordinarily arranged, fresh-cut flowers, the air heavy with the aroma of them, the biggest at the reception desk behind which Ms. Ross was standing.

Her thick, dark hair was swept back in an artful messy bun. Her eyes were expertly and dramatically made up. Her dress fit perfectly. And I would find, when she walked around the reception desk to lead me up the stairs, her shoes cost twelve hundred dollars.

"Ms. Lincoln," she greeted with a small smile, already on the move. "Welcome. We're ready for you."

"Thank you," I murmured.

Ms. Ross's eyes went beyond me. "Can Mr. Arthur take your coat?"

I shrugged off my coat and handed it to a man that had moved out of the shadows of the cloakroom just off from the reception desk.

He said nothing. Just disappeared from whence he came.

I moved silently up the thick-carpeted steps behind Ms. Ross.

"I hope you enjoy our program tonight. It's already begun, as you know."

I was still murmuring when I replied, "I'm sure I will."

"Midori, vodka and Fresca, correct?" she asked when she reached the top.

I cleared the last step behind her. "Yes."

"Excellent," she replied.

We moved down the hall that was handsomely appointed, intimately lit and it had a number of doors leading off of it, all to the right side.

She led me to the middle one, the only one with double doors.

She opened one side and stood out of my way for me to precede her.

I walked into the social viewing chamber and heard it immediately, the hall and reception being soundproofed, but the viewing rooms absolutely not.

I looked to the floor to ceiling one-way window and felt my mouth tighten.

Ms. Ross got close, read my look and gave her expert opinion. "It looks like this scene won't last much longer."

I stared at the women through the window. Considering the cost of membership…hell, considering I was even there, I did not judge what people did, what they liked.

But a woman performing cunnilingus on another woman didn't do anything for me.

Man on man, absolutely.

I just was not turned on by same-sex play if they were my sex.

I looked from the window to the chamber, which I'd been in only once, when I'd taken a tour after being cleared for VIP membership two and a half years ago.

Again intimately lit, there were five segmented seating sections with low walls separating them, the flooring theater-style. The front four sections on two rises having two comfortable chairs in each section for relaxed viewing and a table for drinks and snacks. The seating section at the top rise sat six.

My drink was at the bottom level, closest to the window and the right wall.

"We surprisingly had another booking come in after yours," Ms. Ross informed me.

I looked her way, not thrilled at this news.

"A new member, I'm afraid," she carried on. "He's been notified of the rules, of course. He's also been here more than once and behaved accordingly so you both should be able to enjoy your viewings without concern and with minimal interruption."

"When is he due to arrive?" I asked.

"Sometime between now and midnight," she answered.

A vague arrival. Something else I didn't like.

"He orders his drinks when he's here," she continued. "So I'm afraid unless you want us to interrupt you to inform you of his arrival, you'll have no warning prior."

I nodded, offering no reply, and made a move to the steps that led down to my seat.

"Enjoy," she murmured to my back.

"Thank you," I returned, not glancing at her when I did.

I moved to my seat, stowed my clutch, took a sip of my drink and then pulled out my phone to check email and otherwise kill time while the women finished their scene.

The club, obviously, was a sex club. Intensely private and relatively secret ("relatively" because they had to be known to attract members), it was independently owned.

All players in all scenes were freelance, auditioned and paid well.

There was a member section which had an entry from the street, but, like VIPs, all members needed to pass a vetting process, pay a yearly membership fee but also pay an hourly or nightly viewing fee. Non-VIPs could show when they wished without a booking, paid for their drinks at the bar and sat in a common viewing area with their brethren.

The scenes were played out on the upper floor. The lower floor for non-VIPs was simply a nightclub. There was music, liquor, dancing and men and women behind screens performing dances that hinted at the real thing, that real thing being something that could be found beyond security up a set of hidden stairs.

Obviously, there was also the VIP section, which had its own entry and a higher level of service, providing much more discretion and vastly superior accommodation.

The owners paid Benito Valenzuela for protection and assistance in making certain the club was not discovered by law enforcement.

This protection was at one time paid to Marcus Sloan. Seven years ago, in the days when Sloan was still acknowledging my father's existence, he'd sold that protection to us. This was why I knew of the club.

In a brutal takeover that meant we lost one man and two more were injured, three years ago, Valenzuela had taken over.

After that, I continued my membership because it continued services I appreciated at a caliber that was more than acceptable. I did this even if the club was under Valenzuela's umbrella.

Benito Valenzuela was not the most couth individual on the planet. In fact, he was one of the foulest people I'd ever met. He reminded me of my grandfather, including the fact he'd convinced himself he was the opposite of vile when he was not.

My father and my sister didn't know I continued to belong. Neither would be pleased, though it would be Dad, as usual, whose displeasure would be communicated in a way that I would have no choice but to desist doing something he did not like.

But in my life where I had very little I enjoyed and absolutely nothing I looked forward to, the club served a variety of purposes.

It was a secret defiance to my father, and even my mother, the former who would be furious if he knew I went there, the latter would be horrified.

It was also mine.

Mine.

Georgie didn't go there. Dad didn't. None of our men went for fear of Dad's (or Georgie's) displeasure. And certainly none of my legitimate colleagues or acquaintances went there.

So I could go and not run into anyone who encroached in my life.

A life that was less of a life and more of a *world*.

I understood there was a real world. I knew it existed beyond the bounds of the world in which I lived. But the boundaries of my world, or more aptly put, the *bonds*, meant it seemed alien to me. There but not there. On the cusp of my existence but as unattainable as Mars.

This meant the club—what I did there, what I saw, what it made me feel, the time I spent, everything there—was mine. Just mine.

I didn't have that. Not in any other part of my life. In truth, my father had only just four years ago stopped approving every clothing and accessory item I bought to wear in the pursuit of Shade business. Although I was now free to clothe myself, that freedom was significantly lacking in every other aspect of my life.

Further, I liked watching. There were some scenes that did nothing for me, like the current one playing out. There were other times nothing caught my attention.

And there were times when a scene or a player *did* catch my attention.

But the bottom line was that the club still was a place I could be that was my own. I could enjoy a drink, relax, and for a few hours be away from everything and just be...*me*.

And if there was a scene I liked, it would set me up for much more pleasurable things later.

Of course, I was giving myself these pleasurable things. But pleasure was pleasure and I didn't have a lot of that either so I was happy to take what I could get.

As the cunnilingus was unfortunately reciprocated, making the scene last longer than expected, I discovered I didn't have much email and therefore enjoyed the mindlessness of several games of solitaire on my phone when the dimness of the window and the lack of sounds caught my notice.

I looked to the window to see they'd darkened it in preparation for the next scene just as I heard the door behind me open.

I sighed.

I preferred a private salon simply because it was private. I knew many used those salons for a variety of purposes, alone or bringing a partner or partners. But when we'd owned protection, I was made aware they had cameras everywhere, including in the viewing rooms. This was for security purposes and VIPs were assured that staff very much understood discretion and that all tapes were wiped when the club closed at three in the morning (something I knew they did in our time—during Valenzuela's time, anything could be happening).

I might like to watch but I didn't fancy anyone watching me.

I also enjoyed prolonging it. If a scene worked and I enjoyed it, waiting to take care of the need it ignited was half the fun.

So that wasn't why I didn't wish to have company.

I simply didn't wish to have company.

I didn't bother looking over my shoulder. I didn't care who was arriving but also the person arriving likely wished the same thing.

I heard a pleasantly deep man's voice say, "Dewar's. Rocks."

"Yes, Mr. Grant."

No noise after that undoubtedly because the carpeting muted him moving to his seat and Ms. Ross would never in a million years make too much noise closing the door behind her.

However, I only vaguely considered those thoughts.

I was still stuck on the pleasant deepness of the man's voice.

I wanted that. I wanted that to let my mind take flight. I wanted the next scene I viewed to be stirring and to use that voice and my imagination to make some fabulous man up in my head who had a pleasantly deep voice who could do pleasant things to me. Then I would go home and create an even more fabulous fantasy with my hand between my legs.

These thoughts in my head, I heard the swish of fabric that was probably him setting aside a suit jacket, and out of habit at the sound, my head turned left.

I took one look and turned my attention back to my phone.

His voice had a pleasant deepness.

His appearance was so beyond pleasant, it was startling.

I waited, not wishing to be caught looking, and Ms. Ross returned with his drink only moments before the window illuminated for the next scene.

Only then did I allow myself to look at him again.

He had his eyes to the window, the drink to his lips.

I looked away quickly. But this time I'd noticed something so I couldn't help myself from just as quickly casting another glance his way before I again looked away.

I'd been correct.

It was Nick Sebring.

I focused on my breathing, keeping it calm, my eyes to the window, my attention on my thoughts.

In my business, no, in my *world*, one made it a point to know men such as the Sebring brothers.

On several occasions, I had met Knight Sebring, a Denver nightclub owner who also provided protection and client vetting for a stable of ladies of the evening.

We had no dealings with Knight. He had a niche and kept to his niche, making it clear he had no interest in expanding his operation outside the women he had under his protection. Unless a client was exceptionally stupid, Knight also had little to no problems with any of his businesses. He lived quiet and extremely comfortably with his partner, Anya, and their two daughters.

Some years ago, perhaps seven or eight, Nick Sebring had worked for his brother, Knight. There had been a falling out, the reason for which I was not privy. After this Knight cut his brother loose.

It then appeared Nick had lost his way as there was a spell of time where he was either keeping company with a variety of unsavory characters or on the straight and narrow with an office job.

However, four years ago, Nick Sebring had set up his own shop.

This shop included providing a variety of elite services to an exclusive set of clientele who could pay handsomely. In a very short period of time, he'd made a name for himself in this business of acquisitions, deliveries, security, mediation, surveillance, deep background checks, safe-housing, and information collection, dissemination and safeguarding.

Also in a very short period of time, he'd made a fortune doing these things.

Back in the day, Nick Sebring had been known as the incompetent, unprincipled wastrel younger brother of a successful man. Nick also was known to have a fondness for cocaine and a mind filled with nothing but getting laid and living large off his brother's back.

He was no longer any of that.

What he was was a dark horse. No one had expected anything of him except, perhaps, the frequently earned title of baby daddy and an early death due to his own folly.

But now, in our world, he was respected and even feared.

And, in the club in the seating area next to mine, he also *looked* nothing like he used to look.

The few times I'd been on the scene and had the opportunity to see him back then, I'd noted he had been very pretty. Unlike his brother, who was remarkably good-looking in an intensely masculine but entirely offhand way, Nick Sebring had been handsome in a look-at-me way. He'd worn clothes that were loudly expensive, his hair was over-styled and he had a body that was meticulously maintained—not to maintain it, but to get attention.

Now, his black hair was clipped very short, only bits at the top and the front longer and sticking up in appealing ways which invited a woman's touch to arrange or smooth, no matter how hopeless this endeavor might be (or perhaps because of it).

He was tan, my guess, not due to laying by a pool, especially not now when we were heading out of February. The lines emanating out of the sides of his eyes and around his mouth and the nuance of ruggedness barely contained in the elegant confines of a viewing chamber in the club hinted the tan was because he spent time outside.

His stubble was thick and not groomed. He was not a man who forgot to shave that day or had been too busy to do so for a couple. It had been weeks. Though it was not a full grown beard.

I detested facial hair on a man.

But Nick Sebring's looked good.

And his clothes were impeccable—not obnoxiously so, but in an understated way. That didn't mean his sky blue dress shirt didn't catch on his defined biceps or beautifully delineate his broad shoulders, they did—deliciously so.

Since Tommy, unless it was one of the rare occasions where I was in a certain mood and went out to find a man to assuage that mood, it was unusual for me to have a reaction to a male. Not any of them. It was too dangerous.

No-strings-attached and usually no-names-exchanged fucking was one thing.

But I'd learned my lesson.

Three glances and Nick Sebring drew me. In fact, even sitting still I was finding it physically exhausting fighting the urge to look his way. And I was finding it utterly impossible to get him out of my mind.

Thankfully, a noise pierced this thought and my unfocused gaze focused on the scene being played out in the window in front of me.

The whipping post had been set up.

Such was the attraction of Nick Sebring—the whipping post and I hadn't noticed.

If done well, that was my favorite scene.

I reached to my drink and took a sip, forcing myself to take in the players.

The man had the whip. Cat o' nine tails, a beautiful set in braided chocolate and burgundy leather with expanded curved tips, not knots, beads or frayed.

He was in jeans, nothing else, and had a large, muscular body that was most appealing.

A woman was tied to the post. She was also in jeans and nothing else. I saw the red marks on her back and knew she'd taken more than one lash during my inattention.

And when I watched what the man did next, I automatically crossed my legs, feeling my lips part and Nick Sebring flew from my mind.

He ran his lips along the marks on her back.

One. Another. The next. And the next. Slowly. Tenderly.

A devotion.

Once done, he ran the handle of the whip along her hip.

Again slowly, he stepped back, raised his arm and let loose.

The slap of leather against flesh filled the chamber as her head flew back, her quiet moan sweet and short, her back arched.

He moved in and tenderly ran the tails of the whip along her skin. As he did, she relaxed for him. He then worked her neck with his mouth and pressed his bulging crotch into her behind before he again stepped back and let loose with the whip.

And again.

Then he moved back to her.

I'd seen many such scenarios but not one as slow, as drawn out, as tender, loving, sensual as the one before me. A scene where he mixed pleasure and adulation with her pain like they had an entire week for him to bring her to climax and not the length of their scene at a sex club.

They were on display, who knew how many people watching, but they were completely alone. She was completely his. Her adoration of him not in question. And this adoration was not what he could do to her. Not what he gave to her. That was only a part of the love she had for her master.

She loved *him*.

His devotion was the same. Unhidden, completely exposed. Every move he made was entirely focused on her pleasure. On *her*.

She was the center of his universe, at play and not.

After an unusual succession of three lashes, her moan came deeper and I again could not control the direction of my gaze.

It moved to my left.

When it did I saw that Nick Sebring was entirely focused on the scene. Leaned slightly to his right, his elbow resting on the arm of the chair, his hand up, his thumb distractedly tracing his lower lip.

At this sight, my sex, already damp, convulsed.

I wet my lip and bit it, watching his thumb move along his. Wanting my tongue to replace his thumb with a yearning the strength of which I wasn't sure I'd ever felt.

Without warning, his head turned, his gaze capturing mine.

His eyes were a startling blue. Pure blue. Like the ocean.

I wet my lip again.

Those blue eyes dropped to it.

My nipples tightened.

A noise came from the window and I looked that way, seeing the man was now rubbing his partner between her legs. She was working his hand, writhing against her bonds, desperate for every inch of contact he gave her.

I felt my breaths begin to get heavy and tightened my thighs against each other.

The man went from between her legs to her fly. He undid it and pulled her jeans down over her ass. Once bared, he paid attention to it with whip, hand and lips.

I again bit my own lip, this time to hold back the inadvertent noises I would emit at how what I was watching was making me feel.

He pulled her ponytail free, her long, curling, red-blonde hair falling down her back and swaying against skin that had to be beyond sensitized. Seeing this, I felt my own hair trapped between my back and the seat and I wanted it released. I wanted it moving against my skin. I wanted to use it against *his*.

Not the master working his slave before me.

The man with the pleasantly deep voice and ruggedly handsome face beside me.

Sebring.

The master pressed his hand back between her legs, now unobstructed by her jeans.

Her noises became desperate.

His growls of approval became audible.

Witnessing that, hearing it, instantly, my need became uncontrollable.

Utterly.

I looked left and saw Sebring's eyes not on the scene but on my crossed legs.

I uncrossed them and they cut to my face.

His gaze was burning, searing holes right through me.

God, he felt the same as me. About that scene and about *me*.

Seeing that in his eyes, without that first thought, I pushed out of my chair and moved along the low divider that demarcated our seating areas.

I was breaking the rules. I knew my membership could be revoked for what I was about to do.

I didn't care.

I moved around the divider to his section.

The noises from the scene playing behind me filled our space, getting louder, keener, hungrier.

I stopped at the side of his chair, looking down at him.

His head was tipped back, his eyes locked to mine.

Another growl from the window followed closely by the unmistakable noise of flesh hitting flesh.

Master was fucking his slave.

A trill ran down my neck, my spine, spiraling over my ass to tighten between my legs.

Completely unable to stop myself, I bent to Sebring and ran my nose along his cheekbone.

When I started to lift away, my head was captured with his hand cupping the back.

At his move, my heart stopped beating and a surge of wet drenched my panties.

We stared into each other eyes.

His gaze held heat and hunger but also a question.

I felt my breaths come quick and sharp, something inside me firing further just knowing that whisper of a touch was gliding along his lips. Therefore I suspected my gaze held heat and hunger too, but also the answer to his question.

I was correct. I knew because suddenly, he was up and he took me with him.

His hands to my skirt, he yanked it high, exposing my panties. I gasped and leaned to him, lifting my hands and curling my fingers around his hard shoulders.

Without delay, he shoved his hands in the back of my panties and down until they fell to my ankles.

And then I was *up* and he was striding to the wall as I wrapped my legs around his hips, one arm around his shoulders.

My other hand was working between us.

I barely freed him before his hips moved forward probingly. He caught where he needed to be and immediately surged in, filling me.

Oh God.

So completely *filling me*.

I swung my ankles back to hitch my calves on his hips in order to find purchase and ride him as Sebring fucked me against the wall in the club. One hand at my ass, his other one caught the back of my neck, squeezing and giving me a slight shake, telling me he wanted my eyes.

I gave them to him.

Panting, gasping, moaning against his parted lips, his labored breaths scored across mine as I held him tight at the shoulders. My other hand cupped to the back of his head, I rode his driving cock as he fucked me hard.

It took no time at all before I exploded on a whimper, sliding my nose along his before dropping my forehead to his shoulder because I couldn't hold it up anymore, these actions and noises coming nowhere near the enormity of the orgasm I was experiencing.

Regardless, he couldn't have missed it considering how forcefully my body was shuddering in his arms and my pussy was spasming around his cock.

He pressed me to the wall and powered faster, harder, pummeling me as I gasped quietly through my climax and his thrusts until I felt his tongue touch my neck, his hard body go completely still and I heard his deep sigh.

We didn't move, either of us, not for long glorious moments where I did something for reasons I did not understand. I did something I never, not ever, *not ever* allowed myself to do. For reasons I could not fathom, I did something I knew it was pure insanity, pure *torment* to do.

I believed.

For one magnificent second, connected to Nick Sebring, I *believed*.

I believed in a better world.

I believed I could feel complete.

I believed I could have someone by my side.

I believed I could feel safe.

I believed I could be happy.

I believed I could be loved.

I believed in a dawn coming where I would open my eyes and have all of this only for it to lead to another day dawning where I'd have it and then another day...

And another...

And another...

And another...

Until I no longer existed on this world.

Thus I made an uncontrollable noise of loss when Sebring lifted me away from him and our connection vanished.

The moment was over too quickly.

Way too fucking quickly.

As always.

I dropped my legs.

He put me to my feet and stepped back.

Lifting my eyes to his, mine I knew shuttered, his equally blank, I shimmied down my skirt.

He did his fly.

It was me who looked away in order to walk to my panties. I bent as ladylike and dignified as I could to nab them before I shimmied them up as best I could. I smoothed my skirt over them when I was done and walked to my seat. I took the last sip of my drink in a way I hoped appeared casual before I grabbed my phone, shoving it in my purse.

I tucked my purse under my arm, turned and moved back Sebring's way.

I again caught his gaze as I walked to him standing where I'd left him but turned to watch me, shoulders against the wall, arms crossed on his wide chest.

I dipped my chin as I walked past him and began to make my way up the rises, thinking now I'd lost the club. The only thing that was mine. Like Tommy, being foolish, thinking I could have something I wanted and going for it, I'd lost the only thing that was truly mine.

I could never come back.

Not because I'd broken the rules. Sebring would have to complain and I had a feeling he would not be doing that.

But because I'd made a huge mistake fucking a man who existed in my world. A man who had the power and resources to hurt me if he so wished. A man my father could hurt if the whim struck him.

And it would.

This I knew with absolute certainty I could not have. I could not do. I'd learned that.

I'd *learned* it.

"I want more of that."

It was the pleasantly deep voice which was far more pleasant now due to being roughened by sex.

He wanted more.

Of me.

My heart turned over, my stomach flip-flopped and for another nanosecond, I believed.

I turned to him, my mouth opening to tell him that would never happen.

It was a grave mistake.

The instant I caught sight of him, I froze.

He was tall.

His eyes were the color of the ocean.

And he made me believe that I could want something, take it and *have it*.

Own it.

Keep it.

Something precious would be *mine*.

Even if that belief only lasted seconds, I'd waited all my life to feel that feeling.

To really, really *believe*.

My feet took me to him.

I stopped a foot away.

I bent my head and opened my clutch, shoving my fingers into the side pocket until I found it.

I pulled out the pen and reached for his hand.

And like a girl at a club who had hopes for everything from getting thoroughly banged to having just met the father of her future children, I wrote my cell phone number on his palm.

When done, without a word, I walked out of the room, pulled out my phone and texted Harry so he could reverse fifty feet in the alley and take me home.

4

Cool Customer

Nick

NICK WALKED DOWN the stairs to find the girl waiting at the bottom, her eyes slits, her arms crossed on her chest, her fury unhidden.

When he got close, she leaned in and hissed, "You fucked her."

The bitch didn't turn off the cameras.

She'd watched.

Aggravating.

Without hesitation, he grabbed her upper arm and dragged her with him toward the back room.

The security guy came out of the vestibule as did the coat-check guy.

"Move another step, you're both looking for a job," he warned.

They stopped, as they would, considering six months ago, the Sebring brothers had secretly purchased the club. To keep it on the down low, both were silent partners. The old owners still ran it with the only change being that they didn't pay Benito Valenzuela protection money. Knight and Nick were perfectly capable of protecting the club.

Valenzuela backed off without a fight considering he had recently drawn Knight's attention and not in a good way. He was smart enough, in his current war with Chaos and the moves Georgia Shade was making, not to court a new enemy.

But as it served Nick's purpose, the staff of the club now knew he was their boss.

Therefore, unimpeded, he pulled his employee into the back room and through it to the door at the rear.

"Nick, you're holding me too tight," she whined, twisting her arm against his hold.

He wasn't. His hold was not tender but it wasn't causing pain.

He knew how to cause pain in a variety of ways.

Deacon Gates had taught him.

He also knew how to contain someone and not to cause pain.

Hettie and Turner had taught him that.

Her fear at his actions and the fact she'd fucked up and was freaked was causing her pain.

He yanked her to his side as he hit the code into the keypad. He heard the latch unlock and pushed the door open.

He looked to the man inside watching a bank of twelve monitors with visuals that shifted every five seconds. Visuals that fed from the thirty cameras throughout the club.

The man took one look at Nick's face and immediately lifted his hands, not at all happy he'd watched his boss fucking a woman considering that boss was right there, clearly about to get in his shit about it.

"She said—" he began.

"Delete it," Nick ordered.

The man instantly turned to the monitors. One cleared then showed the now empty social chamber.

Within five seconds, it blanked.

Without another word, Nick dragged the girl out of the monitoring room and closed the door.

"You're done," he told her. "Pack your shit. Out."

Her eyes got big.

"You're firing me?" she asked.

Fuck, he hated stupid bitches.

He'd smelled that on her the minute he met her. It concerned him, not only for the purpose he bought the place—to get access to Olivia Shade—but because he owned the fucking place and no employer wanted a stupid bitch for an employee.

But she was liked by the old owners.

What she pulled, that no longer factored.

"Yes," he answered, letting her go. "Get your shit and *out*."

"But we——" she began.

"There is no we," he told her.

Her head twitched in shock.

Yeah. He hated stupid bitches.

"But you took me to dinner," she whispered. "And then we——"

"Fucked. You weren't very good so I didn't come back for more. Lesson. Usually, a man takes a woman out, fucks her, wants more, he does something about that and doesn't let three weeks elapse between the first fuck and the next."

"But, you've been flirting with me for——"

He knew what he'd been doing.

He'd needed something from her.

He got it.

He knew she felt his change when she snapped her mouth shut.

"Out," he whispered.

She swallowed visibly but that was the extent of her further wasting his time. She hustled her admittedly sweet ass to get her shit and then she got out.

He pulled out his phone, started a string to the managers of the club and tapped in the text.

Find a new Ross.

He hit SEND and went home.

⸻

AN HOUR LATER, Nick sat on his sofa, foot up, sole of his shoe pressed to the edge of the coffee table, the fingers of one hand wrapped around a glass of Dewar's and ice, his other hand lifted, his eyes to Olivia Shade's phone number written on his palm.

Christ, she was a cool customer.

After walking to him in that fucking skirt with that fucking look on her face that made him absolutely sure he could fucking *smell* the wet drenching her pussy...

Then taking his cock like she did, her eyes locked to his, her hips working his dick...

And finally coming with the demure noises a princess would make while her pussy told a different story and milked him hard.

After all that, walking like she was drifting through her living room in order to grab her panties, put them on, nab her purse and do nothing but nod before she was going to walk away from him.

He had not expected first contact to go that spectacularly well.

He expected eye contact. Maybe a few words exchanged. Enough she'd get he was into her kink so he could lay the groundwork when he ran into her elsewhere.

He didn't expect to fuck her against the wall.

And certainly he didn't expect that fuck to be that outstanding.

He also didn't expect to feel whatever the fuck it was he felt coming off her after her orgasm milked his right out of him.

He had no idea what it was but whatever it was, he stayed buried inside her a lot longer than he'd intended.

And it made him uneasy.

She'd given nothing away after that and it was almost like he'd imagined it.

He stopped looking at her number, leaned forward, tagged his phone off the coffee table and sat back. He used his thumb to program her in.

And there she was. A bold OLIVIA SHADE at the top of her contact.

Her there with him everywhere he went.

A Shade in his life.

He looked across the room to the chest against the wall where the framed picture of Hettie was. A picture that hadn't moved for four years, except for when he moved house and when his cleaning service dusted it.

Fuck.

He put that thought aside, tossed the phone back to the table, nabbed his drink, threw it back, heaved himself out of the couch and went to bed.

LIKE HE HAD a sixth sense (and in his business, he had to), Turner called him the next morning five minutes after Nick's workout.

"You make contact yet?"

Nick looked from his orange juice out the sunny window.

Cold. Warm. February. July. In Denver, the day dawned, odds were it'd be sunny.

"You wanna tell me why you're asking?" he requested.

"One of her boys got dead last night."

Nick's back straightened but his eyes dropped to the stainless steel countertop. "What?"

"Eli Cook, street name Green. Not sure why. Cops say the crime scene, that bein' his apartment, looked like he was packin' to leave town. Not sure why about that either. Don't got a lot of insight into the Shade family dealings anymore, but no word on the street sayin' there was an issue. He had a gunshot wound to his thigh that was not mortal, but was fresh, though not as fresh as the ones that *were* mortal and no one knows jack about that either."

Even though Nick knew all about Green, including who shot him considering he had surveillance all over the Shade warehouse, he had nothing to say so he didn't say anything.

"This is not good, Nick," Turner went on. "The House of Shade has been a house of cards for years now. A cold wind blows, it'll blow away and everything stacked inside will go with it. And I gotta tell you, with them taking desperate measures years ago to diversify dealings, that going so far south it dropped off the face of the earth, and them constantly scrambling with not much coming of it, now Eli Cook biting it for no apparent reason, I feel a seriously fuckin' bitter wind kickin' up."

"Fucked her last night," Nick shared.

There was a pause, then, "Say again?"

"Set it up I was with her last night at the club for the initial meet. Apparently, she liked the scene that was playin' out and wasn't feeling the idea of delayed gratification. She made it clear she was good to go; I took her up on the invitation. We fucked. She gave me her number after so we're gonna do it again. But before that, it was reported to me she called in at just after six to book her viewing. She was there by ten thirty. She left at just after eleven thirty. Tail on her said her driver took her right home and that's where she stayed. When was her boy done?"

"Jesus, Nick. I'm not callin' you to be Olivia Shade's alibi, for fuck's sake. Christ. I can't believe what you're tellin' me. The bitch is made of stone. First contact and you fucked her? How could you even drive your cock in there without it breaking clean off?"

Olivia Shade was not made of stone.

She was warm and soft, smelled good, and her sheet of straight black hair felt like silk.

And if he was another man he knew her green eyes had the capacity to brand ownership. He knew it because, as they held his while he thrust into her, he had to fight giving over to it.

And last but very much not least, she had a phenomenally tight, hot, wet cunt.

"Trust me," he muttered. "She's not made of stone."

"Nick, nature is gonna take its course with Vincent Shade. With all of them. You do not have to use his daughter to get to him."

He shouldn't have told Turner his plan.

But he needed this to succeed and he was going to use everything he had to do that, family, friends, skills…and markers.

And Turner owed him a fuckuva lot of markers.

So he'd told Turner his plan.

"Your concern is heartwarming," he joked, lifting his glass of juice and finishing it, hoping Turner would take his hint and shut up about it.

He didn't take the hint.

"You know this family. You know those two women. You've done such extensive research on them, you might know them better than they know themselves. So you know the Shade sisters have two uses for men. They can take orders and/or give orgasms. Fuck, Georgia Shade uses her cunt as a recruiting tool and to make sure their soldiers toe the line. At least Olivia doesn't fuck where she works but you found out yourself the last three cocks she took didn't know her name and she didn't ask theirs."

She hadn't asked his last night either.

In fact, she hadn't said a fucking thing.

But she knew who he was like he knew the same of her. No one in their world didn't, either way.

"Least last night proves one thing," Nick said. "Not thinkin' she'd even sit in the same room with me much less ride my dick if she knew what went down with Hettie. That close of an encounter, I'd be in a firefight by the time I hit the alley, even if she's hidin' her kink from Daddy and they got about ten soldiers left in their crew."

"We already know that, Nick. Vincent rules that warehouse with an iron fist, but he tried to form a stable of girls six years ago and Georgia lost her mind. With two women set to inherit that dried-up dynasty, whores are not on their agenda. With them not even allowing whores, neither of the sisters knew he was involved in human trafficking. Think that's the only thing that would have the Shade sisters breaking ties with their old man."

That also made him uneasy. The fact that Olivia was his entry to tearing down Vincent Shade's world. To gaining access to Gill Harkin and blowing a hole in his head just like that man had done to Hettie. To dismantling everything *Shade*.

Which meant both sisters would lose everything when neither of them had been involved with what had happened to Hettie.

But they lived that life. They stood by their father's side. They did their jobs.

Sometimes you got away with dealing day to day with the devil.

Sometimes you got burned.

"Nick," Turner called when Nick said nothing.

"Nature takes its course, I'll walk away. But the time is ripe, Eric. So I'll work my plan until that happens or until I get what I need. It's in motion now. There's no other option."

"Please be safe," Turner replied. "At least Georgia Shade has blood pumping in her veins. She likes a good fuck a lot more often than her sister. She likes a good time too. She's got a life and she lives it. But outside of what Vincent tried to do to resurrect their operations six years ago, it's widely considered Olivia Shade is the quiet brains behind their ventures and if it wasn't for her, that family would have disappeared from the scene years ago."

"I did gather this intel before I started this gig," Nick pointed out.

He listened to Turner sigh.

"We done?" Nick asked.

"You get anything useful about that dead soldier, would make some folks happy in the DPD they got an even anorexic lead."

"Right, after I finish bangin' her again later, seein' as the last time she didn't say a fuckin' word to me, I'll ask if she feels like turnin' rat and givin' me somethin' so the cops can nail someone in her crew, or out of it, for making a dead soldier."

"You fucked a woman who didn't say a word to you?" Turner asked.

"Yep," Nick answered.

"And you got her number?"

"Yeah."

Turner sounded more than mildly curious when he asked, "How does that work?"

"We were at a sex club watchin' a guy whip his bitch and work her pussy with his hand. Shit happened and I had her against the wall. After, I told her I wasn't done with her. She wrote her number on my palm. That's how it worked."

"Jesus, made of stone or not, Olivia Shade is fuckin' gorgeous so I'm gettin' hard just thinkin' about her writing her number on my palm. Seein' as I'm at work, not even gonna think about the other."

And Nick was not going to think about why he immediately and unfathomably felt pissed at Turner telling him something about Olivia fucking Shade was making him go hard.

Turner wasn't done.

"And if I was acknowledging the existence of this alleged sex club, I'd ask how much VIP membership costs."

"Twenty-five thousand dollars a year."

"Fuck."

"Lucky you know the owner."

"No I don't."

That made Nick chuckle.

"Stay sharp," Turner ordered.

"Later," Nick returned.

They disengaged.

Nick tossed his phone to the counter and moved through his place to his bathroom to take a shower.

He was at his desk in his office three and a half hours later when he texted her.

Hotel Teatro. Six o'clock. I'll text the room number later.

He did not identify himself.

She made him wait.

In fact, she didn't reply until he'd sent his assistant to check in, got the room number and texted it to her.

Which was at four fifteen.

And when she did, she only texted, *6:00*.

That was it.

A cool customer.

But absolutely not made of stone.

5

FUNNY

Olivia

8:15 a.m. — Nine Hours Earlier

Sitting at my desk, I wasn't working at my computer.

I was staring at my cell phone.

This was stupid.

Insane, really.

But I was and I was doing it in hopes he'd call or at least text.

As I'd been doing since I got home last night, late, wanting him to say something, *start* something, give me a reason to explain why I believed, why I responded to him the way I'd done.

This was insane too and not simply because, to start something, something minimally real, something somewhat normal, would be dangerous but also because I'd been the woman sitting next to him at a sex club who got up and made my way to him, making it clear what I wanted.

A quick, hard fuck with a stranger.

Did something real or normal start like that?

I had no idea.

I just doubted it did.

But I was wanting it, hoping for it, glancing then staring then glaring at my phone like I could make magic happen and get it.

And I needed to stop doing that.

Perhaps in the heat of the moment in an intimately lit sex club after getting an orgasm from a woman he'd never met, Nick Sebring would think he wanted more.

In the light of day, he probably thought differently. And even in the world in which he lived, if he didn't already have a steady woman who I'd assisted him in cheating on last night, he'd be looking for one who was absolutely not like me.

The woman he would look for would probably be like his brother's woman, Anya. Exceptionally beautiful, warmth radiating out of every pore. A woman who owned and operated a salon and had nothing to do with Knight's business. A woman so far out of our world, the only reason I knew what she looked like was because I saw her in her private section in Knight's nightclub, Slade, when I went there for a drink and to pick someone up to fuck.

I resolutely turned from my phone to my computer, where my email was on the screen.

I grabbed my mouse and hit refresh even though I'd only sent the email to David ten minutes earlier. A carefully worded request that was really a demand that he send all the accounts and other pertinent reports by noon that day.

Not surprisingly, David had not replied.

My eyes slid to my phone.

This had to stop.

I straightened in my chair, looked back to my computer and got to work.

―☒☒☒―

Three Hours, Fifteen Minutes Later

My phone sounded.

My eyes shot to it before I snatched it up.

I stared at the text long enough for the screen to fade to blank.

Hotel Teatro. Six o'clock. I'll text the room number later.

Oh God, he'd texted.

God, he wanted to see me again.

I touched my thumb to the button on the bottom of my phone to engage it. I went to texts.

I was about to reply when I stopped.

Sebring wanted one of two things.

A fuck from me, this time since we'd have a bed and privacy that fuck (maybe) lasting longer.

Or, less likely but still an option, he wanted to start something minimally real and somewhat normal.

Outside of what I knew *of* him, I did not know the man. I knew he looked good, sounded good and felt *great*.

But I knew nothing else. We hadn't kissed so I didn't even know how he tasted.

What I did know was that no man deserved the kind of hassle I could bring into his life.

I closed my eyes, feeling that realization settle around my heart so heavy, it felt like it was struggling to beat.

This surprised me since I lived with that sensation every moment of every day of my life. Except for some reason this heavy felt a lot *heavier*.

I put my phone down and turned my attention back to my computer.

It was half an hour later and I was at the espresso maker across the room finishing making my second espresso of that morning when I heard the tone from my computer telling me I'd received email.

I went back to my desk and saw an email from David.

No attachments. No accounts. No reports. No files at all.

Simply a one line, two sentence email.

Perhaps we can make a meeting to go over what you need. Next Tuesday at 4:00?

We did not need to make a meeting. And it was Wednesday; the next Tuesday would give him a whole week to hide whatever it was he was intent on hiding and play on his history to recruit my father to shut me down.

I knew it.

So I wasted little time firing back, *You may have another hour on your deadline. Please send what I requested by 1:00. If you don't, Gill will be at your office to collect what I requested at 1:30. Thank you.*

I sent it.

659 1635

Ten minutes later, I got a phone call.

It was David.

I ignored it.

At five after one, I started getting the files.

I opened them immediately and began going through them.

Three Hours Later

IT WAS FORTUNATE David sent what I requested (except a good sight more than I needed), this keeping my mind off the fact that Sebring wanted me to meet him at Hotel Teatro and that I wanted to meet him at Hotel Teatro very badly even though I would not be doing that.

But, since David sent far more than what I requested (this suggested he was burying me under information so I wouldn't find evidence of wrongdoing), I was very busy.

Therefore I was engrossed in going through the order manifests of one of our legitimate companies when I heard the knock on my door.

My "Come in," was distracted.

I kept my gaze to the computer as I heard the door open and shut.

It took several seconds before I realized someone was in my office but they had not spoken.

I swiveled in my chair to turn my attention to the door.

Tommy was standing there.

Standing there looking at me.

Standing there looking at me with an expression on his face I could read.

I held his gaze, not believing what I saw, not wishing to experience the wash of raw putrescence it sent flooding through me, then fighting back the rage that rushed through in its wake.

With everything else—shockingly not the least of which being my brief but affecting encounter with Nick Sebring—all of it piling on and being too much, for once I did not control my reaction, consider every move available and then move forward cautiously (or, as was often the case, not at all).

I surged out of my seat and quickly made my way to the door.

ORLAND PARK PUBLIC LIBRARY

"Liv—"Tommy began.

He shut his mouth when I sliced my eyes to him.

"You should've called me."

I made it to the door and hauled it open.

"It was a direct order," he said.

I stopped and asked, "Dad? Or Georgia?"

He didn't answer even as he did.

His eyes moved across the hall.

Without hesitation, my feet moved across the hall.

"Liv!" he clipped.

I ignored him and knocked loudly at her door, didn't wait and pushed through.

"Fuck! Get the fuck out!" Georgia, back to her desk, knees up, bent and spread wide, taking Gill's cock, twisted her head to glare at me.

I looked from my sister to Gill.

It was not the first time I'd noted my sister's favorite soldier was large, built and exceptionally handsome in a pug-like, blunt, brutal way.

It was just that I was so angry, I might like watching but that absolutely didn't include my sister, so I noticed it with far more abstraction than usual while catching him fucking her.

"Go," I ordered, looking in his eyes, not anywhere else.

"Are you *insane?*" Georgia demanded to know.

I kept my eyes on Gill who was bent over my sister but he had his head tipped back to look at me.

"Go," I repeated.

He held my gaze then looked down at Georgia.

After a moment, he slid out and straightened, tucking himself back in his pants.

I stepped to the side of the door in Georgia's office, attention to the floor, giving them both privacy to get themselves sorted.

I saw Gill's legs walk by me as he left.

He closed the door.

The instant I heard it click, I looked to Georgia's desk. She was now standing behind it, leaning into her fists spread wide on the top, her expression enraged.

"Do not ever do that again," she whispered.

"Was he going to Sloan?" I asked.

"Confirm that you will not ever do that again," she replied.

That meant Green was not going to Sloan.

"Was he going to Valenzuela?" I pushed.

"Liv, *confirm* that you will not *ever* do that *again*," she repeated.

"So neither," I surmised and finished, "And you had Tommy kill him anyway. Tommy. *Tommy*."

"You are not hearing me—"

Suddenly, I bent toward her, hissing, "*No*. I'm not hearing you. I do not give that first fuck you're pissed." Her brows shot up at this rarity and I leaned back, asking, "Tommy?"

"Fuck, Liv—"

"Tommy!" I snapped his name like a whip, aiming my lash her way.

She pushed away from her desk. "He gets orders just like Gill."

I shook my head. "No he doesn't. Tommy doesn't. Not from you. Tommy's mine."

Her face lost some of its anger and her tone was softer when she said, "He isn't yours. He hasn't been yours for a long time. And you know it, babe."

"He's mine, Georgie," I reiterated.

"He isn't, Liv."

I leaned forward and was again hissing. "*He's mine*."

My sister's voice was actually gentle, as was her gaze on me, when she returned, "He wasn't even yours back then."

My torso shot back like she'd struck me.

"He does what he's told," she continued. "He doesn't get special treatment. He doesn't get the clean jobs because the boss's daughter gave him her cunt and her heart. It should have been a long time ago I stopped letting you protect him. Keep him for yourself. Try to keep him clean. The time for that to stop is now. A job needs to get done, no matter how dirty, he proves allegiance by doing it quickly and doing it well just like anyone else."

"So," I began, "Green isn't stupid enough to turn on us, he just lost his patience because he needs money to actually feed himself, he takes off and you send my ex-boyfriend to whack him to make a point?"

"A point that needed to be made. Not only to Tommy but out there." She threw an arm wide before she pointed at her desk. "And in here, to *all* our boys."

That speared through my heart.

— 53 —

"It was you?" I asked.

"It was me."

"Not Dad?" I pressed masochistically, but holding on to hope that she was taking orders too.

Just like Tommy.

She shook her head, her manner still gentle. "No, sis. Not Dad."

She hadn't relayed the order.

She'd given it.

I stood just inside the door of her office, silent.

Defeated.

Tommy, my Tommy, had killed a man. That man was Green. My man. My soldier.

It wasn't like Tommy was clean. Before and after there was a Tommy and me, he'd done things. Many things. Including that. He was a gangster, like me. That was part of the business.

Though, I'd never killed anyone nor ordered an execution. But I'd sat through listening to orders being given with and without saying a word against it.

But since there was a Tommy and me, it was Gill or another member of the crew.

It wasn't Tommy.

Not my Tommy.

"He gave up on you."

Her quiet words set my entire body to trembling.

Even so, I retorted, "Dad had Gill pouring acid on his face."

"Dad himself poured boiling oil on your back and you didn't give up on Tommy," she shot back.

I looked away, the trembling worse, the pain resurfacing. Vast assortments of pain. Entire collections.

She was right. We'd been found where we thought we were safe in Baja. We'd been dragged back. And the torture hadn't been just for Tommy for overstepping his bounds, daring to fall in love with the king's princess, taking her away.

The torture had been for me too.

We both had a lesson to learn.

Everyone associated with Vincent Shade had a lesson to learn.

But I'd been first.

There was a small area of skin on Tommy's left cheekbone that looked like it was melting.

He'd endured that for five minutes and renounced me. Promised it was over. Accepted his punishment of working by my side and never again touching me. Ending forever what we'd had. And last, committing his future to my father's sister's daughter.

He'd married my cousin three months later.

But for ages, Tommy had watched the oil poured along the small of my back, my upper hips, and I had not renounced him. He'd shouted. Cursed. Fought against his restraints. Begged them to burn him.

But when they turned to him, he hadn't endured his long.

I'd endured it silently, focusing as best I could on making new plans. Plans for when it was over, we were healed and it was time to try again (this time successfully). The oil dripped on my back while I decided our next destination. How we'd get there. How we'd cover our tracks. At the same time hoping with each drop gliding pure agony, I was proving to my father that I loved the man I was accepting torment for so he'd find it in him to simply let us be free.

"Liv, sissy, you need to give up on him too," Georgia told me gently.

Her words brought me back into the room.

"He's a soldier, nothing more. He's not yours. He's *ours*," she went on. "And he needs to do his job."

She was correct.

In this world where we lived, she was absolutely correct.

It was just that I didn't want to live in a world where things like that were the way you lived.

"Right now I hate you," I whispered.

Her shoulders slumped slightly, but that was all she gave to me.

"It isn't the first time," she replied.

She was again absolutely right.

She was my sister.

But she was also her father's daughter.

And I *detested* him.

"No," I agreed and watched her fight the flinch. "And I'm sure not the last."

Still holding my eyes, she started to round her desk. "Liv—"

"Fuck you, Georgia," I bit out and she halted at another rare reaction from me.

"I'll give you time," she offered.

"Excellent call," I returned, reaching out a hand to the doorknob. I opened the door and started through but turned back to share, "David's hiding something. I'm leaving for the day and working from home for the foreseeable future. I'll cover his duties while he's out of commission. Until I find out what he's hiding and how bad it is, you need to use your inestimable skills to shut him down. I'm sure I can count on you doing that."

"Liv—"

I raised a brow as I interrupted her. "I can't count on you to do that?"

Her mouth got tight before she forced out, "It's done. I'll go with Gill personally."

I made no reply.

I walked across the hall, trying to ignore Tommy leaning a broad shoulder against my doorjamb.

"Liv," he said quietly as I moved his way.

I made no response.

He shifted as I got close so I could enter my office.

He entered it with me and closed the door behind him.

"Liv," he repeated.

Stopping behind my desk, I did not sit. I turned and looked at him.

"Now is not a good time."

Something flashed across his face I'd seen a lot over the years. Too much. He should have learned to hide it. If not for him, for me. I'd learned how to do it for him.

Now, I wondered if he didn't do that just so he could manipulate me.

That something was pain.

"She's pregnant."

At his words, my throat closed.

"Georgia has recovery plans. They might work this time. That woman your dad gave me to coming up pregnant…" It seemed he was going to say something else but shut it down in order to say, "I need to take care of my family. I needed to make that statement of loyalty. I—" he gave his explanation, much of which *again* I already knew.

But now he was in with Georgia and knew of her "recovery plans?"

It was worse than I thought.

And...

His *family?*

"Please be quiet," I requested.

The pain in his eyes deepened.

"We need to talk," he said.

"I disagree," I replied.

"It's always only been you," he whispered.

"Funny," I returned instantly. "When I was getting thoroughly and satisfyingly fucked against a wall last night, it wasn't even a little bit about you."

He flinched.

I didn't feel that flinch.

I was over this.

All of it.

All of Tommy, our tragic history, or nonexistent future.

All of *everything*.

I couldn't let it hurt me anymore.

I had to move on.

"I'm sure you have work to do," I noted leadingly.

"Liv—"

I knew my face shut down to the extent it shut him out because I made it so.

"You need to go and do it, Tommy," I ordered.

His mouth went hard.

We stared at each other.

I tried to recall his face those days in Baja when we were happy. When we thought we'd made it. When we were sure we were free.

I couldn't pull up that first vision.

His wife, my cousin, was pregnant with his baby.

Yes, time to move on.

I watched as Tommy nodded and walked out the door.

I turned and bent to my computer, putting the files I needed on a flash drive.

While I was doing this, my cell sounded.

I looked at it and saw a text that simply had a number on it.

Sebring.

Hotel Teatro.

The room number.

I stared at the phone.

I would never have anything minimally real and somewhat normal with any-one. Not Nick Sebring. Not anyone.

What I could have with anyone I wanted, absolutely *anyone*, was a fantastic fuck.

I snatched up my phone.

I typed in *6:00*.

I hit SEND.

Then I shut down, locked up and got the hell out of the filthy, dingy, obscene house that Clive Shade built.

6

TUSSLE

Nick

In the hotel room, Nick heard the knock at the door.

He moved to it, looked out the peephole and felt the corners of his mouth hitch up when he saw her.

Fuck, those big green eyes, perfectly arched dark brows, the olive tint to her skin, the expert way she shaded under her cheekbones...

She was a coldhearted criminal but she was one that was very easy to look at.

And even easier to fuck.

He opened the door.

He was going to say something but he didn't get the chance when her hand darted out and she caught him under his jaw, using it to push him in and around until his back hit wall.

She stared up at him, her hand wrapped around his jaw, her expression holding an emptiness that was so extreme it was almost like a void he could fall into and get lost forever.

He heard the door swish closed and latch.

Then she was up on her toes, her head moving toward his, those green eyes dropping to his mouth.

She didn't get her lips to his before his tongue was out, as was hers, both of them colliding and tangling before her mouth slammed to his just as her body pushed in, pressing hard, forcing him tighter to the wall.

He shoved out. Gripping her wrist at his jaw, he yanked it down, twisting and slamming her against the wall, slanting his head to deepen an already deep kiss. Their tongues again clashing before he actually took her mouth.

But he took her mouth.

And like she'd done to his, he consumed it.

His fingers still around her wrist, he yanked it around his back, using his body to shove her tight to the wall, pressing his hardening cock against her stomach.

She arched, and moving quickly, whipped him around so his back was to the wall and she took over the kiss. Tearing her wrist from his hold, she curled her fingers around his throat just as she cupped his hardening crotch with her other hand.

Fucking *hell*, this woman was *hot*.

But he was done playing.

And he was done kissing.

Her mouth, that was.

He pushed her away. She struggled to regain control.

She lost this struggle when he caught her hand and dragged her down the short hall into the room.

She lost her footing when he gave her hand a strong tug and she fell into him with a soft gasp.

He let her hand go, caught her hips and threw her four feet onto the bed.

That got him another soft gasp which took his cock from hardening to rock-solid and throbbing.

He bent over her, holding her now intense green gaze, spanning her hips with his hands. Shoving backwards, he found the hook of her skirt, released it and pulled down the zipper.

He moved his fingers to curl them into the sides of her skirt's waistband. With a vicious tug that took her hips and panties with it, he yanked off the skirt.

Chest to the bed, eyes to her cunt, the black curls neatly groomed with a precision that meant her wax technician was a master with possible OCD issues, they were also glistening with wet.

Having the tussle at the door, seeing the utter perfection of her pussy, smelling her, watching her legs part in invitation, her knees shifting up, Nick couldn't have gone gentle if he'd wanted to.

Luckily he didn't want to.

He bent his neck and devoured her.

Fuck, she tasted just as perfect as she looked.

As he fed, he felt her excitement ramp. Tasted it. Ate it. Gave her more. Consumed the result. Drove her to the edge.

And when he had her there, he stopped and moved over her.

Not surprisingly, she used both the pump she already had planted into the bed and the calf she had wrapped around him to flip him and then she was straddling him, pushing up, her hands already to his fly.

Normally, he would not allow this.

Her face flushed with need, her manner urgent, even desperate, all that surged through his blood, his gut, straight to his cock.

So he allowed this.

She tugged his pants down, grabbed his dick, guided it to her and took him home.

At the beauty of her sheathing him, he gritted his teeth against the urge to let go and release way too fucking early. Bucking his hips, he watched how much she liked taking him, her head thrown back, her shining, straight mass of silken black hair swaying.

Then she dropped forward into a hand in the bed by his side, locked eyes with him and rode him violently as he watched until she gave it to herself and she kept doing it until she forced it from him.

Fucking spectacular.

He came down buried inside her, his eyes opening to see her still resting in her hand in the bed, her body moving gently with her still-labored-but-evening breathing, her dark hair framing her oval face, her straight bangs brushing her lashes, her green eyes locked to his trying to brand him, make him hers.

No way in fuck that was happening.

But he'd take more of this.

A lot more.

That said, the woman was going to learn how to give up control.

Not surprisingly, without a word, she swung off his cock, moving immediately toward the side of the mattress.

Nick focused on pulling up his trousers, doing the fly and angling off the bed. By the time he was up and had turned his attention back to her, she was on her feet, facing him, arms twisted behind her to do up the skirt she'd put on.

He held her gaze.

"We got all night, Olivia," he informed her.

Not even a hint of a response to him calling her the name she hadn't given him.

Then again, he knew she knew him; she'd make it her business.

She also knew he'd do the same with her, even before he sat next to her the night before.

Her expression might not have changed but his words spurred her to action, this being walking his way.

She stopped. Her eyes still on his, she lifted a hand and touched his chest lightly with just the pad of her middle finger.

It lasted half a second.

Then she dropped her hand, turned and walked away.

He heard the door close behind her and he couldn't stop his smile.

Fuck yes, a seriously cool customer.

And the hottest fuck he'd had in his life.

10:45 The Next Morning

NICK TYPED IN the text and hit SEND.

Teatro. Six.

Forty-five minutes later, he received, *Room number?*

He smiled at his phone and didn't fuck around with waiting games.

He texted back, *Later.*

Olivia didn't reply.

When his assistant checked them in, he sent the room number.

Olivia texted back, *6:00.*

6:47 That Evening

He was ass to the chair watching her ride him and he didn't even know how she maneuvered him there.

The kiss tussle started them off again the minute he'd opened the door to her.

This time it segued into a bed vs. chair tussle, one he somehow lost.

Fuck, she was going to make him come again, climb off and take off.

This would not allow him to move forward his plan.

Fortunately, he was stronger than her and could do something about that.

Her sexy noise of frustrated surprise made his cock jerk and his balls tighten as he stopped her mid-ride, pushing up to his feet with his arms around her.

Their eyes clashed as he carried her to the bed and, serious as fuck, as shocking as it was, he nearly burst out laughing at the uppity annoyed princess look she had on her face.

He controlled his reaction and then set about controlling her expression when he fell to the bed on top of her and started fucking her.

Hard.

She enjoyed control.

She also liked taking cock.

Proof she liked to give *and* receive.

Nice to know.

This didn't last long. She manipulated with eyes, hands, mouth, noises, and best of all, squirming until she'd pulled off his cock and turned underneath him. Wedging herself up, she offered herself, ass in the air.

He was a guy so he didn't delay, took his knees and accepted her offer.

She reared into him, her neck twisted, eyes cast high, watching his face as he fucked her on her hands and knees in front of him.

She was still fully clothed, her skirt pushed up her hips, her blouse on, the pointed toes of her pumps rooted in the bed.

He was still fully clothed too.

But from what he could see of her round ass and sweet thighs, he was going to find a way to fuck her naked as soon as possible.

Starting now.

Continuing to take her, he shifted his hands from hips up her ass until his thumbs moved from smooth, supple skin to encounter something he wasn't expecting that took his attention away from repeatedly burying his cock in her pussy as hard and deep as he could manage it.

She instantly pulled so far forward, he lost her and his eyes went from his hands under her skirt to her face.

She twisted to her ass, scooting back, her eyes another invitation.

He followed her. Stopping her movements with an arm around her waist, he pulled her up.

She took hold of his dick, guiding him in.

When he caught at her wet, he impaled her.

Driving his other hand in her silky hair, he clutched it and yanked her head to him so he could drive his tongue into her mouth as he fucked her against the headboard.

Fifteen minutes later, they'd both come and he was ass to the bed, back against the headboard, pants up but undone, cock still pulsing but tucked away, eyes on her shimmying her skirt over her panties.

He didn't say a word, but watching her, he couldn't beat back his grin.

When he gave that grin to her, her eyes dropped to it and it almost looked like her movements stilled for a second.

But it was only a second before she went to a hand and then knee in the bed to reach him.

She kissed the side of his neck, pulled back, looked into his eyes then pushed off the bed and walked away.

Nick heard the door close right before he heard his own chuckles.

He'd fucked the woman three times.

And she hadn't spoken a word.

—⁂—

Hotel Teatro, 6:04 The Next Evening

HE OPENED THE door and she came through with intent.

Ready for her, he wrapped an arm around her waist, taking a wide step back. He shifted them sideways then pushed her into the wall. He pressed the door closed and flipped the safety latch just as she tried to shove against his hold and get away from the wall.

He let her push him back but went back farther in order to give himself room to do what he intended to do.

Which was what he did.

Lifting her up wrapped around his middle, feeling his lips twitch at the angry, surprised noise she made, he walked her into the room. He swung her around like they were swing dancers doing a lift and she made another noise, this one just surprised, before she landed on her back on the bed.

He landed on her and that was when he heard and felt her breath leave her in a puff.

"Right," he began. "Let's start different this time."

No void expression.

Her eyes were shooting fire.

Not the kind that she wanted to use to brand him.

The kind that told him she was pissed right the fuck off.

Nick again fought laughing.

She said nothing.

He didn't laugh but he did smile, moving his hand to her face, cupping the side and dropping close.

"Hi," he whispered.

Her gaze had dropped to his smile but after he said that word, it lifted to his.

He again had the void.

He missed the fire.

But he got her voice.

"Hi," she whispered back.

Necessarily, due to the fact it was a whisper, it was soft.

Surprisingly, it was a lot more.

Too much more.

He decided that was good enough.

So he slanted his head and took her mouth.

Twenty-two Minutes Later

THEY'D BOTH CLIMAXED.

Her face in his neck, his cock in her cunt, him on his ass, his legs up, cocooning her, she tried to shift off.

Nick allowed it to a point.

When he was done, he caught her ankle.

She stilled her movements and lifted her eyes to his.

"We're not done," he told her.

She held his gaze. She did this for a while.

Then she licked her lips.

After that, she shifted again.

Toward him.

When she got close, he wound his arms around her and took her to her back.

He also took her mouth.

Later, he took something else with his mouth.

And later, for the first time, she took something of his with hers.

He also managed to get all their clothes off and, without a fight, she let him ride her start to phenomenal finish. They took their time, both coming harder and both taking longer to recover because of it.

He left her in bed to hit the bathroom.

She was dressed by the time he came out.

This did not make him happy.

"Olivia—"

She moved quickly to him, lifted a hand and touched her fingers to his lips before they slid across his cheek and hair then down and around the back of his neck.

Only then did she open her mouth to speak.

"Tomorrow, Sebring."

She started to move away.

He caught her at the waist and hauled her back, angling his head as he did.

As happened often, their tongues collided before their lips did.

They kissed hard and uncompromisingly. Battling. Seizing. Claiming. Going at it. Giving it all they had.

With no one winning.

But still, they both broke contact as the victor.

"Tomorrow," she repeated, pulled from his hold and walked away.

⸺

5:27 The Next Evening

"Don't go Unka Nick!"

His five-year-old niece, Kasha, was yanking on his hand, her expression set to stubborn, her eyes—Knight's eyes in a face shaped like Anya's—irate and trained on him.

He swung her up in his arms and she tried to beat back the giggle but did not succeed.

"I gotta go, princess," he told her.

She forgot she wasn't getting what she wanted and she gleamed.

She loved being a princess.

Fuck, he had to stop thinking of Olivia Shade doing princess shit.

Kat and Kasha, his nieces, were his princesses.

Olivia Shade was nothing.

Except a fuck, a really good one…and a means to an end.

"You don't gotta go. Daddy's making steaks," she reminded him.

He looked to Knight who was in the kitchen with his older girl, Kat.

But Knight's attention was on his younger brother.

Nick looked back to Kasha. "I'll have a steak next time around."

She got irate again. "But I want you to have one *now*."

"Geez," Anya's voice came out of nowhere. "She's her father's daughter," she finished her mutter, moving out of the hallway into the living room. She stopped close, her attention on her girl. "Uncle Nick said he had to go."

Kasha crossed her arms on her chest. "Unka Nick should *stay*."

"Put her down, Nick," Anya ordered and the instant she did, which was the second Nick moved to acquiesce to her demand, Kasha wrapped her arms tight around his neck.

He started quietly laughing.

"Unka Nick is *staying*!" Kasha declared.

"Yeah, he is," Knight put in.

Nick looked to his brother.

So did Knight's woman. "Not you too."

"Me too," Knight decreed then looked down at Kat. "Baby girl, can you help Daddy and put out another placemat for Uncle Nick?"

"Yeah, Daddy!" Kat, Knight and Anya's first, almost eight-years-old, always daddy's little helper, agreed immediately and jumped to do as asked.

"Knight, he has somewhere to be," Anya called.

"He can be there a couple hours later. Now he's having dinner with his family," Knight returned.

"Maybe he wants to have dinner with his family *next* weekend," Anya returned.

Knight's eyes settled on his woman and his, "Baby," was a warning.

Anya's glare stayed glued to her man in a way Nick knew she was telling him he could shove his warning right up his ass.

He forged into the silent breach.

"I'll stay."

"*Yay!*" Kasha screeched.

"Yay!" Kat yelled.

Anya's head whipped his way. "Don't give in to him."

He looked down at his smiling niece then at her mother. "Too late."

Anya rolled her eyes.

Nick moved to the kitchen and planted Kasha's booty in a stool at the bar beyond which her father was cooking. "To have dinner with you, gotta make a call," he told her.

"That's allowed," she decreed.

He was again chuckling when he glanced at Knight before he moved out of the space, down the front hall and into Knight's office.

He pulled out his phone and called Olivia.

The call (and not a text) was a test. A test he suspected would go to voicemail because she'd said exactly five words to him since they'd met so it was not likely she'd answer the phone.

If he had to guess, his voicemail would eventually get him a text that said she wasn't going to wait for him to have dinner with his family in order to meet up with him later. Alternately, she wouldn't communicate at all and he'd eventually lie in bed at Hotel Teatro, pissing valuable time away waiting for her only for her not to show up.

What he didn't expect was her to answer on the third ring.

"Sebring," she said as greeting, her voice soft just as the five words she'd said to him were, except now she wasn't whispering.

He liked the sound. Especially having it wrapped around his name.

Fuck.

"Olivia," he replied. "Listen, I'm having dinner with my family. I'm not gonna get to the hotel until eight. Maybe later."

"Are you checked in?" she asked.

"No," he answered.

"My turn," she stated.

He blinked at Knight's desk.

Her turn?

"I'll text you the room number," she went on.

"Right," he pushed out, trying to hide his surprise and not sure he'd succeeded.

"By your——" she started but abruptly stopped, said no more though she didn't disconnect.

"By my...?" he trailed off on a prompt.

She didn't take the prompt for several beats before her soft voice again came at him.

"By your family, I'm assuming you mean Knight and his girls."

"Yeah."

He heard an almost indistinct noise.

Relief.

That pissed him off.

Why, he had no clue.

He wasn't the fucked-up one in this scenario, working for his dad who was a gangster who did seriously jacked shit including ordering the head blown off a female undercover FBI agent at all, much less right in front of the man who loved her.

"Not tied to anyone and fuckin' you," he bit off.

"We don't exactly chat in order to get to know each other," she replied.

"You hell bent on taking control of my dick the minute you hit the hotel room, that's not on me," he reminded her.

There was another hesitation before she suggested, "Maybe we should take a break for a couple of nights."

"Uh…fuck no," he denied, after years of waiting to put it in action, not about to let anything delay him further in carrying out his plan. "About now I'm in the mood to tussle with you and see who comes out on top."

She didn't say anything.

"You gonna text me a room number?" he asked

"Yes, Sebring," she answered in that voice that was almost goddamned delicate.

Which was annoying.

Because it was not annoying.

It was beautiful.

And a fucking turn on.

Shit.

"See you in a couple of hours," he replied.

"Okay," she said.

She might have said more but he disconnected before he heard it.

He turned to rejoin his family to see Knight leaning against the doorway.

"You in over your head?" his brother asked the second he caught his eyes.

"Absolutely," he answered without hesitation.

"Worried as fuck about you," Knight told him.

"Don't be," he replied.

Knight shook his head, pushed from the door and looked down the hall before he entered the room.

"I do not know this woman and since before you even started this shit, I've been askin' around. No one knows her. She's unknowable. Mysterious pussy can be good. But mostly, mysterious pussy is just a trap," Knight shared.

"Not me caught in a trap, brother," he reminded him.

His words did not reassure Knight.

"You gotta control this situation completely, Nick. You gotta be one hundred percent on the ball. I don't need to tell you that father of hers is a fuckin' lunatic. You know that better than anyone. And this has not changed in four and a half years except it's gotten worse as the man gets more desperate. I didn't finally get my brother in a way I love havin' him, givin' him to my woman, my girls, to have some bitch outplay him and take him away from all of us."

Again, Nick was pissed off.

"I won't get outplayed."

Knight opened his mouth but didn't get anything out.

"Don't say more," Nick warned. "I wanna eat a steak with my two princesses, my brother and his woman. You broil a fucking good steak and I love my princesses. I do not need to be in a shit mood while doing it 'cause that'd spoil everything."

Knight gave him an intense look that melted into his lips quirking.

"I got my brother the way I want him too, Knight," Nick continued. "I fucked it up with you. With Anya. I worked to earn that back. I got it. Do you think I got what I spent the afternoon with out there, then my niece is throwin' attitude to keep her uncle close for dinner, and I'd do shit to lose that or anything I earned the last four years?"

During his speech, his brother lost the lip quirk and the intensity came back.

"No," he answered.

"Trust me," Nick urged.

"You need me, you do not hesitate. Yeah?" Knight asked.

He nodded.

"Shit, need to check the steaks," Knight muttered, turned and walked out of the room.

Nick gave it time, mostly doing this because he could still hear her voice and he was still dealing with the fact he liked it.

Then he walked out of his brother's office to go have dinner with his family.

In the middle of it, he got a text with a room number.

He felt Knight's eyes on him when he looked at the text.

He didn't reply to the text.

He also hadn't lied to his brother.

Fucking Olivia Shade was so good he was in over his head. He knew it. He just didn't care, happy to take from her everything she was prepared to give on the path he was negotiating, not giving that first fuck she was taking everything she could milk out of him along the way.

But when he took that text while eating the steak his brother put in front of him, his mind flashing on what exactly he intended to take from Olivia Shade in an hour and how much he'd enjoy her milking everything she could out of him, he had no idea.

No fucking clue.

No fucking clue that before dawn hit the sky on a new day, he wouldn't be in over his head with Olivia Shade.

He'd be drowning.

7

DROWNING

Nick

THEY WERE BOTH on their knees, her back to his front and she was taking him.

And she liked what she was getting.

She had one arm lifted high and wrapped around his head, her neck twisted, her lips parted, her breath coming in pants, his jaw to her hair.

She was in shadow. Before session two—this session—she'd turned out the lights in the room. But the curtains were open, the lights from the city the only illumination in the room.

Outside of it being him knocking on the door, it had been just like it always had been. Hot, fast, hard. A clash. A grab. Taking all you could get and giving only accidentally while doing it.

She'd got her mouth on him. She'd blown him. Before she made him come, she fucked him.

She came hard while she did.

So did he.

He took advantage and gave that back, taking as he did.

Now he was fucking her.

And, Christ, her tight wet cunt was astounding.

He pushed forward with his chest and she got his message, dropping to her hands in the bed. He curled over her, arm wrapped around her, hand cupping her tit, fingers pinching and tugging.

She reared under him.

Out of necessity before things took a turn he did not want them to take, he broke their usual silence.

"You need to come," he growled.

To his shock, immediately, she gasped, "In a second."

He pounded into her, pinching hard and tugging harder at her nipple.

She whimpered.

Fuck.

She didn't make a lot of noise outside breathing heavily.

That sounded nice.

Too nice.

"Olivia, you need *to come.*"

She twisted her neck and caught his eyes, hers scorching even through the dark.

He fought the brand.

"Fuck me, Sebring," she ordered.

He let her tit go and slanted his arm up her chest, curling it around her shoulder. His eyes on hers, he held her steady and *fucked her.*

She bit her lip, let it go and closed her eyes, turning and dropping her head.

Finally submissive in her orgasm, he drilled her and she took it, but not for long before he exploded in her sleek wet.

He stayed buried, coming down, liking it as she spasmed around his dick, not knowing why what happened next would happen next.

Maybe after two orgasms she was sated.

It being later than normal, maybe she was tired and off-guard.

Maybe she was getting used to him.

But when he pushed his hips into hers and took her to her belly before he pulled out, rolled off and rolled her on top of him, what happened next happened.

She shoved her face in his neck and pressed her chest into his in what felt like a body hug without the arms.

Then he felt her sigh against his skin as she relaxed on top of him.

She always smelled good, and right then that was no different, except it was better. This was because, mingled with her perfume, the products she used in her hair and the natural fragrance of her skin, he could smell *them* on her. A nuance of him and the scent of sex clung to her, heavy and exquisite.

Her hair always felt good and right then spread across his chest and shoulder that also was no different.

And her body always felt good, but he'd never had it like it was right then.

And it was not good—in fact it was entirely fucked that he liked it like it was right then maybe better than any way he'd already had it.

He took a guess at the reason behind her actions, shoving the rest of his thoughts in the back of his mind, and advised, "You liked that so much, you need to submit more often."

It felt like she relaxed even more at the same time he felt something weird against his throat, like her cheek moving with a smile.

He almost caught hold of her hair to pull back her head to see if that was the case when she snuggled into him.

Fucking *snuggled* into him.

It was not a burrow but it wasn't deniable as a cuddle either.

He felt his body still.

What the fuck?

Olivia Shade, made of stone, she comes, she fucks, she *comes*, then she leaves...*snuggling?*

Even though that happened, she made no response.

"You gonna do that?" he asked and explained, "Submit."

Her shoulders moved in a slight shrug.

Back to silence.

He wanted her voice.

As risky as he knew it was, he pushed for it.

"Definitely hot, you on your hands and knees in front of me, head bent in submission, takin' me."

She gave him her voice and he automatically soaked it in.

"I was coming," she pointed out.

"I *made* you come," he corrected.

"I can't really argue that," she murmured.

"And doin' it, you definitely submitted."

He was right, he knew it. He knew the difference.

He had a feeling she did as well when she attempted to stop their conversation with, "Quiet, Sebring. I'm recuperating."

He felt his lips twitch up.

"Good call. Plenty of energy so I can fuck you submissive again," he muttered.

Another body hug without the arms and then he felt her lips trail his collarbone.

Shit.

He should let her go.

This time, *he* should get up, get dressed and get the fuck out of there. He was getting in too deep. The first actual conversation they'd had and it was happening.

He had to step back and get control.

He didn't. He slid his hand up into her hair, fisted it gently and gave it a tug.

She lifted her head and he saw her face, shadowed but visible by the lights of the city.

"You dug that scene, master and slave," he noted about the scene that she *definitely* dug when they met at the club.

As a response to that, she lifted her hand, cupped his jaw and slid her thumb along his lower lip before her eyes caught his in the shadows.

"We should book a salon," she suggested softly.

They were seriously fucking doing that.

But that wasn't what they were talking about.

"Changin' the subject, Olivia," he noted.

"Are you asking me if I liked to be whipped?" she asked.

"Whipped. Spanked. Caned. Cropped. Some or all of the above," he replied.

"I have no idea," she told him. "Do you?"

"Think you're missin' in your desire to cow me that I'm tryin' to do the same to you."

"No, Sebring," she said in that fucking voice. That fucking voice that now that he had, he had to brace against because he liked it too much. "I am not missing that."

"Not sure this works, two tops with neither of us feelin' good thoughts about bein' a bottom."

She dipped her face close as she again slid her thumb along his lip in a gentle way that felt good just as it felt claiming before she moved her hand down so she could stroke his jaw.

"I don't know. Seems you don't mind when I top you."

"Prefer it when I top you. And I've noted, especially just now, you don't mind it either."

He felt her lips touch his.

Then he felt, actually *felt* her smile.

And he wished the lights were on so he could see that in those green eyes.

"Strange that we don't seem ill-suited," she remarked.

Seriously?

"Ill-suited?" he asked.

"Ill-suited," she answered, then went on like he needed an explanation. "Not a good match."

"I know what it means. But who says 'ill-suited?'" he asked and felt another smile.

"Me," she whispered against his lips

He felt that whisper there and in his gut and he knew. He knew he was better when the woman didn't talk.

He was about to do something about that when she asked, "Are you saying you think we should stop meeting?"

"No," he replied swiftly and continued, "My guess, we're gonna have to fight that out another way, a way we both like. A discussion about it is not gonna earn us jack. But what I'll say now is you aren't gettin' dressed and leavin' my ass here. For once, we're actually gonna use a room one of us is payin' for for more than half an hour. I would prefer that be one of the times I paid for it but I'll take this time. And we're usin' it partly because I'm wiped and need to sleep and partly because I'm not done so when I wake up, I wanna wake up and fuck you."

She remained silent so he kept talking.

"And before the next time we meet, I want you to think about your kink. You liked that whipping, you can't deny it. I do not wanna take it, but I enjoy giving it. You're up for a test, we'll break you in easy."

She didn't sound offended when she stated, "That's not going to happen."

"Olivia, you practically mounted me at the club watchin' that man with his slave."

"I'm a top, Sebring."

"I'm not taking a whip."

"Hmm…"

Fuck.

He wanted her tied for him and he knew he wanted it not just because that was one of the many things he liked, but because, from what they'd already had, he wanted that *from her*.

Not because she was Olivia Shade, a woman he wanted to cow before he gained her trust so he could get the information he needed to take his revenge against her father.

Because she was Olivia, a top, and mounted over her watching her drop her head and take his cock, he wanted her *cowed*.

He rolled so she was off him, her back to the bed, him pressed down her side.

"What are you doing?" she asked.

She again didn't sound offended.

But she did sound surprised.

"Told you, wiped. Gettin' some shuteye. You are too. We wake up, room service breakfast and Sunday morning fucking until checkout."

"Sebring—"

"Go to sleep, Olivia."

"Se—"

He found her mouth and kissed her hard.

It shut her up.

She also melted into him and kissed him hard back.

He broke it, tucked her face in his throat and repeated his order. "Go to sleep."

"You're leaking out of me."

Fuck.

That reminded him of something.

With no talk until now, the conversation hadn't been had.

It had to be had.

"You on the Pill?" he asked quietly.

"Obviously," she replied matter-of-factly. "Are you clean?"

"Yeah."

"Good. Condoms are a nuisance," she murmured.

Jesus.

This woman.

"You clean?" he asked.

Now she sounded offended.

"Of course."

That was when he smiled as he muttered, "Right."

Even more offended, she snapped, "I am."

"I believe you."

"You said 'right,' like you didn't."

"I said 'right,' like, okay. Right. You're clean. You're on the Pill. Topic done. I can fuck you and come inside you and all's good."

"Right." Now she sounded like she didn't believe him.

His body was shaking as was the bed when he wrapped her tight in his arms and heard his humor when he noted, "Now you're full of shit."

"Whatever," she muttered.

"You gonna go clean me from you or are we gonna argue about who's bein' sarcastic and who isn't?" he asked.

"I'm going home," she told him.

Shit, he had to get her past this. If he didn't get in there, and not just in her cunt, he'd never earn her trust and get what he needed from her.

His arms tightened further. "Are we gonna fuck tomorrow night?"

"Yes. At the club, if we can reserve a salon. If not, it's back here."

"Can you explain why we can't pass out here and fuck in the morning *and* again at the club tomorrow night while we hopefully watch a bottom submit knowin' you want to try that with me but talkin' shit because you wanna convince me you like top?"

"I—" she began to make some lame excuse.

Fuck, he was wiped.

Which meant he was done.

"Clean up and come back to bed, Olivia," he said on a sigh, loosening his arms.

"Not good with orders, Sebring."

"Don't give a fuck, Olivia."

She didn't move.

He did, this being a hand to her ass, giving it a smack.

Her body jumped before she went solid in his arms.

"You just smacked my ass," she announced haughtily.

Total princess.

He liked it.

Fuck.

"Seein' as it was me who did it, I already know that," he pointed out.

"Well, what you might *not* know is that I'm not fond of sarcasm or men who are smartasses *or*, and this one *especially*, men who smack women's asses," she informed him.

He tightened his arms around her again, rolled to his back, taking her with him, and when they were in position, he said to the ceiling, "Fuck. If she keeps yappin', not gonna be able to break her in easy 'cause I'm gonna have to gag her to shut her up, tie her to bed to control her, and she's gorgeous with a great body. Seein' her like that for me is gonna make me wanna play with her 'til she submits and I'm never gonna get any shuteye."

"If you let me go and stop chatting with the ceiling, I can clean up, come back and you can get some *shuteye*."

He let her go instantly but did it with a smile, a smile that came even if he was not at all happy at the same time he felt a warm hit his gut at learning she could make a joke.

She scrambled off him.

It had been happening.

She was hot when they were fucking.

Cute when she was a princess.

He could feel the tug but he could deal with both.

So it had been happening. Her pull. Reeling him in.

But he was keeping his head above water. Barely, with their conversation proving she could exacerbate the princess cute that he liked, make a joke, and throw some effective attitude.

What he couldn't deal with was what happened next.

And it wasn't her warning as she slid out of bed and walked toward the bathroom, "By the way, Sebring, so you don't waste time or effort, I'm never going to submit to you." Something, if he'd had the ability in that moment to pay closer attention, he would take as the challenge it was.

No, it wasn't that.

It was her miscalculating her position when she turned on the bathroom lights.

She hadn't meant for him to see.

But when she turned on the lights, at what he saw, it hit him like a bullet.

It was *her* that plunged the room into darkness that night when he'd started taking off her clothes.

And it was always *her* who shifted, writhed, pulled away, repositioned them if he ever got close to getting his eyes on her back.

Or touching her there.

So he knew it was a miscalculation when he caught sight of her when she flipped on the light before she closed the door because she didn't want him to see.

Fuck, the woman was usually dressed before his dick stopped being hard.

And right then, when he got his eyes on her back, that was when he went under, lungs filling with water, sinking like a dead weight, knowing he'd have to fight to resurface.

Careful of this guy, Turner's voice from memory suddenly slammed into his head. *He does not fuck around when he gets hold of someone. He's pissed and done with you, before you know it, you got a bullet in your brain. He needs somethin' from you or he feels like playin', he likes to burn.*

To burn.

To fucking *burn.*

Nick stared at the door not seeing it.

He also didn't see Turner in his memory during one of the many briefings he'd had with Nick and Hettie.

He didn't even see the photos in that file of Shade and Harkin's handiwork on others.

No.

Nick stared at the door seeing the same thing he saw in those photos but on Olivia.

The pink, melted mess of scars at the small of Olivia's back and her upper hips.

He likes to burn.

Christ, was that some terrible accident she'd endured?

Or had her father burned her?

They knew nothing about her. No one did. If she didn't exist out in the open, she'd be Deacon before he'd met his Cassidy.

She'd be a ghost.

But she did exist out in the open. She drove to work. She drove home. She went out shopping. She had her nails done. She took a Pilates class. She went to dinner or lunch with her mother. Also with her sister. She went to the club. She occasionally caught a film, but always by herself. She also didn't hesitate to go to dinner by herself. Her sister visited her house. She visited her sister's. He'd seen her with Gill Harkin. Tom Leary. Eli Cook. Other members of her crew.

But never her father.

Nick had been surveilling her on and off for four years and they'd kept tabs on her before, when he was working with Hettie and Turner.

He'd never seen Olivia with her father.

Not once.

He'd also never seen her smile.

Not at lunch with her mother, occasions that she hid (poorly) were obligatory. There was no love between those two. There was *nothing* between those two.

Not even when she was with her sister, someone it appeared she held some affection for (if not much, or if it was, she wasn't overt about it).

No smiles.

Definitely no laughs.

Nothing.

Made of stone.

But not made of stone.

She didn't like smartass men or sarcasm, hugged without her arms, snuggled, was offended he'd think she had an STD, used words like "ill-suited," was absolutely going to submit to him and get off on it, and she was capable of making a joke about him talking to the ceiling.

And she'd smiled into his throat.

And against his lips.

He'd felt it.

He'd felt them all.

Last, she'd been burned.

Badly.

Burns that were signatures of her father's favorite method of torture, something Nick knew for certain because he'd seen it in a goddamned FBI file.

That was no accident and it was no coincidence.

Her father had burned her.

Her father had scarred his youngest daughter.

But why?

And now she lived like a ghost but out in the open. Not like her sister who could loosen up and definitely enjoyed her life.

No.

Nick was the first man she'd fucked more than once in four years.

Again, why?

Both women were in their thirties, and as far as anyone knew, neither of them had a steady man in their life, nor did it look like that was imminent for their future.

And again...

Why?

A mystery.

She had been before, he knew it, so did everyone.

But his game was not solving the mystery of Olivia Shade so when he went into it, he didn't care she was a mystery.

Now, that burn...he did.

"Fuck," he whispered into the dark.

The bathroom door opened and it opened after she turned out the light.

He watched her shadow walk to the bed.

There was an unusual hesitancy in her soft voice when she said, "I think I should go home, Sebring."

His response was to push up, reach across the bed, tag her hand and yank her into it.

She fell hard on him.

He didn't give a fuck.

He tangled his limbs in hers and both of them in the covers.

"Shut up and go to sleep, Shade."

She shut up but her tense body told him she was nowhere near sleep.

He tested her, sliding his hand down her spine.

Before he could hit scar, she rolled to her back, taking him with her so he was on top, both his hands trapped under her.

She'd rolled him on top.

She hadn't done that. Not once.

He settled in, doing it shifting one arm out from under her to put some of his weight into it at her side, the other hand he moved to her hip where he stroked.

"See?" he joked. "Not as top as you think you are."

She sighed.

He grinned and kept stroking her hip.

He was wiped but she fell asleep before him, relaxing under his body and his touch which he used to smooth not only her hip, but her side and in, avoiding her scar, to slide up her back and hold her to him.

As she melted into sleep, Knight's words came to him.

Mysterious pussy can be good. But mostly, mysterious pussy is just a trap.

His brother was right about both.

But he'd missed one.

Mysterious pussy could also just be a mystery.

And Nick was now drowning in the mystery of Olivia Shade.

Which meant he had no choice but to solve it so he could surface.

And maybe survive.

8

HAVE A CARE

Olivia

I HEARD MY PHONE ringing and my eyes opened.

I saw mattress covered in a rumpled white sheet, sunlight and a hotel room.

I also heard something more.

This being Nick's voice saying quietly, "Yeah."

My eyes shifted up.

He was naked and standing by the bed, his head turned to where the noise was coming from my cell that was in my purse on the dresser across the room.

"Large pot of coffee, orange juice, a bottle of champagne, fruit plate, granola and yogurt," Nick said, still talking low, and I saw he was on the hotel phone. "That's fine. Right. Thanks," he ended and I watched him hang up.

I heard my phone stop ringing but Nick walked that way.

My gaze followed and I enjoyed watching him move.

Since we'd met, I'd had no occasion simply to take him in.

And right then I saw his casual confidence in manner also was reflected in his movement, not to mention in his nudity, all being extremely appealing.

I tensed when he picked up my clutch.

It would not make me happy if he dug into my purse. I hadn't even had the occasion to watch him walk, unless that walking was dragging me, lifting me to throw me across the room to the bed, or while he was inside me, again to put me in bed.

We were definitely not at a place where he could help himself to the inside of my purse even if it was only to help me out by bringing me my phone.

And we'd never be at that place.

Considering the fact he'd been talking quietly, he likely thought I was sleep.

So if he helped himself to my purse, it would be for curiosity and not to help me out at all.

My purse in his hand, he turned back toward the bed and I closed my eyes, suddenly more concerned about him discovering me watching him than him looking through my bag.

I felt the bed depress.

I felt a gentle hand at my hip over the covers.

And I felt him give my hip a light sway and his breath on my cheek when he whispered, "Olivia, wake up. Someone's tryin' to get in touch with you."

I opened my eyes.

His blue ones were smiling.

God, I could open my eyes to that every day.

I'd give my life to have that.

"Hey," he greeted.

Damn.

This had to stop. What we were doing had to stop.

Immediately.

Even having that thought and knowing it was an imperative one, I didn't catapult myself from the bed, haul on my clothes and dash out of the room, leaving with iron determination never to respond to another text from Nick Sebring again.

No.

I said, "Hey."

Something amazing happened to his eyes as his hand slid up my hip.

In the light of day, something I'd never seen him in, I found I could swim in those eyes.

Swim in them forever.

Yes.

This had to stop.

Immediately.

I should have stopped it last night. The night before. The one before that.

Instead, last night, I'd stayed. In the dark, powerless against the pull of a living daydream. Being normal. Having something real. Cuddling with a man after you'd had great sex with him. Speaking to him. Falling asleep with him.

So I'd made a big mistake.

I'd stayed.

And right then, he was coming closer.

I pushed back and dropped my gaze to his fingers wrapped around my clutch resting on the bed between us.

I looked at him again. "You have my purse."

His head tilted to the side and he pulled back a bit.

I completely ignored the pain even a three inch retreat from Nick caused.

"Your phone's been ringin'," he informed me. "Just stopped. But it's the third time it went this morning."

I felt my brows draw together and I shifted up, holding the sheet to my chest and looking to the clock on the nightstand.

Just after nine o'clock. Late for me. Early for anyone to call repeatedly on a Sunday.

Those kinds of calls were never good.

"Damn," I whispered, reaching for my clutch that I noted with gratification I also ignored that he hadn't opened. "I need to see if something's up."

His hand disappeared. I grabbed my purse and got out my cell while he spoke.

"Ordered room service. They say half an hour, forty-five minutes."

"Right," I murmured, seeing three missed calls and three voicemails, all from Georgia, all coming in the expanse of ten minutes.

This made me unhappy.

Since our altercation, I'd avoided her and she'd avoided me. I'd done this by not going to the warehouse. She'd done this by not confronting me about not going to the warehouse.

Obviously, she was done avoiding me. The problem was, I wasn't done avoiding her.

This wouldn't matter. If she was done, I might be able to say a few words to make my feelings clear, but eventually I'd have to find a way to be done too.

I pushed up to rest my back against the headboard, taking the sheet with me, looking Nick's way.

He was still sitting on the edge of the bed.

He was also looking at me.

"I have to call my sister," I informed him.

"Unh-hunh," he muttered but said nothing else and didn't stop looking at me.

I should probably ask for privacy. Nick Sebring had a business that involved a variety of specialties. Information was one of them. Anything I had to say to Georgia or Georgia had to say to me was none of his business. But he'd be listening because it could be *somebody's* business.

The intriguing thing about this was, he didn't hide he intended to pay attention. He didn't offer to leave. He didn't pretend he had his mind on other things.

I liked that. It was honest. I didn't have a lot of honest in my life and getting it was refreshing.

And the good news was, as far as I knew, he didn't have superhuman hearing. I could have a conversation with my sister and control what he heard. She could speak as she wished. He'd not hear it and she'd have no clue I was with someone.

I looked to my phone and made the call.

I raised my knees and stared at them as I listened to it ring.

"Where the fuck are you?" Georgia greeted.

"Happy Sunday to you as well, dear sister," I replied.

"I'm not in the mood for *you* to have a mood," she bit back instantly. "Where are you?"

She'd never know that. Not if I could help it.

"Can I ask why you're asking?" I queried.

"Because I'm at your house with coffees from Tex and donuts from LaMar's, both I'm delivering as an apology and you're not answering your door."

Coffee's from Fortnum's Used Books made by a crazy man named Tex were the best coffees perhaps (I had not researched it extensively) in the world. And I had not encountered a better donut in Denver (and I *had* researched this extensively) than LaMar's.

This was quite the apology and Georgia knew it.

I still didn't care.

"I'm not there," I told her.

"I kinda got that, what with you not answering the fucking door I've been pounding on for the last ten minutes. This settles it. I need a key to your pad."

She'd asked that before.

I had little privacy already.

No way in hell I was giving my sister a key to my house.

I looked to Nick. "I'm also not going to be there for a while."

He grinned a very attractive grin and shifted down the bed.

I wanted to pay attention to what he was doing but Georgia's voice came at me.

When it did, my focus went to her and my eyes went back to my knees.

"We need to talk," she stated.

"I'm not ready," I replied.

"Right. Then we still need to talk and when I say that I mean about David. I shut him down and shut him out. He hasn't been able to get into his office since Wednesday. He's complaining to Dad, saying work isn't getting done. Dad's up in my shit about it. You've had days. You find anything I can give to Dad so we can move that along?"

I felt Nick's hand glide around the top of my ankle.

I kept my gaze to my knees.

"Not yet, considering half the time I'm spending looking into that situation and the other half I'm spending doing his job so things don't get delayed, pile up or missed. Though, I do feel that I'll need to spend time in his office. There are things there I'd like to review."

"So you're finding something," she guessed.

"I have so much, it's impossible to find anything without taking weeks, something he well knows, his responsibilities something he can't be away from for a weeks-long audit. It wouldn't be smart, naturally. The work he does has to continue to get done. But further, Dad would never allow it."

Nick's hand, which was drifting up the inside of my calf, stopped.

I looked to him.

He was down the bed, on his side, head in his hand, elbow in the bed, other hand under the covers, head tipped back, eyes on me.

Listening.

Intently.

"You're right," Georgia informed me. "Dad wants him back in the office on Monday."

"I need at least another week."

"I can probably buy you a day. That being *this* day," she returned. "So my suggestion, get your ass home, grab this coffee and the donuts I got you and get to David's office."

"I'm not working today."

"Li—"

I looked to my lap and my words hissed through the air like a whip. "I'm not working today."

"You're gonna have to get over that shit," she warned.

"I'm over it but I'm in the middle of something else," I retorted. "That being the stunt David pulled, a stunt the simple fact he pulled it should buy me at least another week of assessing the situation. You can't get Dad to accept that and he sends him back to his office, so be it. Not the first time such a decision has been made, the consequences of which might not be promising."

Georgia was silent because she knew I spoke truth.

Nick's hand started moving back up the inside of my calf.

By the time it hit my knee, I felt his touch in my pussy.

My eyes went to him.

He was no longer listening intently.

His attention was aimed at my breasts.

I looked down.

My hand with the sheet had slipped. I wasn't exposed fully but there was a lot to see.

I shifted the sheet up.

Nick's hand started moving much faster down the inside of my thigh.

"Are we done?" I asked my sister.

"We need to have lunch this week," she told me.

"Pick a day just as long as it's later in the week, text me where to be, I'll be there."

"Okay, Liv. And—"

Nick cupped me with his hand.

I cut my sister off. "I have something I need to do. Enjoy your Sunday."

"Li—" I heard before I disconnected, hit the button at the side to turn the ringer off and tossed the phone to the bed.

I was about to lunge at Nick when something moved over his face.

No.

More than one something. It looked like he was at war with himself.

One side won, leaving his expression sharp.

"You know what I do," he said quietly.

I held my breath and nodded.

"Have a care, Olivia."

More honesty.

I'd mentioned David's name. And Dad.

There were things he could read in that but David was the legitimate side of the business. No one would have interest in that.

But still, what Nick said was the first indication he gave that he wasn't just out for a fuck or whatever else he could get from me.

But that he was looking out for me.

I stared into his eyes.

Then I lunged.

I did not need years of visits with a psychologist to explain to me that I had zero control in my life so that was why I liked control in bed.

The partners I'd chosen, none of them had seemed to mind. All of them had seemed to like it. They had provided varying degrees of pleasure depending on their talents. They appeared to receive the same.

It wouldn't matter if they didn't. I never saw them again so their opinion of my performance meant nothing to me.

The battle for control with Nick was entirely different.

There weren't varying degrees of pleasure.

There were varying degrees of *dizzying* pleasure.

Everything was a contest from kisses to touches to the ultimate fuck, with each contest having two opponents.

And two winners.

I'd spent the last four evenings banging Nick Sebring, and until last night, getting dressed when it was smart and getting the hell out.

But that morning, in the light of day, both of us naked, Nick talking quietly on the phone to order breakfast that included champagne, seeing his grin, our banter of the night before I knew I shouldn't engage in but couldn't help myself, falling asleep under him, something else I knew I shouldn't allow but I didn't stop—our fucking went manic.

For my part, I needed that time to turn things back. To reduce him to a tool, a length of warm, hard flesh, a stiff cock, all there simply to get me off.

This was what I always tried to achieve with Nick. Effort that was wasted because I spent every moment between being with him until being with him again thinking about being with him.

I suspected his game was much different. I didn't know his game but I knew there was one. I was not *just* a fuck. But I was also not the woman he intended to take to dinner with his brother and his family either. If I was, we wouldn't be meeting at a hotel. If I was, he'd ask me out to another type of dinner, a getting-to-know-you one.

So that morning, in the light of day, I had to win. I had to reduce him to a length of warm, hard flesh, a stiff cock and nothing else in a way I could keep him in that place until this was over.

If I didn't, over coffee, champagne and a fruit plate, all would be lost because I would get lost in the desperate desire to swim forever in Nick Sebring's eyes.

And as we engaged in our intimate war, Nick played safe like he always played safe.

Bigger and stronger than me, he could overpower me easily and make this a scene I would not enjoy.

He never did that unless it was safe for him (which meant safe for me) to win his point.

As for me, I always took advantage of this handicap.

Like I did then after we both tired of the scrimmage. Ready for more, I got him to his back and climbed on top.

I tried to ignore the beauty of his collarbone carved in a wide rise on either side of the apex of his throat. The smooth, sculpted bulges of his pectorals. The rippled swells of muscle over ribs. The flat but indented plain of his stomach and downward pointing angularity of his hip muscles that led to the spread of dark hair that fed to then bedded the root of his perfectly formed cock.

I just guided that beautiful cock to me and watched between us as I took him. Made him fill me. Plunging down and rearing up, frantic and reckless in my need to ignore all that was him lying beneath me and drive myself straight to orgasm like he was any man with any cock I could use to get me off.

And it was getting me off.

I was panting with the burning need to reach the end as well as the effort I was expending to take me there when I saw his ab muscles contract, veins popping out along the hard flesh from black pubic hair to his navel.

God.

Just seeing that…

Almost there.

But he was curling up.

My eyes cut to him and I lifted a hand to his shoulder, forcefully shoving him back down.

And I rode.

One of his hands curled around my hip.

I knocked it away.

And I rode.

A blue flash fired in his eyes and he moved again to press up, lifting several inches off the bed.

I curled my hand around his throat and shoved, taking him back down.

I kept my hand there, held tight, eyes locked to his…

And I *rode.*

But it had happened. I saw it. I felt it. It was everywhere. It filled the room. It marked his frame. His expression. There was so much of it, I felt it sink into my skin.

I'd taken it too far.

This was proven when, with a feral growl that I could swear originated in his shaft and tore out of his throat at the same time it ripped from my pussy straight through me, his eyes dark and riled, he wrapped an arm tight around my waist. He flipped me to my back. I then found my wrists captured and pressed deep into the bed, his face an inch from mine, his cock pounding brutally between my legs.

And it…

Was…

Astounding.

"Knees high," he grunted.

Without a thought outside what that would give to me—or what *more* it'd give to me—I lifted my knees high.

Oh yes.

It gave me *more*.

"Legs wide," he bit out.

I acquiesced but not enough.

His thrusts turned savage.

My breaths started to hitch.

"Legs...*wide*," he growled.

I spread as wide as I could.

"You submit."

It was a question and an order.

"Yes," I whispered, unable to say more, speak louder.

It was coming.

"You submit," he repeated.

My legs tensed. My neck muscles strained. My eyes closed.

His fingers tightened around my wrists.

"Olivia, do you submit?"

I forced my eyes open half a centimeter.

But my lips moved on their own.

"Yes," I gasped. "I submit."

"Fuck," he groaned, pounding deep, his lips now brushing mine.

It felt good. I kept taking it. I kept loving it.

But as I did that, most of my attention was taken by experiencing the colossal orgasm that had me so in its thrall, my entire body was tight as a bow, straining to experience it in its totality at the same time contain it so its ferocity didn't send me flying apart.

On the way down, I was able to pull myself together to enjoy the final thrusts that led to the violent shudders of his climax, doing this feeling his growly sigh against the flesh of my neck.

His hands never released my wrists.

I wrapped my legs around his hips and felt his weight. His heat. I smelled his hair. Our sex. I felt his cock embedded in me like it was made to be there.

And I stared at the ceiling knowing I'd lost.

But all could not be lost.

I couldn't endure it again.

And I wasn't going to let another man endure it.

I allowed myself that moment of him pinning me to the bed, his body my whole world, my legs wrapped tight around his hips like it was my right to hold him to me.

Then he released a wrist.

I released his hips.

His head came up and his sated eyes caught mine.

"Unh-unh," he muttered, not happy I let him go.

"I need to clean up," I declared.

His head tipped slightly to the side. "You never clean up right after."

"I need to clean up," I repeated.

He grinned at me.

That was two that day.

Both of them sublime.

I had to get *out of there*.

"You're freaked."

"Sebring, get off."

He shoved his hand in at my back, still grinning. "Totally liked bein' pinned to the bed, taking your fucking."

"Get off," I demanded.

His grin got bigger.

It was a smile.

His eyes danced with it.

Oh God.

Those eyes got closer.

God!

"Fuckin' loved it," he whispered.

His hand shifted down.

I went completely still.

His hand kept going down.

No!

I bucked violently.

"Off," I demanded.

"Olivia."

"Get off me!" I snapped.

He didn't move.

Except his hand.

I felt my lower lip tremble and to stop it, I pressed both lips together as his fingers trailed the scar at my back.

No.

"Off," I whispered.

He seemed distracted, but at my word, he looked to me.

"Olivia—"

"Get off me."

"I saw them last night."

I shut my mouth.

His gaze dropped there then lifted back to my eyes.

"How'd it happen?" he asked like it was a normal question. Like my scar wasn't an unspeakable shame, declaring to the world what I was, what was in my blood, who I belonged to.

I didn't speak.

"It looked bad," he noted.

My mouth was filling with saliva so I forced myself to swallow. He watched my throat work then returned his attention back to my face.

"Does it still hurt?" he asked.

"No," I lied shortly.

Or semi-lied.

The pain was there.

It just wasn't physical.

"Then why won't you let me touch it?" he asked.

"It's hideous," I pointed out the obvious.

"Only caught a glimpse of it but it just looked like a scar to me."

Yes, to him that was all it would be.

"Scars aren't attractive," I remarked.

"Anything about anyone is attractive as long as they're the kind of person who can be attractive however that comes about. Including scars. You got beautiful hair, Olivia. Unbelievable eyes. An amazing body. That scar's just a part of you. It's not hideous. It's like you. It's fascinating."

There was beauty in what he said, and that beauty intensified if he actually believed it and wasn't spouting rubbish.

Still, my response was, "That's easy for you to say, not having such a scar or having the time when you earned it."

Everything about him changed. Focused. Grew alert.

And his voice was deceptively low in a way I didn't know him well enough to read when he asked, "Earned it?"

I'd said too much.

"Will you please get off me?" I requested.

"Yeah, I'll get off you," he agreed surprisingly easily. Then he shared it wasn't easy. "If you promise to get up, clean up, not hide your scar while doin' it, and come back to bed rather than gettin' dressed and hightailing your ass out of here."

"Perhaps we should get a few things straight," I suggested.

His lips twitched.

That was attractive too.

God, he had to get off me so I could *get out of there*.

"You think?" he teased.

Nick playful.

He was good at it; he'd started that demonstration last night.

No.

Days ago when he forced me to say "hi" to him in that way that was unbelievably titillating at the same time sweet.

Yes, Nick was good at playful.

"You're a fuck," I declared.

He seemed unoffended and no less amused.

"I think I got that the times you climbed on, got off, got dressed and took off."

"Since you're a fuck and I'm a fuck, there's no need for us to sleep together. Eat together. Or share unnecessary discourse."

Now more amused.

"Unnecessary discourse?"

"Talk," I snapped.

"I know what it means," he shared. "Though, just to point out, I want you coming back to me so we can eat, get our second wind, and because we don't have a lot of time before we gotta check out, you can suck me off. Then we can go.

Later, when we hook up again, I'll return the favor. That's us being just fucks to each other. Now, room service shows and you wanna drink champagne, eat fruit and do it silently until you get on your knees between my legs, have at it."

That was both titillating and funny.

I didn't get a chance to experience either to its fullest (not that I'd allow myself to do that).

Nick kept talking.

"You wanna be quiet, that'll be a nice change. Most bitches talk your ear off, either determined to drill it into you how interesting they think they are or cover how little they got between their ears by talking relentlessly. Honestly, this is part of why I like you being just my fuck. Not that you get that we're just fucks, which is definitely a bonus. But you're quiet and I could use the break."

This was not amusing.

"I feel the need to be offended for the sisterhood," I informed him snootily.

His amusement increased significantly.

"Have at it," he allowed. "Though, you intend to do that with a lecture, maybe I'm good you leave before room service gets here."

"And yet now, I have a burning desire to stay."

He let loose another smile.

And I again knew I should go.

There was a knock on the door.

Nick twisted his head to look that way and then turned back to me.

He gave me a quick kiss, then, "It's fruit plate, champagne and blowjob time."

Without another word, he slid out and knifed off me and out of the bed.

He nabbed his jeans on the way to the door.

He disappeared down the hall.

When he did, I shot out of bed, snatched up the closest piece of clothing (which unfortunately happened to be his Henley) and darted into the bathroom, closing the door behind me.

I cleaned up.

I used the amenities provided to brush my teeth.

And I did all this knowing when I walked out of that room I should get dressed and walk out of the Hotel Teatro never to walk in again unless I was dining at the Nickel.

This meaning never seeing Nick again.

He could be playful. A smartass. Honest. Hot. Funny. He could look out for me.

And he'd seen my scar and he didn't find it hideous.

I needed to disappear from his life.

I didn't do that.

Like my mind was not my own, my body controlled by that mind, I walked out of the bathroom, sipped coffee, drank champagne, nibbled from a fruit plate and lectured Nick Sebring on the fact that women who talked incessantly were probably very attracted to him and therefore nervous and he should be kinder.

I also shared some other things about the sisterhood I felt he should know, particularly my views on men smacking women's asses.

He'd grinned at me through some of it. Said sarcastic things through other parts. Was a definite smartass on more than one occasion. And throughout this, he was playful.

And highly appealing.

So after room service, I got down on my knees and sucked him off.

But truthfully, I liked his dick. It was pretty and he tasted divine.

So I would have done that anyway.

9

AESTHETIC

Olivia

LATE THAT AFTERNOON, after leaving Hotel Teatro (checking out ten minutes after Nick and I battled it out in a final kiss before he walked out our hotel room door), I was at my computer in my home office paying my bills.

My phone rang.

I looked to it, my stomach flipping, my heart leaping and I closed my eyes tight.

What was the matter with me?

Don't answer, Livvie. Don't answer. Do NOT answer, Livvie.

My hand darted out and I answered.

"Hey."

"Hey," Nick replied. "No salons open tonight. I'm not feelin' the Teatro. Come to my place. Seven. I'll feed you before I fuck you. I'll text the address."

His place?

He'd feed me?

Not a chance.

"Sebring—"

He interrupted to ask, "You like spaghetti?"

Yes, I liked spaghetti.

But more, I desperately, even feverishly wanted to know if he was a good cook.

Naturally, I didn't share either of these.

I stated, "It really shouldn't matter to you if I do or don't considering I'm your fuck for the evening."

"An evening when I intend to eat spaghetti," he returned.

"If that's the case, I'll come over at eight," I replied.

There was a brief hesitation before he suggested, "I think we should define this fuck business you think you got goin' on."

For some reason I found that funny.

I could not allow him to make me laugh.

"A fuck hardly needs defining, Sebring."

He ignored me. "You seem to be good with climbing on my dick, climbing off it and going home."

"Yes, that would be how I define a fuck," I confirmed.

"Right," he said shortly but was far from done. "Not askin' you to share your darkest secrets, Olivia, sure as fuck not gonna share mine with you. But you are not hard to look at. You're sharp and smart and funny. And straight up, I'd rather sit around eatin' spaghetti talkin' to you while lookin' at you before I fuck you than sit in my place by myself waitin' for you to show and climb on my dick."

All that was nice.

I could not allow that to feel nice.

"Seb—"

"We don't gotta be friends," he said. "That doesn't mean we can't be friendly. This is no strings. I'm not lookin' for attachments. I think we both get with who we are in our world it wouldn't be smart we formed one. That shit never works. Not for anyone."

He certainly had that right.

He didn't need me to confirm that, he kept going.

"You got your gig with your family business and that in no way interests me. I do not want your gig or your family in my business. But we're adults. We both got our heads screwed on straight, or at least I do and with your need to establish boundaries, I'm gettin' yours is too. There's more than one way to enjoy someone. You just wanna offer me your body, I'll take it and be down with that. But I'd rather get the opportunity to look at you for longer periods of time than what I get fuckin' you. If that comes with us having a few chats that don't go beyond surface, I'm down with that too."

He was handing me an option, marking the path so I wouldn't get hopelessly lost.

An option I knew I shouldn't take.

"I like spaghetti," I announced.

Damn.

There was a smile in his voice I would have preferred to see aimed at me when he said, "Seven."

"Right."

"Later, Olivia."

"'Bye, Sebring."

We hung up.

Ten minutes later, he texted his address.

I finished paying bills.

Then I spent way too long finding the exact perfect outfit with shoes and accessories and primping with the intent of looking utterly, amazingly fabulous at the same time hoping my outfit came off like I was doing nothing important, just heading over to some guy's house for spaghetti and a fuck.

I did all this convincing myself the path was marked.

But knowing in the deepest recesses of my mind that I was already lost.

BEFORE I LEFT, as Harry had taught me (in case of emergency, which I decided to think of this as that), I carefully took off the tracker my father had placed on my car.

I also checked to see if any of the boys were in their usual places when they randomly sat and watched my house.

When I saw all was clear, I headed out.

But even with my sat nav, I got lost on the way to Nick's.

This was because I did not trust my sat nav because I did not expect him to be living in the location at which it was pointing.

It was across the tracks LoDo, to the northeast along South Platte River, beyond Confluence Park and amongst a bunch of dead end streets, train tracks, supply warehouses and large self-storage units.

Even in this urban no man's land, his building was well-kept, exceptionally so, if nondescript considering it had been a warehouse prior to its resurgence to what it was now.

It was a new renovation. I knew this because it looked it, there were very few cars in the parking lot (two, exactly) and there was a sign out front that said units were for sale.

The building was painted light gray with darker gray and black detailing, this detailing being mostly brickwork and some signage but also a variety of iron stairwells on the outside of the building (there were four, one on each side).

The huge windows were multipaned, likely how they'd always been, but it was obvious they'd been switched out for new.

The parking lot had to have been redone completely, considering the fact it now had green space with fledgling trees that would one day be beautiful and throw a great deal of shade.

And the lighting around the building did not invite the unwanted there for nefarious ends, as could be found in this neighborhood where there wasn't much population and not much happened after close of the scattered businesses.

I followed the signs to the unit Nick's text gave me and slid my Evoque into a spot outside it that was next to one of the two cars in the lot, a red Jaguar F-TYPE coupe.

The car was gorgeous. It was also totally Nick—handsome, hot, fast and sleek.

I wanted to ride in that car with Nick.

I was never going to ride in that car with Nick.

This knowledge weighed heavily on me as I looked to the top of the iron stairway and saw a large, square, warehouse door to the side of which were big, modern, black metal letters that said UNIT 8.

"What are you doing, Livvie?" I whispered.

But even doing so, without delay, I pushed open my door and swung my carnation pink patent leather Jimmy Choo, spike-heeled pump out.

I got out of my car. I beeped the locks. I walked up the iron steps. And I stood in the recess, knocking on the big, square door.

I dropped my hand and my head, staring at the pointed toes of my fabulous pumps peeking out from the bootleg hems of my expertly faded (because I bought them that way), low-rise jeans.

"I should not be here," I whispered to my toes.

You are not hard to look at.

I squeezed my eyes tight.

You're sharp and smart and funny.

I swallowed.

And straight up, I'd rather sit around eatin' spaghetti talkin' to you while lookin' at you before I fuck you than sit in my place by myself waitin' for you to show and climb on my dick.

Maybe I could do this.

Because he could do this.

He didn't want any attachments.

He knew the boundaries.

He wanted nothing to do with my family (smart man) and he wanted my family to have nothing to do with him (again, smart).

He knew. He knew he existed in our world the way he did, which was providing integral services to people who could afford them.

And he knew I existed in our world as part of my family's business which was just plain toxic in our world and any other (thus he wanted nothing to do with it).

He'd keep me on the straight and narrow.

I heard a loud noise that sounded like scraping steel and then another one that sounded like heavy steel rolling on steel. I lifted my head and watched the door slide to the side.

Like last night when he'd shown for the first time wearing jeans, a Henley and a leather jacket rather than opening the door in a dress shirt and nice trousers, Nick Sebring was at home in comfort.

Thus casual.

Tonight, not a nice Henley and faded jeans.

Faded jeans and what appeared to be a cobalt blue V-neck cashmere sweater.

At the sight of him my clit started tingling.

"Yeah," he whispered and the tone of that word made my gaze go from his wide chest to his face.

My stomach turned over.

His eyes stopped traveling the length of me and cut back to my face.

"Rather look at you while I'm eatin' spaghetti than do it alone," he finished.

That felt nice.

No, I should not be there.

"Uh...hey," I pushed out.

His mouth quirked, he took one step toward me, grabbed my hand and pulled me in.

I heard the sound of scraping metal again as the door was being rolled back as well as the bolt being turned.

But I was looking around the space.

Deeply distressed, thus deeply attractive gleaming wide plank floors.

To the right, a couple of steps up through a wide exposed brick arch, a room that held a king-size bed. This space was large and illuminated only slightly by a modern lamp on the nightstand that gave off a reddish-pink glow as well as the outside lights coming in the huge arched, multipaned window that was at the front of the unit.

His bedroom area held masculine, sturdy, wood furniture, all with minimal design but what design it had held a bent toward a modern that would turn classic, not go out of style.

To the left, a seating/TV area with another enormous window and beyond that, colossal open space. This space included a kitchen with stainless steel countertops and appliances, black cabinets and an enormous butcher-block topped island. It also included a modern dining room table with high backed chairs that seated six, as well as an area beyond that was set up with a desk facing the room, a desk that, from the scatterings on its top, was used.

The back wall was also exposed brick.

Inward and to the right was another wide brick arch with step up that led, from my vantage point, to space that held workout equipment.

I took it all in, noting the only incongruous piece in the entirety of the place, including incidental furniture, rugs and wall art, was a beat-up old La-Z-Boy recliner in the seating area.

Even the mouthwatering smell of garlic and spices that was wafting from gleaming and steaming pots in the kitchen, the enormous-bowled, fine-stemmed, tall red wineglass and breathing bottle of wine sitting on the bar and the plethora of salad paraphernalia, foodstuffs and half-drunk glass of wine on the butcher-block island were utter perfection.

It was like a professionally dressed movie set for the interesting hot guy with trustworthy eyes and a fantastic body who the heroine was sure was too good for her. Until, of course, he convinces her she's worth the time he's going to spend getting her in his king-size bed in his fantastic bedroom space and making beautiful love to her.

A movie where, at the end, he'd have no problem leaving that fabulous unit to buy a four bedroom house in a trendy country setting (that's more like a suburb) whereupon they'd immediately adopt a Labrador puppy and start making a family.

When in real life the man who owned and decorated (or oversaw the decoration) of a place such as this would have zero tolerance for a clueless heroine he had to train. Instead, he'd only have eyes for a woman confident in every aspect of her life. He would also never end up in a trendy country setting that was actually a suburb. He might eventually end up in a mini-mansion much like mine or a country house that had already been completely refurbished so he could start raising horses without delay, but *never* a trendy country setting.

And if he adopted a dog, he'd pick whatever breed struck his fancy, as long as it wasn't too happy-crazy-bouncy and the dog was fine with either going with him everywhere he went like a hot guy canine sidekick or being chill hanging out and waiting for Dad to come home.

These thoughts inanely running through my head, I glanced around noting they'd used the raw materials of the warehouse beautifully. Nick's space being a bachelor pad for a man with money and taste. But a woman could easily make the space feminine and marvelous.

Too bad he lived in that building. I would be in the market for something (hopefully soon, though no offer from the second viewing and actually no additional viewings from anyone) and I could work with a space like this.

I felt his eyes on me and looked up to him at my side.

"Impressive," I noted.

"I can die happy, you approve," he muttered, but there was no sting to his words because even in the subdued lighting of his space I could see his eyes were amused.

He was teasing.

I ignored that and declared, "Though, I feel I must inform you that the La-Z-Boy skews your aesthetic."

My flippant remark was a mistake.

The biggest one I'd made in my life.

Because the second I finished uttering it, Nick's arm shafted up. Before I knew what he intended, he'd hooked it around my neck, using it to yank me to him. I collided with his long, solid frame just in time to hear and feel him burst out laughing.

His laughter was as deep and pleasant as his voice.

And then some.

A lot of some.

So much of some I wanted the sound and feel of it to last a lifetime.

Unfortunately, it did not. His arm at my neck released some pressure and I felt him shift so I looked up at him to see he'd adjusted to look down at me.

"It's my dad's. Been my dad's since I could form a memory. Dad loved that chair. No fuckin' clue how many NASCAR races and football games he watched in that chair, probably thousands. Remember him holding me on his knee when I was fuckin' around and climbed the cabinets in the kitchen to get something, knocked over a glass pitcher that broke, then fell on the glass pitcher, gashin' open my leg. Deep. Long. Twelve stitches. Dad held me there while Mom wrapped a bandage around it before they took me to the doctor." His eyes drifted beyond me as he finished, "Got a million stories like that about that chair."

I did not like where this was going.

I so much didn't like this, continuing to do things I knew I shouldn't do, I noted gently, "As lovely as that is, I'm not feeling good thoughts about that chair being ten feet away."

He stilled.

Completely.

Except his eyes.

They came right to me, working, shifting, going from blatant shock to melt to sweet warmth until he closed them from me and they were hidden.

"He's not dead, Olivia," he explained quietly but without inflection. "Mom got sick of that chair. Said it was an eyesore. Redecorated the whole fuckin' family room with the sole purpose of getting shot of that chair. The minute we heard it was goin', Knight and me started fightin' over who would get it. Anya put her foot down that she would not inherit that ratty-ass chair. So, not havin' a woman to bust my balls, for once in my life with Knight—and that is not an exaggeration—I won. Though, sayin' that, that chair is worth negative five hundred dollars and it cost me a fuckin' arm and leg to ship it from Hawaii, it's butt-ugly, fucks with my aesthetic and on a wet day, it smells. So I'm not real certain how big a prize I got."

"It appears you may have much the same relationship with your brother as I do with my sister."

His arm around my neck tightened as he started moving, drawing me farther into his place.

"Somethin' we have in common, outside we both like control, you in those shoes and you in those jeans. Though I 'spect the reason why I like you in those shoes and jeans is different than the reason you like 'em."

"I suspect you're right."

He stopped us by the wine, released his hold on me, gave me an amused gleam out of his blue eyes and ordered, "You pour. Then you're on salad duty. I got bread to sort and shit."

After that, he sauntered comfortably around the bar in a pad that might be perfect, but to him it was home, to get to the bread, which was part of the food-stuffs arranged on the island.

I put my purse to the bar, shrugged off my jacket, poured wine and asked, "You want more?"

"Top up would be good," he muttered, reaching a long arm out to nab a bread knife from a knife block at the back counter.

I moved around the bar and topped up his wine. Then I assessed the salad stuff. After that, I assumed salad duty, keeping an eye on Nick who was very much sorting the bread. In fact, with an ease obviously born of practice, he was making homemade garlic bread, including microwaving crushed garlic, butter and olive oil, brushing, sprinkling bits of cheese and broiling.

I looked to the bubbling sauce.

"Homemade bread, does that mean homemade sauce?" I asked.

"Didn't have time," he muttered surprisingly, a mutter that alluded to the fact that, if he did, he could also have made homemade red sauce. "And hope you like meat," he went on. "Sauce has got ground sirloin and Italian sausage in it."

"I like meat," I assured him.

His attention came to me on that but fortunately he didn't treat me to some coarse, schoolboy, low-intellect comment.

He just gave me a look telling me he had one on the tip of his tongue and he was saving me from it.

"Thank you," I replied to his look.

Another mistake.

He again started laughing.

It didn't start with a surprised bark leading to audible hilarity with his shaking body pressed to mine making me feel we could have something that was beyond normal straight to amazing at the same time it was heart-stoppingly real.

But it was nearly as pleasant.

I concentrated on the salad.

All the veggies were fresh and high quality. With the latter, as was the wine.

"Did you shop for this?" I asked the tomato I was cutting into wedges.

"Found out no salon openings, called you, then yeah, I went to the market," he answered.

He just didn't throw this together.

He'd shopped.

God.

"Speaking of salons, booked us Wednesday night."

I turned my attention to him. "I can't Wednesday night."

He lifted his brows.

I answered his unasked question. "Duty supper with my mother. After it, I have a habit of going to the emergency room to ask them to check my heartbeat, in other words, if there is one, and call in the on-call dentist to examine the possibility I've grown retractable fangs. This, since I'm relatively certain a vampire begets a vampire and so far in my lifetime those traits have been latent."

More deep, pleasant laughter from Nick, this time with twinkling ocean blue eyes aimed at me.

And it was then I knew I was working for it.

I needed to get smart and fast. He might be able to respect boundaries but I already knew my heart had no clue what they were.

"Not close with your mom," he pointed out the obvious, eyes still twinkling my way.

"How'd you guess," I murmured, looking away and tossing tomato wedges into the greens.

"Olivia," he called.

I looked to him.

"I'll book it another night but we're not scheduled to be there until ten thirty. Do your duty. Later, meet me there. I'll examine your gums a way you'll like better, and you turn vamp, there's a lot of places I don't mind you suckin' me."

I shook my head and again looked away, allowing a slight curve to form at my mouth.

"Christ, she *can* smile," he teased, reminding me my life didn't offer me many occasions to do this, and to play it safe with Nick Sebring, I shouldn't let him give them to me.

Thus, the curve evened out.

My name didn't sound close to teasing when he called, "Olivia."

I didn't look from the salad. "I'm hungry, Sebring. Feed me then fuck me. Then I need to get home. I have a busy week next week."

There was silence broken only by bubbling from the stove before I heard end-of-cooking noises as I focused on the finishing touches on the salad.

I was done and about to go wash my hands when I felt Nick fit his front to my back.

He didn't wrap his arms around me and hold me but there was warmth in his closeness all the same.

"We both like what we got," he said softly into my ear. "That means you'll be here again. So you gotta know, the invitation is open for you to stay after we fuck. You feel you need to make your point by leavin', your call. But I figure with the way we fuck we're not gonna be done with each other for a long time. I like you at my side in bed because that means I get more in the morning. You want that too, stay. You're not in the mood, go. If I got shit on I need to give attention to first thing in the morning, I'll share that we need to see to business and I'll walk you to your car. But outside that, you need to know, the invitation is always open."

I twisted my neck and lifted my eyes to him.

I didn't know what to say. What he just gave to me was more than anyone had given to me in my life, outside Tommy. And what Tommy and I had had been dangerous and stupid and we both knew it even if I was just figuring out the full extent of that years later.

So I just said, "Thank you."

Nick nodded, touched my waist and moved to the stove.

We ate spaghetti with a spicy meat sauce, fantastic garlic bread and a delicious fresh salad.

In other words, Nick could cook.

He insisted we leave the dishes but we took the wine to his bedroom.

We fucked combative, fast and rough.

I won.

After, Nick did as promised and returned the favor of what I gave him that morning after room service.

But his ended with more fucking and me getting another orgasm.

Although I got another orgasm, that time, he won.

And after that, because to be smart I had to make my point, we got dressed and he walked me to my car.

We kissed hard and greedy at my driver's side door.

And I nearly ran into a streetlight as I watched Nick in my rearview mirror as he jogged up his steps while I drove away.

10

A Goddamned Squeeze

Nick

10:38 — Wednesday Night

SHE WAS LATE.

Nick was not happy.

He looked at his phone to the text he got from her fifteen minutes ago that warned him she would be.

A dinner with her mother should not last this long. He knew. He'd sat through watching her do it more than once.

Shit.

Olivia Shade.

He was fucked and getting more fucked by the day, and not in ways he wanted.

This included the fact that the last two nights, later than their normal meets, at his invitation she came to his place. Once there, she immediately tried to climb on his dick (he allowed her to be successful before he stopped allowing this). He gave it to her and she gave it to him. After she was done, at her choice, they got dressed and he walked her to her Range Rover.

She had not retreated. She spoke. The sex was just as aggressive, but with their conversations, the outing of her scars, there was a trace more intimacy.

And she was learning to give him full access. She definitely came out of the moment if he touched her scars, but she fell back into it faster and faster and no longer tried to avoid it.

But other than that, she was giving him nothing. No in. She accepted his invitation to be friendly but only accepted it to the point she was comfortable with it, which was not much.

At this early point in his plan, Nick should be down with that. He assumed with her remark she'd "earned" her scar that her father had given it to her. He did not know this as fact, but with her shame around it, shame that felt deeper than her simply being a woman who had what she considered a flaw that marked her, it was a good assumption.

There was a story behind that scar and it had to do with Vincent Shade.

That mystery he would solve along the way.

Olivia sharing that she might be one of the few people in the world who'd understand the struggle he'd had coming to terms with his relationship with his brother and handing him the shock of her softheartedness when she thought his father died were unexpected things he knew he had to guard against.

So Nick had needed to step back.

When this was over, when he'd earned her trust and used it to gather enough information to bring down the House of Shade, the best case scenario for her was that he'd walk away and she'd remain standing. There was no doubt she'd hate him, but she'd remain standing.

Another scenario, when he had what he needed and made his move, she went down with her father, not literally, as in taking a bullet, but figuratively, as in enjoying a long stay in a prison cell.

The worst case scenario, she'd shield her father in a way where she did go down. Literally.

He already knew from what he got from her he'd work for the first.

But he had to be all in with his plan, so if she worked against him on that, he'd have to roll with it.

And take her down.

He'd given her two nights to back off and get her shit together, through doing that giving it to himself.

Now it was time to go back in.

He was impatient to do that.

In order to control the feeling, he also had to admit to himself that he was impatient to see her again.

This meant they needed to fuck, and a lot, so he could work that feeling out.

Eyes to the scene in front of him, a guy getting it from three girls, something that didn't hold Nick's attention (he'd prefer the guy being absent and just the three girls), knowing she was going to be late and that would last at least another quarter of an hour, when the call came in from his boy, he took it.

So he was surprised, in the middle of it, when he heard the door open behind him.

He had to roll with it.

Regardless, in order to gain her trust, he had to give her the impression she had his.

Therefore, even as he cast his eyes over his shoulder and watched her walk his way carrying a green drink in her hand, wearing a slim-fitting, expensive-looking turtleneck, one of her signature skintight skirts (just seeing the folds at her sex making his dick start to get hard) and another signature—her pumps, he kept talking.

"Call the boys. Three more to come to you. Set two men at the perimeter, another man inside. And tell Lee if this shit goes south, he owes me another fuckin' marker. Where he finds these women *we* gotta keep safe, I don't know. It's starting to be a fuckin' joke."

His gaze aimed up, locked to hers as she moved in front of him. He then turned his head to watch her fold gracefully into the chair beside him.

"It'll take at least twenty minutes to get three more guys here, Nick. And Stark reported the threat is imminent," his boy reported.

Giving an important situation his attention, Nick looked to his shoes, his legs stretched out, his feet crossed in front of him. "Okay, Casey, then stop talkin' to me, get the boys there, even if they show as reinforcements, and do your job."

"There could be casualties."

"Just as long as those casualties aren't my guys or the woman you're keepin' safe, I'm okay with that."

"Right, Nick. I'm on it."

"Later. And report back."

"You got it."

He disconnected and looked back to Olivia to see her attention on him.

She arched one haughty, princess brow.

"Work issues?" she asked.

Cool customer, hot as fuck.

And cute.

Shit.

"There are a few arms in my business that can be more than your average risky," he answered.

"I see," she said in her soft voice, turning her head away and lifting her drink to take a sip.

"Melon?" he guessed at her drink.

"And vodka," she murmured against the rim of the glass.

He was hoping it was just pussy-booze, like Midori, something that was lame that she liked that he would find unappealing about her.

But no.

She had to have the added vodka.

"There's a new Ross," she noted.

"Hmm..." he muttered noncommittally, being the reason why they'd employed a new Ross at the club and not about to explain that.

He reached to his whisky.

She turned to him again. "I'm surprised. I've been a member for years now and they've had no turnover in staff."

He shrugged. "Shit happens."

She looked to the scene in a way he knew she didn't see it, murmuring, "I don't like it."

"The woman could have found a higher paying job, or she got married, or a hundred other things, Olivia. Your business is not hers, her business is not yours. It's the way of the club."

She nodded at the scene but said nothing.

"You wanna tell me why dinner with your mother lasted nearly four hours?" he asked.

"I was ambushed," she replied.

He felt his neck start to itch.

Ambushed?

"Say again?" he pushed.

She looked to him. "I was ambushed. It was not dinner with my mother. It was dinner with my mother, one of her friends and her friend's son."

That was when Nick felt his jaw tense and his repeat of, "Say again," was gritty.

"It was a fixup," she explained offhandedly.

But the blazing streak of jealousy Nick experienced at her words was alarming. And unhealthy.

And last, so severe and unexpected, he had no tools at hand to battle it in order to ignore it.

Completely oblivious to all of this, Olivia kept speaking.

"We all had dinner and he was under instruction to take that further, which meant I had to have drinks with him after. Mom and her friend left. He bought me a drink that unfortunately led to two which unfortunately led to him sharing rather openly he was interested in fucking me but also interested in taking me to dinner. In order not to earn the wrath of my mother, which I would incur if I did not give him the attention she thinks he deserves, I had no choice but to drink the drinks he bought and make plans for dinner. However, since I already have plans for intercourse, I refused that part of his invitation."

Nick felt his jaw get tighter to a point a muscle danced in his cheek all the way up to his temple.

"You made a date with this guy?"

She shrugged and looked back to the scene. "This is new, Mother matchmaking. As with any motherly attention she turns my way, she'll lose interest in it soon enough."

"You made a date with this guy."

This was a statement voiced in a way that her attention shifted swiftly back to him.

Her eyes moved over his face slowly before she whispered, "Yes, Sebring."

He studied her for any signs he was the player getting played.

As was her norm, she gave him nothing.

"You date him, you do not fuck him," he ordered.

She twisted her torso, turning fully to him. "Sebring—"

"You take me ungloved. You've never taken me gloved. You make a habit of that with all the men you fuck?"

Her shoulders straightened and her eyes darkened. "Absolutely not."

"And I believe that…how? I fucked you against a wall and took you repeatedly for days, all without protection, all before you even said hi to me."

"This is rather late timing to share your concerns," she remarked.

"Answer my question," he demanded.

"That is not a common occurrence."

"Is it uncommon?"

Her soft voice was a strained snap when she replied, "It's singularly unique."

"I gotta believe that, Olivia."

"I have to believe the same, Sebring."

"Wasn't me walked your way, beggin' with my eyes for you to fuck me," he pointed out.

He felt the searing fire which was indication she had a formidable temper she had not yet unleashed as she stood, announcing, "This is done."

She bent to put her drink down and turned to her purse but he caught her before she grabbed it and had her in his lap before she could make a move to stop him.

She twisted at the waist, planting a hand in his chest and pushing hard.

"I said this is done," she reiterated.

"What's done?" he shot back. "You bein' pissy I'm askin' pertinent questions after you strut in here tellin' me some guy wants to fuck you and you made a date with him while you're fuckin' *me* and doin' it takin' me ungloved? Or somethin' else."

"*We're* done," she retorted sharply.

Fuck!

He felt those words too many places, including his balls, his gut, spearing into his temples and burning around his heart.

He wanted that reaction to be about Hettie. He wanted it to be about his plan. He wanted it to be about vengeance.

But Olivia Shade never smiled, she fucked strangers in a way it was clear that was the only connection she'd allow herself and she had nasty scars on her back.

And Nick was drowning in all that.

So in order to control that too, Nick had to admit to himself it wasn't just about Hettie, his plan or vengeance.

It was about Olivia Shade.

"Uh…no we're not," he denied.

She stopped pushing at his chest and dipped her face closer. "Do not pretend for one moment what started us was by my invitation only. Yes, I invited you to that ride. But that invitation went both ways."

"You took the walk," he noted.

"You made it clear it was a walk worth it to take," she retorted.

"Not sure why we're goin' over this when the point is, you're still takin' that walk every time you come to me. You're takin' that walk, you do not take another guy."

Both her brows shot up. "Are you saying you want exclusive?"

"Woman," he growled, his hand moving up her back to fist in her hair so he could pull her face to within an inch of his, "you take me *ungloved*. Fuck yes, that's gotta be exclusive. We fuck, I fuck *you*. Not a parade of guys you're fucking."

He felt more of the heat of her temper as she lost control.

"And now I say *fuck you*, Sebring." The pressure came back from her hand at his chest. "Let me go."

He held her fast. "Not a chance. You are not done with me and I sure as fuck am not done with you."

She pushed harder. "I'll say it one more time, let me *go*."

He jerked her closer. "You tellin' me you feel so much nothin' for me that you *wanna* expose me to whatever shit your mom's friend's boy could give you?"

"I'm telling you that you don't get to make assumptions about the woman you think I am because I was drawn to you to start what we started the way we started it," she shot back, her delicate voice tight with anger, and he couldn't deny it and she wasn't hiding it—hurt. Hurt he did *not* like to hear. Hurt she felt enough to force her to make a mistake. "I'm telling you I haven't taken *any* man unprotected. Not even Tommy."

Nick felt his body still.

But doing it, he felt hers lock.

Not even Tommy.

Tom Leary? A Shade soldier?

A fucking Shade soldier it was known wide felt the wrath of his king and got the drip of acid on his face to learn his lesson. A lesson people knew he'd learned just looking at his face but no one knew why he'd learned it.

This thought shifted from his head when suddenly, her body flew into motion.

Fuck yeah. She'd made a mistake.

He moved instantly to clamp her tight to him.

She emitted a noise of desperation when she found herself immobilized, her arms wrapped round her front, her wrists seized, the only thing she could move was her legs and they were positioned to his side so any movement was ineffectual.

He needed to dig into her comment about Tom Leary.

But he felt at that juncture it would be an error to focus on the mystery of Olivia and not the forward movement of his plan.

"No one but me?" he asked.

"Sebring," she bit off.

"Why me?"

"Let me go."

He shook her slightly. "Why me, Olivia?"

She looked to him, mouth tight, eyes holding unhidden anger and frustration, both, he suspected, for herself but aimed at him for her mental health.

"You're of my world. You get it."

"I know of Tom Leary, Olivia," he probed gently. "He's of your world too."

She gave a slight toss of her head that if their situation was not as intense as it was would have been fucking adorable. Enough to make him laugh or at least smile.

Instead, it just registered as fucking adorable, which was bad enough.

"He's *in* my world. There's a difference."

"I get that," he muttered.

She glared at him, too dignified to fight when she knew she was beaten.

He held her glare and it was fucking adorable too.

His eyes dropped to her mouth.

"Fuck, I want you to ride me hard right now."

He watched her lips part.

His gaze cut up.

Anger and frustration gone, hunger all there was in her expression.

She felt him hard against her thigh.

And she wanted that too.

His hold loosened. "Climb on, Olivia."

There was no war as to who would be on top, not this time. Necessity dictated she take the top unless he wanted her on the floor (and in that room he would absolutely not take her there) or again at the wall and he was in the mood to watch.

But they were them. The war was had, this being who got to pull and tug what piece of clothing on the other.

But he got her skirt up, her panties off and she got his cock out.

Then she got it in her.

She could have the top.

But he was taking control.

And he did. To her eyes widening, her cunt soaking, his hand fisted in her hair, his other arm around her waist driving her down on him as he thrust up.

He shoved her head to his, their foreheads colliding.

She held on to his shoulders, as he moved her on him, moving under her, Olivia bucking through the ride, their gazes locked.

"Sebring," she breathed.

That was the first time she gave him that.

He liked his name on her lips when his cock was inside her way too much. So he angled his head and took her mouth.

They kissed.

They fucked.

They came.

A live sex scene played out behind a one-way window as they did it and neither of them paid any attention.

They had both come down, he was still inside her and holding her, his hand now gentle in her hair, having allowed her to slide her forehead to his shoulder.

"I won't fuck him," she whispered.

He relaxed.

Completely.

And gave her a squeeze.

A goddamned squeeze.

He couldn't stop it.

He knew why. He knew it. He knew he was fucked by it.

He shouldn't care who she fucked.

But he did.

It wasn't (all) about going ungloved.

It was much more than that.

Fuck.

Shit.

Fuck.

Yeah, he was drowning.

And he had to resurface.

Soon.

11

A PERFECT GODDAMNED WORLD

Olivia

12:32 – Friday Afternoon

I SAT ACROSS FROM Georgia at Rioja, barely having my ass to the chair and my purse set aside before I grabbed my napkin to shake it out and put it on my lap. This was my indication, regardless that she chose Rioja, a place I'd normally wish to linger, that I wanted this to go quickly.

"David's disappeared."

At her announcement, I casually finished laying my napkin on my lap and shared, "Not surprisingly, since he'd like to be somewhere far away to enjoy the seven million, six hundred twenty-three thousand, two hundred forty two dollars he stole from us."

Her brown eyes went wired and her mouth got tight.

Georgia and I shared Dad's straight black hair and olive skin. She got his brown eyes. Mom's eyes were blue. I had no idea where my eyes came from. I just always liked the fact that there was something of mine that was none of theirs.

"I just finished finding it all half an hour before I left for lunch," I went on. "And at this point, as petty as it is, considering I've been sharing my concerns about David for years, I would very much like to say 'I told you so.'"

"Please be careful, Liv. I'm suddenly not in a good mood."

I wisely decided, considering her moods occasionally could be like our father's, to be careful. Thus I looked away, seeing a waitress coming our way.

Georgia already had a martini.

I ordered sparkling water with lemon and lime and a glass of Prosecco.

"I would suggest that as soon as possible Gill and or Tommy are dispatched to bring him back. And it would be helpful when they did that they bring back as much of our money as they can," I stated when the waitress moved away.

My sister's still angry eyes narrowed on me.

"Tommy?"

I tipped my head to the side. "He does need more responsibility, doesn't he? Seeing as he has a growing family he needs to take care of. It's time he stopped stagnating and moved up the ranks."

Anger and sisterly tenderness warred in her features as she started, "Liv—"

I turned my attention to my menu. "Let's order. I have a good deal to do and I have plans this evening."

She said nothing. The waitress came back with my drinks. We ordered.

Then she said something.

"It's been years. And now you're over Tommy that easily?" she asked, watching me closely.

"I'll never be over that," I answered then went on foolishly, bringing up a topic I knew all too well I shouldn't bring up, "A heinous lesson that was learned when there was no need to teach it. But still, although never to be over the lesson that was Tommy, I'm over Tommy."

"You guys stole two million dollars," she said carefully.

Yes. I was foolish to bring it up.

I did not want to go over old ground.

But I was so used to doing it when the frequent occasion occurred that my sister tried to explain gently what had been demonstrated not-so-gently, out of habit, I couldn't stop myself from asking, "How can one steal one's own money?"

"Nothing is anyone's, babe, you know that. If it's Shade, it's *all* the Shades'."

I nodded. "Oh yes, I do remember that being mentioned while boiling oil was being poured on my back."

She flinched.

I kept talking.

"Okay, it has to be said that we're at a stalemate about this that we should call for eternity. I'm over Tommy. I'm *really* over discussing this. It's clear you agree with Dad that I did wrong and deserved to be punished."

She tried to interrupt. "Liv—"

But I persevered.

"I've made it clear that I felt as a human being I should be free to work and earn my own money and have the right to pursue happiness with whoever I choose without threat of imprisonment and torture. I'm afraid I have rather strong feelings about that ideology, no matter how brutally I was proven wrong. Thus, we won't come to an agreement or even a compromise. So allow me to live my repression with some dignity."

She leaned toward the table and lowered her voice as she said, "Like I've said a million times before, we keep discussing this because you need to be careful about shit like that, sis. I'm not happy David stole from us but I'm glad you found it. Dad'll be seriously pissed about David but he'll be pleased you seem more on board, sorting that out, calling the order to get Gill and Tommy involved, taking care of family. But, you keep going the way you're going, saying the shit you say, behaving the way you do, not letting that shit go..." She let that hang and finished, "You have to know, Dad doesn't trust your loyalty."

I let my eyes widen in faux shock.

"Really?" I asked sarcastically. "You can't be serious, Georgie. Gee...that must be why he still watches my house."

"You learned the loyalty lesson once," she hissed, but she said it like she wished she didn't have to. "The way you carry on, Liv, he's not sure it sunk in."

"I did learn *a* lesson," I agreed. "However, I will note that the lesson taught did not buy loyalty. It bought hatred. And in order to end this discussion once and for all, I'll stop pussyfooting around and say it out loud. I loathe that man. Since he never liked me much, I returned the favor. But after that, I *hated* him. The only reason I do what I do is not loyalty to him. It's because it's the only livelihood I have. Then there's the small fact I have absolutely no other choice. And last, the only good part about it all, I do it because I love *you*."

She sat back at my last, her face growing soft.

I watched her reaction wishing I didn't love her. It might make some things much easier.

But I did because she was my sister. I did because she'd always, as best she could, took my back.

And her showing so readily how much it meant to her was another one of the reasons why.

"Needless to say," I sallied forth, "we need the money back that David stole so if you'd like to take a break from our pleasant conversation at this juncture to give that order to Gill, I'll wait. Or, if you'd prefer I do it, I'll take that opportunity now."

"I'll do it," she muttered, reaching for her purse.

I sipped Prosecco while she did, trying not to think how different this was—having this conversation *again* with my sister, talking about a business I did not want to be in, harking back *again* to all that happened which should be history, but I had to admit (regrettably due partially to me) it had not yet been laid to rest—doing all that with something to look forward to in my imminent future.

This being dinner at Nick's that night, something I'd agreed to last night under some duress while fucking in his bed.

Not painful duress.

A different kind.

But (I told myself) the fact remained that I had survived a dinner at his place without anything catastrophic happening. And the same with fucking there every night since, except when we were at the club. Not to mention an ugly conversation with him that still made my heart race because it seemed it was spurred by jealousy he shouldn't feel and a demand from him of exclusivity I should not have given in to.

Yes, I'd survived all that.

And I'd survive lunch with my sister.

So dinner again with Nick should be a breeze.

Our meals were served while Georgia was still issuing orders to Gill.

I didn't feel in the mood to be polite, but the truth of it was, I now had two jobs, mine and David's, so I needed to get moving. Therefore I didn't wait before I started to eat.

She joined me when she was done on the phone.

"Unless you prefer otherwise, I'll explain things about David to Dad," she offered, tucking into her pasta.

"That'd be fine," I agreed, willing to agree to anything that offered me the opportunity not to be around my father. But definitely not being there when he heard his trusty friend/employee was an embezzler.

"We've other things to discuss," she told me.

"David left a mess so let's discuss them. I have a great deal to do," I replied.

"I've set up four labs," she announced. "As of two weeks ago, they're all fully functional. We'll have product by the end of next week."

I stopped with my fork halfway to my mouth and stared at her.

"Sorry?" I whispered.

"Four labs," she repeated. "It's taken time and some resources. But the people I have dealing with it know what they're doing, they source good shit and they cook good shit. Your boys will have product, and a lot of it, by the end of next week. They need to get their shit together to unload it because it's gonna keep coming."

"Product?" I asked.

"Ice and E," she stated casually, and equally casually shoved food in her mouth.

I looked side to side before I leaned her way and hissed, "*Georgie!*"

I did this for a variety of reasons, including the fact I was just hearing this now and she was calmly discussing cooking meth and ecstasy at fucking Rioja!

"I told you I had a plan," she replied.

"Does Dad know of your plan?"

She said nothing.

Oh God.

"One," I began to count down all the things wrong with her going forward with this to the point of production. "Valenzuela hears we've got labs, we're at war."

"We have territory we've kept. We'll work that careful not to infringe. If we can keep it from him and are smart in selling for long enough, when it's time to expand, we'll have soldiers to fight or he'll be smart enough to let go some turf. And anyway, we're *producing* and I'm assured what's cooked is very good. He might find it in his interests to start buying from us."

She was insane.

Benito Valenzuela did not have *partners*. He didn't make *deals*. If there was something he wanted or something was happening he did not like, he performed hostile takeovers, the hostile part defined as hostile because it was underlined in blood.

I didn't argue that. She knew that, this being why she was insane.

Instead, I stated, "Two, when Dad finds out, he's going to lose his mind."

She shook her head. "He'll come around."

"You know what he finds acceptable," I reminded her. "And those two products in our menu are not that."

"It isn't the eighties anymore, Liv," she told me exasperatedly, like it was me making the rules when it was not, never was and it never would be. "He has to swing with the times. We can't get our hands on coke or H because Valenzuela has it tied up. I had to get creative. Furthermore, it's ridiculous Dad thinks cocaine and heroin are *elite* drugs and Shade only deals in elite. There *are* no elite drugs. Drugs are drugs. Drugs are money. And we need money."

I glanced again side to side before I retorted, "I know it isn't the eighties, Georgie, but this is Dad and he thinks he's *king*. You don't move forward on something like this without discussing it with him. On that alone he's going to lose his mind."

She dropped her fork and leaned toward me. "We don't do something, we lose hold. *All* hold. Soldiers. What little territory we have left, and you know there isn't much. We gotta rebuild. We had to do that five years ago, seven, ten, before you or I even took our offices at the warehouse. So it's safe to say that right now, the time is so ripe to do it, it's rotting off the goddamned vine and *I'm* not gonna rot with it."

At her vehemence, and frankly, the veracity of her statements, I shut my mouth.

"I know he's not going to take it well, that's why I didn't talk to him about it in the first place," she carried on. "But he has no choice. It took me years to sort out all the shit I needed to sort out under the nose of Valenzuela and Seth Townsend's boys still sniffing around, keeping tabs. Not to mention that fucking motorcycle club, the Nightingale men, Delgado's commandos, those two fucking Sebring brothers and every other player who keeps tabs on the Denver streets."

"It's impressive, Georgie," I told her the truth, but keeping my face perfectly impassive, especially after her mention of Nick and Knight.

Her annoyed, frustrated eyes warmed.

"And the boys will be relieved," I went on.

She nodded, again picking up her fork. "They will. Dad will too, he gets over it and gets with the program. It'll help, you sussed out this thing with David, taking care of the family. We get the legitimate side producing again, rebuild our stronghold in the turf we've got left, start pushing for more. Valenzuela has a soft spot for me. I've been buttering him up for months." She grinned and finished, "Finally, for the House of Shade, I see good things."

She shoved pasta in her mouth and started chewing, still grinning.

I was not grinning.

I did not see good things.

I saw labs that were always in danger of being sniffed out by rivals or law enforcement and wondered what steps Georgie had taken to be certain those labs were not tied to anything Shade. Another conversation we would have, just not one at a public restaurant.

I also saw our boys who would soon have product on the street and this would not go unnoticed, not by anyone. Those "anyones" would wonder where we got it and our boys obviously were more vulnerable with product in stock than they were when our cupboards were bare and I didn't feel we were in any place to keep them protected.

And Georgie could, at times, control our father and guide him. At other times, if he felt like not letting something go, he made things uncomfortable. And there were even other times when those things should be made uncomfortable for Georgie, but since she was his favorite and his heir, he transferred his displeasure to me.

The only thing I had to hold on to was that my sister wasn't dumb and she knew all of this. Even desperate, I didn't think she'd move forward stupid and she always did what she could to protect me.

So maybe it would work out.

She was right. Our legitimate dealings were much more successful than we knew, something now we would directly benefit from when we did not before because David was skimming a good deal off the top. And this also made laundering our other money easier.

So perhaps things were looking up.

I wanted to hold that hope. I wanted to believe, at least in that.

But I couldn't shake the idea that there was no end to the downward spiral of the House of Shade. I couldn't shake the feeling that the end of our world as we knew it was near. I couldn't shake the thought that end was not going to be a good one.

For any of us.

9:23 – That Evening

NICK ROLLED OFF me, rolling me with him.

I tried to turn the other way to start preparations for making my escape but he held tight.

I put pressure on his hold, saying, "I need to go home, Sebring. I have to work this weekend."

"You're distracted."

I stopped pushing, tipped my head back and saw his eyes on me, doing all this feeling more alarm than I should (which was to say, any at all), that he hadn't enjoyed what we'd just done because he thought I was distracted.

"No, I'm not," I denied.

He gave me a small grin but did it with an unusual look in his eyes. "Okay, let me rephrase. That was hot. I dug that. But it took work to get you there and it doesn't normally take that kind of work or *any* work because you're always all in from the start."

Okay, so it was good. He enjoyed it.

There being nothing to worry about, I started putting pressure on his hold again, murmuring, "I'm just busy."

His hold went strangely solid even as he let me go with one arm to put his hand at my jaw and force my attention back to him.

"Just yes, no or kind of," he said in a tone of voice that made me brace. "You okay?"

That was when I understood his grin that was small and the look in his eyes.

He was worried about me.

I stayed braced, this time against how nice it felt for my heart to trip over itself at the thought anyone could worry about me.

Especially Nick.

"Yes," I answered. "I'm fine."

"Okay, Shade," he muttered, his hand gliding back, his fingers sifting into my hair. "But just to say, that could be a 'no' or 'kind of' and you don't have to lay it on me as to why. I still can help make it better by fuckin' you again. Or I could take you out so you can slam back as much melon crap and vodka as you can stomach and you got my promise I'll get you home safe no matter how shitfaced you get. Or we can just zone out in front of my TV."

I fought the desperate desire I suddenly had to know what programs Nick "zoned out" in front of at the same time I felt the intensely pleasant feeling it caused that he offered me anything to make things better if I wasn't okay.

I succeeded in doing this and replied, "That's appreciated."

I felt his fingers curl in my hair as he slid them down and used the backs to stroke my neck through the tendrils.

And as he did this, his touch and the new look in his eye made me brace again.

"You got someone?" he asked quietly.

"I do believe we've had a discussion about exclus—" I started.

"Not someone to fuck," he cut me off. "I know you got that, him bein' me. Someone to work shit out with."

That didn't only make me brace; it made me tense from top to toe.

"Sebring—"

"You tight with your sister?"

"Of a sort," I felt it safe to answer.

He read my answer for what it was. "So you're not. Not for shit like that. Not for when you need someone."

I forced my body to relax on top of his when I shared carefully, "You know that can't be you."

"I get that," he returned instantly, now sounding disgruntled. "We know where we are. But you're not tight with your sister, not that way. You're not tight with your mom. I'm not askin' for it to be me. What I'm askin' is, is it someone for you?"

It wasn't someone for me.

In trying to come up with a reply, I knew I accidentally gave one when his eyes narrowed on me and he bit out, "Fuck."

"I'm fine," I assured.

"Right," he stated shortly, his unhappy expression uncharacteristically unhidden. "I'll pretend 'cause we are what we are that doesn't mean dick to me. Sayin' that, it sucks knowin' there isn't anyone you got for you."

My heart tripped again because that felt good too.

I had to put a stop to this.

"This is the part where it's important we remember the limits of what we have," I shared in a whisper to gentle my words but also to hide the pain his words caused because I liked them too much for safety.

"You look at me with that sweet, sad look in your eyes, Olivia, and you say those words to me…"

He shook his head and I thought, even hoped he was just going to let that hang.

But he kept talking.

"You fuck me like you can't get enough of me and you give me you like you want me to drown in your pussy and then you tell yourself you believe that it stops there. You do that, I got no choice but to give that to you. But I can get what we are to each other and still give a shit about you. And that's where I am right now, with that sweet, sad look in your eyes, lyin' on top of me after just havin' you. And that's where I was with you two days ago with your mom shovelin' shit you for some reason got no choice but to swallow. And even before, you tryin' to hide your scar from me."

Before I could break in to stop him, relentlessly he went on.

"And I'll let you think you're bullshitting me that I'm just cock to you when you didn't hide your pain for me when you thought my dad was dead. You need that, I'll let you have it because you give me no choice."

"You telling me it's bullshit isn't exactly letting me have that, Sebring," I pointed out when I had the chance to wedge words in, but I got no more out.

"Oh yeah," he said like it was a continuation and I hadn't even spoken, "and I'll try to pretend you're stone-cold Olivia Shade two seconds after you've been a smartass."

Hesitantly, I shared, "I wasn't being a smartass. I was simply pointing out an incongruity in your statement."

He looked to the ceiling. "Christ, I'm tellin' her if she needs me, I'm there however she needs that to be, and she's spoutin' words at me like 'incongruity.'"

She needs me, I'm there…

I couldn't focus on that.

Instead, even more hesitantly, I began to ask, "Do you not get that word or——?"

His eyes cut to me and his arm around me squeezed hard with annoyance. "Yes, I get that word."

"*Oh*…kay." The first syllable came out in a wheeze because he hadn't yet loosened his hold.

He studied me.

Then he slid his arm up my back until his hand caught under my arm and he pulled me up his chest so we were eye to eye.

"The point is," he said softly, "we've established *we get it*. There are lines we don't cross. We both know why. We both got shields up to protect ourselves and each other from the shit in our lives. But that doesn't mean we can't give a shit and that doesn't mean we can't be decent to each other when the need arises."

"I…I…" I didn't know what I wanted to say, so I finished weakly, "I actually am fine, Sebring. I have some things on my mind but I'm fine."

He scowled at me.

I wanted to shut this down. I wanted to stop myself from feeling what I was feeling because it felt too good.

But he was right.

We got it.

And if that was true—and he believed it was—and if I could convince myself of that—then we *did* get it.

So I could have it.

"However, if needed, I'll be certain to get shitfaced safely with you or…" I shrugged, "other."

"You do know you can be cute," he remarked curtly.

I could?

"No," I told him.

"And it's fucking annoying," he declared, sounding like it was far worse than that.

I had the deep desire to smile.

Instead, I pressed my lips together.

His eyes dropped to them and he suddenly looked *well* beyond fucking annoyed.

His gaze came back to mine.

"And, just sayin', in a perfect goddamned world, I'd know who taught you it wasn't okay to be happy, not even for the length of time you'd give yourself to smile, and I'd fuck them right the fuck up," he declared, his words and their tone proving he was *definitely* beyond fucking annoyed.

But still, I liked he had that emotion for me.

And liking it, I felt my body melt on his as I whispered, "Sebring."

"Now," he rolled me to my back, "with all that shit, I'm *not* fine." His mouth came to mine. "So we're fucking until I feel better."

"Okay," I agreed, sliding my arms around him, perfectly fine with giving at least that to him.

So I did.

We fucked.

And by the time he walked me to my car, I didn't know how much better Nick felt.

But outside of leaving him, I felt great.

12

REARVIEW MIRROR

Olivia

5:26 — Saturday Evening

My phone rang, I looked at it and didn't bother fighting it.

I answered it.

"Hey," I greeted.

"Hey," Nick replied. "Got somethin' that came up. Can't do dinner tonight."

My heart sunk.

"Text you when my shit's done. You can come over or I could come to you," he finished.

My heart got light.

I wanted him to come to me. I wanted his presence in my house, the memory of him in my bed.

But I did not want anyone who might be watching to see him come to me or see his Jag in my drive.

"Text me," I said. "I'll come to you."

"Right, later."

"Later, Sebring."

We hung up.

I finished what I was doing at David's office and headed home because I had to make myself dinner and then be ready for Nick whenever he was ready for me.

—✂—

11:38 — Saturday Night

WHEN THE TEXT came from Nick (that text being, *I'm home*), I should have let it go. It was late. Much later than I expected. Too late and thus rude to be texting a woman who you want to come over so you can fuck her.

I should absolutely not let him think I was up, waiting for him.

And I should never give him the impression a late summons such as that would get me in my car, driving the streets of Denver just to get a dose of him.

What I should do was answer it the next day, saying I'd gone to sleep and missed his text.

Or better yet, not answer at all and make him communicate with me.

I knew all of that.

However, the only thing I could muster was allowing twenty minutes to pass before I checked for signs anyone was watching the house and then I went to the garage to take the tracker off my car and I headed out.

I felt slightly better when I was barely on my way before another text came in from Nick.

You awake?

I didn't text him back and not just because I was driving.

I went to his house. I parked. I walked up the iron stairs.

He had the door open by the time I made the top.

I barely walked through before he slid the door to at the same time he shoved me to the side.

He pushed me against the wall.

I was about to push back when I froze because Nick didn't go for a kiss.

Or he did.

But he went for a different kind of kiss.

He dropped to his knees in front of me.

I drew in a sharp breath as I felt my hips jolt when he yanked my jeans and panties down to my thighs.

I dug the back of my head into the brick of the wall when I felt his tongue dart out, forcing itself into the tight juncture between my legs.

And I felt my jeans bite into my thighs as I automatically tried to force my legs wider to give him more access.

Nick didn't need more access. He was doing just fine thrusting his tongue into my close wet.

Yes.

Oh God, yes.

He was doing just *fine*.

"Sebring," I breathed, and lost his tongue as he surged up.

But I got his eyes and I got his finger as his gaze caught mine and he shoved his finger tight against my clit.

My eyes closed and my lips parted.

That was when Nick finally kissed me.

1:02 – Sunday Morning

"FUCK," NICK GRUNTED.

I'd had my bare ass to the top step to his bedroom, my legs had been around his hips as I took his cock, but I'd pulled off, squirmed up, turned to crawl out from under him to force him to follow me to the bed.

He didn't follow me to the bed.

He wrapped an arm around my belly and yanked me back, pulling me between his legs. My thighs pressed together but bent at the hips, he rammed back in.

I moaned and pulled forward against the strong hold he had on me but only to drive myself back.

I heard his noises, thick and deep and greedy, mingling with my own, which were soft and desperate, and a wave of wet hit between my legs as a shaft of electricity shot from clit to nipples.

I drove back harder.

Nick thrust in faster.

I was close and I wanted it to happen together.

I tossed my hair to look over my shoulder at him.

"Come," I ordered.

His liquid blue eyes came to me as he kept fucking me. "Do not come."

"*Come,*" I hissed.

He pulled out.

"No!" I snapped.

He straightened, taking his feet and taking me with him, my ass in his hips, my back to his front.

I tried twisting in his arms.

Instead, I fell forward to the bed as Nick fell with me.

I tried to regain my knees and add my hands under me.

Nick used his weight to subdue me, his strong thighs to push between mine, and then he was filling me again, thrusting deep with me on my belly.

I stilled just so I could fully experience that beauty.

He didn't still but shoved a hand under me, straight down, finger to my clit.

"Now *you* come," he demanded in my ear.

I lifted my hips to get more of his cock at the same time I undulated them against his finger.

"Sebring," I gasped.

"Come," he ordered.

My entire body started trembling.

"Fuckin' *come*," he growled.

Shuddering under him, I came.

Spectacularly.

2:24 — Sunday Morning

NICK HAD ME pressed against my car, one arm around me, his other hand in my hair at the side of my head.

"You're a fuckin' nut," he muttered, looking amused.

"I am?" I asked, sounding confused.

"Olivia, you're drivin' home instead of sleepin' in my bed and wakin' up in a few hours on a Sunday, a day I think it's a law is supposed to be lazy, which means I'll fuck you slow then make you breakfast. And, just sayin', I make fucking great cinnamon French toast."

I'd had more than spaghetti from Nick, it had all been good, so I knew without a doubt he made great cinnamon French toast.

I also knew I wanted to taste it.

But what I knew most of all was that this was all I had left to hold on to in order to keep sane, smart and stay safe.

Leaving.

We could text. We could phone. We could make plans. I could eat with him. I could fuck him. We could chat.

But I was not spending the night.

"Maybe some other time," I told him.

He looked at me, mouth twitching, head slightly shaking, knowing there would be no other time.

"A fuckin' nut," he muttered again, not sounding broken up about it and still looking amused.

I liked seeing him amused even if I wished he sounded broken up about me not spending the (whole) night.

Before I could come to terms with those contradictory emotions, he bent in, brushed his mouth to mine, moved back an inch and said, still with mouth twitching, "Seven tonight, babe. Pork chops."

It was then I realized why he wasn't broken up and why he was amused.

Because he knew in just fifteen and a half hours, I'd be back.

Okay, maybe I was a nut.

I imagined Nick made superb pork chops.

But I was stuck on cinnamon French toast.

"Perhaps we can have breakfast for dinner," I suggested.

His body started shaking as his mouth stopped twitching and began smiling. "Got a rule about my French toast. That bein' you gotta earn it by makin' me come in the morning."

I wondered how many women had earned that.

Just as quickly as I wondered that, for peace of mind I stopped wondering.

"Hmm…" I murmured.

His smile got bigger as his laughter became audible.

And his eyes were dancing in the parking lot lights when he whispered, "A fuckin' nut."

I liked that. It was a sweet tease, saying he found me amusing which meant a lot to me.

Too much.

So much it hurt when he again moved in, touched his mouth to mine, but this time, when he moved back, he let me go.

"Drive safe home," he ordered.

I nodded and made myself move immediately to get in my car.

And it hurt again when I watched through my rearview mirror as he did as he always did, jogged right up to his place instead of standing in the parking lot watching me drive away.

Maybe, I told myself, when I came back the night after he watched me drive away, I'd stay.

Maybe.

Then again, I figured he jogged right up to his place because he didn't want me to see him watching me drive away.

Or, like it would have been if I was in his position, he didn't allow himself that intimacy but instead, forced himself to turn his back on what we had and jog away.

※

8:27 Sunday Night

"This is ridiculous," I declared, eyes to the TV.

"It's awesome," Nick replied.

I turned my head to look at him sitting on the couch beside me.

We were meant to eat pork chops in front of the TV instead of where we usually ate, at his bar. This was because there was a program Nick said he wanted to watch.

And we'd done that.

But now our plates were on the coffee table, as were Nick's bare feet (mine were tucked up under me at my side on the couch), and we were on episode two of Nick's program.

A program that was ridiculous.

"I can say with relative certainty, Sebring, that if a lunatic had hold of just one, but most especially *five* nuclear weapons, pretty much every country's government on this earth with the resources to put a stop to him would expend those resources to put a stop to him. Not just a single man who unfathomably has been expelled from the CIA for being *too good at his job* and his gay, deaf hacker sidekick who types faster on *seven* different keyboards without once saying, 'Crap, missed a key,' than a transcriptionist with twenty years of experience."

After I quit speaking I noticed Nick staring at me with an expression on his face that was so beautiful, I had to stop breathing so I could take it in fully.

Then he burst out laughing at the same time his arm shot out and he caught me around the neck. When he had hold of me, without delay he yanked me so I went up and over my legs tucked to my side toward him and slammed into his side. Then he slid his arm down so it was around me, holding me close.

It didn't need to be said I should have fought this. If I couldn't fight it then I should have pushed away.

In fact, Nick and I should be fucking so I could be leaving rather than us hanging out watching TV.

But we were watching TV and I wasn't fighting it.

I was done fighting it.

We had what we had and it was good.

And it kept getting better.

It had only been a couple of weeks but it was clear Nick had his life, I had mine, he didn't share or pry, I didn't either. It didn't feel surface, what we had, but it also didn't run deep.

What it did feel was safe.

Since he could do this, I was beginning to believe I could too.

So I relaxed into his hold and allowed myself to enjoy the sound, look and feel of his laughter.

When he'd controlled it (slightly) he focused on me.

"Right, babe, what do you watch?"

"Documentaries."

His brows shot up.

Then he again burst out laughing.

Vociferously.

That time, I stiffened.

"It isn't *that* funny," I declared into his laughter, and even if he kept doing it, I didn't stop talking. "In fact, it isn't funny at all. Documentaries are interesting. There are even ones they dramatize, where actors play characters in history. There was a really good one about the men who made America. It was fascinating."

Still chuckling, Nick dipped his face to me. "Olivia, I can guaran-damn-tee it was not as fascinating as an ex-special forces, ex-CIA badass and his gay, deaf hacker sidekick chasing after a lunatic with five nuclear warheads."

"When you say it like that, it sounds stupid to argue," I retorted but didn't let it go. "I still could argue it."

He nabbed the remote on the table beside him, hit pause on the program and looked back at me.

"Right, I got this whole season taped. We watch a couple more episodes tonight. You find something you like that I can DVR, I'll set it and we'll watch it tomorrow. Then we'll compare."

From what I'd heard (since obviously I had no real experience), this was a surprising offer from a man, especially a man in your life (as it were).

"You'll try something I like?" I asked to be certain I'd heard him correctly.

He was holding me so I felt as well as saw his shrug.

"Sure."

I liked that.

I liked it so much and I was so comfortable in Nick's hold in Nick's place after eating Nick's pork chops, I smiled at him. It was small but it came right out.

And his eyes dropped right to it.

As did his touch, like it was a gift but he feared it was a mirage that if he didn't touch it, it'd fade away.

So he touched it, his hand to my face, his thumb sweeping over my lips while his eyes watched.

Of course, with his intensity, the smile withered to nothing.

He lifted his gaze to mine.

And my heart squeezed at the look in his eyes and the quiet, sad tone of his voice when he whispered, "Sometimes you kill me, baby."

To get away from his sudden sadness, something I hated that I'd forced on him after he'd been laughing, which was something I loved giving him, I allowed my eyes to drift away.

He wasn't done.

"No. A lot of the time."

I drew in an unsteady breath and leaned forward. "I'll take the plates to the sink."

He didn't let me go.

In fact, his hold tightened.

"Olivia," he called.

I braced before I looked back to him.

"Leave it," he ordered. "Relax," he kept ordering.

Then he gave me a squeeze, turned his attention back to the TV and again grabbed the remote.

He rewound until we were back to where I'd started talking and he hit play.

I left the dishes. I relaxed. And over two and a half more episodes, I watched a lone, ex-special forces, ex-CIA operative and his gay, deaf hacker sidekick get closer to saving the world from a lunatic who managed to get his hands on five nuclear warheads.

They got so much closer, the next four nights, along with the documentary I chose (which, frankly, was not nearly as fascinating), we watched the rest of the season.

Plans for nuclear obliteration of London, Tokyo, Rome, New York and Sydney were thwarted.

And I had to admit, when they were safe, I was relieved.

Not only that they were safe.

But that the program had been picked up for a second season.

—————

11:54 — Friday Night

I PLANTED MY chin smack in the middle of Nick's pecs and lifted my eyes to his.

He had his head propped on several pillows, his neck bent and his eyes were already on me.

"Did they have casualties?" I asked.

I watched his head give a slight jerk as his brows inched together.

"What?" he asked back.

"The…your…" I felt funny but for some reason persevered. "Your boys. You were talking to one at the club the week before last. You spoke of casualties. Was…were…" I wanted to trail off and let it go, but like before, I couldn't stop myself from pushing forward. "Did it all come out okay?"

His lips hitched up.

"Is Olivia Shade asking me a question, sharing concern about my business and my boys so, by extension, doing the same about me?" he teased.

I looked away as I shifted to get my hands to the bed to push up, murmuring, "My mistake. Time to leave."

I didn't push up.

My back hit the bed and I couldn't move because Nick was covering me at the same time grinning down at me.

"No casualties," he declared. "The reinforcements got there on time. The bad guys showed, saw they were fucked, didn't try for the girl and instead retreated after my boys engaged. They were probably waiting for their own reinforcements. When they retreated, my team moved her out and put her in a different safe house. We found out her brother has a big mouth and that's how her first location was discovered. Now the job's done, she's safe and I got paid," he shared.

"I'm glad," I returned snappishly.

He didn't stop grinning, in fact, he started quietly laughing as he replied, "You sound it."

"Though, your story over, it's now *really* time for me to leave."

He stopped grinning and laughing.

"Get off me, Sebring," I ordered.

He studied me.

In the middle of doing it, he lifted a hand and trailed a finger down my hairline as I held my breath because that, like most everything from Nick, felt nice.

After that, without another word, he got off me.

We dressed.

He walked me to my Evoque.

We kissed hard and rough at my driver's side door.

I got in my car.

And in my rearview mirror I watched him jog up the steps to his place as I drove away.

13

Beauty Bound

Olivia

3:48 – Thursday Afternoon

"Just text the ingredients, Olivia," Nick said into my ear as I drove to the warehouse.

"I'll bring them," I returned.

"Babe, I'm goin' to the grocery store before I hit home."

"And I have to drive to your place before I hit your home so I can stop by the grocery store."

"No need for us both to go."

This was true.

"You're always feeding me," I pointed out.

"Yeah, that's the rule. Your ass is in my house, I feed you."

I made a turn, muttering, "You have a lot of rules."

"My ass is in your house, you make the rules."

It was only the second time in our time together he'd mentioned being at my house.

I felt a thrill at the very thought.

Then it felt like I hit a wall with a painful thud when I remembered that'd never happen.

"Maybe we should chat about that later," I murmured before saying louder, "But I'm making dessert tonight and I'm buying the ingredients for the dessert I'm making."

"Fuck, got another call comin' in that I gotta take so I can't continue this stupid fuckin' argument with you," he replied semi-distractedly.

"Which means I'm bringing dessert."

"Whatever. Six?"

"Six, Sebring. See you then."

"Later, Olivia."

We hung up.

I saw the warehouse and felt my stomach go from warm and happy at talking with Nick to roiling with sick.

It was the first time I'd been back since the whole thing went down with David. This was because it was easier doing David's job at his office in the Denver Technical Center, known by locals such as myself as DTC. It was also because I hated the warehouse and I hated my father, who only had one office, that being in the warehouse. Therefore working elsewhere I could avoid him a lot easier.

I was parking in the spot that had my name on it when my phone rang again.

I looked to it in hopes Nick was done with his other call and had called me back so we could continue our ridiculous fucking argument about dessert.

It wasn't Nick.

It was Dustin, the fixup my mother perpetrated.

I sighed.

Dustin and I had spoken, just enough for him not to share with his mother (who would share with my mother) that I was blowing him off, not enough for me to actually fix a date with him.

However, this was something he was pushing more for as the days went by, our conversations became longer, his interest in seeing me again was more firmly communicated and I was beginning to run out of excuses.

I was, indeed, busy at work. But mostly, I was fucking another guy (that being after we ate together and hung out together) who I preferred to spend time with so I didn't have time for Dustin.

I looked from my phone to the warehouse and decided one thing that annoyed me and reminded me my life really wasn't my own at a time.

I let the call go to voicemail.

I would find it was really not my day when I made my way up the stairs that were open to the large, loud loading area where many men were being loud while loading things and I nearly bumped into Tommy at the top. This happened when I opened the door to enter the hall off which the offices were located.

"Liv," he murmured, not moving, his arm out to hold open the door.

"Tom," I replied, shifting to scoot by him.

He caught my arm.

I froze, my gaze cast to his hand on my arm.

I lifted it to him.

Even with the order I was giving with my eyes, he didn't let me go.

"We have to talk," he shared.

"We'll make a meeting," I replied.

His fingers tightened. "Not talk like that."

I raised my brows, allowing mild curiosity to infuse my features.

He got closer. "Shit's gone down. I shared somethin' with you. Haven't seen you since. It's fuckin' with you, I know it and I gotta know you're good."

"I'm good," I assured him immediately, pulling at my arm in his hold.

"Liv—"

"Tom, let me go. I've got things I need to do."

He didn't let me go.

He kept hold of me with one hand as he let the door swing closed and lifted his other to lightly touch the marks on his face before he dropped it.

"I got a life to live and one choice how to live it, honey, but I gotta live it and you know I want kids," he shared gently, but albeit gently, they were things I already knew.

I knew he wanted kids because *we* were going to have kids. Three of them.

And none of them were going to be gangsters.

"Then it's good your wife is pregnant," I remarked.

His chin jerked into his neck.

"Now, unless you're intent on talking me into holding her baby shower, and just to remind you, she and I are not that close, I'd like you to let me go," I requested, pulling again at my arm.

He didn't let me go.

He got even closer.

This meant I got even more annoyed.

"I know you're hurting, Liv," he declared.

"I'm not hurting, Tom. I'm busy. Now let me go."

"There's shit we need to talk through, probably needed to talk through way before now but no matter the time that passed, it was always too raw. But we can't avoid it anymore. And with things changing the way they are with the business, it could mean change between—"

"There's nothing we need to talk through," I interrupted. "There's just one thing you need to do and that's let me go."

"Honey—"

I felt the icy-heat of my anger flash.

"Fucking let…me…*go*," I snapped.

Tommy blinked.

Then he let me go.

Even released, I was no less displeased, and in our new roles in our world, Tommy needed to know that.

So I shared it with him.

"You don't obey an order immediately again, Tom, this will not make me happy."

He stared.

"Now, get back to doing whatever you need to be doing," I finished curtly, gave him a sharp nod of my head, yanked open the door and I walked into the hallway.

I heard the door close, drowning the noise behind me.

The second indication it was not going to be my day was when I barely lifted my head from watching my feet take me toward my office and I saw my father walking my way.

Damn.

"Olivia," he called.

"Dad," I replied.

I stopped at my door.

He stopped with me.

I took him in.

Seeing him for the first time in weeks, I noted that he looked old.

He'd been good-looking. Average height, sloped shoulders, but he'd had a strong-featured, interesting face that was classic enough to be handsome, rough enough to give him an edge.

All that was melting. Booze. Broads. Three wives, none (but the first, my mother) lasting long but all of them lasting long enough to be a pain in everyone's ass (that including my mother, in perpetuity, unfortunately). Living large.

There was a reason when you lived like that you wanted to die young, because you didn't want to get to the point where you were wearing your life on your face.

As sick as it made me, and it made me sick, I couldn't help but think, regrettably this long since had not been my father's end.

"I hear you're seeing someone," he announced.

My heart stopped beating.

Had I missed a tail on my way to Nick's?

Dad didn't notice I needed resuscitation.

"Finally, your mother and I agree on something," he stated.

What?

"Sorry?" I asked.

"Dustin Culver," he answered. "Good match for you. I like it."

I heard the door to the loading floor open and looked that way to see Gill walking in.

Gill was back.

I wonder what that meant about David.

Dad saw him too because, without another word except, "Good-bye, Olivia," he walked that way.

I watched him, feeling strange in a way I very much didn't like and I continued to watch him as he and Gill disappeared through the door.

The noise had just again been drowned out when I heard, "Yo."

I looked to Georgia's office door to see her standing in it.

She was looking down the hall.

"Did I hear Dad out here?" she asked the hall.

"Yes," I answered, and she looked at me. "He took off with Gill."

"Come in here," she ordered and didn't wait, she walked into her office.

I sighed and followed.

I shut the door behind me and wandered to the chairs in front of her desk.

She was already seating herself behind it.

I made a point that I didn't intend to stay long by standing at the back of a chair and putting my hand on it.

She didn't seem to care about my point. She was preoccupied, shuffling papers around on her desk like she was looking for something at the same time talking to me.

"A quick brief," she started. "Our supply is exceeding our demand. I knew it would but our boys have gone without so long, they're itching to turn product. It's far too soon for us to challenge Valenzuela territory so Tommy suggested expanding outside Valenzuela's influence, namely some turf that's weakly protected in Fort Collins and Greeley. Tommy's taking off tomorrow with Miguel to look into that."

"And what did Dad say about all this?" I queried.

My back straightened when she replied nonchalantly, "I haven't told him yet."

She had to be joking.

"What?" I asked.

She glanced at me then back to whatever she was looking for on her desk as she repeated, "I haven't told him."

"But, Georgie—"

"You're not going to tell him either."

"Georgia—"

All of a sudden, she locked her eyes to mine. "You're not. And you're gonna quit fucking around and make a date with that fucking Culver guy."

"What?" It was a whisper this time as I felt a chill snake down my back.

Dad and Georgia mentioning Dustin when neither of them spoke to Mom so neither of them should know?

What was going on?

She didn't answer my question. She released my gaze and went back to whatever she was doing at her desk, but again she did this talking.

"Gill hasn't found David. This is frustrating. With all that's happening here, we need him so I called him home. I've contracted with Raid Miller to find him. You'll deal with cash for Raid. I already gave him half, but you know the drill. He'll want the other half on delivery. You know his fees. Raid doesn't fuck around so we'll have David soon. Arrange for the cash to be in my safe as soon as possible. As he works this, I'll communicate with Miller."

"I always work with Raid."

She again gave me her eyes. "This time, I'm working with him. Now, Dad and I discussed it and we want you full-time doing David's job. I'll deal with some of the stuff you do. Tommy's going to take over the boys."

I stared at her, wanting to believe this was a boon, considering David's job was entirely legitimate. That was, it was legitimate outside me using some things to launder money, none of which David was "officially" in the know about so he could "officially" deny it and keep our money safe should something happen to any of us. This was in order for us to have that money when we got out of whatever jam we found ourselves in or to use it to fight our way out of that jam.

This now was a joke considering David stole a great deal of it, but it was supposed to be a financial safeguard should we need someone to cover our assets, as it were.

His job wasn't exactly exciting but there was much to say about the fact that doing it couldn't land me in prison.

Not to mention, I hated my job and not only because it could land me in prison.

I also hated the warehouse.

David's small but swank office in DTC, his assistant and his part-time book-keeper were tons better than the warehouse.

But there were a lot of changes happening with little to no discussion. Dad was not in the know about some of them which made me extremely uneasy. And Georgia could get in her head, get focused and be abrupt or vague because of it. But her manner now was demanding and dismissive, the former she could be, of a sort. The latter, rarely.

And last, I took care of the boys and my doing it was the only reason they'd stuck by us so long. I never discussed Tommy with them but I had concerns about them respecting him enough to take orders from him. But at the very least, there should be a transition so I could build that if it wasn't there.

"Your reward for finding David's bullshit," Georgia went on. "Now, like you always wanted it, you're clean. We'll do monthly meetings but you stay clean. Dad feels, and I agree, that we've learned from this that the person who does David's job should be in the family. That's you."

"I..." I shook my head then quickly nodded it. "Okay, Georgia. But—"

I got no further.

"Clear what you need to clear from your office and we'll make a meeting for you to go over whatever you have to go over with me," she ordered. "But I want you officially out of the warehouse by next Friday."

I nodded again. "Right, but I think we should talk about transitioning—"

"And make a date with Culver," she spoke over me, obviously in conclusion because her attention went back to her desk and her body language stated she'd dismissed me.

But she'd again mentioned Dustin which was strange and disturbing.

"Are you talking to Mom?" I asked with disbelief.

"We've both extended olive branches," she shocked me by saying. "I'm not going to be taking her shit over martinis anytime soon but I've given her voodoo doll a rest."

So it was Mom who'd shared about Dustin.

And likely Georgia who shared it with Dad.

"Georgia," I called.

"What?" she asked, locating what she needed, a folder, and picking up a pen as she opened it and focused on whatever was inside.

"Georgie," I said quietly.

She shifted her attention to me.

"You need to talk to Dad," I advised.

She said nothing.

I kept advising.

"I agree with looking into expansion outside Valenzuela's territory, but we should sell to locals who can distribute. We shouldn't put our own men there. And please be patient. Don't push too soon too fast."

"I hear you, Liv, but, babe, got shit to do," she replied.

I tipped my head to the side. "Is there something you aren't telling me?"

"Outside the fact Dad lost his fucking mind at that shit David pulled, he's eager to have him found and to put a line under that, including getting our fucking money back, and he was surprised and pleased you sorted that shit...no."

There was no hesitation, no shift in her eyes.

I fancied Georgie could lie successfully to anybody.

But not to me.

So I relaxed.

Okay, maybe all was good.

"I should help transition the boys to Tommy," I told her.

"It's already done."

I didn't like that.

"Georgie—"

She lifted a hand my way. "You're too easy on them, Liv. They're good. They've got money coming in, product going out. And Tommy's definitely watched you for years. He knows those boys and how to handle them. It's already working."

I could believe that.

"Right, then I'll let you get to it," I murmured, turning to leave.

"Thanks" she said to my back, but distantly. She was moving on.

I moved on too, only glancing at her marking on the papers in that folder before I closed the door to her office and moved to mine.

It had been weeks so it felt weird being there. Especially right then, with the unexpected but definitely not unwanted news that my job description had changed. Changed to something I greatly preferred doing. Something safer. Something that maybe in doing it, I might get an hour or two's sleep at night, having a clear head and feeling moderately (but not completely, never that) clean.

It was something that should make me smile.

Hell, it was something that should make me twirl with glee.

I did not twirl with glee.

Because it was unexpected. And it was swift. There had been nearly zero discussion about it with me, and my sister could be decisive, but she wasn't stupid, she knew I had the most level head of all of us and she talked things through.

She hadn't talked it through about the labs before she put them in operation either.

Not with me.

Not with our father.

Something was changing and as much as I wanted it to feel right, it felt wrong and it did nothing to make me feel any less like the world as I knew it was shifting under my feet.

And, even more than usual, I was powerless to stop the results of that shift.

Even if it meant the earth opened up and swallowed the whole of me.

10:42 – That Evening

"Hey."

My eyes moved from their contemplation of Nick's super-cool reddish-pink glow light to his face.

He was curled up, head and shoulders to a pile of pillows in his bed at his headboard, his chest on display, his lower body partially tangled in sheets.

Somehow, between orgasm and post-orgasm cuddling-esque maneuvers (as we did them, Nick didn't cuddle, I didn't either—we both still did) to now, I'd shifted position.

I had some of his sheets tangled around my legs, partially around my ass, but my back was exposed, including my scar, and I had my arm on his gut, my chin to my arm, and my attention to the doom I sensed hovering in my world.

When he got that attention, I decided first things first and shifted the sheet so it covered my ass and the scars.

I watched his eyes shaft that way briefly, his mouth tightening in what appeared to be mild frustration. This was something he did whenever I showed any indication of embarrassment about my scar. Though, I had to admit, me doing that was happening on a rarer occasion. It was just that I felt vulnerable right then for some reason.

It was also something he wiped clean from his expression when he looked back to me.

"You're a million miles away," he noted.

"I want you to be someone else," I blurted.

He blinked before he smiled, his body faintly shaking, his smiling lips muttering, "And she knows just how to gut a guy."

"Someone I can trust," I explained.

His humor instantly fled.

"In fact," I went on ridiculously and definitely stupidly, "it'd be good if there was a single fucking person on this godforsaken planet I could trust."

Knowing that was ridiculous and stupid, but it feeling good to get out anyway, I decided that was enough and it was time to go home.

So I pushed up and twisted around to exit the bed.

As I was learning with Nick, I shouldn't have wasted the effort. If I dropped a bomb like that, he'd not let it go and make it so I couldn't either.

So it was not a surprise I found myself on my back, more tangled in the sheets, now hopelessly so, and if that wasn't enough, a good deal of his weight was bearing down on me.

"You okay?" he asked.

I looked up at him and I did it hard, searching, trying to find anything, absolutely anything that would tell me where he was at, *really at*, with me.

But all I could see was marginal concern, the rest he held hidden.

Which told me where he was at with me.

Which was precisely where I was at with him.

And lastly, it was exactly where we'd always be.

I was never okay but that wasn't for then or ever, for him or anyone. It was just what it was and it was all for me.

So I weighed my words and gave him what I thought was safe.

"It's just that I learned some interesting things today which could lead to good or it could..." I shrugged, "not."

"Let me guess, Olivia Shade is not an optimist," he remarked.

I almost smiled.

Instead I confirmed, "My glass has always been half empty. That is, when there was anything in the damned thing at all."

I watched his features at war again, definite concern and also curiosity, those along with what appeared to be a hint of unease.

But he settled into the concern.

"Wanna make a deal?" he asked quietly.

I felt my neck muscles tense as I felt us shift to dangerous ground.

"Sebring," was all I said.

"Half an hour, you let it all hang out, you give me what you got, lay it all on me. You're worried, you let it out. You want advice, I'll give it to you honestly. Cone of silence. It goes no further than this bed. It's just you and me. And after that half an hour, it's forgotten. We'll never speak of it again and you can trust it's buried with me. And you can trust that, Olivia. Swear to fuck. You got half an hour where you are not you and I am not me. We're other people, something else to each other and you can know down to your soul during that time that you've got what you need from me and you got it safely."

I stared into his beautiful blue eyes set in his handsome face before my gaze drifted. To his spiky dark hair. His corded neck. Even his well-formed ears. Taking him all in, wanting that. Wanting it, and really having it, even if only for half an hour. Wanting it like you wouldn't believe.

I could taste that want in my mouth.

I even fancied I could live forever feeding on just those thirty short minutes with him being everything I needed him to be, naked, his weight warming me, his cum still inside me, tangled up in his sheets, safe in his bed, safe, *safe*, safe to unload on *somebody* even a hint of the shit that buried me.

And the tingling in my throat hurt so bad, it felt like it would strangle me, knowing how bad I wanted that, and using his words—knowing how down deep in my soul I could never risk it.

Which meant I could never have it.

Not with him.

Not with anybody.

But that pain wasn't about anybody.

That pain was about not ever having it with Nick.

"Olivia," he whispered and the way he said my name I knew at least some of what I was feeling was leaking out of me.

"I have to go," I whispered back.

"Spend the night," he urged gently.

God, I wanted that too. To again sleep beside Nick. To wake up next to him. I fought that want every night. Every single night, I fought a want I wanted *badly*.

To have it just one more time.

One more.

I shook my head and swallowed against the pain.

He dropped closer, his hand coming up to stroke the side my neck.

"Change the deal. Take the whole night. We got until morning to be what you need us to be," he pushed. "Swear to Christ, you're safe right here. I can give you that, Olivia. I can give you the night. I promise you that."

The night.

Heaven.

Bliss.

For me, an eternity.

I shook my head again.

"Whatever it is, you don't give it to me, what'll you do with it?" he asked.

I shook my head again.

"Give it to me," he whispered.

"I have to go, Sebring."

"Give it to me, Olivia."

"Please get off me."

We stared at each other.

He stroked my neck.

I battled the burn in my throat.

Finally, he dipped his head, his nose gliding along my cheek until he touched his mouth to the skin just in front of my ear.

And then he shattered my world.

"You didn't take that deal and I get that, Olivia. It's smart. I know, I'd do the same thing," he said there, his lips skimming against my skin. "You didn't take what I was offering but in this moment, I gotta say something. I'm gonna say it once and it's what you need know."

With that introduction, he pressed closer and gave it to me.

"If you let whatever you got inside you loose, you'd make a man incredibly happy. You'd be a dream he couldn't build. You'd be everything. You should not be fuckin' a man who can give you nothing. You should find one you can trust who knows nothing for certain in the world except you're his everything. I want you to come back to me tomorrow night. And the next. And the next. But I hope like fuck one day you disappear and I never hear from you again, no one ever hears from you again. And I hope that because I'll know that'll be the day you get what you deserve. Bein' able to let loose with a man you trust who thinks you're his everything."

When he stopped talking, I turned my head and drew in a slow, deep breath, taking him in, my nose brushing his skin, knowing, the day I died, my last thought, my last feeling, the last scent I'd experience was going to be the memory of that breath.

Drawing in what I wanted but could never have.

Drawing in Nick Sebring.

Drawing in a Nick Sebring who'd just told me that man who I could trust who would think I was his everything was not nor ever would be *him*.

Then I whispered, "Sebring, please get off of me."

It felt like I took more of his weight, like his powerful body slumped in defeat, right before he got off me.

And unfortunately, so gently to the point it was tenderly, he helped extricate me from the sheets and put me on my feet.

I got dressed. He did too so we could dance our dance, one neither of us enjoyed, one neither of us had the strength to stop.

In other words, so he could walk me to my car.

We stood at my driver's side door and I wanted a hard, rough kiss to remind me of what we were.

But I knew I wouldn't get it.

I didn't.

Instead, he lifted both his hands to cup my face and got deep in my space.

"You'll be back tomorrow night?" he asked.

"Yeah," I answered.

"Yeah," he whispered like it hurt to say.

"You do know, Sebring, that you should also be fucking a woman who can give you more than me," I pointed out.

He'd already shattered my world.

But that was when he destroyed me.

"Funny how I can't for the life of me figure out what that more would be."

Slowly, I closed my eyes.

I felt him shift before I felt his lips touch my forehead.

I opened my eyes.

"Tomorrow night, Olivia."

I nodded.

He let me go and stepped away.

I got in my car and only glanced at him briefly to lift my chin before I drove away.

For once, I didn't look in my rearview.

But I made sure I was well away when I allowed myself to pull over and dissolve into tears.

The only thing I had, the only thing that gave me the strength to sort myself out, get back on the road, get home, get to bed and keep breathing was I knew.

I knew I had something to look forward to.

I knew I'd be with Nick the way I could have him and the way he could have me the next evening.

Only a few hours away.

Only a few hours.

And I'd again have Nick.

—◦◦◦—

Nick

NICK STOOD AT the top of his steps and watched the dark streets until he couldn't see the back lights of Olivia's Range Rover anymore.

Only then did he go into his unit.

He slid the door closed behind him and bolted it.

He stared at his place.

It was a great place. He liked it. He'd worked hard for it. He'd earned everything in there.

Gone were the days he tried to find the easy way, living under the shadow of Knight, deciding, since he could never beat his brother he might as well use him to get the good things in life.

Now they were his but only because he made it that way. He'd worked hard. He'd done it.

So yeah, he liked his place. He liked his car. He liked his clothes.

He had it all and he liked it all.

He had it all.

The look on Olivia's face after he offered his deal blistered his brain.

Fuck, he did not have it all.

And Olivia Shade was not a mystery.

With the time they'd spent together, he now knew so down deep it was the fucking air he breathed that Olivia Shade was something of exquisite beauty not allowed to be what she needed to be.

Beauty bound.

She was not a ghost who could be seen.

She was a hostage in a lavish cage.

Like how she got her scar, he could not know this with any certainty since he could never ask because she'd never tell.

He still knew it right to his balls.

It was not his job to set her free.

It had nothing to do with him.

She was not his end game.

He had to let her be.

He had to end it with her and find another way.

He had the power to save her from one ugly thing that infected her life.

And he was going to save her from that.

He was going to save her from Nick Sebring.

14

HABIT

Olivia

5:12 p.m. — The Next Day

I STARED AT MY phone.

I was at David's office, now my office, working, trying to catch up. Until I shifted it to Georgia I was still buried under two jobs.

I wasn't thinking about work.

Normally by now, Nick had texted me. Told me when I was free to come over. Usually sometime around six and usually including telling me what he was going to be cooking.

No text.

I waited. I worked. I worried.

I went home at close to seven and still there was nothing from Nick.

I made myself a big salad, ate it all alone in my huge kitchen, and close to nine, texted, *Are you okay?*

I eventually went to bed.

It was the first night in three weeks I'd hit my bed without first hitting Nick's so Nick could hit me.

I tossed and turned all night, my phone by my bed.

Dawn came.

And from Nick, there was nothing.

—∞—

8:36 p.m. — Three Days Later

I KNOCKED AT Nick's door.

The Jag was there. The huge windows that, on the stairs, in his recessed entryway or even from the street I could not see into, were lit, the soft glow from the bedroom, a brighter glow from the living room.

I heard nothing.

He didn't answer the door.

I looked to the large signature bows of the black Valentino platform, peep-toe pumps I wore.

Those bows, so simple, still a thing of beauty.

At least there was some beauty in the world I could own.

I looked to Nick's door.

He was in there.

But we were over.

He was the smart one.

The strong one.

Thank God one of us was.

I walked down the steps with my head held high. We were friendly. He'd stopped communicating. Now I was just an acquaintance he'd fucked who was checking on him.

I had no proof but still, I knew he was fine.

I could move on.

Yes, I would move on.

Nothing to look forward to, not anymore.

But that was okay. Naturally, I'd keep breathing.

It was habit.

I made it to the bottom of the steps, went to my car, got in and drove away.

I didn't even look up to Nick's unit.

He was already a memory

⸺※⸺

Nick

NICK STOOD AT the window, teeth clenched, muscle jumping in his cheek and he watched her walk to her car.

Total poise.

Like a princess.

His princess.

The adult one.

"Shit," he whispered.

She got in her Range Rover and drove away.

And she did that not once looking up.

Not once.

That was good.

If she'd looked, he wouldn't have been able to stop himself going after her.

It was better this way for everybody.

Especially Olivia.

⸺※⸺

7:19 p.m. — That Next Friday

NICK STARED AT the texts on his phone.

Are you okay?

Missed yesterday. Tonight?

Sebring, is everything okay?

After that, nothing.

His head shot up and his mouth got tight when he saw Turner had slid on the stool next to him. He'd slid off that stool five minutes ago to use the bathroom. He'd returned and Nick was so deep in thought about Olivia, he didn't feel him come back.

"Responses kinda slow, Sebring," Turner murmured, eyeing him closely.

Nick didn't reply. He looked away from his friend, lifting his drink to throw the rest of it back, his eyes catching on a woman's at the end of the bar who was looking at him.

She gave him the smile that was his opening.

He looked away and threw back his whisky.

He returned his attention to Turner.

"I need another way to get at Harkin and Shade," he told him.

Turner held his gaze, his lips now thinned.

They unthinned so he could ask, "Are you serious?"

Nick saw the bartender pass, got his attention and jerked up his chin before tipping his head to Eric.

The bartender nodded.

Nick looked back to Turner. "Olivia's not gonna work."

"Because she doesn't know dick that'll help you or because you like havin' your dick in her too much to use her to help you?" Turner asked.

"We're not discussing that," Nick stated. "You don't have any ideas, all right. You got thoughts on Olivia you feel like sharing, that's not happening."

"Seems there's a pattern with you, work a job, get pussy during it, you fall for it."

Nick turned fully to Eric.

"Careful," he warned.

Turner tilted his head to the side mockingly. "Careful, me talkin' trash about Hettie or careful me talkin' trash about Olivia fuckin' Shade?"

"You hear me say we're not talkin' about this?" Nick asked.

"I hear you say we're not talking about Olivia fuckin' Shade," Eric returned.

"Yeah, that's what I said," Nick confirmed.

Turner's expression shifted from seriously annoyed to pissed before he clipped, "Jesus, brother. She's Olivia *fucking* Shade." He got close and bit out low, "The daughter of the man who ordered Hettie executed."

Nick's response was just as low. "I might be wrong but I think I remember that better than you."

"Seems to me, you protectin' that bitch, you mighta forgot it."

"Careful," Nick repeated, this time in a whisper.

Turner leaned back. "Are you fucking serious? Hettie was yours but she was also a member of *my* team. She got whacked under *my* watch. And you get that, Nick. I know you do since you were a member of that team too."

Their drinks were dropped on the bar and Turner glanced at the bartender as they were.

Nick didn't take his eyes off Turner and only spoke when the bartender was gone.

Then he asked, "You know what Tom Leary did to earn his acid?"

"Denver lore, brother," Eric gritted out, still pissed. "Leary a walking, talking lesson to any soldier who done Shade wrong."

"Yeah, I know that. But do you know *why* he earned his acid?"

"Not thinkin' Shade gave a shit what the lesson was for, just that the lesson was learned and not just by Leary but anyone who'd clap eyes on him."

"Olivia's back is burned to shit."

Nick watched Eric's head twitch violently.

"What the fuck?" he asked quietly.

"Not acid. No clue what it was but it left scars and a lot of them. A fuckuva lot more than Leary earned. Look at Olivia's, feel it in my scrotum, the pain that had to come with gettin' those scars."

Turner's brows went up. "Her father?"

"Could be an accident. Could be a lot of shit. That is, could be if her father wasn't Vincent Shade and known for doin' that crap. But she said she 'earned' them. You have an accident, you ever use that terminology?"

Eric turned to his vodka rocks and lifted it, muttering, "No."

"She never smiles," Nick said as Turner took a drink.

His friend gave his gaze back to Nick but he didn't speak.

"Not true, twice. Fucked her countless times, had her at my place every night for weeks. Ate dinner with her. Watched mindless TV. Saw her smile twice and both of them barely counted. Felt her smile but didn't see them. She'd never let me in, Eric. Not because she's protecting her father, because, if she does and she gets caught, what'll she get? She knows. I saw those scars so I fuckin' know. I'm not gonna fail in my mission but the slim chance I do and she gets caught between him and me, he'll make her pay. And I'm not gonna be responsible for that."

"She's part of his business, Nick," Turner reminded him.

"She hates her mother. I get a sense she's relatively tight with her sister but that only goes so far. But she never talks about him. It's like he doesn't exist. And it's not because we were both keepin' shit to ourselves because that's the way it is with people like us. She's the most inaccessible person I've ever met. But if she opens up even minutely, lookin' into her eyes when it's there, it's like falling into a pit of misery."

"Jesus," Turner muttered.

"Yeah," Nick muttered back, remembering that look in Olivia's eyes and shifting to the bar to grab his drink.

"If it's her father who did that to her, why doesn't she leave?" Turner asked.

Nick threw back a healthy pull before answering.

"The entirety of the small of her back to along the top of her hips. Not a lot of space but too much for what happened to it." He turned his eyes to Turner. "Mutilated, man. Not even a centimeter of healthy skin. That at the hands of Daddy. Whatever she did to earn it, she learned. That lore in Denver?" He shook his head but said, "She learned it. Fuck yeah, Eric. She learned. But she learned privately. And she's shit scared of it happening again. She's bound, man. A prisoner in tight skirts and expensive shoes who lives in a mansion."

"You take him down, you're not gonna save her," Eric stated.

"I won't walk over her to take him down either."

"She's gonna know it's you," Eric pointed out.

Nick felt his mouth get tight and turned back to his drink.

She was. There was no stopping it.

"Nick," Turner called.

Nick looked to his friend. "She will. And she'll definitely get where I was at when I started things with her. But she'll also know I didn't end it that way. And she'll know it was her that earned that respect. It might not be much, but it'll be something."

"Buddy, she's your best way in there," Eric reminded him.

Nick threw back more whisky and didn't respond.

"Murder has no statute of limitations," Eric went on. "You testify against Harkin, he'll get the death penalty, takin' out a federal agent."

Nick looked again to his friend. "Not that I haven't shared this with you a hundred fuckin' times but maybe this time you'll let it sink in. I come out as the confidential informant I was and openly rat on Harkin, Shade feels nothing. And it's not just Harkin but Shade who's gotta pay. And Georgia Shade is a wildcard, but she's a Shade. She'll be about retribution. And I'm not big on the idea of entering WITSEC, if that's even offered to me for the low-level player that is Harkin. I'm also not big on puttin' my family's asses on the line. That happened once because of Vincent Shade, I'm not gonna let it happen again. I don't disappear into witness protection and a miracle happens and no Shade wreaks vengeance, a rat in my business, I'll lose every client I got. And I kinda like to eat, Eric."

Eric's lips thinned again, not a big fan of anyone talking to him that way, but he still got Nick so he also nodded.

Nick turned away and said no more.

Eric fell silent with him.

Minutes later, Eric broke the silence.

"I think of a way in, we'll talk."

"Appreciated," Nick muttered into his glass, lifted his eyes and caught the bartender's attention.

He got another drink.

So did Eric.

He caught the girl at the other side of the bar looking at him two more times.

He went home alone.

※

11:17 – That Night

NICK STOOD AT his kitchen counter, his fingers wrapped around another glass of whisky, a framed photograph held in his other hand.

The picture was of Hettie. A woman who looked like a girl. A pretty girl. A mature girl.

But a girl.

When she was alive, Nick had thought she'd always look like a girl and would do just that until the day she died. He'd thought this thinking that day would be decades in the future.

But in the end, in a way he hated, it had turned out he was right.

Blonde hair, it had been thin-ish but it was soft. Big blue eyes. Freckles on her nose.

She could act like a dork. She was sometimes klutzy. She had no problem being a big goof.

She could also take down a two hundred and fifty pound man who was six inches taller than her.

She looked so far from FBI it was hilarious.

Which made her perfect for undercover work.

He stared at her picture in its frame, something he'd had out for years. Something he'd put away when he'd started inviting Olivia over.

And he stared at her picture realizing that over the years, she'd become a part of the décor. He hadn't paid much attention to the fact, in one pad or the other, she'd been on the chest he now had at the wall between his bedroom and the workout room for years.

She was a memory.

She'd died and he'd vowed to himself she'd never be reduced to that.

But she was a memory.

A happy one.

The wound of the shock of her brutal death fading, the rest, the good times, had floated to the surface.

Hettie smiling. Laughing. Joking around. One of the guys but in a way that was all girl. Giving great head. Fucking up the eggs. Acting like she was having an orgasm the first bite she took every time he cooked for her.

Hettie. A happy memory.

But a memory.

And he stood there looking at her and her freckles and he did it for once not missing her fucked-up eggs.

He did it wishing he'd taken a fucking photo of Olivia.

"I'm an asshole," he whispered to the picture.

You're not an asshole, sweetheart. We both know oh-so-fucking-well you can't control who you fall in love with, Hettie whispered into his brain, and his back went straight.

Fall in love?

"Jesus, shit, now I'm a lunatic," he muttered.

With determination, he turned his attention to his whisky.

He downed it.

After he did that, he thought maybe he wasn't a lunatic.

Maybe he needed to stop fucking drinking.

On that thought, he walked the picture to the chest but he didn't put it on top where it used to be.

He slid it in the drawer where he'd hidden her when he'd had Olivia.

And he forced Hettie out of his mind as he moved to his bedroom.

The problem was, he tried to force Olivia out of his mind too.

He succeeded with Hettie.

But as she'd been doing since that night he decided to save her from him, Olivia kept him awake all night.

※

6:23 — Sunday Evening

"Okay, you want to tell me why it looks like you haven't slept in a year and you're all broody?"

Nick turned from his contemplation of the lights of Denver that he could see from his place staring out the floor to ceiling windows of Anya and Knight's condo.

He saw Anya had sidled close.

He hadn't felt her approach.

Fuck, he had to get his head together. Turner, Hettie *and* Deacon had taught him better than that.

He looked across the expanse of sunken living room to the other side of the space where the kitchen was. Knight and his two girls were there too, cooking. He saw Knight smiling, Kat giggling and Kasha in her own world, not helping her father and sister, but for some reason she was in the middle of the kitchen twirling.

There it was again. Knight was a natural at everything he touched.

Even being a dad.

There were parts of that that weren't really a surprise. Their mother, back then fucked way the hell up, had had Knight and named him so he'd be her protector.

But not in a million years would Nick guess his brother would be comfortable in a kitchen with two little girls, letting one twirl happily in her own world while making the other one giggle.

And not in a million years would Nick guess he'd be happy seeing his brother had that, content in his place being a part of it, and not feeling less because of either.

He turned back to Anya.

And Anya, being his in a way he would also never guess he wanted, but in a way now he wasn't sure he could live without, that being the sister he'd never had, he laid it out.

"I don't think of Hettie anymore."

She looked confused and spoke cautiously, "I…well, I can't tell by the way you said that. Is that good?"

"I don't know," Nick replied. "Is it good not to think of someone you loved who you watched get shot in the head?"

Her face registered a minor wince and he wished he hadn't laid it out so bluntly.

Before he could apologize, her eyes swept to the kitchen and she moved closer.

"Eventually, to heal and be able to move on, you have to stop thinking about her," she told him softly.

Nick looked to the lights of Denver.

"I think it's healthy, Nick," she kept on and then assured, "And it's not a betrayal. Honey, you know…" he felt her get even closer, "it's been years."

"There's someone else," he murmured.

"Good," she replied.

He turned to her. "I can't have her."

Her mouth turned down. "Bad."

Nick looked back to the night. "Maybe I should just get the fuck outta Denver and start over."

"Well, although an option, I do think Kasha would pitch an unholy fit at the very thought. Kat wouldn't be far from her sister in that, but she'd be quieter about it. And your brother would lose his mind."

Nick loved that at the same time it felt heavy.

He also felt Anya's fingers curl around his.

"But you have to take care of you," she whispered.

He looked down at her and dipped his face close. "Could you fall in love after Knight?"

She was still whispering but it was fierce when she said, "Never."

He felt that muscle in his jaw tick.

"But that doesn't mean I wouldn't—" she tried to go on.

It was jacked as shit, but after their beginning and how Nick had acted out during it, now Nick couldn't stomach even thinking about the idea of Anya with another man.

So Nick cut her off, "We should stop talking."

"If you feel something for someone else, Nick, that doesn't mean—"

"How about feeling everything for her?" Nick asked, definitely laying it out now. Laying it out for Anya and admitting shit out loud he hadn't even admitted to himself. "When that was only supposed to be for Hettie. What does that mean?"

She looked confused again, and uneasy to the point of looking frightened. "It means I don't understand why you can't have her."

"For her safety."

"That makes no sense."

He shook his head again. "Unfortunately, I can't explain further."

"No, Nick, what I mean is, there is no safer place on the planet for a woman than with the man she loves."

Nick stared at his brother's woman, unable to speak.

She jolted him out of his silence with just, "Nick—"

"I was right there and that place wasn't safe for Hettie when they took her life," he stated.

"Unfortunately Hettie isn't here to confirm what I'm going to say but I figure she'd disagree," she replied gently. "If her life had to be taken, you being there when it was was the only safe thing she had in her last moments."

Anya was right. Hettie would confirm that. He knew it the way her eyes never left him. He knew, even unable to save her, he gave her something just by being there and her knowing he loved her and just how much as Harkin raised the gun to her head.

"Your new girl—" Anya went on.

"It wasn't supposed to happen with her. It shouldn't happen. It *can't*," he told her.

She glanced briefly toward the kitchen again before looking to Nick and declaring on a squeeze of his hand, "And those are the times when you know it's real. When it shouldn't be. When it wasn't supposed to be. When you aren't supposed to let it. And there's nothing on this earth that can stop it." Her tone went cautious. "Isn't that what happened with Hettie?"

"This is different," he shared.

"How?" she asked.

"As much as I love what you said, babe, I am the last thing that's safe for this woman."

"I don't understand."

"And I love that you don't," Nick said, jerking his head to the kitchen. "That means he protects you from that, Anya. You don't feel it. All you feel is what he gives you to make you safe. But there are women out there who are not as lucky as you and we're talkin' about one of them. Life is complicated and it's ugly and that ugly can be extreme. I got a job to do and she's in the middle of that. If she knew she had a choice, she'd have the choice of ugly or uglier. And I'm the latter."

"I know life is complicated, Nick, but love isn't."

"And my brother gives that to you too."

"No, it's just the way it is and you had a version of this with Hettie where you two had no business being together and neither of you cared. An agent and informant falling in love during a dangerous operation?" She shook her head. "You both knew that was risky for a variety of reasons. You both went for it. You had what you had and now I hope you're glad you took that shot because the world made it so you didn't have it for very long but at least you can rest in the knowledge that you both had the courage to go for it. What's different with this girl?"

"What's different with this girl is the same. I don't handle shit just right, one, the other or both of us could get dead. I had that once, Anya. Not big on experiencing it again."

She stared up at him.

Then she said, "Nick, honey, we really need to find you a girl who isn't at risk of mortal danger." She started to look comically desperate when she suggested, "Maybe we should all start going to church."

Even in his mood, Nick couldn't bite back the bark of laughter at the thought of Anya dragging him *or* his brother to a house of God.

Then again, she'd be doing it to try to find a woman to fix him up with but that made it no less funny.

"Mommy, what's funny?" Kasha yelled across the living room, and when Nick looked that way, he saw she was already on her way to her mother and uncle to find out closer to the source.

"Grown-up stuff, baby," Anya answered.

That made Kasha's face set which meant they were going to have to make something up because she wasn't going to let it go.

But as Anya turned her attention to her daughter, Nick turned his to his brother.

Knight didn't hide his relief that his woman had made Nick laugh. Nick had tried to hide his mood but he knew he was shit at it.

Knight also didn't hide his continuing concern when Nick caught his eyes.

However, Knight did eventually hide it when Kat got his attention.

It would be much later, when the girls were in bed and Anya was shuffling around in the kitchen on the phone with her friend Viv that it would be Knight's turn.

The music playing low, both of them on the couch in the sunken living room, both of them with drinks, Knight murmured, "Somehow, she tied you up."

"I'm untied," Nick lied.

Knight appeared to be proceeding cautiously when he said low, "Seems you got a thing for the girl you can't have."

He didn't proceed cautiously enough.

"Not a twenty-somethin' asshole with my eye on a pretty girl who'd fall in love with my brother. And back then, when I first knew Anya, you didn't exist for her. Until you did. Then it was all about you."

Now Knight didn't appear pleased. "We don't have to go over this, Nick."

"Then don't talk shit you don't know, Knight," Nick returned.

"I don't know, share with me," Knight invited.

"Only got it in me to spew that once tonight, brother. Anya got it. She can give it to you."

His older brother studied him before he repeated, "She's tied you up."

"I'm loose."

"You didn't get loose for you," Knight observed.

"Nope. Not for me. Perfect world, she'd be here tonight so I could give Kasha a shot at makin' her smile."

"Kash is good at that."

"She broke through with Olivia, I'd buy her a human-size Barbie car."

Knight held his gaze and whispered, "Fuck, she tied you up."

"She'll never be happy, Knight, I know it. And yeah, that ties me up."

"You wanna make her happy."

"She'll never be happy."

"You wanna make her happy."

"Yeah, in that perfect world that doesn't exist, I'd wanna make her happy. But we don't live in a perfect world, Knight."

"I do, certain times a day, those bein' when I walk over that threshold," he stated, jerking his chin toward the front door.

He liked Knight had that. Nick had started his life after his father got their mother out of all her shit. Knight didn't start his life like Nick did, his mother clean and sober and not whoring.

Yeah, he was glad Knight had that.

He was glad his dad found his mom and cleaned her ass up and he was glad his dad gave that to Knight.

And he was glad Anya gave him everything else.

But that was for Knight.

"Some people don't get that, Knight."

Knight again studied him before he said, "Get this done. Just take these guys out."

"They need to hurt."

"Just take them out."

"Four and a half years, Hettie's just a memory. I promised she wouldn't become that. I failed. I had no choice. I'm human and that happens so I can survive, not be the walking dead, stuck in the past. Deacon taught me that and I learned it. Too good. But I have to finish the job she started. I promised that too. And that's a promise I gotta keep."

"Brother, do you have any clue how all the shit you're sayin' does not jive? Olivia Shade is wound up in that mess. You take those guys down instead of takin' 'em out, she goes too. She might not be happy now. But I've seen the woman in her tight skirts and heels. She'll be a lot less happy wearing an orange jumpsuit being someone's bitch."

"I'll figure it out," Nick muttered.

"Fuck," Knight muttered in return. "Do not get your shit jacked trying to save hers."

"There is no way to take care of my shit without jacking hers. I just gotta jack it so she ends up just hating me and not doing it wearing a fucking orange jumpsuit."

"Fuck, maybe *I'll* take these fuckers out," Knight irately told his drink.

Nick watched him take a sip.

When he was done, he got his brother's attention when he said, "Maybe this is penance for me bein' an asshole. Havin' it good growin' up, unlike you, unlike Ma, and still givin' her shit. Dad shit. You shit. Actin' like a motherfucking twat. Maybe that's it. Why it was the way it was with Hettie. Why shit went down the way it went down with Olivia. I don't know. I could think on that for millennia and never know. I just gotta keep movin' through it and hope I find a life where I walk over some threshold into my version of the perfect world."

Knight opened his mouth to speak but he didn't get in there because Nick didn't stop.

"What I do know is, I might have been an asshole twat, but I learned not to be that. I also learned other things. From you. From Hettie. From Dad, Mom, Anya. And something Hettie gave me was how to read people. And I know to my balls, brother, that Olivia Shade deserves a lot more than just being saved from an orange jumpsuit. Her father being responsible for Hettie's death, my mission to make him pay, to finish her job, bring him to justice, it can't be me who gives her more. But to my balls, Knight, I know she deserves it."

Knight heard him. Knight always listened. It was just in the last four and a half years Nick noticed he did.

And this time when his brother heard him, Knight offered, "You want anything from me?"

"I want this done so Olivia can be free to find herself some motherfucking happy. But you can't help with that so you're doin' what I need you to do. Just bein' the big brother I never let you be."

"Not a hard job, Nick," Knight said.

"Not anymore," Nick replied.

Knight gave him another look then took another drink.

After that, thankfully, they dropped the subject.

Nick went home.

He did not sleep.

Knight

8:23 — The Next Morning

AFTER MAKING LOVE to his woman and with her curled close, Knight had slept soundly.

But he woke with things on his mind.

So he made the call.

And he gave the order.

"Find everything. Do it invisible. Give it to me. And however you do it, it never leads back to Nick or me."

"You got it," Sylvie Creed, one of his closest friends and an ex member of his team, being ex because she now lived in Phoenix with her husband and kids, replied.

Knight hung up feeling better.

Sylvie and her man Tucker, both PIs, two of the best in the business, would get him what he needed.

Which meant they'd get what Nick needed.

Nick wanted to do this on his own.

He could do that.

He didn't need to know until it was time to know he had help.

15

AN EYE

Nick

10:12 – Tuesday Morning, Two Weeks Later

"NICK, THAT RALPHIE guy is on the phone again."

Nick looked from his desk to Bernadette, his assistant who was hanging from both hands on the doorjamb, her torso swinging inside his office while her lower body remained out of it.

He gave her the same answer he gave her the last three times over the last week and a half that this Ralphie guy had called.

"I'm hopin' I'm makin' this clearer than the last three times I said it, Bernie. That bein' I do not want to take a sales call from an art gallery, *any* art gallery or *any* sales call."

"I told you," she stated irritably. "He's not *sellin'* you something. He says someone bought something for you and he needs to make an appointment with you to install it."

"Bullshit, Bernie, it's a gimmick to get me on the phone."

"I thought that but the reason he keeps calling back after I tell him we're not interested and we don't want to be on their call list is that he *insists* someone bought some painting for you."

Nick looked back to his desk, ordering, "Find out who supposedly bought me some fuckin' art so I can call them and tell them I don't need any fuckin' art."

"Righty ho, *jefe*," Bernadette replied.

Jefe.

Jesus.

She called her husband Dante that too.

Why he hired a smartass assistant, he had no idea. She'd even been smartass during the interview.

Perhaps it wasn't karma kicking him in the ass for being a twat while he was growing up and staying that way well into his twenties.

Maybe he got off on the pain.

He put Bernadette out of his head and was about to make a call when she showed at his door again ten minutes later.

"Goin' out to get coffee, want one?" she asked.

"Got a meet with Hawk in half an hour, I'll be gone before you get back, so no," he answered.

"Feel like springin' for coffee for me and all the boys?" she pushed. "It'll be a write off. Not to mention team building."

He sighed and did what he did a lot with Bernadette because apparently he *did* get off on the pain.

"Hit petty cash."

"Gotcha," she muttered, grinning and swinging back out only to twirl around in the hall and catch his gaze again. "Oh, yeah, and that Ralphie guy said the painting is from some woman named Olivia Shade."

Nick went still.

Bernie kept talking.

"So, totally a sales call. You don't know any Olivia Shade."

"What was the gallery again?" he asked, his voice so low it seemed it made no noise.

Apparently, it didn't.

"Come again?" she asked.

"The gallery," he bit out. "What's the name?"

Her head twitched. "Do you know an Olivia Shade?"

Nick leveled his eyes on her.

"No," he stated firmly, her eyes flared and he knew she took his meaning which finally reminded him of why he'd hired her. "Now tell me the name of the fucking gallery."

"It's called Art," Bernadette answered. "That one downtown. Close to Larimer Square."

"Thanks," he replied, turning to his laptop.

She disappeared from the door.

Nick found Art's website and the number. He called it.

"Art, Ralphie speaking," a man answered.

"Ralphie..." Fuck...was an adult male seriously allowing himself to be called that name? "This is Nick Sebring. My assistant—"

"Well thank goodness, Mr. Sebring," Ralphie interrupted. "I'm so glad you called. You *must* have this piece. It's *fabulous* and *dying* for a new home. Ms. Shade seemed rather taken with it for you. Though, it's large and part of our service includes delivery and installation. So I've got my calendar open right here and if we can—"

"Tonight, five thirty," Nick declared.

"Oh...well, let me see. I can—"

"Tonight," Nick said. "Five thirty."

There was a brief pause before, "Of course, Mr. Sebring. Tonight. Five thirty."

"Right, do you need my address?"

"If you don't mind."

Nick gave it to him. Then Nick exchanged only the briefest of pleasantries before he hung up on him.

After that, he ignored the tight in his chest and went to his meeting.

◆

5:57 — That Evening

"I SEE MS. Shade has an eye," Ralphie stated.

Ralphie was a good-looking but definitely gay guy who was standing beside Nick, studying the large painting that had been installed over his chest between the two arches.

Yes, she had an eye.

Jesus.

The princess could pick paintings.

"Oh!" Ralphie cried then reached inside the jacket of the expensive suit he wore. "She left this for us to give to you," he stated, pulling out an envelope and offering it to Nick. "There you go. Now, if you're happy with it, we'll leave you to your evening. But if you need anything, an adjustment or you simply want us to hang it elsewhere, don't hesitate to call. However, just saying, that painting was *made* to hang *right there*. But if you want it elsewhere, we live to serve."

"It's good. Thanks," Nick muttered, taking the envelope at the same time reaching to get his wallet to tip.

Ralphie was engaged in gesturing that they could leave to the two men he brought with him who did the carrying and installation while Ralphie ordered them around. But when he turned his attention back to Nick, he shook his head, and to make his point absolutely clear, he lifted both hands and wagged them side to side as well.

"We don't accept gratuities. But the thought is appreciated."

No gratuity.

These days with tip jars out at gas stations where the attendant didn't move from behind the cash register, this was a surprise. But a good one.

He made a mental note of that on the very off chance he needed more art.

Nick nodded and walked him to the door.

The man barely cleared it before he rolled it shut and bolted it.

He then looked down to the envelope.

NICK SEBRING, was written on the front.

She had slanted, flowing, unusual, almost artistic handwriting.

He turned his eyes to the painting.

It was enormous, filling the space.

It was also amazing. The canvas painted entirely in a deep blue hue that reminded him of the ocean, this only interrupted close to the bottom with a series of sweeping, undulating lines in peaches and reds with some browns and blacks.

They looked like lines and Nick could imagine many missed it.

But he saw it immediately.

With some of the curves, swells and circles, definitely the coloring, the lines were an abstract of a man and woman fucking.

And an unusual choice for Olivia, the woman was on her back.

He wanted to smile at that.

He didn't smile.

He looked to the envelope, tore it open and pulled out a card in thick, creamy stock, the front embossed in a traditional monogram of OSA.

He briefly thought about the fact that, with his research, he knew Olivia's middle name was Amalie. And seeing that monogram, he thought her name was the most beautiful name he ever knew.

Then he opened the note and read,

Nick —

With your words the last time we were together, you gave me what you needed to give me.

With this painting, I'm returning the same thing.

It's a poor demonstration of what it needs to say, but at least it's something.

I hope one day you find the woman you couldn't build in a dream. You deserve that.

But I want to thank you for what you gave to me. Including being the one who had the strength to stop what could amount to nothing.

Though, I will admit, when we were together it didn't feel even a little like nothing.

When you find her, make sure she makes you happy. If she's not beyond a dream, find the one who is. Don't settle for anything less. If you did, the last hope I have in this world would be dashed, proving my pessimism for eternity.

Be well, Nick. And be happy.

Yours,

— Livvie

She had never, not once, called him Nick.

He had never, not once, called her Livvie.

But he had been her Nick.

And he had not made it safe for her to give him Livvie.

He stared at the note, reading it again.

And then again.

Including being the one who had the strength to stop what could amount to nothing.

Saliva filled his mouth.

Though, I will admit, when we were together it didn't feel even a little like nothing.

He looked to the painting.

The last hope I have in this world would be dashed...

He pulled out his phone. He did it not thinking.

He kept not thinking when he pulled her name up on his texts.

He used his thumb to type out the words.

He hit SEND.

He ignored the return texts she sent.

Instead, he set about waiting.

16

REDUCED TO THAT

Olivia

I WAS NEARLY FRANTIC, but definitely panicked as I drove to Nick's.

So much so, I almost forgot to take the tracking device off my car before I set out.

I remembered. And I looked to see if anyone was watching.

Only then did I take off.

But I did it fast.

His text scared me.

Come over. Now.

He'd never been demanding. Not like that. Not in a text. Not even over the phone. In fact, although he could be somewhat bossy, he was normally laidback, and except for the argument we'd had at the club, he was always in a good mood.

Come over. Now. did not say good mood.

It was also not somewhat bossy.

It was imperative and demanding.

Especially when we hadn't had any contact in weeks.

My return texts of *Are you okay?* and *Sebring, answer me* received no response.

So I took off to do as he said.

Worried.

He had a brother. His brother had a family. Nick also had employees.

Other than that, he'd asked me if I had anyone but I'd never asked him. And our relationship was such he didn't share about all his friends, buddies he might meet for a beer, high school sweethearts he still kept in touch with.

He might not have anyone either.

In fact, in our world, there were very few anyones you could truly trust.

And he might need someone.

Especially if he needed someone because something had happened to his brother or his brother's family.

Knight Sebring kept himself and his business to himself.

That didn't mean there wasn't danger to his business. If anyone hurt any of the girls he provided protection for, it was known his retribution was swift and brutal.

That might mean enemies.

But it could just be life. A car accident. An illness.

Anything.

Life happened all the time and my experience was most of what happened during the living of it sucked.

So yes, I was worried. I hadn't heard anything but that wasn't unusual. Even back in the day when I was directly involved in the life, with my position in it, news reached me slowly. Now, it might not reach me at all.

God, what if someone went after Knight's Anya?

Or one of their daughters?

This was a terror of mine. It made no sense. After what had happened with Tommy, I decided never to have children.

But sometimes I woke up at night in a cold sweat, having dreamed some enemy of my father or Georgia had decided they should pay through my babies.

Or that I'd done something and my father or Georgia used my babies to pay.

No, I never intended to have any children.

I was also worried because Nick's text could be construed not as upset, but as anger.

I'd bought him that painting. It had been days ago now and I'd heard nothing.

But maybe he didn't like it.

That said, he had a right to refuse it and I'd told the handsome Ralphie who worked at the gallery to be certain Nick knew he had that right. So it wasn't like I was forcing it on him.

But maybe he didn't want memories of me. Maybe when he found the girl he couldn't build in a dream, he didn't want to look at a five thousand dollar painting and remember me. Maybe he thought I was being clingy by giving it to him after he'd ended things so definitively, even if my note didn't say clingy.

However, none of that prompted an angry *Come over. Now.* just so he could share that with me. He could simply tell Ralphie he didn't want it and continue to ignore me.

So no.

I didn't think that was it.

I just hoped whatever it was—Knight, Anya, one of Nick's nieces—that it would be okay.

And I tried not to think about how much it meant that if it was Knight, Anya, anything, he had called on me.

By the time I swung in the spot beside Nick's Jag, I was so frantic, it didn't register I was back at his place. A place I never thought I'd be again. But even so, it was a place I thought of daily, even hourly, wishing I'd have the chance to go back, just once more, but better, whenever the spirit moved me because in the perfect world of daydreams, it, like Nick, belonged to me.

No, I didn't think of that.

I just quickly got out of my car, closed the door and felt my heart slam in my chest when I looked up to Nick's unit and saw his door already rolling open.

He always knew when I arrived, probably heard my car, but he never opened his door before I hit the stairs.

This made me do that: hit the stairs and fast, running as best I could in skirt and heels.

Nick met me halfway up.

And the pain in his face sent a slice of terror through my heart.

"Nick," I whispered, stopping on the step beside him, lifting my hand to rest it on his chest, my eyes glued to his. "Oh God, sweetheart. What's happened?"

For some reason as I spoke, I watched the pain score deeper.

But he didn't answer. He tore my hand from his chest, his fingers closing around mine so hard they hurt. He then dragged me up the steps so fast, I tripped and almost fell.

He didn't seem to notice. He just kept dragging me until he'd pulled me into his unit. He stopped abruptly to slide the door closed.

The jerk his sudden stop sent through my arm made me fall into him, but I didn't care.

I was all about Nick.

When he bolted the door and turned to me, I yanked my hand from his, lifted both to his chest and leaned in. So intent on him, I didn't notice him walking forward, hands to my hips, shuffling me back.

I just begged, "Talk to me."

He didn't talk to me.

He stared down at me, the blue of his eyes openly turbulent, the frank honesty of emotion something he'd never given me.

Which meant it had to be bad.

"God, honey. What's happened?" I whispered.

He didn't answer.

"Is it Knight?" I asked cautiously.

Vaguely, I noted him stopping us so we were just standing there, touching but unmoving.

"Anya?" I pressed carefully.

"You don't intend to do it," he stated.

I stared at him, confused.

"Sorry?" I asked.

His fingers dug into my hips and he declared, "You want me to be happy."

I felt my head twitch, now more confused.

"I...I don't get it." I shook my head. "I mean, yes. Of course. I want you to be happy. Though, I don't get—"

"But you don't intend to do it," he repeated.

At what I thought he was saying, my heart twisted and I had to curl my fingers into his shirt at his chest to help support me.

"Sorry?" I breathed.

"You don't intend to do it."

I let him go in order to shift away.

Nick's fingers went from my hips and his arms rounded me.

Tight.

Slamming me into his body.

"Sebring—"

He bent his face close to mine and barked, "*Nick*," so fiercely I winced.

I tensed as I asked, "What's happening?"

"Got your painting, Olivia. Got your note," he explained but it didn't explain anything. "You want me to be happy. But you don't intend to do it."

I didn't intend to do it.

He was right; I didn't intend to do it.

What he would never know was that I'd die and kill to have the privilege of making him happy.

It just wasn't an ability life afforded me.

"We both know I can't be that for you," I reminded him.

"Yeah," he bit out like he had to expel the word because it tasted beyond foul. "What you know that I don't is that you can't be that for anybody."

I went completely still.

"Can you?" he clipped but didn't wait for my answer. "You can't be that for anybody."

"Sebring—"

His arms gave me a squeeze. "*Nick*."

I shook my head. "Why are we—?"

"Good question, Olivia. Why? Why can't you be that for anybody? Why can't you be happy?"

We hadn't been together for weeks.

How had he figured so much of this out?

I cautiously tried to pull away.

His arms got tight and this time they didn't loosen.

I stopped trying to pull away.

"We're rewinding," he decreed. "I know why you can't be that for me. I know why I can't share why you can't be that for me. What I wanna know is why *you* think you can't be that for me."

"You can't share and I get that. You have to get why I can't share."

"No, I don't."

"You have to."

He bent close to me. "Your father is a piece of shit. Planet'd be better if he was obliterated from it. Not sure about your sister, but thinkin' she's much the same. Know you got soldiers who deserve a bed in the dirt."

At his words, I wrenched in his arms but he held fast.

I again went still and kept my hands between us to give as much distance as he would afford me.

"That's part of why I can't have you. But you're not about that. You're not them. You haven't shared that with me. I still know it down to my balls. You know it too 'cause you live it. So why won't you let yourself have me?" he asked.

You're not them.

Yes, he'd figured me out.

"Sebring—"

He lost it.

"*Nick!*" he thundered, giving me an abrupt, rough shake.

"Nick," I whispered, pressing my hands into his chest, not to get away but in a gesture I hoped was soothing.

He stilled and the tumult of his eyes calmed.

God, just that, his name and a simple touch from me and he calmed.

Was he that attuned to me?

"Who burned you?" he whispered back.

Oh no.

I closed my eyes.

"Livvie."

My throat clogged.

No one called me Livvie.

No one.

Livvie didn't exist.

Not for anyone.

But me.

"Baby, who burned you?" Nick pushed gently.

I opened my eyes.

"Who burned you?" he pressed.

I stared into blue.

"Who burned you, baby?"

"I can't be with you," I told him.

"Who burned you, Livvie?"

"I can't be with you, Nick."

"Who burned you?"

"I can't be with you because my father is a piece of shit and I care about you too much to have his stink settle on you."

Nick went silent.

But the room went wired.

He heard me and he got me.

Every word.

He got me.

He knew who burned me.

He knew, my father burning me, there was no me. There was just Vincent Shade's daughter, and me not even having me, I couldn't give myself to someone else.

I felt the electricity snap against my skin, but for Nick I had to force out my plea.

"Let me go."

Nick didn't move or speak.

I slid my hands up and curled them around either side of his neck.

"You need to let me go, sweetheart," I whispered.

He moved then.

He slammed his mouth down on mine and kissed me.

I didn't bother fighting it. It had been weeks since I'd seen him, touched him, heard his voice. If I couldn't fight it to stop something from starting that I knew for the both of us was unhealthy, the need I had for him after weeks without him was impossible to beat.

So, no.

I didn't fight it.

I kissed him back.

He moved us toward his bed.

On our way we tore at each other's clothes. I heard ripping. I knew I popped some buttons off his shirt. I didn't care about either.

I just needed him.

We fell to the bed partially clothed. We made frantic but light work rectifying that.

If before sex had been a battle for control for us, now it was war.

It wasn't hungry.

It was wild. Frenzied.

Abandoned.

I had no thought. Not one. Not about anything but what I was feeling and what I could make him feel.

In return, Nick's intensity cocooned me. The world melted away. There wasn't even his bedroom. His bed. These were incidentals. They existed without existing.

It was just him. The noises he made. The feel of his body. His smell. His hands on me. Mine on him. Our tongues. Our teeth. His cock. My pussy.

Reduced to that, safe in Nick, trusting in that moment that was just him, only him, nothing else existing, I eventually gave in and gave him everything.

I gave him the real me.

Safe with Nick, I submitted.

Relaxing into the position he'd earned, his hand wrapped around the back of my neck, my cheek pressed to the bed, arms under me, ass in the air, taking his cock, he felt my capitulation and drove in faster.

"You mine?" he grunted.

"Yes," I whispered.

He had me.

So he claimed more.

I felt his thumb invade my ass.

My eyes drifted blissfully closed and my body started trembling.

"You mine?" he growled.

"Yes," I breathed.

His hand at my neck held me down while he fucked my ass with his thumb and my cunt with his cock.

"You mine?" he bit out.

"Yes," I repeated. "Yes, Nick. Keep fucking me. Please. Keep…*fucking*…me."

He kept fucking me and my trembling turned to shuddering, the violence of it growing more and more as I felt him take me and listened to our noises fill the room. The sound of our fucking. His low grunts. My heavy breathing.

Suddenly, I knew I was going to lose hold on it, my orgasm was going to overwhelm me and I couldn't let that happen. I had to keep it together. I had to live that moment for eternity. It couldn't be over. I'd never have it back. I'd never be nothing but Nick's. I'd never have him all to me.

"No," I whispered, the word breaking, trying to lock against his thrusts so I could freeze us in time, keep my climax at bay, have what we had right then forever.

"Livvie?"

"No," I whimpered. "Don't...wanna...lose you," I panted.

His thumb slid gently out of my ass and his hand at my neck moved in, around and down until he had it hooked at my chest.

He pulled me up as he kept powering up inside me, his lips now at my ear.

"I'm right here," he said.

I closed my eyes.

He pulled away, turned me, dropped me to my back in the bed and grasped my hips, yanking them up and into him so he was crouched back on his knees, again inside me, taking me.

I opened my eyes and his gaze held mine.

"Right here, Livvie."

I felt the tears rise in my eyes as I reached out, planting a hand in a slap against his abs, feeling them work as he drove into me, his gaze locked to mine.

"Nick."

"Right here, baby."

I threw my other hand back, pushing it against the headboard and driving myself down on him as he took me.

"Fuck," he grunted, his face darkening.

He was close.

My hand at his abs curled in, my fingernails scoring flesh.

I was closer.

His cock rammed deep.

"*Fuck*," he groaned.

"Nick," I whispered then arched uncontrollably as my body shattered while Nick kept fucking me, doing it gripping my hips hard, yanking me to him, sighing deep, all while shooting inside me.

Simultaneous orgasm.

Beautiful.

If I was going to lose him, lose that moment, that was the perfect way for it to happen.

I was just coming down when I felt his warmth cover my torso and I realized he'd fallen into me, his face in the pillow at my side.

I put my hands to him, moving, stroking, memorizing, feeling my frame jerk lightly with the aftershocks, my lips parted, eyes closed, breath steadying.

"You're fucking spending the night," Nick growled into my neck.

My body had felt liquid.

At his words, it turned solid.

He lifted his head.

I opened my eyes. "We can't—"

He cut me off. "We're gonna figure it out."

"There's nothing to figure out."

He looked over my head, muttering, "I'm not findin' this part of you bein' a fuckin' nut cute."

"Sebring," I called quietly.

He looked back at me, a mixture of sex and irritation on his face.

I liked that look so much I felt my pussy convulse.

He felt it too.

"Christ," he bit out, his hips bucking into mine.

"Sorry," I whispered.

"Don't apologize for milkin' my cock," he ordered.

I pressed my lips together and tried not to convulse again at his words.

"You came here tonight thinkin' I needed you."

I decided not to answer and not just because I'd made that clear earlier so he already knew the answer.

"All I did was kiss you and now I gotta take my shirt to a tailor to put new fuckin' buttons on it," he carried on.

I continued my silence, again not just because that did indeed happen and there was no point denying it.

"And now you finally get it that your body is mine, your cunt is mine, your ass is mine, your *everything* is mine and you can trust me to give you what you need because," he dipped closer, "*you can just fuckin' trust me* and you say in the fucked-up mess we've built we got nothin' to figure out?"

"I—"

"Shut it," he growled.

I snapped my mouth shut not because he told me to but because I was getting angry and I'd been taught not to speak when I was angry.

"You're spending the night," he repeated. "Now, have you eaten?"

Have I eaten?

Was he crazy?

I glared at him.

"Olivia, have you eaten?" he asked impatiently.

"We are not doing this," I declared.

"We are," he shot back. "And that discussion has been had. Now, tell me, have you fuckin' eaten?"

"The discussion hasn't been had considering I said one word during it before you rudely interrupted me."

"Did you come here thinkin' I needed you?"

"Did you text me to trick me into thinking you did?" I returned.

"No, I texted you because I wanted your ass here so I could ream it for givin' me that fuckin' amazing painting but writin' that just fuckin' fucked-up note, makin' it clear you weren't gonna search for your own happiness which meant I had to do somethin' about that shit. Which, even if it pissed me off, was good since I was lookin' for an excuse to do that and you gave me one. And then after I reamed your ass, I intended to tag it. That's all done. And you don't gotta bother answering. I know like you know I know that you came here thinkin' I needed you. Which says it fuckin' all."

"Sebring—"

He got so close the tip of his nose brushed mine.

"Livvie, we're gonna figure this out."

Nick on top of me, his cock still inside me, I started trembling but for a different reason this time.

He felt it. I knew it when I saw the rage flash through his eyes before he buried it and forced his arms under me so he was holding me.

"You toe his line," he whispered.

"Sebring—"

"He burned you. You toe his line. You don't ever step over it. You did and you earned his lesson. So now you don't ever step over that fuckin' line. Am I right?"

Caught in his eyes, I let the blue close me in and it was just him again for me.

"He owns me."

The flash of wrath shot through his gaze again before he slid out of me and rolled us to our sides, keeping me close in his arms.

"I own you," he decreed.

"Sebring—"

"Livvie, not ten minutes ago, you gave yourself to me. He can't own you when you belong to me."

"You don't understand."

"I didn't feel the burn but I see the scars so I do understand, baby. But that's done. It was done the minute you walked to my chair in the club. I owned you then. And you own me."

I closed my eyes and dipped my chin into my throat.

God, I wanted to own him. I wanted him to be mine.

And I wanted him to own me.

I felt Nick's lips at the top of my hair.

"We're gonna do this right. Take it slow. Build the trust. Figure it out. And do it smart. You with me, Livvie?"

I tipped my head so my lips were at his throat but I didn't open my eyes when I whispered fervently, "He can't know. It isn't about me. But he can't know. I can't go through it again. Not it happening to me. Watching."

Nick slid his arm up my spine and curled it around the back of my neck.

"Leary," he said quietly.

I pressed my lips deeper into his throat, murmuring, "He can't know."

"He won't know, honey."

"He can't know," I repeated.

"He won't touch me."

"He can't know."

"Shh," he shushed me, his hand at my neck shifting to sift through my hair.

It took a while but eventually it worked. I turned my head so my cheek was to his throat and relaxed in his arms.

"I need to keep you safe, Sebring," I whispered.

"I'm safe, Livvie."

"You need to let me keep you safe."

"If that means letting you go, that's not gonna happen."

I sighed and said, "They watch my house."

"Okay," he replied slowly.

"They have a tracker on my car."

I felt his body grow taut.

"Fuck," he clipped. "Do you——?"

"I take it off before coming here."

"Goddammit," he muttered, then, "Lavish cage," but said no more.

That was when I took a chance and gave him some more of me.

"They don't know about the club. When I go, Harry drives me."

"Harry?"

"A leftover from another time. He's loyal to me. He also knows the drill. He's the one who showed me how to find a tracker on my car and remove it without them knowing."

"Right."

Nick again said no more and I didn't either. I just lay in his arms trying to get back that feeling of just Nick and me.

But the fear kept invading.

Nick felt it.

"He's not gonna hurt me and he's sure as fuck is not gonna hurt you, Olivia. You got no reason to trust that but we work this out, we build it, you'll eventually get there with me."

The fear started choking me and to release some of it, I shared, "He won't let me go easy."

"I don't give a fuck how hard it is on him."

For some reason, I expected there to be more.

There wasn't.

That was it. Simple.

To Nick, it was a foregone conclusion.

No, not even that.

To Nick, it was done.

I was Vincent Shade's no longer.

I belonged to Nick Sebring.

With some surprise, on that simple thought, I felt the tension ebb from me.

He felt it too.

"Now, babe, this time answer me. Have you eaten? Because I haven't and I'm fuckin' starving."

"No," I answered. "I haven't eaten."

"Right," he muttered. His arms tightening around me, he dragged me up the bed so we were face to face. I opened my eyes and caught his just in time for him to finish, "Got nothin' in the fridge. So we're ordering a pizza."

Nick was ordering us a pizza.

I was a girl with her guy, spending the night at his place, fucking and ordering pizza.

Normal.

Simple.

Real.

The last of the tension shifted out of me.

"I hope you have beer."

His concentration shifted and he muttered, "I'll run out and get some."

"Sebring?" I called.

His attention focused again on me.

I had something to say but when I got those blue eyes, I couldn't get anything out of me.

So I did the only thing I could do.

I moved to him and touched my mouth to his, my eyes open and I hoped communicating.

I had a feeling he read me because one hand glided in my hair, the other one glided down to cup my ass and he rolled into me, taking my lip touch and turning it into a hot, hard, rough kiss.

He ended the kiss by rolling us again, him to his back, me on top of him, whereupon he immediately smacked my ass and muttered against my mouth, "Now go get me the pizza menu. Famous's. Top drawer, left back of the kitchen."

I heard not a single word out of his mouth.

"You smacked my ass," I declared, eyes narrowing.

"Do it again, you don't get me the menu. And grab my cell on the way back. It's in my slacks."

I pushed up.

He came up with me and brought me down, twisted so my torso was pinned under his, back to the bed, lower body on its side so he could smack my bare ass again.

I felt my eyes get round before they went squinty.

"You gonna do as you're told or you gonna fight me?" he asked.

He looked like he was struggling against smiling.

"You're getting off on this," I accused.

"You're getting off on it too, Olivia, and don't deny it 'cause I'll just have to prove it and that'll delay pizza which would be annoying."

"I—" I began to snap but his hand cracked against my ass again right before it soothed it sweetly and his mouth came to mine.

His deep voice was gentle and just as sweet when he asked affectionately, "Livvie, go get your man the pizza menu and his phone. Okay, baby?"

He ended that request sliding his hand in, his fingertips gliding between my legs, one whispering across my clit.

"Okay, Nick," I breathed.

His eyes smiled and he gave me a short, rough kiss before he let me go.

I got him the menu and his phone.

Holding me in his bed, Nick ordered pizza.

He left me in his bed when he got dressed and went out to buy me beer.

He came back and we ate pizza, drank beer and then fucked, slow and long and beautifully.

And I fell asleep with Nick in his bed.

I woke up there too.

Both the falling asleep and the waking up I did with Nick holding me.

Normal.

Simple.

Real.

And terrifying.

17

NO LIMIT

Nick

7:28 – The Next Morning

AFTER THEIR SHOWER, Nick lost track of Olivia when he was in his closet pulling on trousers.

He found her in his kitchen, wet hair just as it was dry, straight as a sheet, bangs spiky against her eyebrows, wearing his shirt from the day before barely buttoned up because there weren't many buttons left.

She was doing something and he hoped it was making coffee.

But he saw her purse on the bar where he put it after he retrieved it the night before from where she'd told him she'd left it in her car.

"Got your phone on you?" he asked, moving toward the kitchen, his eyes to her purse.

"Yes," she answered.

"Gonna take it today, honey. Have one of my guys look at it. Make sure they got nothing on it to track you."

He felt her gaze and turned his from her purse to see panic etched in her features.

Like last night, he beat back his response not only to having the knowledge confirmed her own fucking father burned her, but also the asshole kept tabs on her to control her.

Instead, he swiftly moved around the bar and pulled her in his arms.

"It's gonna be okay," he told her.

She rested her hands on his biceps, her head tipped back, her expression not assured.

"Do you think they know I'm here?" she asked.

If they knew that she was visiting him, now or before, they both would be very aware of it.

"No," he answered and gave her more, "And even if they did, if they got that info just off a tracker, they wouldn't know who you were visiting. I own this unit 'cause I own the building. A company I'm a partner in did the renos. But the unit, the building, my car, nothin' is easy to trace back to me. For business purposes, I erased myself a long time ago. Just makes shit easier. Only people who know I exist are the IRS but even that's a juggernaut I pay three CPAs to straighten out so they don't audit me. So, unless they're standin' outside watchin' and see me open the door, they won't know who you're seein'. And I got security on this building, watched twenty-four seven, so if we had company, I'd know that too."

She relaxed against him, but only slightly.

"We have a lot to talk about," she remarked.

They really fucking did.

"We'll do it."

"Sebring—"

"Shade," he cut her off, taking one arm from around her to cup her face and dropping his closer to hers. "We'll do it. We'll take our time 'cause we got it. We'll figure it out. In the meantime, I make sure you're safe to move around as you like, not the least of that being making it safe for you to be with me. Starting today. So can you do without your phone for the day?"

She nodded.

"Right. Tonight, you're back here."

She nodded again.

"Six, Olivia. And if I'm not here, I'll give you a key."

"I'm uncertain I have the brute strength to open your door."

He grinned. "It sounds angry but it's a piece of cake."

"Right," she murmured, her eyes drifting to his throat.

"Livvie," he called.

Her gaze came back.

Before he could say more words to reassure her, she spoke and as she did, just the way she did it last night, he caught the look deep in her eyes.

"You'll give me a key."

That said a lot for any man and woman, he knew it.

For them, the level of trust it communicated was out the roof.

And the way she felt about it wasn't right there for him to see, but she gave it to him because he put in the effort to look deep.

"I'll give you a key," he confirmed quietly.

She leaned into him, her soft body yielding to his hard.

"Fuck, you gotta stop bein' sweet or I'm gonna need to fuck you against the island and I got zero time this morning," he warned. "I need coffee and to get a move on."

"Okay," she said in her soft voice.

"Now make coffee," he ordered.

She rolled her eyes.

She'd never done that.

Now she was being sweet with her body and her normal just plain cute.

He moved his hand down, catching his shirt, yanking it up and he was about to swat her ass when he felt it was bare.

"Fuck," he grunted.

"Sebring?"

He curled his fingers into her ass cheek.

Her lips parted and her lids lowered.

Fuck.

Without another word, he turned her and bent her over the island, yanking up his shirt and seeing her bare ass.

"Fuck," he groaned, his hardening cock going solid.

"Sebring," she whispered, and tipped her ass.

An invitation.

Christ.

His princess.

"Goddammit," he muttered. Powerless against her pull, he undid his pants. "Hold on," he ordered.

She shifted her hands to the sides of the island.

He drove his cock into her wet cunt.

Fuck.

He took her hard and fast. She came for him hard and fast. He shot deep, did it hard but luckily not quite as fast.

When he was done, still breathing heavily, he turned her, lifted her and planted her ass on his island, shoving in so he was between her legs. When he got to where he wanted to be, he kissed her.

And when he was done with that, he stayed close and held her tight as he said quietly, "Like you in my shirts, Liv, but so I can fight the urge to spend every minute I'm awake fuckin' you, panties would be good."

"Hmm…" she murmured as reply, her beautiful green eyes even more beautiful hazy with sex.

She was totally not going to wear panties.

Yeah, she owned him. He told himself he'd resisted the brand but she'd burned it deep weeks ago.

Admitting that and still powerless against her pull, Nick kissed her again.

Then he put her on her feet.

She wandered to his master bath off his bedroom to clean up.

By the time she was out, he'd finished the coffee she'd started making and he'd gotten her a key.

He poured himself a travel mug.

She grabbed her cell and gave it to him. She also wandered to the door with him.

He kissed her there and muttered, "Bolt this after me."

"Yes, master," she teased.

"Already late. Don't tempt me," he warned.

Her lips twitched up, not a smile, not completely but it was something.

He'd take it.

For now.

"Six, babe."

She nodded.

He left Olivia Shade in his house without him there, rolling the door closed himself.

He heard the bolt go.

Livvie safe inside, he walked to his Jag.

※

11:56 — Late That Morning

"OKAY..." KNIGHT SAID, his voice vibrating.

Nick watched his brother take a breath in through his nose.

Then he finished, "*What?*"

His brother was in his office, the door closed, Nick was giving him a full brief. He'd just shared about Olivia's scars.

Many would misunderstand Knight Sebring's purpose of providing administration services, including client vetting as well as protection, to a stable of call girls. Most every human being would think he was doing it for the ten percent he got, making money off pussy.

He was not doing it for the ten percent.

He was doing it because he was Knight, a name that defined him, a baby born to a whore with the intent to use him as a shield. Knight had protected his mother for as long as he had memories. It was the first thing he'd learned to do.

Shit like that was hard to shake.

Needless to say, that being him, a woman being burned for any reason was not big with Knight Sebring.

"You heard me," Nick said quietly. "We aren't that far with figuring shit out so she hasn't shared the story direct, but from what she said, she had somethin' with Tom Leary and her dad didn't like it. Made his point. She says her dad owns her and she's terrified as fuck he's gonna find out about us and hurt me."

"He burned her."

"Knight, brother, need you to focus."

"He *burned his fucking daughter.*"

Nick fell silent.

He gave Knight a few beats to pull his shit together.

Then he said softly, "I feel this, brother."

"I know you do," Knight gritted out.

"You can drown in that, Knight."

"I know you can."

"I can't let you take me there. I can't drown in that. I gotta stay focused. So you need to lock it down or I'll let it loose. Now I got two missions and the new priority is Livvie. I let that loose, I fuck it up and neither of us are safe."

Knight looked to the wall behind Nick.

He drew in another breath through his nose.

Then he looked back at Nick.

"Just take these motherfuckers out," Knight clipped.

"Olivia's owned. Georgia is a wildcard."

"You're worried if you end Shade and his soldier, the sister'll come after you or your girl," Knight stated accurately.

"I've watched both those women closely for years, Knight. Georgia does not give the impression she's doin' anything she does without anything but gettin' way the fuck off on it. And if that's the family dynamic, that it's cool to force loyalty through pain, there's no tellin' what she'll do. Georgia is the heir to the throne. I gotta know as in *know* what kind of woman she is before I take that on 'cause I gotta decide how it's gonna go with Georgia. I get this done, Olivia is free. Not her and me buying a new enemy who's a threat."

"Right, then I got somethin' to share with you that's gonna piss you off but you're gonna have to roll with it because it also works in your favor," Knight told him.

Nick stayed silent but he did it tensed.

"I set Sylvie and Creed on this," Knight said. "They've been in Denver for two weeks, workin' Olivia for you."

Nick looked to his desk in an effort to control his reaction.

"I know you wanted to do this just you, but she had you tied up," his brother explained.

Nick looked to Knight.

"The House of Shade is finding its footing," Knight informed him. "They got labs producing shit, men putting it out on the streets. Olivia has been moved out of the warehouse, into the legit side of the business. And Raid's been—"

"I got every office in the warehouse bugged, Knight. I know all this shit. And Raid told me himself when Georgia called him in to find David Littleton. He found him. He turned him over. And David Littleton hasn't been seen since. The labs are on Turner's radar. Comings and goings and deliveries being monitored. But none of that is linked to any of the Shades physically or on paper. Georgia has it compartmentalized. Even her closest men, Harkin and Leary, don't deal with those labs directly. And Vincent Shade doesn't even know they exist. So until one of those fuckers slips up, I cannot use any of it to hurt the House of Shade."

He took in a deep breath and finished.

"You dragged Creed and Sylvie up here the only time of year it's worth livin' in Phoenix and you did it for nothing. I have it covered."

Knight looked impressed.

Nick tried not to be annoyed.

"For some reason, Georgia isn't saying shit," he went on. "Vincent doesn't know she's reestablishing a foothold in the Denver drug market. I don't know why. But my guess is, she's been frustrated for years with his incompetent management, not to mention he's made it clear she's his heir, but he's dismissive and condescending both to her face and in talking about her to others. If that was me, I wouldn't put up with it for long. I reckon she's feeling the same since she's put up with it for seriously long, is fed up and setting up for a takeover."

"That makes sense," Knight said.

"The problem with that is that if Georgia is the brains and the power behind their now-successful but illegal operations, and her father doesn't know shit, I got nothin' to feed to Turner to take Vincent Shade down."

"Sylvie and Creed report Harkin, who has for a long time been considered Shade's most trusted lieutenant, is no longer Shade's man. Not only him but also Tom Leary are both tied to her skirt. So you get dirt on Georgia and you gotta jump that gun to keep your girl safe, least you can take Harkin down because they're tight so we know he's in deep with Georgia Shade and her production labs."

"The plan never was to take Harkin down, Knight. He was following orders but he pulled the trigger. The plan has always been to take Harkin out."

Knight's gaze on him was intent but he said nothing against Nick's decree.

"Thank fuck Marcus and my protection hasn't worn thin," Knight muttered.

That was a definite "thank fuck" considering the fact that once Knight and his crew extracted Nick four and a half years ago, Knight as well as Marcus Sloan made it clear, and they did that widely, that Nick had their protection. They also made it clear that if anything happened to him, it would be blood for blood until there was nothing left of anyone who harmed him, including and especially anyone with even remote ties to the House of Shade. And both Knight and Sloan could guarantee that, with far more men in their armies who were loyal for real reasons.

They'd also shared Nick was no longer connected to the FBI and his cooperation with them in the first place had been about the girls being trafficked, something known wide through Denver was a family thing.

They didn't lie.

Officially.

What Vincent Shade didn't know that eventually blindsided him didn't matter.

Shade had let Nick be and Nick had been careful not to fuck up as he carried out his plan. As far as Shade was concerned, Nick had learned his lesson through Hettie and was returning the favor of letting Shade be.

And in the meantime, Nick had built his own threat that included a loyal army. But he knew if Shade found him a threat, Shade would ignore that. He'd even ignore Knight.

But he would not get in the face of Marcus Sloan.

"In your listening, Georgia Shade have any clue what went down with Hettie and the FBI?" Knight asked.

"No one mentions it except Shade, Harkin and Leary, but only in Shade's office. Never Georgia. Definitely not Olivia. Don't listen myself, but reports state she doesn't even know much about what's going down with the labs, has been fully removed from the illegitimate operations, her ties to the soldiers have been cut and she's not in close communication with the warehouse anymore at all."

"Sister protecting sister as one builds up to a takeover?" Knight asked, his brows going up. "Or sister cutting out sister as she builds up to takeover?"

"No clue," Nick answered, his mouth tightening after he did.

He had no bugs in Olivia's new office. But he got a report on her conversation with her sister weeks ago, including Georgia's not-gentle nudges for Olivia to start seeing Dustin Culver.

It was a strange fixup considering Culver was an attorney with no ties to anything illegal in any way except a few semi-dirty clients who weren't much to get excited about. And Nick had no idea why Georgia was pushing that because, outside her nudges, neither Georgia nor Shade had mentioned Culver.

After he broke things off, Olivia not a focus of his plan, Nick didn't know if she'd started seeing him.

Or fucking him.

That got scratched on the top of the list of shit they were discussing that night.

"Nick," Knight called.

Nick focused on his brother.

"Want you to take a chance on finding someone, bein' happy. Not real thrilled you picked the way you picked, not your girl, a tough road you both gotta travel. But I've already found what I need. I know how it feels. You find what you need, I'm happy for you and I've got your back. But is that all you wanted with askin' me here? To tell me you found a woman you wanna try to make happy, your neck's on the line and the woman you're claimin's neck's on the line? Or do you want somethin' from me?"

"I called you here because I wanted you to know my decision about Olivia. I called you here because you need to know that's the path I'm on and it's gonna be bumpy. And I called you here because, along that path, I might need you and I needed to give you that heads-up."

"To launch this operation, you pulled in your buddy Turner, a fuckin' Fed, and every other marker you got out there and you asked nothin' from me." Knight smiled. "I was feelin' left out."

"Think, over the years, I've asked enough of you."

His brother stopped smiling and stated, "You don't got much left to learn. You set about learning it and you didn't fuck around doin' it right. But one thing you do still gotta learn is, when it's family, Nick, there's a limit to the shit I'll eat. But there is no limit to the love I'll give."

Nick kept his mouth shut but he did it to swallow against the lump that was all of a sudden blocking his throat.

Knight let that go and pushed up from his seat.

Nick pushed up with him.

"Want her ass at Anya's and my place for a steak, soon's you can," Knight demanded.

"They watch her, brother," Nick told him.

Dark flashed in his brother's eyes before he said, "Clear her of a tail and get her ass to Anya's and my place for a steak, Nick. Soon's you fuckin' can."

"Right. It isn't just that. You need to give me time. She's closed up tight. Face value, she's cool to ice-cold, man. You don't know the warm under that surface, she isn't easy to like."

"Kat and Kasha'll break that down. They don't, you know to dump her."

"I'm bein' serious, Knight."

Knight tilted his head. "This woman's the woman you're willin' to put your ass out there to get her safe, puttin' the mission you been livin' and breathin' for four and a half years in jeopardy, she's gonna be at our bar eatin' steak more than once over the years. I think we can look past her bein' a little cool and uncomfortable with us the first time around. So get her ass to Anya's and my place, soon's you can."

"Jesus, you're a bossy motherfucker," Nick muttered. "Then again, you always were."

"You don't know the half of it," Knight muttered back, but did it grinning.

He probably didn't know the half of it. What he did know was that he didn't want to.

Nick grinned back. "Get out of my office. Got shit to do."

Knight didn't stop grinning as he moved to the door.

Before he opened it, he stopped and turned back.

"Anya made it easy. Fell for me, gave me the beauty of her, didn't make me work for it. Not even a little. Not a lot of women like her would put up with a man like me. Who I am. What I am. How I am. What I do. Barely a hesitation, she was all in. I needed that. Life I was born into, I needed something that important to come easy."

Nick again remained silent, held his brother's eyes and let Knight give him what he needed to give.

"You, brother, you started life havin' it easy," Knight continued. "Got a lot of love for you so this is difficult to say but I'm gonna say it. I like you gotta work for what's important. If you work for it, you'll get it. You'll get why it was worth the work. You'll never forget that. And you'll finally get to where I am now after you wade through all the shit, knowin', when you finally have it easy, just how worth it was to keep wading through. But bottom line, I know you're a man who's got the balls and the guts and the heart to stick it out and wade through."

Nick gave it the time he needed to let his brother know that sunk in and it meant something to him.

Then he gave him shit.

"You done with heartfelt big brother lectures?"

Knight's mouth quirked on his, "Fuck you."

"You wanna meet my girl, safer for you to come to us at first. But I'm no one-trick pony so it isn't gonna be steak."

"Now he disrespects my steak," Knight muttered.

"Get out. Got work to do."

Knight grinned and turned.

He was almost out the door when Nick called his name.

He had men out there, Bernadette.

He didn't care.

"Just so you know, love you too."

A different kind of dark flashed in Knight Sebring's eyes before he shook his head, grinned again and disappeared.

Nick got back to work.

⌇

6:02 – That Evening

THE MINUTE HE heard the growl of her engine get close, Nick slid open the door and stood at the top of the stairs.

Even though he'd warned his security company to keep an eye out for any car he'd inventoried as being used by her father's crew or anyone not associated with the building showing on the cameras repeatedly, he scanned the area. At the same time he did this, he watched her get out of her car, go to the back, grab the handles of some brown paper grocery bags and move gracefully up the stairs.

When she hit the landing, he hooked her with an arm and shuffled her in.

He was kissing her by the time he had her over the threshold. He kept doing it as he slid the door closed.

He only lifted his head when he'd turned the bolt home.

"Groceries?" he asked.

"I'm cooking."

That night weeks ago when he'd ended things, she'd made some crazy-ass dessert that included a slapdash layering of nothing but brownies, heavy cream whipped with a packet of instant vanilla pudding and mini-Reese's Peanut Butter Cups. It was fucking amazing but even professional eaters could only shovel two spoonfuls of it in their mouths before they started lapsing into a diabetic coma.

He'd watched someone he loved die and was tied to a chair, facing certain death just instants before being rescued. He had not let that paralyze him. He let it feed him. Therefore, since then, he'd done and seen a variety of some serious shit.

Nick didn't fear much.

After one encounter with the results of her efforts in his kitchen, Olivia with groceries put the fear of God in him.

He shuffled her toward the kitchen, stating, "Maybe we should establish kitchen boundaries."

"Dear God, more rules from Nick Sebring."

"The one and only time you made something in my kitchen, I nearly lapsed into a sugar coma to the point it was touch and go I could fuck you."

Her body locked, successfully stopping them from moving as she declared haughtily, "That's the all-American dessert. Any proud, red-blooded American should easily be able to consume a huge bowl of that with a smile before they went off to plant a flag somewhere or win a gold medal or something."

"That is not the dessert of champions, baby."

"It most certainly is."

"My arteries hardened just looking at it."

She glared at him.

She was being cute and funny so Nick hugged her close and shoved his face in her neck as he burst out laughing.

He stopped laughing when she whispered in his ear, "I fucking love it when you do that."

He lifted his head and looked down at his unsmiling princess who was again giving him something deep in her eyes.

"Drop the groceries," he ordered.

"Sebring—"

"Drop the fucking groceries."

She stared at him but she didn't have to look deep.

He was giving it to her surface.

He watched her lick her lips as he heard the thumps of bags hitting the floor.

That was when Nick picked her up, took her to bed and fucked her.

Much later, he left her in his bed, naked, sated, dozing, tangled in his sheets. He retrieved the bags. He stopped paying attention to what he was putting away after he unearthed a packet of thick-cut bacon, a bag of seasoned, frozen curly fries, a jug of canola oil and huge bottle of Ranch dressing.

He made bangers and mash with homemade gravy, flash boiled fresh haricot vert and peas.

They ate in front of the TV, Nick in jeans and a tee, Olivia again in his shirt.

This meant after they ate, they didn't do any talking. They didn't figure shit out. He found his hand moving up the inside of her thigh and he discovered no underwear.

So they fucked on the couch. Then moved to the bed.

And Nick fell asleep holding Livvie.

Finally, two days in a row, what he'd wanted for weeks he got.

That being falling asleep doing just that.

And waking up the same way.

18

NOT TO FIT

Olivia

9:15 – Friday Night

"I'm so sorry," I whispered.

I was chest to Nick's abs, in his bed, my arms crossed lightly on his pecs, my head tipped back, my eyes to his where he was lounging against his headboard.

He was fiddling with a lock of my hair.

He'd just told me about his mom, his dad and his brother. About how his mother had been a junkie prostitute, Knight born into that, his father a john who fell in love with a hooker.

His father had also been an enforcer, in the life with power behind him both through his fists and the man he worked for. So he could keep her pimp cowed while he pulled her and her boy out and got her clean.

Shortly after he was successful with this, they got married, had Nick and Nick's dad officially adopted Knight.

"Nothin' to be sorry for, Liv," he replied. "I didn't feel it. I didn't live that. I was just the asshole kid they made and had to put up with while I figured out they all went through hell to give me safe and normal while all that time I was feelin' left out they had that bond from the struggle."

He'd shared that too. How he'd been a jerk to his whole family. To friends. Even to Anya when she and Knight were starting out.

"It's very wise for anyone to figure that out, Sebring," I told him. "No one likes feeling left out and you were too young to get that what they shared was not something you'd want to be a part of. They were just your family and you didn't fit. It hurts not to fit, most especially with family. So of course that's all you'd feel until you were mature enough to sort that out."

"I took it too far and it lasted too long," he muttered, gaze to his fingers twirling my hair.

"Yes, you took it too far but that's only unforgiveable if it genuinely lasted too long. You're the man you are now. They know that. You're in each other's lives. So it obviously didn't last too long."

He looked to me and the warmth making his blue eyes liquid felt like it settled in my soul.

"What's that about wise?" he asked softly.

That settled in my soul too.

His voice still soft and now gentle, he asked, "You know how it feels not to fit, don't you, baby?"

We were doing what Nick said we'd do. Taking it easy. Taking our time. Figuring it out. Not pushing it. Just living it. Getting used to each other.

Giving me that, since we started again, this was the first time he took things someplace heavy.

We needed to share. We needed to figure it out.

Even so, when he asked questions like that, I knew he already got me.

I shrugged to indicate he was right. "Ever the pessimist, I sensed a long time ago that wouldn't happen and gave up wanting it."

That tendril of my hair wrapped around his finger, he stroked my jaw with it, his tone still gentle but now also careful. "That scar your dad's way of tryin' to make you fit?"

He'd given me what he'd given me, something nobody knew about the Sebrings. In giving it, he'd been thorough, honest, and quite a bit of it wasn't pretty.

In-depth detail like that of their lives and histories would be all over if it was there to be had. It was detail that gave insight about why Knight did what he did.

It explained the history the brothers shared. None of it put him or his brother in jeopardy but any information could be used in a variety of ways.

But this information, bottom line, wasn't anybody's business.

Nick had given it to me. Open and frank, he'd just given it to me, handing me parts of him that in our world could be twisted into weapons that could be used to hurt him, Knight, Anya, his family.

He'd given it to me.

Trusted me.

And that meant everything.

"I ran away with Tommy," I declared.

Emotion instantly blazed in Nick's eyes that I read and maybe my reaction wasn't healthy.

But I loved it.

Because it was jealousy.

That said, I also had to assuage it.

"It's over now. Long done. Long dead. But back then, we were in love. We went to Mexico. We were going to run a Jet Ski business and make babies. We were stupid and young and hopeful which made us more stupid. Dad found us. Dragged us back. Taught his lesson."

My eyes drifted away from his as my words kept coming.

"He told Georgia it was about the money we supposedly stole. But we hadn't stolen anything. Some of it was mine, some of it was Tommy's. I think Dad told her that so she'd not question what he was doing. The lesson he was teaching. But he taught it and not just to me. To Tommy. But he also taught it to Georgia. She might be in denial but she learned it. It wasn't about the money Tommy and I took with us. It was about me and even Tom."

I looked back to Nick, and lost in my story, I kept telling it. But even looking right at him, I barely saw him.

"My father owned us and we were not free to do what we wished or be with who we wished. We were not family. Tom was not a soldier who disobeyed orders and had to be punished. We were tools who needed to be available to him for whenever he wished to use us. Minions. Slaves. We did as told and nothing else. And Georgia's three years older than me. She saw men and even had some who were steady before that happened with me and Tommy. Not after. She learned the same as me."

Still stroking my jaw, Nick held my eyes but he didn't say anything.

So I asked, "You know what's strange?"

"Everything about that is strange," Nick noted quietly.

He probably wasn't wrong but I didn't know that life.

I didn't share that verbally, but I knew Nick still got me when he asked, "But what do you think's strange, Livvie?"

"He doesn't give a shit about me," I told him. "I haven't seen him in weeks. He doesn't care. He hasn't phoned. Asked me to report in. Sent an email. Requested I meet him for lunch. Asked me to come over for dinner. It's just about control. He's perfectly fine knowing I'm where he wants me to be doing what he wants me to be doing. But that's it. He's nothing to me for reasons that are obvious. But I'm nothing to him too. And that doesn't make sense for the simple fact I'm his child. It seriously doesn't make sense for the not-simple fact that he taught me the lesson he taught me."

"No, it doesn't," he agreed, and I noticed his eyes intent on me. "Does that hurt?"

"No."

"Baby, he burned you. Your dad. Your father did that to you. I can't comprehend that. And it wasn't for some jacked sense of family devotion and loyalty that he did that."

"It doesn't hurt, Sebring."

He stopped stroking my jaw and cupped it, starting with ill-concealed disbelief, "Olivia—"

"It would hurt someone normal," I whispered. "I'm not normal. It isn't like a phantom limb, something you had, used, needed and missed when it was gone. I never had that. I never had love. Devotion. Loyalty. You can't miss something you've never had. Even when they had me tied down and he was pouring the oil on me, my mind wasn't even there. I felt it happening but it was just something happening. It hurt. It hurt unbelievably. But I wasn't there. My mind was where it always was. Somewhere else so I could survive and not go totally fucking crazy."

I stopped talking.

Then I went still.

Because Nick was still. The air was still. The room was still. In fact, I fancied the earth stood still as he stared at me, the rage that he'd successfully tamped down before burning blatant in his gaze.

"Nicky—" I whispered, inching up his chest.

"You're out of that warehouse, yeah?" he grunted.

"I…" I nodded uncertainly because I hadn't told him yet about my change in job and I didn't know if he was telling me to *get* out or confirming I *was* out. "Yes. Do you—?"

"Babe, I know everything," he declared, answering the question I didn't completely get out. "Just get that. I know about your sister's labs. I know Raid Miller found the man whose job you're doin' now. And I know since Raid brought him back that no one has seen that man."

I felt my eyes grow huge but Nick wasn't done talking.

"It's my business to know everything. I got a lot of ways I find shit out and I use those ways. I do not trade in information very often. That's sticky and you gotta keep tabs on everything, beware of shifts in the underbelly, because you could cross someone you don't wanna cross when they're nobody but they end up somebody and allegiances in our world change daily. But I still gotta know. I make my money getting things for people. Delivering things for people. Providing safety in a variety of ways. Knowledge is power and to do my job and make it so my guys can do theirs and do it safely, I need as much of that as I can get."

"Okay," I said when he stopped talking.

"So I know."

"Okay," I repeated.

"And I want you to stay away from that warehouse," he ordered.

"I can't, Sebring," I shared, watched frustration flash in his irate eyes and went on, "I'm out of my warehouse but I have a meeting with Dad and Georgia next week. They want me doing what I do in DTC but they also want reports about what I'm doing. David, the man who did it before me—"

"Jacked your shit and stole a shit ton of money."

Automatically I started to push up from his chest.

Surface information was one thing. It was rife on the streets. Anyone could gather it in a variety of ways.

But detail like that?

His arm that was resting on the bed shot around me and held me where I was.

"Liv, it isn't a secret," he told me.

"Did Raid—?" I started to ask, not believing that. Raiden Miller was a bounty hunter and a good one, part of that being he was the soul of discretion.

"The man disappeared and Harkin went after him. Harkin is clumsy and has never been known for finesse. But your dad thinks he can do and say whatever the fuck he wants wherever the fuck he wants. He spewed his anger wide about Littleton fucking him and what he intended to do with him when he got him back. So like I said, not a secret."

"God, Dad is such a fool," I whispered to Nick's throat.

"Liv."

I looked to his face.

"You know what happened to David Littleton?"

I shook my head, sharing, "In our crew, David wasn't the first to disappear. I might be privy to certain decisions but I'm rarely privy to the mechanics of carrying them out. Those functions of the business were never a part of my role."

"Keep it that way," he ordered.

I nodded readily, seeing as following that order wouldn't be difficult.

"Your sister is making moves," he declared. "No one knows why she's doin' some of the shit she's doin' but everyone is watching. *Everyone.* You watch your ass and you steer as clear of that as you can. You with me?"

I nodded.

"And you do not share that with her," he warned. "She doesn't already know she isn't flying under radar, she's a moron. Don't know your sister but what I do know, she doesn't give the impression of bein' a moron. You are not in that. Part of what we gotta figure out with us is what goes from this bed, this house, what we got to out there. But I'll state right now that I am absolutely not a conduit to makin' your family safe by sharin' information. You with me?"

I nodded again.

"Say the words, Livvie," he demanded firmly but also managed to do it tenderly.

I gave him the words. "I'm with you, Nick."

I expected him to relax.

He didn't.

And he didn't because he was worried about me.

"That means minimal time at the warehouse," he stated.

"It already isn't my favorite place so I already avoid it, honey," I assured him.

"Keep doin' that," he grunted. Then, "What happened with that fixup?"

I knew exactly what he was asking.

I bit my lip and pressed up farther.

Another flare of anger in his eyes before he did an ab curl and I found myself on my back pinned to the bed by Nick's body.

"You went out with him," he growled.

I had. I'd gone out with Dustin three times since Nick ended things with me. Twice I managed to keep it at drinks. But there was a dinner.

And several kisses.

No sex. Not even making out.

But we had a date the next evening.

"We were kind of over, Sebring," I reminded him.

"End it," he bit out.

"I—"

"End it, Liv. Immediately."

I felt my eyes get big.

"You mean...*now?*"

"You want me to get your phone?"

He meant now.

"Sebring, I'm seeing him tomorrow night. When I do I'll—"

I snapped my mouth shut when he asked in a scary tone, "Are you fuckin' shitting me?"

"I'll explain during dinner," I promised. "He's a decent guy. It's—"

"End it now, Liv."

"You know," I started tersely, "it doesn't make me very happy when you interrupt me."

The minute I quit talking, he rolled off me and the bed.

I snatched the covers up over me before I pushed up to my elbows and watched him walk naked through his bedroom to the living room. I then watched him grab my purse from the coffee table, open it and dig through.

I got distracted by his wide chest, his cut abs, his thick thighs and his very pretty cock as he walked back to me.

I got undistracted when his weight hit me again and my phone was digging into my palm because he was pushing it there.

"End it now, Livvie," he demanded.

"It's going to get back to my mother," I told him.

"You're gonna date a guy when you got a man so you don't have to put up with your mother?" he asked incredulously.

My eyes slid to the side as I muttered, "You don't know my mother."

"Liv." My name vibrated with meaning and it was dangerous meaning even if the vibration was physical and slid along my skin rather pleasantly.

I narrowed my eyes at him. "We get along. He's a decent guy. He's interesting. He's into me. What reason do I give to end things? I can't tell him I'm with you, that'll get to Georgia, then Dad, and we both know the results of me doing something Dad has not stamped as approved aren't pretty."

"Say you got a new job and you gotta focus on it. Say you're not feelin' it with him. Say you're in a place in your life right now where you can't be about a relationship. I don't know. I got a dick. That shit comes easy. Just work it."

Oh no he didn't.

I gave him a chance to take it back.

"You got a dick and that shit comes easy?"

"A man wants shot of a woman, he doesn't fuck around worried about her feelings. He gets on with it, and baby, I see your face screwin' up to lose your shit about that but think about it. Why drag it out? There's no point. You're not asking for a divorce after bein' married to him for a decade. You haven't even been seein' him but for a coupla weeks. In some shit, life's too short to waste time bein' sensitive."

"You know, the absolute worst part about that is you're right," I snapped.

He grinned but through his grin ordered, "End it."

"Fine," I bit off.

He laid on me.

I lay under him.

He didn't move.

I couldn't move.

"A little privacy?" I requested.

"Uh...no."

I blinked at him.

Then I got angry(er).

"I'm not lying. I said fine, I'll end it. So I'll end it. You can go away and that's what I'll do. End it," I promised.

"Gonna eat you while you talk to him so you'll remember who owns you and make that shit quick so we can get on with our night."

My stomach dropped in a good way.

"Now, phone him, baby," he ordered, sliding down my body.

"Sebring—"

He pushed one of my legs wide at the same time running his hand down my inner thigh.

His body fell through.

I quickly lifted up my phone and engaged it.

Nick kissed the inside of my opposite thigh.

My lip quivered and I hit buttons on my screen.

I put the phone to my ear.

Dustin answered on the second ring.

Nick lapped at me.

My voice was throaty and strained as I made up some excuse I forgot what it was seconds after it came out of my mouth, ending things.

I did note, albeit vaguely, Dustin sounded disappointed and it seemed he was going to push it but instead he asked, "Are you okay?"

"I'm fine. You're a good man and saying things like this to a man I respect isn't easy," I replied, then swallowed the noise I wanted to make when Nick sucked deep at my clit. I forced out to finish, "And I'm coming down with a cold."

Dustin said more and it was nice because he was a nice man.

But mostly, I hurried it along so I could get him off the phone and I could concentrate on Nick going down on me.

I managed this, hitting the button to end the call and tossing the phone to the bed beside me, my other hand moving to Nick's head to hold him to me.

But he lifted away.

I got up on an elbow to look down at him to see his eyes on me.

"It over?" he asked.

"Yes," I answered impatiently.

His face got lazy as he whispered, "Good, baby."

Then he rolled, doing it clamped on to me, forcing me with him so we ended with him on his back and I was up, straddling his head.

He yanked down on my hips.

I rode his face.

It wasn't a lie I'd told Dustin. Breaking things off with a nice guy wasn't easy.

It was just, for the first time in my life, as luck would have it, doing something not easy led to a reward.

A really good one.

And that led to another reward.

Sleeping next to Nick Sebring.

So for the first time in my life, it was worth it to do something not easy.

It made me feel almost happy.

Except for the part that I feared down deep in my bones that it would end for both of us in misery.

19

CLEAN UP ON AISLE FIVE

Nick

8:03 – That Next Monday Morning

NICK BARELY GOT to his desk in his office before his man Curt was at the door.

"A minute?" Curt requested.

Nick caught the look on his face and lifted his chin.

He didn't take his seat behind his desk while Curt moved in and closed the door.

He walked to Nick's desk and stood opposite it.

"Georgia Shade ordered a sweep of their offices this weekend," he reported.

The itch that was beginning to creep up Nick's neck stopped.

"Standard practice for them, Curt, you know that," he replied. "Bugs are good. They've been in place without detection for years now."

Curt's voice dipped. "Different kind of sweep, Nick. Whoever did it located all of them like he was goin' right to them. We got nothin' from that warehouse since noon yesterday."

That itch crept back.

"Like he was goin' right to them?" Nick asked.

"Took him an hour to sweep our shit clean," Curt told him.

"Anything heard before that?" Nick asked.

"Georgia giving the order. She didn't say a name. We got no clue if the guy who pulled them is on the Shade crew or if he's freelance. But he didn't fuck around."

Nick and his man held each other's eyes.

This was not good.

It meant a leak.

There was no leak in Nick's crew but shit happened. New allegiances were bought or coerced. He'd have to expend the effort to make certain that was true.

Knight's crew was tight. No way in fuck any of Knight's men would share what Nick had told his brother. But it wouldn't get that far. There was no reason for Knight to share that information with any of his crew, and until there was, he just wouldn't do it.

The only other person who knew he was on this job and knew how he did that kind of job, which meant knowing the kind of equipment Nick used and being able to make an educated guess where it might be placed, was Turner.

Twice while Nick had been working that situation with Hettie for the Feds, Nick's position as a CI had been compromised.

The first nearly got him dead. Hawk Delgado, with the help of Sylvie and Tucker Creed, had intervened, working another job and in doing so, forcing the bust of a small-time player in the larger operation Turner's team was targeting. Nick had gotten away and Turner and his crew had scrambled and covered Nick.

The second almost had the same ending, with Hettie getting dead and the operation never coming to fruition due the players backing off because of Federal heat.

Nick would stake his life that Turner wouldn't fuck him.

That didn't mean someone on his crew wasn't playing both sides.

Obviously, in both incidences, questions had been asked. How Nick had been made. How Nick and Hettie got put in the position that had ended Hettie's life.

Internal investigation, everyone came up clean.

Nick had never liked that, but taking that on was not his mission.

Getting his shit together, sorting his life, settling in with Livvie and finishing the job he started with Hettie and vengeance for the early end of her life was.

Fuck.

Now he had to take that shit on.

"You want us to send a guy in to replace our shit?" Curt asked, taking Nick out of his thoughts.

"No," he answered, not liking that he had to give that answer. But they had a leak, it was too risky. He didn't like not having ears on the House of Shade. But at least Olivia wasn't in that fucking warehouse anymore. "I gotta look into some shit, I'll let you know," he finished.

Curt accurately took his cue from Nick's words, nodded and walked out the door.

Nick pulled his cell out, sat in his chair and stared at his phone.

He wanted to contact Turner. He wanted to give him a heads-up that the internal investigation of his team was shit.

Turner had a snake in his garden.

But Nick needed to clear his own men first.

And when he went to Turner, he had to have solid info to give him.

Nick ran his thumb over the screen and put his phone to his ear.

"Nick," Knight greeted.

"Sylvie and Creed still in town?" Nick asked.

His brother's tone was more alert when he answered, "No, but they can be."

Nick drew in a breath.

Then he stated, "I got a couple of jobs for them."

—※—

Olivia

2:25 – The Next Thursday Afternoon

I MOVED DOWN the hall of the warehouse toward Dad's office, hoping our first monthly meeting went quickly so I could get out of there.

I did it thinking how easy it was getting used to living clean. Just walking down the hall, it felt like the grime of the place in all its incarnations was settling on me, clogging my pores, making it hard to breathe.

Gill nor any of our other boys were outside Dad's door but I heard voices inside.

I knocked.

I received no reply. Not a "come in." Not a "go away."

I was early for our two thirty meeting, but not that early, so I expected Georgia was in there, maybe Gill, Tommy, Miguel, whoever, and they were just waiting for me.

What I did know was that if Dad didn't want me in, I'd get a "go away."

I turned the handle and walked in.

I stopped dead at what I saw, thankful that a lifetime of training blanked my face and any telltale line of my body.

"Come in, Olivia, this won't take long," Dad said irritably, his hand waving at me, his eyes annoyed and on the man sitting in front of him.

I didn't want to go in.

But I needed to go in and not only because Dad was waving at me.

So I went in.

The man sitting in front of Dad looked at me. His eyes slid down the length of my body in a way that exacerbated the feel of filth coating me and he turned back to Dad.

"I'm done waiting, Vincent," Drake Nair declared, dismissing me.

Drake Nair.

I knew the man and part of what I knew was that he would disappear.

Then resurface.

As far as I knew, he'd disappeared for some time.

Now he was back.

I wasn't the only one who knew Drake Nair. Everyone in Denver knew Drake Nair.

Everyone in Denver knew he wasn't that bright, but he was wealthy, and rich men, smart or dumb, could pay to get a job done.

They also knew he was a slimy weasel.

And last, everyone in Denver knew Drake Nair hated Knight Sebring.

I did not keep tabs because Nick was just a name for me back then, but I still knew it had to be years since I last heard of anything happening in the Sebring/Nair war.

Word was, Nair played dirty (not surprisingly).

But Knight Sebring had always prevailed.

I didn't know much of what it was about, outside Knight and Nair were once partners and then they were not.

I just knew with Nair's latest lengthy disappearance the bad blood seemed to have died down.

But now I had a very bad feeling mostly because I had no idea my father knew Drake Nair and I didn't like him, his history, his hatred of Knight Sebring and the coincidence this all was right now sitting in my father's office.

"You're a fool, you go after that again," Dad told him.

I moved across the room to Dad's grubby windows, pretending their discussion mattered little to me but doing that listening closely and fearfully.

"Don't give a shit the protection the brother has. They're tight. The brother gone, that'd sting," Nair returned. "Easy hit. Whack Nick. Deliver a big blow to Sebring. Seriously, Vincent, you cannot have a problem with that."

I fought hard to keep breathing, looking out the window, hoping I was giving the appearance their conversation wasn't that interesting to me when now I was listening so hard it was a wonder my ears weren't bleeding.

"Our histories, respect, you sitting there," Dad said. "You talk stupid shit, Drake, I don't have time for that."

I felt the tension in the room rise and looked to Nair because of it.

His face was twisted with distaste. "Was pussy, you backin' down from that years ago."

Very much not good.

Dad would not like being called pussy.

It was time for Gill to be involved in this scenario.

I moved two steps from the window, sliding my purse off my shoulder, my eyes glued to Nair.

I felt my father's gaze and looked to him.

He seemed reflective as he studied me for a few moments before he shook his head.

I nodded, moved the strap of my purse back up my shoulder and stepped back.

Dad looked again to Nair. "I showed you respect. You wanted time, a meet, I gave it to you. You sit in my office and not give that back?"

"My shit got fucked right along with yours, the Feds shut that down," Nair returned.

The Feds?

What on earth?

"I need resources if I wanna make Sebring hurt," Nair said.

"This is not my problem," Dad replied.

"The resources I need are not money. I got that and I'm good with givin' it up," Nair stated then stressed, "*A lot* of it."

Surprisingly, Dad didn't deign to respond to that.

"Take him down, when I get those bitches he stole from me back, I'll cut you into a percentage of his gash," Nair bartered.

Dad glanced at me before he sat back and declared, "We're done."

Nair glanced over his shoulder at me. Looking into my eyes but for the briefest moment, he took in my breasts and hips before he looked back at Dad.

"Word is your girls ain't stupid. They know easy money and easy money to be made off pussy."

My lip curled.

"You have daughters one day, come back and repeat that," Dad shocked me by saying.

I was not shocked because Dad was in that business. He wasn't, never was and I knew that.

I was just shocked that he was intimating he wasn't because of his daughters.

He shocked Drake Nair too. And amused him. I knew by the noise of the incredulous hoot Nair made.

"We're done, Nair," Dad decreed, doing it appearing bizarrely like he was getting antsy. "I've got a meeting with my daughters."

"I'll come back, you come to your senses," Nair said, pushing up from his chair.

"I would suggest it isn't me who needs to come to my senses. Both the Sebrings are untouchable and that's been demonstrated to you especially because Knight Sebring has made that point personally and *repeatedly*."

Well, at least that was a relief.

"We partnered up good in the past, Vincent, *repeatedly*," Nair retorted. "Both of us did well workin' together."

They did?

That was news to me.

Unhappy news.

Nair wasn't finished.

"And it'd be smart you don't forget that because word is, you haven't been smart much for a long time and you need good partners and you have since Leon put you in your place."

I held my breath.

No one, not a soul, mentioned Leon Jackson to my father.

No one.

Dad's voice was rumbling with contained fury when he said to me, "Our guest has lost his way to the door, Olivia. You can call Gill now to show him that way."

"Valenzuela finally stops fuckin' around, chews you up, spits you out," Nair hissed, jerking his finger through the air at Dad with each "you," he then turned and jerked it to me. "Valenzuela puts *you* on the auction block, I'm buyin'. Cover you in my cum then make that pussy work for me." He turned back to Dad. "And everyone in Denver knows Valenzuela's biding his time. That shit's gonna go down. Make no mistake. Only one who's in denial about that is you. You hearin' me?"

"Our history," Dad whispered, "gives you sixty seconds to get your fat ass out my door."

"Fuck you," Nair spat. "You had the balls to do it, you'd—"

I was desperately tugging my phone out of my purse.

I was too late.

Nair stopped talking because Dad pulled the gun out of his desk.

"Right," Nair taunted, grinning an oily grin.

I quickly searched for Gill's contact on my phone.

The door opened.

Georgia started in.

Dad pulled the trigger.

Nair's head exploded.

He just *had* to pull out his .45.

I closed my eyes, swallowed the sick that surged up from my gut, turned back to the window and dropped my phone hand.

"Seriously?" Georgia asked, not hiding her exasperation. "Our cleaning bill is out the roof already."

"Reschedule," Dad barked. "And clean that shit up."

I opened my eyes and stared through the grime at the parking lot.

"Olivia?" Dad called.

I turned my head his way. He was now close to the door.

He held my gaze and nodded, seemingly communicating something weighty, like for some reason he was proud of me.

I felt my flesh crawl.

Dad turned away, walked out and slammed the door behind him.

I looked back out the windows.

I then heard Georgia say, obviously into her phone, "Yeah, Gill. Call Henrietta. Get some heavy duty bags. Clean up on aisle five."

I sighed.

"Liv," she called to me.

I looked to my sister.

She had a hip hitched, her phone up in front of her face, her eyes to it, thumb moving on her screen.

"How're you fixed for next Thursday?" she asked.

Good God.

My family.

Nick

5:38 – That Evening

JOGGING DOWN THE stairwell to get to the underground parking lot of his building, Nick made his fourth call to Olivia that day.

He was concerned.

It was his third call, the first, that morning, she'd answered. The last two that afternoon, she had not. But he'd also texted three times, all that afternoon, and none of those she'd answered.

He had no ears at that warehouse.

And he had a leak.

She had a meeting that afternoon at that warehouse.

She worked with vipers.

And she was his.

They found that out, they'd strike.

He had no choice but to let her go to work every day with that threat hanging over their heads, a threat she didn't fully understand.

But with his access cut off to the House of Shade, and Sylvie and Creed just back from Phoenix and on the job, Nick was keeping closer tabs on his woman.

So yeah, she didn't reply, he got worried.

Now, with spotty reception, he felt relief when she answered. He also immediately decided to put a man on her, everywhere she went, unless she was with Nick.

"Sebring," she said in greeting.

"You okay?" he asked.

"Not really," she answered.

He jogged faster. "What's happening?"

"Not for the phone," she stated, her voice breaking up as he got deeper underground, but he heard her.

Fuck.

She knew her cell wasn't tracked. He'd told her after his boys went over it.

She still had something she couldn't say on the phone.

Fuck.

He pushed through the door. "I'm coming home. Where are you?"

"Sucking back melon shit and vodka at your bar."

"Be there in twenty."

"All right, sweetheart."

He disconnected, got in his car and probably pissed off a fuckload of people as he made the thirty-minute, rush-hour drive to his place, doing it in twenty.

He jogged up his steps taking them two at a time.

He pulled open the door, shut it behind him, bolted it and strode swiftly into his unit to see her at his bar, tight skirt still on, high heels kicked off, the evidence of her recent activities littering his kitchen, hand wrapped around a green drink.

"I'm cooking and you can't argue since it's mostly done," she declared.

It smelled awesome which probably meant each bite was going to shave a year off his life.

"You're home early," he noted, making his way to her.

"Even though my father thinks he owns me, I do tend to be allowed to make my own hours. So today, I gave myself the afternoon off to go to the grocery store, get the provisions and beat you here to start cooking because our monthly meeting about the family business was postponed due to unexpected circumstances."

He stopped close and she tipped her head back to keep hold on his gaze.

Watching her hair glide off her shoulders and fall down her back, seeing how soft her slim-fitting sweater looked up close, having her mouth right there, he wanted to kiss her.

But he didn't quite get what was in her eyes.

"What's makin' you not really okay, Livvie?" he asked quietly.

"I have good news and…I think…good news," she announced.

He felt his head jerk.

Then he warned her he was losing patience by saying, "Liv."

"My guess is that you know Drake Nair."

Nick felt his body go solid.

He knew Nair.

He knew Nair as an adversary of his brother's.

He also knew Nair as a total and complete asshole.

He further knew Nair was mixed up with the human trafficking business that got Hettie dead.

Last, he knew in all the getting to know you and figuring things out he and Olivia had been doing between fucking and just being together, he'd not figured out how to explain he intended to destroy her father, kill a family henchman and he'd first met her through carefully planned machinations because he intended to use her to start that plan in motion.

What he did not know was why Olivia seemed aloof while bringing Nair up out of the blue.

"Yes," he confirmed tightly. "I know Nair."

"Well…" she flipped out a hand, "he's dead."

Nick stared at her.

"Say again?" he asked.

"Around about the time he told Dad that when Valenzuela chewed him up and spit him out then put me on the auction block and Nair was going to buy me, come all over me and then put me out for sale, Dad blew his head off with his .45. He could have picked his nine millimeter, which would have been far less messy. But Dad doesn't do the clean up or even order it, so he doesn't mind messy."

Nick felt the muscle jump in his cheek as his hands formed fists.

Although stunned at the suddenness of it when Nair had been a pain in the ass for a fucking long time, Nick was not at all pissed Nair was dead.

The guy was a dick. He'd fucked with Knight in seriously shitty ways. And he was a memory that Nick didn't like having since Nick had used the man back when he was an asshole to try to drive his brother and his woman apart.

But he *was* pissed because he felt grateful to Vincent Shade for taking him out due to all of those reasons but especially because Nair spouted that shit in front of Nick's woman.

And he was pissed because he didn't like feeling grateful to Vincent Shade at all.

"A rare, as in *unique* demonstration of fatherly affection," she declared, lifting her drink and taking a sip. She went on after she lowered it again. "That being said both in terms of it as the first demonstration of fatherly affection I remember in, I don't know...*ever* and blowing a man's head off with a .45 is just a jacked-up, crazy, lunatic way to demonstrate affection."

"Are you okay?" Nick asked, his voice still tight.

"Yes," she answered casually. "I was far enough away. No blood or brain matter hit me."

"Livvie," he whispered, his warning gentle this time that her bullshit needed to stop.

"Who does that?" she whispered back and he saw it happening deep in her eyes.

She was losing it.

Nick shifted closer.

"Georgia just called Gill, ordered a cleanup and asked when we could reschedule our meeting. Now who does *that*?" she asked.

He lifted both hands and framed her face.

"Nair was awful," she said. "Everyone knows he's awful. But now he's *dead* and I'm just supposed to go to the grocery store and go home and make dinner and that's it?" She shook her head in his hands. "A man is dead."

"Livvie—"

She lifted her hands too, curling them tight around either side of his neck.

"I don't want this to be my life," she whispered fiercely. "But now, I don't want it in *your* life. Don't you see? Don't you see now why I can't do this? Why I can't have you? Why I can't have *anybody*?"

Before he could react to that, as in put a stop to where she was heading, she let him go, pulled out of his hold, jumping off the stool and taking a big step away. Throwing an arm out wide to take in his kitchen, she kept talking.

"Honey, I'm home," she called out sarcastically. "Oh good, sweetheart. Taco extravaganza for dinner and, oh, by the way, this afternoon, Dad murdered someone in front of me."

"Liv—"

She bent toward him, the movement so abrupt it appeared painful.

"That's *insane*," she hissed.

"Baby—"

She leaned back. "And what do you do? You can't call the cops. Or you can. Then, as retribution, my dad makes you dead or I'm dead or your brother's dead or the mother of his children is dead or—"

He took two strides to her, yanked her in his arms and ordered, "Livvie, stop."

She held herself stiff then sagged so deep he had to take most of her weight.

"We can't do this," she said into his chest.

"I'm getting you out," he declared.

She went stiff again.

Then her head jerked back and she asked, "What?"

"I'm getting you out."

"Nicky," she whispered, her hands coming up, going into his jacket and curling into his shirt at the sides of his waist.

She did that but said no more.

His family called him Nicky when he was a kid. He loved it until it was the time in a boy's life to hate it. No one had used that name for years. Decades.

He loved it again from Olivia.

"I don't know how I'm gonna do it, I'm just gonna do it," he stated. "I'm gonna do it so you're safe, I'm safe. Everyone's safe. No worries. Just free. You just gotta give me the time to figure it out. And as much as I'd like to see that happen right now and do that by callin' the cops and lettin' them know your dad committed homicide today, I'm thinkin' my plan's gotta be more intricate than that. So we brave it out, suck it up, eat taco extravaganza, whatever the fuck that is, and I'll get you safe as soon as I can."

"I'm not sure that's possible," she replied.

"I am," he returned quickly and firmly.

Her eyes registered surprise.

Then her mouth whispered, "You believe that."

"Absolutely."

It took a few beats. It came slow.

But that was when pure beauty entered her gaze.

"Why is it that you believing makes me believe?" she asked in her gorgeous, delicate voice.

"Because I'm the man who's gonna eat taco extravaganza, whatever the fuck that is, just because you made it. I'm also the man who's gonna put the effort into making you come for me after, more than once, even though it's highly likely taco extravaganza is gonna sit in my gut like an anvil. And I'm also the man who knows every day I wake up you mean more to me than you did the day before. And I'm the man who knew you meant a fuckuva lot to me yesterday, so you meaning more today means everything. And I'm the man who's got two priority missions. To get you free of a life you hate and to get you to a place that you smile, frequently and easily."

The beauty in her green eyes didn't leave.

But it did get watery.

So Nick had no choice but to lift a hand to her cheek so he could catch the wet that leaked out with his thumb.

"Right, that's why you believing makes me believe," she said, again with that soft, sweet, gorgeous voice. A princess voice. His princess's voice.

"That's why," he confirmed.

Wet leaked out of her other eye where he didn't have a thumb to catch it. Seeing as he didn't want to take his arm from around her, he had no choice but to sweep it away with his lips.

This he did.

She slid her arms around his middle and held tight.

Since he was there, he dropped his forehead to hers.

She took in a deep breath that hitched.

He just stayed close.

She got it together.

He pulled away a couple of inches but only to look toward the kitchen.

He did a quick inventory and looked back.

"An entire bottle of French dressing?" he asked.

"Trust me," she answered.

"Boxed mac 'n' cheese?" he went on.

"Trust me."

"What *is* taco extravaganza?" he asked dubiously.

And then it happened. A moment he knew he'd never forget. Not in his life.

She gave it to him.

Open and out there and once it was, for the first time, it didn't fade away.

She smiled as she repeated, "Sweetheart, *trust me*."

Oh yeah.

Fuck yes.

She owned him.

He'd never been owned.

Not even by Hettie.

But he was hers. All hers.

Olivia's.

He knew it in that instant because he also knew in that instant he'd do anything, absolutely anything, beg, borrow, steal, kill, crawl, lie, cheat, die, eat taco extravaganza...

All just for her smile.

8:58 — That Night

HER CHEEK TO his thigh, his hand in her hair, she was flat out on the sofa at his side while he had his feet up on the coffee table and they were watching TV when he heard Knight's car.

"He's here, Liv," he muttered.

"Pause, honey," she muttered back.

He paused the program and she pushed up.

She'd brought the groceries.

She'd also brought a bag and was now casual in soft, black, loose-fitting drawstring pants and a gray ribbed tank.

"I'll start the dishes," she said.

"Help when I get this done," he replied.

She reached out to touch his collarbone through his tee before she glided to the kitchen, no less graceful in bare feet.

He went to the door, turned the bolt and slid it open.

He walked out to the landing, sliding the door closed behind him, seeing his brother nearing the top.

"Not feelin' big on this habit you're gettin' of summoning me," Knight stated, still two steps down.

"Livvie's here," Nick replied.

"And?" Knight prompted when he hit the landing and stopped.

"And until shit is sorted, I got the opportunity to be close and bein' that, know she's safe when every day I gotta suck it up when she goes to work for those lunatics, I'm takin' it."

Some of Knight's irritation faded.

"Wouldn't call if it wasn't important," Nick went on. "And would tell you over the phone if I could risk it."

"I gotta get to the club so you wanna lay it on me?"

"Vincent Shade murdered Drake Nair today."

Knight's head jerked back before he ordered, "Repeat that."

"After I got her through freakin' out that her bein' in my life means this kind of shit bein' in my life, she briefed me. Nair was with Shade to try to get him to partner up, percentage off the backs of your girls when he takes them over after he takes you out. To make that sting, he had plans of putting a hit on me. Shade didn't feel like taking up that offer. Nair got ugly. Shade shot him in the face with a .45."

"Jesus," Knight whispered.

"Good news is, that recurring headache is done for you."

Knight watched him closely. "Any bad news?"

"Mention of the Feds which confused her, though not enough for her to snoop around to find out what it means. She doesn't much care what her dad did or does outside of the fact she hates all of it. But even though she now knows my end game is to get her clear of that mess, she doesn't know how that game started. So it's good she isn't snooping around because not only have I not figured out how I'm gonna get her clear, I haven't figured out how to tell her how that game started."

"Fuck, Nick," Knight muttered.

"You got any ideas?" Nick asked.

"No, brother," Knight answered quietly. "Feel for you on that. That's gonna be an uncomfortable conversation."

"Unh-hunh," Nick mumbled.

"Advice, sooner rather than later," Knight said.

"Right," Nick mumbled that too. He drew in breath, looked to the door and then looked to his brother. "You wanna meet her?"

Knight's focus intensified. "Absolutely."

It was the perfect moment. She knew Knight was coming. She knew why. She had to figure Nick wouldn't keep him out in the cold. And Knight couldn't stick around so Olivia didn't have to be on the spot for long.

The first meet over, the next would go easier.

He slid open the door, and if the sound it made wasn't enough of a warning, he called out, "Babe, you wanna say a quick hi to Knight before he has to take off?"

If Nick had to guess, he would have said she'd ice over. Stone-cold. Polite, definitely, but distant in her princess way that might be borderline insulting.

He was shocked as shit when she walked from the kitchen toward them, her hands engaged in rubbing a dishtowel to dry them, doing this almost obsessively, her eyes on Knight, the wide hems of her pants too long.

She tripped, fortunately close so when she went flying, he could lunge and catch her before she hit the deck.

The dishtowel floated to the floor as she latched on to him and he brought her up straight and close, her head jerking back to look at him, her face beautiful and horrified.

No stone-cold princess there.

"Shit, fuck," she whispered.

No stone-cold princess there either.

The laugh he tried unsuccessfully to bite back scraped up his throat over the roof of his mouth to make an amused scratching noise coming out of his nose.

"Brother," Knight admonished when he heard it.

Nick held on to his woman and she held on to him as they both looked to Knight.

"I...um...hi, hey...um, hello," she stammered.

And no stone-cold princess there.

Nick's body started shaking.

She turned and glared at him, unlatching the arm she had wrapped around his back so she could smack his shoulder blade.

His amusement came low but audible.

"Shut up," she muttered under her breath.

"She can be cute," he told Knight.

Knight was staring at Nick's woman, his lips quirked up, and Nick reckoned his brother already got that.

"And a fuckin' nut," Nick went on.

"Nicky, shut up," she hissed.

Knight's brows rose and his gaze cut to Nick.

"Nicky?"

"Now you shut it," Nick replied, still laughing low.

Knight smiled at him then turned that to Olivia.

"Nice to meet you, Olivia. And sorry I'm doing it when I gotta go."

"I...me too, nice to meet you that is. As well as sorry you have to go," she said swiftly and with obvious nerves.

"We'll get together soon, you meet my Anya and my girls, yeah?" Knight suggested.

Olivia tensed against him but nodded and said, "Yes. That'd be nice."

"Right, gotta go," Knight murmured and looked to Nick. "Got the door, brother. Stay warm. Thanks for the news and later."

"Later, Knight."

Knight nodded to him, gave another smile to Olivia then turned and walked out.

"Oh my God, I tripped in front of your brother and said fuck," Olivia whispered in horror the minute the door slid closed.

He pulled her to his front and shared the obvious, "It was cute."

"I said fuck," she repeated.

"Baby, he's heard the word before."

"Undoubtedly," she returned. "And undoubtedly it's not a surprise coming from me considering the fact his brother's girlfriend is a gangster's daughter."

Fuck.

He finally got it.

He pulled her closer.

"He doesn't think dick that's bad about you."

"You sure, you know, considering you called him earlier to ask him over in order to report his nemesis is dead at my father's hand?" she asked sarcastically.

"He was born in your world. There's shit he gets about you that I'll never get about you. I don't give a fuck about it. He sure as fuck doesn't give a fuck about it. And he is who he is and you know who he is. So bein' who he is, he doesn't judge," Nick returned resolutely.

That shut her up.

"Unless you're an asshole or a twat, then he judges," he continued. "And you aren't either."

She pressed her lips together.

"You were cute," he repeated.

She looked to his shoulder.

He gave her a shake.

She looked to his eyes.

"So shake it off," he ordered.

"Okay, Nick," she said softly.

"Now, I think the challenge you issued my digestive system has been bested so I can fuck you without passing out or throwing up."

She frowned.

He ignored that and decreed, "Time to do that."

"Just to share an important tidbit as we figure our stuff out, your ridicule of my cooking is not amusing to me, Nick Sebring."

"Babe, you emptied a *bottle* of French dressing into ground beef seasoned with taco seasoning, *fried* flour tortillas, dumped mac 'n' chees on that, the beef on that, sour cream, cheese *and* guac on that and set that shit in front of me. It was the best thing I've ever tasted. And if a nutritionist saw it, they'd be apoplectic."

"Life is short and it mostly sucks so who cares what a nutritionist thinks?" she shot back. "You have to have some things you enjoy. I eat fruit. I eat veggies. I do Pilates two times a week. I walk on a treadmill for an hour four times a week. Every once in a while you have to treat yourself to such as taco extravaganza. It makes life worth living."

"How about we find other ways to make life worth living, like orgasms and mindless TV?" he returned.

"Is there a limit to things that you can have that make life worth living? Because if there is, I've got you, that's a *huge* boost, but I still don't think I'm even close."

I've got you, that's a huge *boost.*

Fuck, that felt good.

Really good.

"Totally fucking you now," he declared, grabbing her hand and dragging her toward the bedroom.

"Sebring, the dishes aren't done."

He pulled her up the steps, "Shade, don't care."

"Sebring—"

He stopped and yanked her around.

"Get naked," he growled.

She glared at him stubbornly.

He knew how to break through that so he did it, taking off his shirt.

Her glare wavered as her eyes dropped to his chest.

His hands went to his belt.

Her hands went to her tank.

He beat her to naked.

In the race to orgasm, she beat him.

But with that, Nick never minded finishing second.

20

WADE THROUGH SHIT

Nick

6:13 – The Next Morning

JUST AFTER COMING, instead of collapsing on Livvie, he rolled, bringing her with him.

She gave him her weight, her thighs gripping his hips, her face in his neck, her breathing heavy, her soft body fluid in his arms, still coming down from her orgasm.

Christ, weeks he'd had her and every fuck was better than the last.

One of many indications, if they could wade through the shit, their future was bright.

But first, they had to wade through the shit.

To that end, he tightened his hold on her before either of their breathing had evened and told her quietly, "Starting today, gonna put a man on you, baby. Everywhere you go."

He felt her tense against him, he fucking hated it, but he kept going.

"He'll be unobtrusive. But even with him on you, when I text or phone, want you to answer. If you can't right away, do it as soon as you can. Yesterday you didn't and it made me uneasy."

"Okay, Nick," she agreed.

He let out a breath.

Then he hit the next possible pile of shit.

"You sleep okay?"

She lifted her head and looked at him through the dark before dawn.

"Yes," she lied.

He slid a hand up her back.

"Baby," he started gently, "every night I've had you, you been restless."

"I'm not a good sleeper."

"Shit in your head?" he asked.

"I…" She stopped whatever she was going to say and answered simply, "Yes."

"Can I help with that?"

She laid still on him for a beat before she dropped her forehead to his.

He slid his hand all the way up her back to tangle it in her hair.

"Livvie?" he called.

"I think you just did," she said, sliding her head down so she had her nose pressed against the hinge of his jaw.

"Sorry?"

"Helped with that. I think you just did, Nicky," she told him, words in her soft voice he felt hit him hard in the gut.

So his "Good," was gruff.

They fell silent and held on.

Unfortunately, he had to roll her to the side and pull out of her.

"Shower time, Liv," he muttered.

"Okay, sweetheart," she muttered back.

He pulled them out of bed.

Having waded through that shit, he took them to the second best part of the morning.

Their shower.

*

5:22 – *That Evening*

NICK'S PHONE RINGING, he took the call and put it to his ear.

"Sebring."

"She's got a tail on her," Jed, the man he set on Liv that day, said. "Dude followed her from office to home. He's hangin' around, watchin' her house."

"He make you?" Nick asked.

"No," he answered. "But he doesn't look like he's leaving."

"Fuck," Nick muttered, that itch creeping up his neck again, his mind hoping that this was what Liv told him it was, standard procedure. His bugs being pulled, his gut was telling him something else. Then to Jed, louder, "Thanks, man. Stick around, yeah?"

"You got it."

Nick hung up then reengaged, calling Olivia.

"Hey, honey," she answered.

"You had a tail. He's watching your house."

She didn't reply for several moments before he heard a low, "Damn," and he knew she'd gone to a window and tagged her watcher.

"I'm comin' to you," he said.

Her tone was sharp when she started, "Sebring—"

"He won't see me," he assured.

"Are you positive you can pull that off?" she asked.

"Yes," he answered.

Again, she didn't reply for another several moments before, "I'll unlock the doors to the pool. Do you think they know I'm not around and that's why I have someone on me?"

"No clue, babe. But we'll keep better track of shit from here on out."

And they sure as fuck would.

"Right," she replied.

"I got some things to do at the office. I'll let you know when I'm on my way. Also still got my man on you, he's watchin' your watcher. That situation changes, I'll let you know."

"Okay, Nick."

"Later, Liv."

"'Bye, sweetheart."

They hung up. He did the things he had to do, texted her, left the office and parked on the street three blocks from her place. He approached from the alley, went in through her back gate (doing it making a mental note to buy a lock for it) and entered the house through a side French door by her pool.

She was standing at the end of the hall, watching him approach.

He saw her standing there but mostly he was taking in her place as he approached.

He got within four feet—and it took him a while to do that—when he said, "Tell Jeeves I'll take my whisky now."

He watched her body twitch.

And he stopped dead when she busted out laughing.

Fucking hell.

Fucking.

Hell.

He'd never seen her laugh.

It changed her. Entirely.

Gone was his cool, poised, exquisite princess.

Her laughter was soft, even delicate, like her voice, but it transformed her face, the line of her body.

She no longer was the cool-as-shit, hot-as-fuck piece of ass only a half percent of the male population would have the balls to approach because, even if the promise of her screamed it was worth the risk, every vibe she gave said you'd crash and burn.

In her place was the sweet-as-hell, hot-as-fuck piece of ass it wouldn't matter if you crashed and burned because she'd lay that hurt on you like velvet and you'd end up with her number anyway because you were invited to hang with her posse to watch the game.

He still had that Livvie when he made it to her.

He pulled that Livvie into his arms.

She lifted her hands to either side of his neck, curled her fingers to hold on lightly, and still quietly laughing, she tipped her head back and caught his gaze.

"Hey," she greeted, green eyes light and dancing.

Fuck, he was so fucking falling in love with her.

"Hey," he grunted, feeling warmth and contentment, unease, frustration and impatience.

And he was feeling these last because he was pissed he had to sneak into her house from the alley. Pissed he had to have a man on her. Pissed he had to worry if she didn't text back right away. And pissed he couldn't put her ass in his car and take her out to dinner so he could show the whole fucking world the beauty he'd earned.

Her laughter faded, but this time he had himself to blame for the brevity of her happiness.

"Sebring, what is it?" she asked, studying him closely.

"We're goin' to Vegas."

She blinked at him.

"Sorry?"

"Next weekend," he stated. "Do what you gotta do. Sort that shit. But we're flying to Vegas Friday night, stayin' until Sunday. You and me somewhere we can fuck like we fuck but do it bein' able to leave our bed, go out and eat and gamble and drink and whatever the fuck we wanna do and it doesn't matter who sees 'cause no one is watching."

She melted into him, not hiding even a little bit she liked that idea.

"Next weekend. Vegas," she agreed.

"Next weekend. Vegas," he confirmed.

Her happiness came back, not through laughter, through a sweet smile.

"I'll sort my shit," she promised.

"I'll sort mine," he did the same.

"Okay, that's a plan. Now, I haven't been home in a while so we have a choice for dinner. Heated up canned clam chowder or Chinese delivery."

"Is that a choice?" he asked.

"Right," she murmured. "Chinese delivery."

He let her go with one arm, pulling her around to his side and walking her into the gigantic space that was the front of her house. "You got menus?"

"Yes," she answered, moving from his hold to head to a drawer.

He stopped at her bar. "I get it if you feel like Chinese. But don't you have a personal hibachi chef, you know, after he slides one of these motherfucking huge marble slabs off to get to his grill?"

She threw him a look, her eyes still light, her lips tipped up.

"Or maybe you can call your pizza maker to duty. Your wood fired oven outside or what?" he pushed.

She turned away from her drawer and came to him, tossing a menu across the vast expanse of thick, gorgeous, expensive-as-all-hell countertop.

"You should count yourself lucky you're handsome, tall, built and a very good sex partner or your smartassedness would be problematically aggravating."

"Sex partner?" he teased.

"Look at the menu, Sebring."

"Smartassedness?" he kept teasing.

"Menu," she ordered.

"Problematically?"

She rolled her eyes to the ceiling.

He started grinning.

"Baby, get over here," he ordered through his grin. "Haven't kissed you yet. I'll look at the menu after I do that."

She rolled her eyes back to him. "And again with the lucky when you're equally problematically domineering."

"You're not getting over here," he noted.

"I'm engaged in trying to figure out why I have to get over there when you're perfectly capable of coming to me."

"Because you're used to rambling around this palace and I'm not. I need to conserve my energy for the tour you're gonna give me after we order Chinese."

That got him another upward curl of her lips.

He'd take it. Gladly.

She also got her ass to him, came close, pressing her front to his side as she rolled up on her toes, tipping her head back, and he rounded her with his arm.

She offered her mouth. He took it.

And when they broke, she stayed close and advised quietly, "The ginger chicken and Mongolian beef are superb. And the Peking pork isn't bad either."

"I'll order it all. Chinese leftovers never suck. You want egg rolls?"

"Yes."

"Soup?"

"Hot and sour."

She was an egg roll and hot and sour girl.

Fuck, woman of his dreams.

Definitely falling in love.

"You got beer?" he went on.

"Yes."

"Whisky?"

Her face fell. "Just Glenlivet but I also have bourbon, Maker's Mark."

"Neither suck, baby," he assured.

Her eyes brightened again.

"Just so you don't forget," he began. "You mean more to me today than you did yesterday."

Her lips parted and her eyes got bright a different way.

"And yesterday you meant a fuckuva lot to me," he finished.

"Nicky," she whispered, the bright at the bottoms of her eyes trembling.

He gave her a squeeze. "Get used to that, Liv. I intend to say shit like that a lot and I don't want you bawlin' every time I do it."

Her mouth turned down and the bright in her eyes changed again.

"I'm not bawling."

"You were close."

"You were being sweet."

"Like I said, get used to that."

"Then you were an ass."

"You should probably get used to that too."

She glared

Nick grinned.

She jerked her head to the counter, snapping, "Order, Sebring. I'm hungry."

"As you wish, baby," he muttered, reaching into his inside jacket pocket to pull out his phone.

He ordered, not letting her go.

After he was done, he stripped off his jacket and she took him for a tour of her house, which was even more massive than he thought. It was also on the market, something he already knew, with barely any nibbles, something that wasn't a surprise considering the fact it was listed for over five million dollars.

The place was worth it, but considering a very small percent of the population could afford it, a buyer would take some time.

And by that time, he knew right then, she'd be selling and moving in with him.

They ate in the family room in front of the TV.

They fucked in her bed.

And Nick didn't get a text from Jed until they were fucking to tell him her watcher had taken off (a text he obviously didn't take until after they finished).

He did not like that.

Then again, he didn't like any of the shit they had to wade through.

It was time he quit fucking around. It was time to form the intricate plan he had to form to get them through the shit and fulfill the promise he made a dead Hettie.

It was time to get done, move on and guide them both to their happy.

But first, because it was his job as her man that he give her more reasons life was worth living, he was going to take his woman to Vegas.

7:48 — Saturday Morning

NICK WOKE FEELING Livvie trailing a finger along his chest. The touch was light, sweet, and it stayed that way as she traced it down to his ribs.

She added her mouth at the base of his throat, it tracked his collarbone.

When he felt her hair gliding along his shoulder, he turned into her, gathering her in both arms, holding her on their sides.

She hitched her leg on his hip, her fingers now trailing his back, her face in his throat.

"Like your place," she muttered, sounding sleepy.

"Good,' he muttered back, not sure why she said that since "good morning" was more appropriate, not to mention, they were waking in her bed for the first time.

Maybe she preferred his.

"It's you," she went on.

"Yeah," he replied unnecessarily, because it was. He spoke at all because she'd stopped but she seemed to be feeling chatty because she continued.

"I feel safe there."

Fuck, he liked that.

He closed his eyes and pulled her closer.

"Good," he whispered.

She pressed even closer, her fingers no longer sketching mindlessly on his back but instead, her hand was pressed tight to his lat.

"But I like you here," she said, her voice softer, huskier, both of these with feeling.

He rolled her to her back, rolling on top, lifting his head, catching her eyes.

Yeah, she was feeling.

A lot.

Nick said nothing.

"I like you in my house," she continued. With her leg hitched on his hip, Nick had fallen through both when he rolled her. Now, she wrapped her calf around the back of his thigh. "I like you here because, if this fucks up, if I lose it, if I lose you, I'll have that."

His gut started burning. His eyes never leaving hers, he wrapped his fist around his hard cock and started rubbing the tip against her.

He felt her warm damp turn wet.

He dropped his face closer.

Her breath came faster, her eyes went slightly hazy, but she still stayed focused and kept whispering.

"This fucks up, I can ramble around here all alone and be happier doing it, just having these memories of you being here with me."

She got that shit out.

Time to shut it down.

He caught at her pussy and slowly glided into Olivia's soft sleek.

She licked her lips, arching her back, her other leg wrapping around his ass, both her hands pressing hard into the muscle of his back.

"This is not gonna fuck up," he growled, gliding out and taking his time, doing the same gliding back in.

"Okay, Nick."

He kept moving inside her.

"We're gonna make more memories. Here. At my place. Anywhere we fuckin' want."

"Okay, honey," she breathed.

"We're not gonna lose shit," he promised.

He kept moving, going deeper.

She slid one hand up and curled it tight around the back of his neck, the other arm she wrapped around him to hold on.

"I'm gonna make it good," he vowed.

She tipped her hips up, gazing into his eyes, now panting.

"You gotta believe," he ordered.

"Believe," she whispered.

He went faster.

She held on tighter.

"You gotta believe, Livvie," he grunted.

"I believe, honey."

He took her mouth. He fucked her cunt. She came hard for him. He shot deep in her.

He stayed on top and tangled his hand in the back of her hair, holding her still as he said in her ear, "No more talk like that. You think like that, you don't sleep. You think like that, you worry. You gotta let that go, Liv. I'm gonna make it all okay. You gotta let it go and believe."

"I'll let go."

"Promise me."

"I promise, Nick."

He drew in breath.

He let it go.

He felt her body yielding beneath him.

She'd let it go too.

Letting it go, it was time to move on.

And it was Saturday. They had time to move on to good things.

So he moved on, doing it lifting his head and again kissing his Livvie.

***

8:27 – Sunday Morning

HIS BACK AND shoulders to his headboard, his knees cocked, feet in the bed, his hand full of Livvie's hair, holding it back, he thrust up, watching her take his cock with her mouth.

"*Fuck*," he grunted.

Twisting her hair gently, he went still so he wouldn't blow.

She didn't.

Without him thrusting, she started bobbing.

Fuck.

"Livvie, only warning you're gonna get," he growled.

Without breaking her rhythm, on an upward glide, she wrapped her hand around his dick as she released him with her mouth.

Then she gave him her hot, hungry eyes as she jacked him.

Jesus.

Fuck.

"Take me there, baby," he ordered thickly, his hand still in her hair, gripping tight.

She stayed between his legs but leaned over him, still jacking him, hand in the bed beside his hip, her beautiful face, gorgeous naked body and fist pumping his dick all he could see.

"Fuck," he grunted, thrusting up, fucking her hand.

She made a noise that was hungrier than the look in her eyes.

"Fuck," he whispered, and closed his eyes as she took him there and he exploded, shooting on his stomach.

She milked him dry, stroked him sweet and he came down with her pressed to his side, feeling her cheek on his shoulder, his hand still in her hair.

He gave it a gentle tug, dipped his chin and caught her eyes before he took her mouth.

Because she tasted good, because he was falling in love with her and because she'd earned it, he kissed her deep and wet and he did it for a fucking long time.

He released her mouth after she released his cock and wrapped her arm around his ribcage.

He opened his eyes to see her looking at him.

"So, did that earn me cinnamon French toast?" she asked.

Nick stared at her.

Then he burst out laughing.

9:02 — The Same Sunday Morning

STANDING AT HIS kitchen counter with Livvie next to him, close, in the curve of his arm, he lifted to her mouth a fork full of the crunch coated, cinnamon French toast smothered in maple syrup that he'd made his girl.

When her lips closed around it, he slid the fork out. She chewed. He watched her eyes get big with happiness and wonder and she again meant more to him than she did the previous day...hell, the previous moment.

And she did this in a way that he knew every moment with her would give him that same feeling.

He wasn't falling in love.

She had him.

He was hers.

She swallowed and instantly asked, "Can I blow you and jack you every morning for French toast?"

"Absolutely," he answered just as instantly.

She pressed deep and dissolved into laughter.

Yeah.

Definitely.

Every moment with Livvie.

She gave him that same feeling.

In a way he knew.

He *knew*.

He knew she'd give him that now...

And forever.

21

WHO DO YOU BELONG TO?

Nick

5:45 – That Next Friday Evening

NICK SAT IN the aisle seat, staring ahead of him, only the stragglers that were sitting back in coach coming up the gangway.

Liv was not beside him.

An hour ago, she'd texted that she was on her way.

It did not take an hour to get from DTC to DIA.

From taking his seat in the waiting area prior to boarding to right then, having been sitting in his seat in first class for the last twenty minutes, he'd texted her three times and phoned once.

He got nothing.

His neck was not itching.

He was coming out of his skin.

They'd made their plans together, bought their tickets separately, and had chosen their adjoining seats on their respective laptops pressed up next to each other at his bar twenty-three hours and forty-nine minutes ago.

Now he was getting nothing.

He looked back to his phone in his hand when it beeped with a text. He pulled it up immediately.

It wasn't a text from Liv. It was a text from Sylvie.

Knight's men clean. Not a surprise. Your boys clean. Again no surprise. Focus now is on the Feds.

As he suspected.

It was good to have it confirmed. It would be fucking great to know, finally, who fucked him and Hettie from the inside.

He didn't reply to Sylvie. He also didn't send another text to Olivia.

He sent one to his boy who was on her.

Where's my woman?

The reply came quickly.

Peeled off fifteen minutes ago when she hit the door to DIA. She had no tail so I thought she was good. She's not with you?

His thumb ready to move on his phone, his head snapped up when he heard a soft, delicate, winded, "I made it!"

He saw Olivia, looking flushed and flustered, smiling apologetically at the flight attendant as she rushed around the corner into the aisle.

Her eyes came to him.

Her smile got bigger.

He slid out of his seat and did it frowning at her.

Not only at her, at the fact she was late, smiling like she hadn't scared the shit out of him, and last, she had no luggage with her.

"Hey, sweetheart," she greeted as she made her way to him. Reaching him, she put her hand to his abs and stretched up for a kiss.

He continued to frown down at her so her smile wavered, her eyes grew confused and she aimed her kiss at his jaw.

She slid into her seat while the flight attendant gave the announcement they soon would be closing the door.

He sat and texted Casey, *She's here, all good.*

He then turned to his girl.

"You gonna wear that outfit all weekend?" he asked as Olivia tucked her purse under the seat in front of her.

She straightened, grabbing her seatbelt and looking to him.

"Sorry?"

"Babe," he grunted. "Luggage."

"I checked it."

He stared at her.

"That's why I'm late," she explained. "Traffic on 225. Just a semi off the road, but everyone had to slow down to gawk. Then I had to check my bag."

"You think to return my texts so I didn't worry?" he asked.

"I told you I was on my way and you know I don't text and drive, Nick," she retorted, her attention to her lap as she clicked her belt. Done with that, she again looked to him. "And calling you or texting you would have delayed me getting to you."

"Checking your bag delayed you too."

She shook her head in abbreviated shakes, like a head shudder, indicating she found what he said distasteful.

Her tone stated the same thing when she decreed, "I don't do *carry-ons*."

"Liv, we're gonna be gone two days."

At that, she stared at him.

Then she lifted a hand in a sweep up her front, ending with a flourish around her head, and asked with incredulity, "Do you think *this* happens with security allowances of carry-on liquids?"

Nick felt his body jerk.

Then he burst out laughing.

"No," she snapped through his laughter. "It doesn't. One day. Two. Three. It doesn't matter. I'd have to be gone *an hour* to do carry-on."

Still laughing, he caught her by the neck, pulled her to him and took her mouth in a deep kiss.

She kissed him back just as deeply.

Even so, when he lifted his head away, she declared, "*That* was a much better, 'Hello, Livvie. I'm excited for our weekend away.'"

"Hello, baby. I'm fuckin' *ecstatic* about our weekend away."

Her mouth quirked and she murmured, "That works too."

He smiled at her.

Her mouth stopped quirking and she smiled back.

The plane started reversing from the gate and the flight attendant began the safety address.

7:45 — Vegas Time

"I HOPE YOU'RE hungry," Olivia said while wandering into their suite at the Cosmopolitan, Nick following, his carry-on over his shoulder, rolling her huge-ass piece of luggage. "Because I'm *famished* and I *need* to inspect that Swarovski chandelier much closer, hopefully doing it holding a cocktail...*oh!*"

The *oh!* was due to the fact he'd dumped their shit, and when she got close to the bed, he'd thrown her on it.

He didn't delay in shoving up her skirt.

"Nick, sweetheart, I'm hungry."

Chest to the bed, hips over the side, he pushed her legs open, looking to her to see she'd lifted up on her elbows.

"So am I."

"But, Nicky, I'm really hungry," she whispered in that voice of hers, words he didn't give a shit about but he still felt them in his dick.

He took hold of the gusset of her panties and twisted them aside.

Her eyes went hooded and her legs melted open.

"So am I," he growled in repeat.

She made no reply.

He dropped his mouth.

Her head fell back.

Nick ate first.

He fed his woman later.

⸻

10:52 — Saturday Morning

THE CURTAINS CLOSED, the DO NOT DISTURB sign on the door, front to front on their sides, Nick lay naked and entangled in the king-size bed with his Livvie.

"The mountains," she whispered into his throat, her body warm and peaceful, her arms holding him lightly, her breasts brushing his chest, her legs entwined with his. "A house in the middle of nowhere but with a town close by so I don't have to drive too far in bad weather to get groceries."

He'd started their day making love.

Now Olivia was in the mood to whisper to him.

Whisper about everything.

Not everything in the sense there were a lot of words.

Everything in the sense the words she was saying said a lot.

But Nick said nothing. He gave back only his silence as indication he wanted more of Liv's everything while he wove his fingers in her soft hair.

"House big, but not ostentatious. Rustic. Homey. Lived-in," she went on quietly.

Nick remained silent as she told him her dream future.

"Good people in town," she continued. "They know me but don't *know* me. Friendly. I'll be friendly back. But my life will be at home."

At that, Nick spoke.

"Kids?"

This time, Liv stayed quiet.

He dipped his chin to see the shadowed top of her head.

"Livvie?"

"I can't," she told his throat.

She *couldn't?*

Reflexively, he stopped playing with her hair and wrapped both arms tighter around her.

"You can't?"

She tipped her head back. "Not safe."

She could.

Because of those jackals in her life, she just wouldn't.

"I'll make you safe, Liv."

She shook her head.

"Not safe," she repeated.

He gathered her even closer, pulling her up so they were eye to eye. "We get there, we get to that place, we want kids, I'll make it safe."

"They can't have anything to use to get to me," she told him and finished, "or you."

"They won't factor in the equation."

"Nick—"

"Livvie, honest to God, don't want to sound like a conceited asshole, but I know I'm not hard to look at and you're fuckin' beautiful. It might have taken me a while to demonstrate I had a brain in my head, but I eventually did. I'm not dumb and you're far from stupid. We get to that place, we *gotta* have kids. It's our duty to this earth to give it that beauty."

In the light eking around the curtains, he saw her lips part, she pressed closer for a moment, only to move slightly away.

He pulled her close again.

"I don't want a child of mine to become me," she said.

"There's nothing wrong with you," he stated, steel in each word.

"You know what I mean, Nick," she replied, each word soft and edged in pain.

"I know what you mean and that's just not gonna happen."

"And maybe my mom thought that before she had Georgia and me, gave up and took off," she noted.

"And maybe your mom is a stupid, weak, useless bitch," he returned. "What's not a maybe is you're *not*."

"Nick."

His name was all she said.

So he kept at her.

"We get there…and just so you know, baby, that's where I'm heading us and I like where we're going…I can't say I'll take you to the mountains so you can disappear. I got a business. I gotta see to that business. And that business is in the city. What I can say is, I'll get you a place up there we can visit. And when we're at home, wherever we're makin' that home, I'll make you safe. And if we get to that place, we're making a family. When we do that, I'll make *them* safe. You'll live free and easy. They'll live free and easy. That's what I can say. And we keep on, we get to where we're headed, you gotta do what you promised along the way and believe."

"Believe," she said like she was rolling that word around her mouth, and even if he'd asked that of her before, and she'd promised she'd give it to him, she looked like she still wasn't sure how it tasted.

Fuck, but that family of hers did a number on her.

"Believe," he said firmly.

He watched her press the side of her head in the pillow and her tone was one of surprise like she'd just noticed something.

"You like where we're going?"

He beat back a laugh and instead gave her a squeeze, sliding his leg deeper between her thighs.

"Uh, yeah," he pointed out the obvious.

"Our duty to give the earth that beauty?"

That wasn't said with surprise.

It was wonder.

"Yeah, baby," he replied.

She shifted her hands flat across his skin from his back to his chest.

"I...well, I like you, Nick."

Instantly, his body started shaking with humor he couldn't control.

"Well, that's good," he replied.

She pressed hard into his chest and whispered, "Please don't laugh."

He stopped laughing.

"I like you, Nick," she repeated.

Fuck.

She didn't mean that.

She meant more.

"I like you too, Livvie," he whispered back, rolling into her.

"And I like where we're going," she told him, almost shyly.

Fuck.

He settled on her. "I'm glad, honey."

"I want three babies."

Oh yeah.

His choice, he'd stop at two.

She wanted to give him three, he'd give her that.

He dropped his mouth to hers.

"You want three, we'll have three," he murmured against her lips.

"Think about the mountains, sweetheart," she replied. "I think we both could use some peace."

He was looking at mountain properties on Monday.

He ran his hands down her back, over the irregular skin at the small to her ass. She didn't flinch, didn't move away, didn't have any reaction at all.

He was getting somewhere in a lot of ways.

"I'll think about it," he muttered.

"Good," she whispered.

He let her say the word then he slid his tongue in her mouth.

She slid her fingers in his hair.

When he was done kissing her, he moved to work her throat as he trailed a hand around and up toward her breast.

"I love how easy it is for you to make me believe," she said in his ear.

Shit.

He wanted to make love to her again, do it slow, make it last.

She got any sweeter, he was going to have to fuck her.

"Baby?" he called.

"Yeah?"

He curled his hand around her breast.

"Shut up."

"Okay," she breathed.

He grinned against her skin and rubbed his thumb over her nipple.

One of her hands convulsed in his hair, tugging it. The other one started gliding down his spine.

Olivia shut up.

So Nick took his time and made love to her.

6:56 – Saturday Evening

NICK IN A suit, no tie, and Olivia in heels and a little black dress that he liked a fuckuva lot, walked out of the elevators at the Cosmopolitan Hotel in Vegas.

They barely hit the public space when three guys walking by them slammed into each other as their eyes remained glued to Liv when she and Nick passed.

Nick looked from the men down to the woman he held close in his arm.

She was oblivious.

Nick was smiling.

They walked right out the front.

They got in a taxi.

And for the first time, Nick took his woman out to dinner.

11:58 — Saturday Night

HER ASS ON a velvet couch beside him, but most of her weight pressed up against him in a bar that felt suspended in a cocoon of crystals, her eyes carefree and happy, Olivia announced, "I need another cocktail."

She was beyond tipsy, heading straight to shitfaced.

Nick didn't mention that to his girl.

He looked across the space, caught the waitress's eye and jerked up his chin.

He felt Liv's hand at his stomach sliding across and he tipped his head down to look at her again.

"Thanks, baby," she whispered.

He didn't reply.

Instead, he drank in that look in her eyes, feeling her pressed tight beside him.

That was his.

He'd earned that.

After he gave himself that moment, he took what he earned, tipped his head down and kissed her.

When he released her mouth and looked back at her face, he knew that wasn't enough.

So the next party that passed by, a couple, he stopped them.

"Sorry," he said. "But can you get a picture?"

The guy with his girl looked to Nick, then to Liv, and nodded, taking Nick's phone that he'd engaged the camera and was offering.

"How fun! Vegas memories," Olivia cried. Her arm already wrapped around his stomach, she burrowed closer.

The guy smiled, his girl smiled. He aimed, touched the button and gave Nick back his phone.

"Have a good night, bud," he said as he put his arm back around his woman and started to lead her away.

His woman waved.

Olivia kept snuggled to him but waved back.

"Thanks, man," Nick muttered and looked down at his phone.

Olivia again burrowed in.

"Ooo, sweetheart," she cooed. "That's a good one."

It wasn't, she was wrong. The first picture of them wasn't good.

It was brilliant.

Olivia tucked tight to his side, her head tipped back, her cheek resting along the underside of his jaw, a big smile on her face you couldn't miss even if you could only see half of it.

Nick had his arm around his girl, looking at the camera, smiling right at it.

They looked carefree. They looked happy.

She looked carefree.

She looked *happy*.

Yes. It was brilliant.

The waitress delivered her cocktail.

"Awesome," she murmured, leaning toward it.

Nick nodded at the waitress.

Having nabbed her drink, Liv leaned back and caught Nick's eye.

"I think it's time to gamble," she declared before taking a sip.

He grinned. "Whatever you want, Livvie."

She grinned too before she swung her drink to the side, reached her mouth up to his and touched it.

Her eyes a hint away, she whispered, "Let's go, Nicky."

They went. He took her exactly where she wanted to go. He did anything she wanted to do.

He gave her everything it was in his power to give.

And he'd keep doing it, in Vegas, in Denver, on the moon if they landed there.

Just to keep his girl carefree.

And happy.

3:32 — Sunday Morning

THE DO NOT DISTURB sign was again on the door.

Nick was slightly inebriated.

Livvie was smashed.

After dinner and then after dinner cocktails, Nick had lost three thousand dollars at craps.

After Nick dropped that load, Liv had won three hundred dollars at the slots.

She crowed.

She also rubbed it in.

So when the door to their room closed behind them, Nick set about evening out their night's score.

In took him a while, and as usual, she didn't play fair.

This time, he didn't either.

But it was a game he knew she didn't want to win.

So when he got her naked on her belly in their bed, he shoved a hand between her legs, cupping her pubic bone. Kneeling at her side, he yanked her up to her knees, ass in the air, as he held her down with a firm but gentle hand wrapped around the back of her neck.

He then moved his hand from between her legs and reached to the nightstand, pulling open the drawer.

In it was a short-handled paddle made of cushioned, soft brown leather that he'd brought with him and put there when she wasn't looking.

He took it out and rubbed it along her ass.

He heard her soft gasp, but she didn't move nor did she protest.

He buried a grin.

Fuck, she was *so* his.

Time for her to admit it.

"Who do you belong to?" he asked.

She pushed against his hand at her neck and pressed her ass into the paddle.

He landed it across her cheeks. The crack rent the air. Her hips jerked then her legs locked but Nick could still see them trembling.

"Who do you belong to?" he repeated.

She didn't move.

He bent over her.

"Olivia, who do you belong to?"

Sneak attack, she reached out a hand and cupped his balls.

That felt so fucking good, he bit his lip to bite back his groan and again smacked her ass with the paddle.

He heard her whimper into the covers. The good kind of whimper. The kind of whimper she made that he felt in his cock.

"Who do you belong to, baby?" he asked.

She gently massaged his balls.

Christ.

"Who do you belong to, Livvie?"

She slid her knees farther out on the bed.

Christ.

He ran the edge of the paddle between her legs.

Her entire bottom half started trembling.

"Who do you belong to?" he pushed, still stroking her.

She strained her ass up farther.

He gave her what she was asking for and again paddled it.

"Yes," she whispered.

Fuck yes.

"Who do you belong to?"

Nothing.

He swatted her.

She slid her hand up, wrapping her fingers around his cock.

No, she didn't play fair and he fucking loved it.

"Who do you belong to, baby?"

She stroked him.

He gritted his teeth and spanked her. And again. And again.

She twisted her head around in his hold, lifting her eyes to his.

"You, Nicky, I belong to you."

"Cock, Liv, now," he grunted, letting her neck go.

She twisted at the waist instantly. Keeping her ass in the air, she swallowed his cock whole.

Fuck.

Yeah.

He growled before dropping the paddle and sucked his thumb into his mouth. He shifted it to her hole, pressing the pad in.

She whispered, "Please, Nicky," against the head of his dick.

He fucked her ass as he watched her suck him off.

Right before he would come in her mouth, he slid his thumb out and ordered gruffly, "Up, baby. Face the headboard, hold on and give me your pussy."

She wasted no time, slid him out and positioned.

He wrapped an arm around her belly, took hold of his cock and positioned the head.

"Who do you belong to, Livvie?" he whispered in her ear.

She twisted her neck and caught his eyes.

Hers were shining green so bright and burning, he felt branded.

No.

Not felt.

He just was.

"You," she moaned, and his hand was forced from between him as she drove down and started fucking herself hard.

Magnificent.

He took over.

She arched her back and let him.

Even better.

Grunting, whimpering and groaning, they fucked, they did it hard, Nick took her there and then Olivia took Nick there.

She was cleaned up, the lights out and he was drifting to sleep when his woman murmured against the skin of his chest.

"Do you, um…have a crop?"

He grinned through the dark at the ceiling.

He'd been wrong.

She was not the woman of his dreams.

She was the woman beyond even a dream.

"I *so* own you," he muttered back.

"Whatever," she returned, sounding disgruntled but doing it snuggling closer.

"Tie you too," he declared.

She made a noncommittal noise but her body pressed closer to him.

"Blindfold," he went on.

"What*ever*," she repeated with added emphasis.

"Gag as well. Plug your ass. Go all out."

Liv shifted against him. "*Whatever*, Nicky. Now shut up."

"You just came hard for me after I paddled your ass then fucked it and you're getting turned on just talking about getting more," he pointed out.

She lifted her head and snapped, "Shut *up*, Nicky."

He aimed a hand and cupped her face.

"You gotta know, baby, you own me too."

She melted into him again, pressing her cheek to his palm.

He leaned to her, touching his mouth to hers.

"Now go to sleep," he ordered when he was done.

She bent in, brushed her mouth along his jaw and then settled back into him.

Liv snuggled close.

Nick held her as she did.

And they fell asleep.

9:25 — Sunday Night

THEY WERE BELTED into the plane, prepared for landing, and Olivia had fallen to the side, her head on his shoulder. Their forearms were up on the armrest and they were holding hands.

"Can we do that again?" Nick heard her ask.

He turned his head and kissed the top of hers.

"Yeah," he answered and shared, "Take you to the mountains, maybe next month."

"That'd be nice," she murmured, tightening her fingers in his hand.

He didn't reply, just watched the flight attendant going about her business.

"I wanna be safe."

He again turned his head, this time to look down at her as she lifted hers from his shoulder and looked up at him.

"I wanna be free," she went on.

"I'll get you there," he promised.

"No, I mean, I…it's…" She shook her head but kept at it. "It's not your job. I need to sort it out. I don't know how I'm gonna manage that…the last time I tried to leave the family, it didn't go too well—"

Nick cut her off, "Babe, it *is* my job."

Her gaze grew confused. "It's my life, Nick."

"Not anymore."

She continued to look confused with the addition of mildly annoyed. "So now that you've decided where we're heading, my life is yours?"

She'd had enough of her life being anyone's.

But she was sort of right.

"No," he answered. "Now that we're on the same page about where *we're* heading, that future is *ours*. It's not just you anymore, Liv. And it's not just me. It's us. That future, our future, is about the both of us. I want you to be safe and free and have your own life, but if I'm not wrong, we're both agreed that life is gonna have me in it. If that's the case, it's my job to look out for you. There'll be times and ways you'll look out for me. But now, with this, with what happened the last time you tried, I want you safe while I pull it off. So this time, it's my turn."

"You're not wrong," she said softly, something new he liked a helluva lot shining from her eyes. "We're both agreed."

He grinned. "I know."

She grinned back, it was small but it came easy.

He still felt it in his gut.

He hoped he made it so her happiness came at him so much, that feeling stopped, at the same time he hoped it didn't.

"Just so you know, I love Vail, but my favorite is Winter Park," she announced. "It's fun and beautiful and not as hoity-toity."

His grin got bigger. "So noted."

"You want me to find a VRBO?" she asked.

"Knock yourself out," he answered.

"You'll have to give me some dates," she told him.

"I get to the office, I'll get them."

She gave him bright, happy eyes and a hand squeeze before she dropped her head on his shoulder again and fell quiet.

He held her hand.

They landed.

Nick hung back so she disembarked before he did.

He knew (and didn't like) that she'd have to get her bag alone and lug it to her car alone.

He simply went to his car alone, something he also didn't like.

Twenty-five minutes later, he slid through the back gate of her house and let himself in one of her pool doors with the key she'd given him. He also turned off her alarm with the code she'd given him.

She joined him fifteen minutes later.

When she did, they shared a drink in front of the TV. Olivia conked out during the news. Nick woke her and helped her to bed.

Her head hit the pillow, she crashed.

But Nick lay with her pressed against him, staring at the ceiling, knowing the time had come for him to get shit done.

He lay there knowing it and wondering how the fuck he was going to get her safe and free.

He lay there knowing it, needing to do it, and also knowing he'd spent a weekend with his woman in Vegas, two two-hour plane rides where they weren't fucking, eating, drinking, whispering about important shit or having fun, and he *still* had not come clean about where he was with her when they began.

It was good they'd had Vegas. She was relaxing into what they had. She was believing. She was trusting.

Tomorrow.

That shit had to come out tomorrow.

They'd needed Vegas.

Now it was time.

Nick had learned a lot since sorting his head and his life.

Unfortunately, the last lesson would be the hardest.

That lesson being he shouldn't procrastinate.

22

THE BRIGHTSIDE

Olivia

10:23 – Monday Morning

I WAS COASTING INTO the parking area around the warehouse when my phone rang. I saw on my dash computer it was Nick so I took the call as I guided my Evoque to a spot.

"Hey," I greeted.

"What are you doin' at the warehouse?" he asked curtly in reply.

He still had a man following me.

His men had to have better things to do. Not to mention it was expensive to waste one following me everywhere.

And having one tail me was a reminder of *why* I needed to be tailed, which wasn't pleasant.

I would be glad when those days were at an end.

"Georgia texted," I began to explain. Having glided into a spot, I threw it in park. "Wanted a meet. Her schedule today is such she couldn't get to me, so I'm coming to her."

"My guy can't get anywhere near that warehouse, Liv," he told me.

"It's just a meet with my sister. Not a big deal. She wants to go over some new investments I'm suggesting."

"I don't like this," he muttered like he wasn't talking to me.

I didn't like it either. I never liked being at the warehouse.

But this would one day come to an end.

I believed.

Nick Sebring was not Tom Leary.

And I was no longer the Olivia Shade I was when I was twenty-five.

I was smart and I was savvy. I had a good head on my shoulders.

And I could make a man like Nick Sebring talk about having a future with me. Babies.

The only thing I wasn't was strong. I had to admit that to myself so I could face it.

I'd had my strength burned right out of me.

No, I'd *let* them burn the strength right out of me.

Then I let them do whatever they wanted to do and I'd quit fighting. I'd quit dreaming.

I'd quit believing.

Now, Nick was showing me another way. He'd once been another man, a maybe not-so-good one, and he'd learned. He'd learned not to be petty and selfish and manipulative.

He'd grown up. He'd become his own man. He'd become the master of his destiny.

And he saw something in me.

I honest to God didn't know what.

But if he saw it, if he liked it, if he wanted a future with it, I wanted to give *it* to him.

I wanted to make it worth it.

I wanted it for myself.

Nick had needed to grow up.

I didn't need to grow up. I was grown up. Too grown up. I felt a million years old.

So no, I didn't need to grow up.

I needed to grow a backbone.

Nick wanted to look out for me. He wanted to find a way to make me free.

I loved that.

But I had to help.

And I had to make that struggle (and it was going to be a struggle) worth it.

Thinking about all of this on the plane, wanting a life with Nick in it, wanting the future he was leading us to, as well as coming to terms with all of this, I also had to admit I was scared shitless.

But I was beginning to understand that having a backbone wasn't about being brave and stupid, jumping in with both feet, rushing to meet the horizon, so as the sun peaked it burned you blind.

It was about being scared shitless, knowing the source of your fears, understanding them, outsmarting them, and going forth to conquer them anyway.

I didn't know what his plan would be.

I just knew whatever it was, I had to find the strength to be with him all the way so I'd feel worthy of being with him the rest of the way.

"I'll be in and out," I assured him. "Georgia's got all sorts of stuff on. She's never been overly interested in this kind of thing anyway. I'll probably be back in my car on the way to my office in half an hour."

"I want you texting me when you're out of there," he ordered.

Patiently, I reminded him, "I don't text and drive, Nick."

"Then pull over, Olivia, and text me, or just call me and talk to me on your fuckin' Bluetooth like you're doin' now."

At that curt demand, and the open disquiet behind it, I felt a chill slide over my scalp.

Even so, I assured Nick again. "I'm just meeting Georgie, sweetheart."

"Just contact me one way or another when you're out of there, babe. Yeah?"

"Yeah, Nick."

"My man will be waiting. He'll pick you up again when you leave. I still want to hear direct from you you're okay."

"All right, honey."

"Right, Liv. Later, baby."

"Later."

He hung up.

I stared at the grungy outside of the warehouse through my windshield, took a breath and shook off the weird feeling Nick's call left me. That done, I threw open my door.

I was walking up the stairs inside the warehouse that led to the hall of offices when a text sounded on my phone.

I kept moving as I grabbed it and read it.

It was Georgia, *See you pulled up. Meet me in Dad's office.*

Along with the lingering weirdness I felt from Nick's call, I didn't feel happy thoughts about that text.

But this was my sister. This was Georgie. Even if Dad was in a snit about something, she looked out for me.

And Dad was leaving me be. In fact, it seemed after I sorted the David stuff and moved on from Tommy, he was coming to terms with the daughter that was me. He wasn't asking me over for cookouts, but he wasn't in my space or my life hardly at all. This, to my way of thinking, was the best gift he could give me.

So Nick cared about me. He didn't like my family. He didn't like me around my family. And he'd long since warned me to stay away from the warehouse so I knew he didn't like me being here.

He was just being protective.

And I could shake off the weird feeling, get my meet done with Georgia (who probably told Dad about it and he wanted to horn in) and get out of here. Get out of here and get back to my life. My real life, the life I lived without all this and with Nick.

I walked down the hall toward Dad's door deciding that instead of looking at this in the sense I was back here in this dingy hall possibly about to spend time with my father, I should look at it in the sense that I hadn't been there in over a week. My life no longer meant I had to come there every day. I only came there occasionally. And I didn't have to stay for long.

In other words, for the first time since Tommy and I failed in our escape, I looked on the Brightside.

Because of this, my mouth curled up in a small smile as I put my hand on the handle of my father's door.

I turned it.

I pushed in.

I walked in.

I saw Georgia coming up out of a chair in front of my father's desk, turning as she did to face me.

I also saw something out of the corner of my eye.

I didn't get the chance to look that way.

Agony exploded from my cheekbone, coursing a path through my temple and eye.

Having received the backhanded blow from my father, I staggered to the side, hand out to catch my fall however that might happen, eyes blinking in an effort to regain focus taken away by surprise and pain.

I hadn't succeeded before the next blow came. This one not a backhand but an open-handed slap across my cheek that cracked hideously through the room, the sound exploding in my brain.

I careened from that blow only to sustain the next one, another slap, followed by another. But that one was a closed-fist crushing punch that landed right on my temple.

Fighting to remain conscious but unable to remain standing, I fell to the side. Slamming into my hand on the silk carpet, my wrist taking all my weight, the throb of pain radiating up my arm, my hip hitting next.

My other hand to my face, cowering away from the possibility of another blow, I heard Georgia cry, "Dad! Stop with the face!"

"Fuck, you fucking stupid, goddamned *fucking* bitch!" my father shouted, on the second "fucking" grabbing hold of my hair in a painful grip and yanking back.

I made a mew of pain, my eyes opening to see his red livid face inches from mine.

"What the fuck's the matter with you, you stupid, *fucking* bitch?" he asked in an enraged shout, his spittle landing on my face. "Christ! How have you not learned? It's simple," he yanked my hair with the last word and then again with each successive one, "you…do…as…you're…*told*."

My head jerking with each tug, my neck stretched taut in a reflexive effort to fight the jolts and beginning to ache, my scalp in agony, I tried to gather a single thought.

All I could do was notice that my sister was approaching.

I also vaguely noticed Tommy was there, not too far away.

And incidentally—so Tommy—not intervening.

"Dad, back off," Georgia said in a calming voice.

Dad glared at me a moment before he yanked my hair one last time, like he was pushing me away from him, before he let me go and straightened.

I swayed with the wrench, flinching against the pain, and righted myself. But I didn't move further because my father didn't shift away and both Georgia and he were fencing me in.

Hazily, my attention drifted to my sister.

"Dustin Culver, Liv," she said.

"What?" I whispered, that being the absolute last thing I expected her to say, not thinking I actually heard her say it and wondering if I was unconscious and hallucinating.

"Told you to date him, sis. Not break up with the fucker," she stated.

I blinked up at her.

"The man's running for state senate next term," my father spat, and I looked to him. "Way he looks. Money he's got. Brain in his head. His pedigree. His education. His ambition. He'll be in Washington in four years, if he doesn't run for governor. He could even fuckin' make a play for the White House. That kinda future ahead of him, you get him addicted to your snatch, leadin' him around by his dick, what's that do for the Shades?"

I wasn't certain I was hearing what I thought I was hearing.

"You wanted me..." I shook my head. "What?"

"Boy got your stepfather out of some shit, because your stepfather is more of a stupid fuck than *you* are," Dad bit out. "Payback, Culver saw you out to dinner with your mother, he wanted a fixup. Your mother saw the benefits of such a union. She chatted with your sister, your sister chatted with me. We all agreed. You see him. You fuck him. You get him wrapped around your finger, you own him," he jerked his thumb at himself, "then *I* own him."

I felt something coming off of Georgia, it was not nice, and since I didn't need more not nice in the present situation, my gaze darted quickly to her only to see her aiming a sour look at our father.

She rearranged her face when she noticed my attention and looked down at me.

"Babe, getting you out of this warehouse? Getting you clean? Next young, handsome, hotshot Colorado senator sent to Washington is not gonna put a ring on your finger, you're managing a crew of drug dealers."

Me moving offices hardly made me clean.

"I'm still a Shade," I pointed out hesitantly.

"No Shade has direct ties to anything…" she hesitated before her lips quirked and she finished, "shady. Not anymore."

Her sister on the floor at her feet having been on the receiving end of four vicious blows from the father we shared, I had no idea how she could find anything amusing.

Then again, as it sunk in that they were whoring me out to Dustin Culver, something she was clearly in on, maybe I did have an idea.

I scooted back several inches, and with as much grace as I could muster, cradling my tender wrist in my other hand, doing my best to ignore the pain burning in my face, I gained my feet. I then shifted away farther, my eyes glancing from my father to my sister to Tommy, doing this also noting Gill was across the room, shoulder leaned against the wall, face blank, watching.

They were all in on it.

My face stinging and I could feel it swelling, I avoided my father's eyes and looked at my sister.

"So I don't manage a crew of dealers. Now I'm a whore?"

Georgia caught herself mid-eye roll at what she clearly considered my dramatics and threw out a low hand. "He's not ugly or fat or stupid. How tough would it be?"

I straightened my shoulders and held her gaze. "Maybe not tough but did it occur to you to explain your plans to me rather than telling me what I was to do without me really understanding *why* you wanted me to do it?"

"I've been kinda busy, Liv," Georgie replied. "I said date the guy. You dated the guy, okay. Then you broke up with him without clearing that with me. *Not* okay."

So now my sister thought she owned me.

I didn't acknowledge her ludicrous reply.

I asked, "And did it occur to you to maybe *ask* if I wanted to get involved with Dustin Culver for a night or two or, say, *the rest of my life?*"

"You might wanna watch your mouth, girl," my father warned.

I looked to my father, taking another step back, which was chicken, but doing it saying, "No, Dad. I wouldn't," which scared the shit out of me saying it but it was very much *not* chicken.

Dad's face screwed up, his body tightened, and mine did too because I knew he was about to lose it.

But I wanted him to.

I wanted him to beat the living daylights out of me.

And when I crawled to the police and pressed charges then went home to Nick with the umbrella of protection he could offer me, I wanted to watch them squirm.

Because I heard things. I did things.

I *knew* things.

I knew better than to turn rat. I had Shade blood running through my veins. That was never going to happen.

But I'd never been one of them. I'd never fit. They knew that.

So they didn't know I'd never turn rat.

I was done.

Utterly finished.

Nick could keep me safe. He'd promised. And even Dad had said he and his brother were untouchable.

He'd make me the same way.

I believed.

I *fucking* believed.

So *fuck them*.

"Tom," Georgia muttered, turning slightly toward Tommy, who was now on the move, coming my way.

"I'd really rather it was Dad who finished the job, Tommy," I told him.

"Quiet, Liv," he murmured, getting close.

Taking my elbow in a firm grip, he turned me to the door.

"Good. You get him to get her outta my fuckin' sight and then you get her shit sorted, Georgie." I heard Dad order as Tommy escorted me to and out the door. "You get me?"

"It'll be handled, Dad," Georgia replied, managing to sound both conciliatory and annoyed.

It'd be handled, my sister offering me up as Shade property.

Oh yes, I was *so* done with my family.

Tommy shut the door behind us and I let him walk me five feet down the hall before I tried to twist my arm free.

His grip tightened to the point of pain, and in surprise, my head shot to the side and back to look up at him.

He'd never touched me like that.

"Tom, let me go," I hissed, twisting now not only to get loose but against the pain.

"Shut the fuck up, Liv," he clipped angrily, not letting go but now manhandling me toward my old office and in.

Everything was still there except my personal effects. The décor. The furniture. Nothing had changed.

And I would find, in short order, that was agonizingly correct.

Nothing had changed.

Not.

One.

Thing.

Tommy pulled me in several feet, let me go and shut the door.

He turned to me and I braced in shock when I saw his face was a mask of fury.

"Are you fuckin' stupid?" he whispered, his tone harsh with rage.

"You know," I returned conversationally, "I don't need you to be ticked, Tommy. My father striking me four times to push the point home about Dustin Cul—"

Suddenly, he rushed me.

I scurried back, hit a chair, hit a table and hit wall, Tommy pinning me there with his body and his anger.

"I'm not talking about Culver, Liv. I'm talkin' about *Nick Sebring*."

Fear slamming through me, I stopped breathing.

"Yeah," he bit off. "Harry told me."

Oh God.

Harry?

I didn't have to verbalize the question. Tommy was more than ready to give me the answer.

"Taught you how to take the tracker off your car. Taught you how to spot a tail," Tommy explained. "Seein' as it's comin' clear you got shit for brains, never occurred to you, he taught you how to spot a tail, he'd know how to tail you without you spotting him."

"But why would he even *do* that?" I asked quietly, unable to make my voice even a normal volume.

"For money. For *me*," he ground out, jerking a thumb at himself miraculously in the minimal space he'd allowed. "For *us*," he went on.

I shook my head. "Us?"

"Fuck, Liv, do you pay attention *at all?*" he asked.

Apparently, I didn't.

But I thought I did.

"Tom, I—"

"Your sister is taking over," he said low, getting even closer to do it. "Your dad's goin' down, Liv. She's maneuvered him right out. He's been so taken up with findin' new sources of horse and blow, comin' up with crazy-ass bullshit schemes like marryin' his daughter to some asshole he's convinced is gonna be the next fuckin' president, for fuck's sake. Not to mention, generally fucking things up doin' stupid shit, like gettin' caught up in that human trafficking bullshit that almost brought us all down. He didn't see it."

There was a lot there, none of which I got to process because Tommy was still speaking.

"Now, when Georgia's in charge of things, and she will be and she will be soon, things'll change. And those things changing means I get you. You get me. She gets Gill. Your dad gets ousted however she's got planned to oust him and she's got plans, Liv. Make no mistake about that. She is *not* fuckin' around. Not anymore."

I stared up at him, lips parted, frozen in disbelief.

This went on for too long and I knew that when Tommy clipped out, "You wanna snap out of it?"

"You get me?" I asked.

He moved away half a step and tossed both hands up in exasperation. "Fuck, Liv, what do you think I've been eatin' shit for the last six years?"

I could not believe this.

"Your wife is pregnant," I pointed out.

"Yeah, and when I dump the bitch, the kid'll still be mine. He'll be raised half the time by you and me, which might suck, but kids deal with that shit all the time. He'll be good."

I could not believe this!

"When you dump the bitch?" I asked.

"Liv, I'm in love," he pointed a finger less than an inch from my face, "*with you. We're* gonna make kids. You're gonna do whatever you do at David's office. I'm gonna run Georgia's crew. And it's all gonna be the way we wanted it to be."

"If it's all gonna be the way we wanted it to be, Tommy, how is my cousin pregnant?"

He shrugged.

Yes.

Shrugged.

Then he explained, "It took Georgia longer than she expected. I kept ridin' her ass. She told me she'd deliver. I saw the fruits of her labors, they came slow, but I saw them so I trusted her. In the meantime, your dad kept givin' me a load of shit for not knockin' up my wife. The bitch I got at home was also givin' me shit. To shut them down, keep a lid on it, make them think I was still cowed and to give Georgia time to do what she needed to do, I knocked her up."

Was I once in love with this man?

"Tommy," I started for reasons I didn't know due to the fact this conversation was moot. Regardless of what he thought, there was no him and me. "You'll remember the way we wanted things to be was not being involved in this life."

"Babe, love you in a bikini on a Jet Ski. Love you in a bikini anytime. But you start havin' my babies, the bikini will be out and you'll have kids to take care of, so the Jet Ski will be out too. That was us bein' young and stupid. This," he pointed to the floor, "is our life."

"It isn't my life," I told him. "Or at least I don't want it to be, Tommy, and you know that."

"It isn't yours," he agreed. "You're right. But it's mine. It'll put food on our table. It'll keep us with the family. You do what you gotta do, babe. You leave the rest to me."

I held his gaze as I stated softly, "I cannot believe you're saying these things to me."

He shook his head in annoyance. "I can't believe you can't believe it, Liv. Fuck. You're the love of my goddamned life."

"Did you think of sharing that sometime in the past six years?" I asked.

"I did every time I looked at you," he answered tersely.

This was, I had to admit, true.

"Perhaps you could have used your words," I suggested. "And/or my sister using hers."

"The less people in the know with that, the better. And she was worried. Worried you couldn't keep your shit together. You're sensitive. Shit bothers you.

You wanted out of stuff, she was diggin' in deeper. We had to keep you in the dark. She saw that shit happen to you and me, she and Gill were gettin' it on, they were tight, things were intense, she knew your dad would shut that down with them. Took her a long fuckin' time, but she got it sorted. For her and Gill and for you and me."

All of this, *all of it*, was a surprise to me. My father, my sister, my ex-lover, none of them thought enough of me, my thoughts, wants, needs, even to discuss my own damned future with me.

That didn't matter.

It was too late and Tommy needed to know that.

"I'm with Nick now and—"

"Right, *Nick*," he interrupted me, spitting out Nick's name furiously. "That's a pile a' shit you created, Liv. Now Georgia's gonna have to deal with him and do it slick 'cause if he's not dealt with right, that brother of his is gonna lose his mind, drag Sloan into it and Denver will be at war. We're buildin' up, we don't need that kind of hassle."

Unease started creeping.

"Georgia hardly has to—" I began, only to get cut off again.

"Babe, you don't know, you would have totally fuckin' lost it, Georgia fuckin' lost it when she found out and that was when her plans went into hyperdrive. But when your dad got messed up in that human trafficking shit, it was not pretty."

He'd been saying so much to me I couldn't believe, I'd forgotten he'd said those words previously.

And I'd forgotten I'd heard them before.

Now I focused on them.

"What human trafficking shit?" I asked.

"The human trafficking shit the Feds were all over. Hawk Delgado was all over. It was so hot, only a moron would get near it. Plus, human trafficking? What the fuck? The guy won't deal meth because it's a poor man's drug, but he'll sell a human being?"

He didn't expect an answer.

He kept spewing hideous words.

"Georgia nearly screwed everything after your dad ordered Gill to whack Nick and his Fed girlfriend..."

My lungs started burning.

"…and now she knows Sebring is biding his time for revenge. Fuck, we just found out he had bugs all over this fuckin' warehouse and they been here a long time, Liv. Fuckin' years he's been listenin' to everything that's gone down here. Every-fuckin'-thing. Who knows the shit he's got on us? We just know it could fuck us, *all* of us, including you."

Nick had been listening.

For years.

Tommy didn't see he was lacerating me with each word out of his mouth, he kept talking.

"Georgia *doesn't* know he used you as an in to get to your dad and Gill. And it sucks we gotta tell her that part. She needs to have to deal with the Sebrings while axing your dad outta the business like she needs a hole in the head. But the guy's a threat and he's gotta be dealt with."

"His Fed girlfriend?" I whispered.

"His Fed girlfriend," Tommy confirmed. "Nick's brother and his buds got him out before Gill did him. But now Gill's got that hanging over his head. You kill a Fed, you're fucked. He shoulda done Sebring first. He didn't. He did her right in front of Sebring. A witness living and breathing and building an army right here in Denver. Sebring's been holdin' that card awhile. Georgia and Gill were gonna be done with livin' under that cloud eventually. Maybe sooner is better than later."

"Gill killed Nick Sebring's girlfriend," I stated and Tommy finally focused on me rather than vomiting words at me.

"Gill killed Nick Sebring's *Fed* girlfriend," he confirmed. "Man was an informant, Liv. A CI. You know how those brothers are about women. Human trafficking is not gonna happen in Denver if either of them can do shit about it. Nick went in. Got tight with this girl. Your dad was desperate. He had partners putting on pressure. The House of Shade needed *something*. He tried to pull that shit off, got wind Nick was a CI and the girl was undercover, he made the order. Sebring's fucking you to get to your family. He even owns that club where Harry takes you to watch people go at each other. Silent partner, him and his brother. Harry needs money and I need information so I give him money and Harry finds out a lot of shit. He found that out when he caught Nick and a bunch of his boys on your ass, watching you. And Sebring's been watchin' you for years, Liv. Fuckin' years. Since that shit went down with his girl. He bought that club, my guess, he was done watchin', ready to roll, sole purpose of the buy to make an opening to get to the only weak link in the House of Shade. That weak link bein' *you*."

His face twisted with jealousy before he finished.

"And he got that right because he got you."

Nick owned the club.

Nick had been watching me.

Nick had been watching me for years.

Nick had been *listening* for years.

Listening to everything.

Nick had been a confidential informant for the FBI.

Nick had a girlfriend that Gill had whacked.

Nick had a girlfriend that Gill had whacked on my father's order.

Nick.

My Nick.

No.

Not my Nick.

He'd never been my Nick.

Not ever.

I looked away from Tommy, murmuring, "I need to get ice on my face."

His voice changed, went low, sweet, and he got close again when he replied, "Yeah, you do. You want me to get it for you, baby?"

Baby.

Tears started to flood my eyes but I took a deep breath to hold them back.

I shook my head, "No, I just want to go home."

"Take you, Liv."

I looked back to him. "I need some time alone, Tommy."

He studied me a moment. It was a long moment, too long. Long enough to make me fear I'd lose it, and I did not want to lose it, not there. Not close to Georgia and Dad. Not in front of Tommy.

Thankfully, he nodded.

"Give you tonight, Liv. Tomorrow, honey, we gotta talk."

I was not talking to Tommy.

I didn't know what I was doing, right then, the next second, the next day, the rest of my life.

All I knew was what I needed and that was that I had to get out of there.

To do that, I nodded to Tommy and moved around him.

I was halfway to the door when Tommy asked, "Babe, you gonna at least give me a hug or something?"

I again looked to him. I was losing my fight to control the tears. I knew this when I felt them start to spill over.

"Liv, baby," he whispered, making a move toward me.

I took a quick step back, lifting a hand. "Don't. Please."

He stopped.

"I need some time," I repeated.

There was a hesitation before he replied, "Okay, Liv. You got tonight. Yeah?"

I nodded.

"We'll talk tomorrow. Sort shit out," he declared.

I nodded again.

"We been waiting a long time but now's our time. It's finally our time. Okay?" he asked.

I made no verbal or non-verbal reply. I didn't have it in me. I just kept looking at him.

"Love you, baby. Always loved you," he said gently.

Maybe he did love me. It just wasn't the kind of love I needed.

I knew the kind of love I needed. I'd tasted it.

It was sweet.

So, *so* sweet.

Ambrosia.

Even if it was a lie.

"Talk to you tomorrow, honey," Tommy said. "Now go home, get some ice on your face. You want me, call me. I'm there."

I nodded yet again then moved as quickly as I could in my tight skirt and heels, pulling my bag I'd completely forgotten I had and somehow held on to throughout it all down my arm.

I got out my keys.

I got out of the warehouse.

I got into my car.

I shoved my sunglasses on my nose, the throb in my face and sting in my wrist completely unnoticed seeing as I was more focused on the ice that was forming around my heart.

I reversed out of my spot.

On my way home, I looked in the rearview mirror once, seeing who I knew (but had never met) was one of Nick's men trailing me. Trailing me like he'd probably done often over the years. He wasn't obvious, but I saw him.

I didn't see Harry but now I knew he could be back there.

He'd played me.

God, I didn't even have Harry, such as he was, a reminder of a golden time when I still hoped. When I still had it in me to believe.

Now I'd learned. Definitely learned.

Gold didn't exist. It was all fake and tarnished.

My phone rang. I looked to the dash to see it was Nick.

That ice crawled up my throat, frost crackling and spreading.

I ignored it as well as the strange coolness of the tears sliding unnoticed down my cheeks.

My phone stopped ringing but it did chirp with a text.

It would do this repeatedly for some time.

But I kept ignoring it.

I was too busy.

Too busy reminding myself.

Too busy reminding myself never, not ever, not *ever* again to forget.

There was no Brightside.

23

DARK

Nick

11:49 — That Same Day

TWEAKED AND PISSED off that he knew Olivia left that fucking warehouse, made it home, but didn't return a single call or text, on his way to her house to check on her, he ignored Knight's first call.

Tweaked and pissed, Olivia not communicating, the second one coming from Knight five minutes later, he took.

"I got shit happening, brother. Something I need to know?" he asked as greeting.

"Late last night, anonymous tip came in. The body of Drake Nair was discovered early this morning in a shallow grave that is absolutely *not* the Shade MO but absolutely is exactly where the tipster said it would be. The cops got their search warrant, they hit the Shade warehouse. Found what they figure is the murder weapon right in Vincent Shade's desk drawer, residue of blood spatter on his carpet. Shade has been arrested. CSI team went in. My guess, more evidence is gonna rack up."

Shit.

Shit!

"Georgia is makin' her move," Nick guessed.

"So it's not you," Knight replied.

"No it's not me," Nick bit out. "I made that move you think I'd do it without tellin' you?"

"I hoped not. Good to know I hoped right."

Nick couldn't let that annoy him. He had more important things on his mind.

"Olivia was called to the warehouse this morning. She left, went home and in between she is not taking my calls or returning my texts. Your sources who gave you all that shit, they say anything about my girl?"

"No word breathed about Olivia or Georgia or any of the Shade crew, outside Vincent."

"You know, Knight," Nick said.

Knight knew. And what he knew was that Olivia was there when that shit went down. She was a witness to her father shooting Drake Nair. A witness that didn't come forward. Murder covered up, that made her an accomplice.

She was vulnerable.

"Not a word, Nick. Nothin' about Olivia," Knight assured him.

"Sylvie and Creed findin' anything for me with the Feds?"

"Nothin'. All clear. So fishy it smells bad, it's so clear. This includes them not seein' any link from the Feds to the Shades. Georgia picked a solid crew, none of them are stupid, none of them are fuckups. Not like the dad. It's a new dawn for the House of Shade. She played the long game and cleaned up along the way. Though, she tied shit tight, Sylvie and Creed have heard Valenzuela is not pleased with Georgia's recent activities. He was amusing himself with her, thinking she was a joke like her father. Her getting her feet under her, he's not amused anymore."

"Shit, shit, fuck," Nick muttered.

"Shit's hot, brother," Knight told him something he knew but he did it quietly.

"I don't know what's goin' down, I just know whatever goes down from here on out might need to be fast, Knight. Lightning speed. You got my back on that?" Nick asked.

"Don't piss me off with stupid questions," Knight answered.

Nick drew in a breath and let it go, parking in the first spot he found close to Olivia's house, a parallel job one door down.

"I'm at her pad, gotta go."

"You need me, I'm here and I'll put out the alert in case we need to break a sound barrier."

Nick wanted to be amused.

He was too worried to be amused.

"Gotcha. Thanks."

"It's gonna be okay, Nick. If it isn't right now, we'll make it that way," Knight told him as Nick knifed out of his car.

That felt good. Having Knight at his back, that felt good.

But he didn't have a good feeling about this. Liv knew he wanted her communicating. He reached out, she knew to reach back. Her non-response was more than a little troubling.

"Thanks, brother, I'll check in soon."

"Right. Later."

They disconnected and Nick tore his eyes from Liv's house when he heard his name called.

He looked to the car where Jed was sitting across the street.

"Stay or go?" Jed called his question.

"Stay," Nick called back. "And get another man here. Eyes everywhere. Anyone approaches this house, they're stopped and I'm notified."

Jed nodded and closed his window.

Not giving a shit, the jig was up because, with shit going down at the House of Shade, he was not going to let Olivia out of his sight, he walked right up to her house.

He tried his key.

It didn't work on the front door.

He rang. He knocked.

She didn't answer.

He turned and looked to Jed who was now leaning against the door outside his car.

Jed pointed at her house with a sharp upward jerk of his chin.

She was in there.

Why didn't she open the goddamned door?

He called her and got voicemail again.

"I'm out front, Liv. Open the fuckin' door," he growled into the phone.

He disconnected and then he texted that same message to her.

He hit the doorbell.

He knocked.

No answer.

Fuck!

He moved around the side of the house, found a foothold in order to jump the five foot tall fence and prowled to a set of French doors that led to the pool. He tried his key.

His temper cooled considerably when it worked.

He opened the door and moved into her space.

Then he moved through her space, going where he thought she'd likely be, the front great room.

She wasn't there.

He called her name.

No answer.

He went back on the move.

She wasn't in her bedroom. She wasn't in any bathrooms.

His temper spiked along with his concern as he instigated a room by room search of the house, repeatedly calling her name.

He found her in her informal family room where she watched television. He'd not seen her in there because the room was dark, the curtains drawn, and she was at the far end of the room.

Having pulled a curtain back, she was standing in it, her back to the door of the room. He almost didn't see her even stepping into the room to look for her.

He felt no relief due to the fact she didn't even twitch when he joined her in the room and she had to have heard him moving around and shouting her fucking name.

"Jesus, Liv, what the fuck?" he bit out as he moved to a lamp on a table by the couch and switched it on to light the dim room. "Tweaked as all fuck, been callin' you—"

She turned.

He stopped dead as rage seared through him.

"Jesus, fuck," he whispered and took the last distance to her in two long strides.

In that time, she slid out from the curtain, away from the window and away from *him*.

Nick stopped moving toward her, instead he turned with her movements.

First things first.

"Who did that to your face?" he growled.

"Dad," she answered emotionlessly.

He ignored the smoldering burn of fury.

Again, first things first, take care of his girl.

"You should have somethin' on it. You got frozen peas?" he asked.

"It's perfectly fine."

He stared at her.

It was not fine. The corner of her left eye was blood red with burst blood vessels, her temple purpled angrily, the cheekbone under swelling and shoving up the bottom of her eye.

With some effort, he controlled his anger and ordered, "Come here. I want a better look at it."

"Actually, if you don't mind, it'd be helpful if you left."

With those words, her demeanor finally penetrated.

Yeah, Liv not communicating…

Seriously fucking more than a little troubling.

"Babe—" he began as he started toward her.

"Though, before you go, you should know that they're aware of your desire to have vengeance for your dead girlfriend so you should be careful. Georgia is dealing with a number of things and I'm told it's highly likely she'll also be dealing with that."

And at those words, Nick stopped dead again, his gut twisting and his heart slamming against his ribs.

When she said no more, he whispered, "Livvie—"

She cut him off again. "I'm very sorry that happened. I was unaware of it, of course. Not that, if I was aware, I could have done anything about it. I can imagine that was very painful. If it occurred as I was informed it occurred and it happened with you there to witness it…" She shook her head. "Actually, I can't imagine. But I'm sorry you have that memory."

He moved cautiously toward her.

To his one step, she took two back.

He stopped.

She did too.

"Let me explain," he started quietly.

"I think I already got it," she returned.

"I know you don't," he replied.

"Not that you asked my advice, but although I haven't been told precise details of plans that have been set in motion, I'm getting the firm impression that, regardless that things went at a snail's pace for some time, they'll be moving quickly from here on out. I'm certain you can take care of yourself. But you may wish not to delay in—"

"Livvie," he interrupted.

She shut up and swallowed, taking another step away from him.

"Your father has been arrested for Drake Nair's murder."

For a beat, she gaped at him.

She gathered back her ice and nodded shortly. "As I said, things will be moving quickly from here on out."

"I need you to come to my place with me," he told her.

She took another step back, saying crisply, "That won't be happening."

He took a step toward her and she again retreated.

He stopped.

"Liv—"

"You need to leave," she declared.

What he needed to do, seriously belatedly, was stop fucking around.

"Liv, it started one way, but you know, you gotta know, where we are now is a very different thing."

She ignored his words.

"Now. If you don't mind. You need to leave now," she said, sweeping out an arm to indicate the door to the room.

"I fell for you."

"It's in your best interest—"

"I fell for you, baby."

"To go immediately."

"Please listen to me."

"You need to leave."

"I'm in love with you, Livvie."

It sliced right through him but she ignored that too.

"You need to leave now, Sebring."

He took another step toward her. "Baby, I'm in lo—"

Suddenly, she leaned toward him, for the first time letting loose the formidable temper he'd sensed, but she'd never lost control enough to let go, and in a shrill voice that pierced through his brain and his heart, she shrieked, "*You need to leave now, Sebring!*"

The pain in each syllable scoring away his flesh, he stopped moving and winced.

He forced a quick recovery and whispered, "Please come to me, Livvie, so I can explain."

"You need to leave. You need to leave. You need to *fucking* leave!" she shouted.

"Let me come to you."

"*Leave!*" she screeched.

The ice was gone but the pain was worse.

He had to get in there.

"I couldn't go through with it. That's why I ended things with you. You got under my skin, Liv. And obviously," he lifted both hands slightly at his sides, careful of even that move, the situation volatile, the outcome meaning everything, he was going cautious to the extreme, "I couldn't get you out."

He watched as she visibly tightened her entire frame, pulling it together, pushing him out.

"She's gonna hurt you," she declared. "She's got acid in her veins, my sister. You're a threat and she'll eliminate you. She doesn't care. She put her father out there for murder. He'll never breathe free again. Her *father*. She won't blink at taking you down."

He started moving slowly toward her again. "I'll be fine. You'll be fine. We'll figure it out. We gotta do it with her, we'll figure it out with your sister."

"Do not come an inch closer to me, Sebring," she warned. She was losing it again, her tone suddenly feral, the green in her eyes flashing.

He had that, not the ice, he could work it.

He had to.

So he kept moving.

"I fell in love with you, Liv."

"That's impossible."

"It isn't. It happened. And you—"

"It's impossible because there is no me to fall in love with. I don't exist."

That made him stop moving.

She continued speaking.

"I breathe. I'm here. I take up space. I eat. I drive. But I have no brain. No will. No strength. No opinions. I do not matter to the point I do not exist."

"You exist for me."

"I didn't when you targeted me as your in to destroy my family," she returned immediately and unfortunately fucking accurately, going on the same way, "I can only assume you knew I had no dealings with that. You could, I'm sure, perform for a woman who was simply a tool. If you thought I had a part in trafficking humans and murdering your girlfriend, not even you could set that aside so completely as to perform so convincingly and *repeatedly*."

He tried to stop her. "Liv——"

"And it didn't matter to you that you were going to obliterate my world. I could not be tied to that heinous business but I was far from clean. If you took my father down, Georgia and I would go down with him. You sallied forth anyway, I meant that little to you. And of course you did. You didn't know me. You only knew I was a Shade. So of course I would mean that little to you. Being what I am, it's no surprise I mean that little to *everybody*."

Fuck, she was killing him.

He had to fucking *get in there.*

"Baby——"

"Little did you know that all you would have had to do was approach me, share what had happened, and I would have been your insider ally, I'm so disgusted by just how despicable my father has proven that he is. And you can well imagine just how disgusted that is, with all I've shared with you during our artificial relationship, since I was already disgusted because I already thought he was extraordinarily despicable."

"What we have is not artificial, Livvie," he told her firmly.

"What we have is a lie," she returned coolly. "Started on a lie, built on a lie, enduring on a lie and now, if you carry on with your bullshit, Sebring, ending on a lie. Now I think you've had your fun with me, I've definitely had my fill of you, so please, get *the fuck* out of my house right the fuck *now*."

"Babe, plea——"

He stopped that time because, with no warning, she charged him. Slamming her hands into his chest and shoving hard, he heard her cry out in pain and whip one hand down before she retreated just as quickly as she came at him. She did this lifting an arm and raking her fingers through her hair so hard it was like she was tearing at it.

And she did all of this shouting, "Can you just *stop?* Can you just *please God stop?*" She shook her head, her eyes brightening with wet. "I can't take anymore. I can't take *anymore*. No more lies. No more schemes. No more using. No more orders. No more bullshit. *No more!* I cannot...take...*anymore!* God!" She tore her hand through her hair again. "I need you *to go!*"

"Livvie, fuck me, baby, please come here. Please listen to me," he begged.

Her eyes locked to his and at the look in hers, Nick's lungs hollowed out.

"I believed," she whispered.

"Let me come to you," he pleaded urgently.

"You made me believe," she accused.

"You know how it started," he replied immediately. "And I can't deny that, baby. I can't deny that, my Livvie. I fucked up. So many times, I told myself I needed to come clean with you. Too many fucking times. I couldn't do it. I knew it'd hurt you. I couldn't do it. But you know it now, so why would I be here trying to convince you I'm in love with you if I wasn't *in love with you?*"

"I don't know," she shot back, also immediately. "Why would you watch me for years? Plant bugs in the warehouse and listen to everything? Why would you own the club without telling me? Why would you sleep with me knowing my father ordered your girlfriend's and your murder? Why would you pretend to begin caring about me when you knew that, nearly every day, I saw the man who carried out that order?"

"I loved her," he shared.

She flinched but didn't miss a beat.

"I can imagine, planning for years to avenge her. She must have been something."

"Liv—"

"I don't believe anymore, Sebring."

"Ba—"

"You want me to believe you care? Even a little bit?" she asked, but didn't wait for him to jump on it, she quickly finished, "Then leave."

In desperation, unable to remain cautious, he moved to her. She moved with him, retreating around the room with each step he took. He didn't speed up, he didn't get aggressive, but he didn't let up.

And he did all this saying, "First, we gotta see to that eye. Then I'll give you some time on your own to wrap your head around this shit and calm down. I'm not leaving, but I'll give you space. You calm down, you let me talk to you, you actually listen to me, I'll get you to see more clearly what's happening here."

"I ask for one thing, even that you won't do," she pointed out. Having put the couch between them, she stopped. "It's over, Sebring."

Shit, fuck, *fuck*.

"It's not over, Liv. I'm in love with you."

"It's over, Sebring."

"And you're in love with me too."

"You mean something to me," she stated and at that, his lungs started burning. They iced over when she finished, "But so did Tommy."

"Liv—"

And that was when it happened.

Defeat slid stark all over her. It was in her face. Her eyes. The line of her frame. It was so extreme, he could feel it in air and taste it in his throat.

"Can't you see you're killing me?" she whispered.

He swallowed past his throat closing and whispered back, "I can't leave you."

"You can't stay either."

"We're not done."

"We never even started."

"Baby, we *did*."

"It isn't for me," she stated.

"What isn't for you?"

"Dawn."

Beyond tweaked, that word made him more so.

"Dawn?"

"I live in dark. Dawn never comes for me. There will be no new day where I wake up complete. Happy. Loved. There is no other side to make my way to. There is no believe. It just isn't for me."

"I can take you there."

"No you can't, Sebring. Can't you see?"

"No, I can't see, Livvie."

"You can't give me dawn and all I can give you is dark."

"That's fucked up and not true."

"It's every day for thirty-one years, except a few, the few I shared with you, and they were all a lie."

"Livvie—"

"Leave."

"Liv—"

"Leave."

"Baby—"

The tears slid down her cheeks and the whisper came again.

"You're killing me."

He said nothing and not just because she wasn't letting him.

"And she's gonna kill you, Nicky," she kept whispering. "I can try to stop her but there's no stopping Georgie. It'll be her or you. I know it. I don't want it to be either. Please be safe. Please get safe. Please get out of here and make yourself and your family safe."

"I love you, Liv."

More tears fell as she replied, "I wish, honest to God, I really wish I could believe that, Sebring."

He held her eyes and watched the tears fall.

Then he made a decision.

"It's gonna gut me to walk outta here not touching you."

Her lip quivered so she bit it.

His stomach roiled like he was going to vomit.

He fought through it and did what he had to do.

"I love you, Olivia. And I can make you safe. I can make you happy. I want a lifetime of nothing but that."

Another tear fell out of her swelling eye but she said nothing.

"I'm gonna walk out of here not touching you and the last thing you're gonna hear from me is that I love you, baby. Fuck, I *so* fuckin' love you."

They stood, her in front of her couch, him behind it, and stared at each other.

Neither moved except for the wet that slid out of Livvie's sad, dead, beautiful green eyes.

"Love you, Livvie," he whispered.

She pressed her lips together.

Nick Sebring watched.

Then he turned and walked out.

24

NO SOUL

Olivia

Fifteen Weeks Later

I LOOKED TO MY list of TODAY as shown to me down the side of my email screen as I heard the noises in the outer office.

On a sigh I turned my attention to my office door.

Georgie came in.

"You know, us getting rid of that shithole warehouse and me getting awesome new offices you won't move into so I don't have to haul my ass all the way to DTC to have a sit down with you is a pain in said ass," she complained instead of offering a greeting.

I didn't reply.

I had no intention of moving into her offices.

Not because, even with the exit of Nick from my life, Tommy did not reenter it and he didn't take very kindly to that. Although this surprised Georgia, she didn't say anything. She *had* (albeit doing it as a means to a current end) encouraged me to get over him. She couldn't be upset I'd actually done that.

And since Tommy was the man behind the less seemly part of Shade operations, he never came to her office anyway.

Which meant, thankfully, I never saw him.

Also not because Gill *did* show at the offices frequently. What happened with Nick and his girlfriend notwithstanding, he was as clean as Georgia (though not as clean as me). He was also officially taking Georgia's hand in marriage. With Tommy managing the boys, he was therefore recruiting them, so her pussy was now out of commission except for Gill's use. They were planning a lavish affair where the flowers cost more than an SUV and her gown was being custom made.

I had no idea my sister had fallen in love with a man seven years ago.

I was fine with that.

I'd had plenty of time to think about it and the decision I'd made was I was fine with anything that kept me out of their loop.

I was also fine with my father being out of the picture. The evidence pointing to the fact that he shot Drake Nair in the head in cold blood overwhelming (because he actually shot Drake Nair in the head in cold blood), he copped a plea. That still put him behind bars for twenty years, which meant he'd be deep in his seventies when he got out.

There was a small blip to this insofar as Dad got a message to Georgia reminding her she and I were present at that particular murder. His insinuation was that, if he went down, he was taking both of us with him, so he needed her to be certain he did not go down.

Considering the fact she'd masterminded his arrest, and he wasn't stupid enough not to know that, he figured she could do something to reverse the situation, and as was his wont, he was using both of his daughters as a means to that end.

Georgia communicated to me precisely what a hassle she felt this was for her. Regardless (mostly, my guess, because she needed me to do the job I was doing for the family, and no way in hell *she* was going down), she negotiated a deal that my father would make it through that twenty years in prison without any issues if he left both of us be.

He'd balked at first. But something I was not made privy to happened in lockup so he changed his mind and made the deal.

He was no longer in our lives.

I had no intention of deepening my relationship with my sister because of that.

I also had no intention of continuing a relationship at all with my father, so I didn't.

And as life was already dismal enough, I didn't need other sources making it more so, therefore when Georgia cut off our stepfather's kickback, I cut off my mother.

She brought me no joy so why bother?

Nothing brought me joy but Mom not only didn't bring joy, she was a pain in the ass.

So seriously.

Why bother?

It was not a surprise when my mother didn't bother either. I imagined it was actually a relief to her. It freed up her social schedule and added time she could berate her employees and control my stepfather.

I went to work because I got paid to do it. I went home to the huge-ass house my father made me buy that it was annoying to try to sell, and since I didn't have to anymore, I took it off the market. I did Pilates. I walked on the treadmill. I had my eyebrows shaped and my pubic hair waxed. I went to movies by myself. I went to dinner by myself.

I breathed.

I existed.

I pushed as far as Georgia would allow me to do so as my only enjoyment.

When I knew I was pushing too far, I toed the line.

The only other blip to getting to that was the unsurprising fact that Georgia had lost her mind about the fact that Nick had played me. She'd been infuriated at Nick for making that move. She'd been more infuriated at me that I'd let him.

The conversation with my sister that came right after the conversation I had with Tommy telling him I was over him and we had no future, regardless of his plans for six years he shared not an iota of with me, was unpleasant to say the least.

But one thing you could say for it, outside of it being done, was that I now definitely knew my place.

My father might be incarcerated but I was a Shade and my life was owned by the head of the House.

I could fuck who I wanted (not that I did) just as long as they were nameless and harmless. If I actually developed feelings for someone, the silent understanding was that I told Georgia.

I might have found this even bleaker than my life if I had any intention to have feelings for anyone.

Since I did not, it wasn't a problem.

In the case of Nick, I had no idea what was happening. That was part of the business she didn't share with me. Although part of the unpleasantness of our conversation was me sharing I would very much rather my sister not put a hit out on the man who had dishonestly won my heart, but he'd done it all the same.

This was taken as a weakness in my allegiance.

I said no further to my sister on the subject.

I'd made my warnings to Nick. He could take care of himself.

Nevertheless, I sent an anonymous letter to his brother at his nightclub, sharing that the danger was still very real and measures should be taken.

That was all I allowed myself to do mostly because it was all I could do.

As I was not of that world anymore, I'd heard nothing. But watching the news and reading the paper daily did not share that a young, vital, handsome man had been found dead.

So Nick was taking care of himself.

That was good.

In the four months since Nick walked out of my house, I heard nothing from him and saw nothing of him, which proved my assertions during our heinous final conversation true.

I did not believe because there was nothing to believe.

I had no earthly idea but my guess would be that a man who loved a woman would not walk away from her and not look back.

So there it was.

And in the four months since Nick walked out of my house, as I had a great deal of time, I spent a majority of that time wondering how I ever believed in the first place.

Quite frankly, there wasn't anything about me to love.

I was quite attractive, but deep down, people didn't love looks.

They loved senses of humor. They loved personality. They loved manner. They loved someone who loved dogs, like they did. Or they loved someone who was passionate about issues, like they were.

Whatever.

There had to be substance to a person to be a person who could be loved.

There was nothing to me. There'd never been anything to me.

Now Nick, he was a person you could love. He teased great and he cooked great and he kissed great and when you spoke, he listened like there was nothing on earth he wanted more to do. He made me laugh. He made me feel. He made me believe there was something to me.

The woman he spent years plotting revenge for, I bet there was something to her.

But me?

I was a woman he could walk out of my house and never again see.

Truth be told, one of the reasons I decided to keep that house was because it was like keeping a bit of Nick with me. It was the only thing I had, memories of the few times he'd been there. Memories, if I was in the mood, I could pretend were based on something different.

Something real.

I'd been right that first day I woke up to him in my bed. Sometimes, if I was allowing myself to wallow (which I didn't allow often, but it happened), I would ramble and remember his joke about the wood-fired stove. I'd remember falling asleep beside him on the couch after we got back from Vegas.

I'd remember right where he was, right where I was, precisely what he looked like when he lied that lie that was so pretty, telling me he loved me.

"Right, I'm here, I don't wanna be here forever, so let's start this. Harry's retiring and he wanted me to ask you personally to come to his party," my sister announced.

"His reinstatement didn't last long," I murmured.

"He wasn't really reinstated, Liv," Georgie murmured back.

No, he wasn't. That was another bit of info I learned years late.

Harry didn't need me giving him the odd job to make his load a little lighter. He was on Tommy's dollar and on Georgia's payroll, part of his duties being looking after (that meant monitoring) me.

An unexpected betrayal that shouldn't hurt as much as it did.

But it did.

"I'll take a pass on that," I told Georgia.

"Babe, you gotta—"

I stared at her right in the eye. "There are a lot of things I *gotta* do, Georgie. All of them you know. So please don't tell me what else I gotta do if it's telling me how I should feel or if I really don't *gotta* do it. You cannot dictate how I feel. Now, as you sign my paychecks, if it's your order that I attend Harry's retirement party, I'll be sure to attend. But I'd rather not."

"We were all looking out for you," she informed me.

She truly believed that.

Which, of course, made it all the worse.

"That would make a great deal of sense, if I was seven," I retorted. "As I was not, it makes no sense at all."

"Liv—"

I interrupted her, "Can we move past this?"

She shook her head in annoyance.

"I don't care that you didn't want Tom back. Tom was patient, sure, but he was also weak. I'm actually glad you're smart enough not to settle for that. He got his opening, and if he wanted to win you back, he could have. Months now, he's done dick. He's excellent in the role he's in. Watching you, he learned from a master, put his spin on it, things are going great. But he's not the man for you and you figuring that out, I'm glad."

I said nothing because there was nothing to say and because I was bracing since I didn't know where this was going.

"That said, I'm your big sis. I was looking out for you. Leading Tom along with the promise he'd get you when he had a purpose to serve, served *my* purpose. It worked out. You didn't give him what he wanted, he's got other shit he wants, so he's not complaining. But again, you, Liv, got something up your ass and you just gotta let it go."

"This is you telling me how to feel, Georgie," I pointed out.

"This is me telling you that we are out of the fire but we jumped right into the frying pan. Valenzuela is up in my shit and things are hot and going to get hotter so you need to strap in, Liv. No way I worked my ass off to get us to where we are to have some psychopath pull that rug out from under me. And you gotta be all in because, however I need you, you're gonna need to kick in."

Marvelous.

"You with me on that?" she asked when I said nothing.

"Is there a choice?" I asked back.

"That's not saying 'I'm with you,' Liv," she retorted.

"It's the best I have, Georgie," I returned.

She sighed a beleaguered sigh.

I sought patience, and as I was a practiced hand at that, found it.

"You know where Sebring is?"

At this surprise question, I made a sharp noise in the back of my throat.

"What?" I asked.

Suddenly, her eyes on me were frightening and her tone was a whisper.

And with that look and tone, as she spoke, I wondered with not a small amount of alarm if I ever really knew her.

"Babe, you do, you spill. Okay?"

I stared at her. Right in the eyes, I stared at my sister.

I suspected she had acid in her veins but I'd also hoped she had a soul.

She had no soul.

Looking right at her I saw it. For the first time I saw it.

Like our father, Georgia Shade had no soul.

"I don't," I told her.

"You do, he contacts you, you spill."

"I understand where things are at with Gill, his ring is on your finger, but—"

It was her turn to interrupt me.

"This, we do not discuss. This is not up for discussion. We have a liability. *We*," she bit off the last word while lifting a hand and waving it between us. "There are no words exchanged when we have a liability. When we have a liability, the crew unites while Momma takes care of the threat. You're either a member of that crew or you're not, Liv. And I think you get where you are if you're not. You can bitch and complain and act superior all you want. It's annoying but it's you and I've swallowed it enough my whole life, I'm used to the taste, so I don't give a fuck. But we got a threat, you close ranks. That's it. No words. It happens. Now, I asked, you got that?"

She asked if I got it that, if I protected Nick, she'd mow me down to get to him.

Obviously, that was not okay.

But I got it.

"I got it," I stated.

"So he's not contacted you."

"No," I confirmed.

She stared at me, clearly assessed I was telling the truth, and nodded.

She relaxed.

I did not.

Her manner might have changed, but the look in her eyes was no less frightening.

"I want you to rethink Culver," she stated.

I sat still and silent, my eyes anchored to hers, not of my choice.

"I've been paying attention to the moves he's making, and one thing in his whole, fucked-up life Dad was right about is that Dustin Culver could be an asset," she continued. "He could be useful. Give it time. A few days. Think on it. We'll talk. When we do, if you don't want to go there, I'll want good reasons, Liv. Really good reasons. So when we talk, if you're not up for giving that another shot, you need to have those reasons. Yes?"

I got that too.

With Tommy no longer in the picture, which meant whatever she promised him in regards to me not something she had to worry about, she now intended to revisit the idea of whoring me out to Dustin Culver due to the possibility he might be useful to the House of Shade. No reason I gave, including the fact I just wasn't into him, certainly not the fact I was in love with one of our enemies, would be good enough.

The decision was made. I already had a mission: get Dustin Culver addicted to my snatch.

No.

My sister had no soul.

"Yes," I said quietly.

"He's a good-looking guy. You two'll be good together," she assured, as if looks were the only thing that mattered.

"You're right. He's not difficult to look at," I agreed.

The scary went out of her eyes and she smiled.

I watched her smile and another part of me—the last part, a tiny part, the only part living, that being the part that was my love for my sister which I thought reciprocated the love she had for me—died.

I did not let this show.

I was a practiced hand at that too.

The rest of our business wasn't nearly as much of a roller coaster ride, and when it was concluded, she left.

I wondered about Bali.

Or Fiji.

Or Timbuktu.

But in case they had someone following my browser history, I did not turn to my computer and do searches.

I'd learned.

I breathed but I did not exist.

This would always be the way.

The thing was, I wanted that way to be somewhere else so, even if I only breathed, I did it in a place I breathed easier.

One thing I learned from my sister *and* Nick Sebring was how to play the long game.

I would not go tomorrow or next month or maybe even next year.

But I'd go. Patient. Smart. I'd go.

Worried she'd try to find me, I'd never breathe free. Georgie had proved even more than Dad that she had no intention of letting go an asset she could use, an asset she thought was hers.

But maybe someday in the far distant future, I'd breathe easy.

And in the meantime, it was clear she was turning her full attention to Nick Sebring.

That was not my business.

He could take care of himself.

I never breathed easy.

But just the thought of my soulless sister deciding it was time to take care of that particular threat…

It was a wonder I could breathe at all.

———

11:13 — That Night

I STOOD IN my great room, staring out the front windows, the old burner phone I used to use when I called the club in my hand.

I'd looked up the number in the phonebook. That way, no one could trace the search.

I'd memorized it.

I shouldn't do what I was thinking of doing.

I couldn't *not* do it.

I looked down at the phone, punched in the numbers and put it to my ear.

It rang four times before I heard a woman answer, "Slade."

There was dance music in the background—not loud, muted. She was in an office at a nightclub.

Knight Sebring's nightclub, Slade.

"I'd like to speak to Knight Sebring," I stated.

"Mr. Sebring doesn't take calls through this line. You have to talk to his PA, Kathleen, during normal business hours. I'm sorry, but if you don't have her number, it's difficult to get to him."

This meant she wasn't giving me Kathleen's number.

"Tell him it's Olivia Shade."

"Ms. Shade, it's unlikely—"

I cut her off.

"He'll want this call and he'll know why he wants this call. What he won't want is to find out an employee got this call and didn't share the information with him the call was placed. He can call me back. But tell him Olivia Shade wants to speak to him. He has tonight to call me. I won't answer any other time." I gave her my burner number and finished, "He has tonight."

I then hung up.

She clearly had a direct line to "Mr. Sebring," because in astonishingly little time, my burner rang.

The small display on the flip phone said, *Unavailable Number*.

Definitely Knight Sebring.

I answered with, "Mr. Sebring."

"Olivia, it's—" Knight Sebring started.

I didn't let him get any further.

"My sister is interested in your brother's whereabouts. He knows that as I've told him before. He's undoubtedly taken measures. Even so, he should know, she's getting impatient."

"Oliv—" he started, sounding irked, urgent and impatient.

I flipped the phone closed.

Before it could ring again, I slid the back open and pulled the chip out. I took it to my sink, dropped it into my garbage disposal and turned it on.

I dug through my trash and buried the phone in it, tucked inside a used food container.

After that, I washed my hands, dried them and took a deep breath.

I'd done what I could do.

All I could do.

Now it was over.

All that was left was unfamiliar territory.

That being hope.

The only hope I allowed myself to have.

Hope that Nick stayed safe.

25

MORNING LIGHT

Olivia

Four Days Later

THE HAND CLOSING over my mouth woke me with an agonizing rush of terror and panic.

"Be calm, Olivia," a deep voice came through the dark, right in my ear, and I could sense him hovering over me on my bed. "It's Knight. I need you to come with me."

Knight?

Knight Sebring?

I turned my head on my pillow to look up at the shadow above me and the hand over my mouth came with me.

"I'm not here to hurt you," he told me. "I'm here to deliver a message. When I do that, what's next is your choice."

I stared at his shadow.

"You gonna stay calm?" he asked.

It took a moment for what was happening to penetrate before I nodded.

He immediately moved his hand.

"Now I need you to come with me."

The shadow disappeared from the bed and moved toward the door. As I watched, I saw weak light coming down the hall. In that light, as the dark line of Knight Sebring's body came into better focus, I saw a petite blonde woman standing out in the hall.

I knew her. Vaguely, but she was in our world. She'd been on Knight's team back in the day as well as running her own PI business. She'd moved from Denver years ago. Now she was back.

Sylvie Bissennette.

What was going on?

Knight disappeared through the door, but Sylvie remained in the hall, eyes to me, face inscrutable.

Whatever was going on, I had no choice but to face it.

I figured it was likely, with my warning the other night, the Sebring brothers were closing ranks.

I was a source of information.

I'd bought that by calling him. I knew I shouldn't do it, but I did.

Now I had to disabuse them of that notion.

On a sigh that I emitted to hide the hard beating of my heart I felt certain could actually be heard, I threw back the covers. With a glance at the clock, I saw it was nearly five in the morning. I was in a nightgown and I had company.

With this in mind, calmly, like I had all the time in the world, with Sylvie's eyes on me, I went to my bathroom and grabbed my robe. Shrugging the taupe silk up my shoulders, I cinched the belt as I walked back through my bedroom toward the hall where Sylvie was still standing.

She said nothing and didn't twitch, not even her expression, as I walked into the hall.

I saw light coming from the family room where my television was.

I headed that way.

It was good I made the trek bracing, even as my heart was racing, my skin tingling, my palms itching, for when I got to that room, it was filled with men.

Raid Miller, I knew.

Why he was there, I didn't know, though I did know he was tight with the Sebrings.

To my shock, even if he'd disappeared from the world where I lived and had been gone for years, the hunter known as Ghost was also there.

As was, of course, Knight Sebring.

And one other man.

For my peace of mind (what there was of it), I was delighted (at the same time, I had to admit, crestfallen) that that man was not Nick.

He was a big bear of a man with blue eyes, brown hair and a frightening scar marring his otherwise overall masculine beauty. A scar that led into his hair causing a streak of white through the brown.

I entered the room feeling Sylvie move in behind me.

Two lamps were on, set dimmed. The curtains were closed, blocking even the little light from the lamps from shining out.

And my television was blue screen.

I stopped in the middle of the room, three feet behind the back of my couch, all eyes on me.

My attention was on Knight Sebring.

Handsome, very.

But not like Nick.

There was hard behind Knight's eyes. Life lived that scarred him in a way that would never leave. He might give it to his girls, where it was safe to allow it to show, but right then there was no light in his eyes. Not like the pure blue light Nick could shine on me.

Light that, if it hadn't been a lie, would have been beautiful.

"Can you explain what's happening?" I asked Knight.

"Delivering a message," he repeated what he'd said earlier.

Before I could ask for more information, he lifted his hand toward the TV, a hand that had my remote in it.

"You get the message, what's next is up to you," he finished just as music filled the room.

Chords on a piano playing over a ticking clock.

Something about that soothing sound, so contradictory to my current situation, made my eyes shift to the TV.

Playing on it was a video of someone driving down a road. The view was not of that someone, but out the car window.

It was a pretty road that had high, green grass swaying against the shoulder.

A voice I recognized started singing just as there was a cut in the tape and then we were still in a car but it was driving through a town. Obviously a small town. An old town. American flags waving on slants outside pretty little houses. Covered sidewalks in the town proper with hanging signs for storefront businesses. Window boxes. Tubs of flowers. Tended shrubs. Sparkling cars parked at slants leading to the sidewalks.

The tempo of the song changed and we were back on the road with the green grass undulating.

Hills in the background.

No.

Mountains.

Mountains.

I stopped breathing.

The tempo increased again and the car turned down a drive.

Unconsciously, I walked to the back of the couch.

I did this because I needed to.

I needed to curl my fingers on the back in order to stay standing.

The tempo changed again as the video cut and we were out of the car, walking. Walking up a path to a house.

A house…

A pretty little house, homey, rustic, lived-in, tucked amongst a forest of big green trees. A pretty little house painted barn red with white trim with big tubs of flowers, window boxes and tended shrubs at the front.

A house in the mountains.

The music built to a crescendo as we took a tour of the house. Its wood floors. Its kitchen with a big farm sink and lots of old appliances that needed to be updated (but I hoped they never were). Its bathroom with an old claw-footed tub.

My breath caught.

A cozy living room with an abstract painting over the fireplace, the predominant color of the painting an ocean of blue.

There were little bedrooms with not much in them.

And another bedroom with a big bed flanked by two nightstands that each held a lamp but only one had a picture frame.

The camera moved closer.

It was a silver frame. A silver frame with a picture in it that I knew was taken in Las Vegas. The picture of a couple nestled in a web of crystals.

The words to the song started beating into my brain.

The video faded to black.

But the picture immediately faded back.

A deck.

A view.

A dawn.

A man's bare feet, ankles and legs in pajama bottoms propped up on the top railing.

I knew those feet.

The camera pulled back.

He also had on a long-sleeved thermal.

His back was to me.

His hair was thick, dark and clipped its usual short.

His ocean blue eyes were turned from me.

Tock, tock, tock...José Gonzalez was speaking to me.

But it was Nick Sebring communicating to me.

I watched Nick's profile as he took a sip of coffee and dawn came over the soft-topped mountains that were not Rockies.

He turned and looked over his shoulder right at the camera.

I drowned in blue.

The screen went black.

In desperation to get it back, my gaze shot to Nick's brother.

He had his on me and his mouth open to speak.

He closed it as he looked into my eyes.

Then he gifted me with a miracle.

In the expanse of a breath, I watched hard dissolve, scars heal and light shine.

"Hurry, honey," he whispered.

I didn't even take the time to nod.

I turned on my foot, my robe rippling out behind me, I ran to my bedroom.

I was hopping up and down, awkwardly pulling on a pair of slacks when Sylvie hit the door to my closet.

"Here to help, babe. What do you need me to pack?" she asked.

I spared her only a glance.

She was no longer looking inscrutable.

She was looking like she was fighting against laughing.

I nearly fell over, tangled in my pants.

I righted myself and answered, "Nothing here I want."

"Nick's ready for you, Olivia, but he's a guy. Not sure he's got your brand of shampoo down. And heads up, he's *never* gonna have your brand of shampoo down. We bitches gotta take care of that shit. Hell, you in his life, the man will forget *his* brand of shampoo. That'll be up to you too."

"Right," I whispered, tearing off my robe, on a mission and not fully processing her impromptu relationship lesson. "Then please, if you will, until I can get to the store wherever Nick is, I'll need you to pack my shampoo."

I turned to the rails and yanked off the first blouse my hand hit.

I heard her muffled chuckle as she walked out.

I finished getting dressed. I then dashed around my closet to get the bare essentials, tearing at hangers, opening drawers and not closing them, shoving things into the first piece of luggage I could grab—a carry-on.

A carry-on bag.

My heart started feeling funny.

I ran to the bathroom just in time for Sylvie to shove a variety of packed cosmetics bags in my lonely piece of luggage.

We moved out of the room, me fast, Sylvie behind me coming slower.

That's when I smelled it.

Gasoline.

I stopped dead in my hallway when I saw him.

Ghost walking toward me, a filled body bag over his shoulder.

Now Ghost—his gaze glancing off me as he passed—his expression was inscrutable.

I sensed motion in the hall and looked down it to see Knight come toward me from the great room.

He approached, stopping in front of me.

"You died tonight, Livvie."

I put a hand to the wall but didn't tear my gaze from Knight.

Sebring.

He wasn't making me free.

He was making me *free*.

"You," I said softly, saying no more.

Knight got me.

"I'll be good knowin' my brother is happy."

My heart kept feeling funny but I knew what the feeling was in my eyes.

Tears stinging.

For me to be free, we were disappearing. No roads could lead to us. Too dangerous.

I was getting Nick.

Nick was losing his family.

I couldn't do that. Nick had worked hard at earning back his family.

"I can't—" I began.

"You think I finally got him, and he finally got you, I'd let anyone keep me away?" he asked.

I swallowed.

That made me feel better.

Knight grinned at me and with that, he was almost as beautiful as his brother.

"You'll lay low. We'll sort shit. Then we'll have a family reunion."

Yes, that made me feel better.

I nodded.

"Not much time," a man's voice muttered and I saw the brown-headed, scarred guy moving down the hall from the back of the house.

He had a gasoline canister dangling from his fingers.

I looked back and caught it as Knight lifted his chin to the guy then grabbed my hand, reaching out to take my carry-on from Sylvie in his other.

He moved me toward the pool doors.

I looked back into a hall that now held Sylvie, Raid, Ghost and the scarred man.

"Thank you," I called as Knight dragged me out the door.

"Don't get bored senseless in the middle of fucking nowhere," Sylvie called back as the door swung closed behind me.

That was *not* going to happen.

I felt my lips start curving.

Knight pulled me down the side of the pool until I started almost running to match him step for step, nearly surpassing him on our way to the back gate.

There was a Maserati in my alley. He helped me into the front seat, threw my bag in the trunk, got in beside me and took off like a shot down the alley.

We were three blocks away before I looked back.

The flames consuming the vast mansion that was so not me (even when I didn't know what me was) were already dancing toward the sky.

"Valenzuela," Knight stated.

I settled back in my seat and looked to him.

"Sorry?"

He looked at me out of the side of his eye quickly before returning his attention to the road.

"Benito Valenzuela murdering her sister'll keep Georgia occupied while we take care of the rest of the business. Same time it does that, obviously it'll keep her from thinkin' she needs to look for you."

They were framing Valenzuela.

I did not want to know and knew not to ask. Filled body bags. Gasoline. It was not for me to know. I knew this because, even if I asked, Nick would have made it so they didn't tell me.

Still, I started, "Knight—"

He didn't look out the side of his eye then, but glanced fully at me before he looked back to the street.

"No matter what you saw, no one got harmed in the making of that scenario, Livvie." He jerked his head to indicate behind us. "That you can trust. Now you just gotta keep trusting and let Nick's plan play out."

I drew in a sharp breath.

This was Nick.

All Nick.

I closed my eyes.

When I opened them I knew two things.

One, I was smiling at the windshield.

And the other, I knew what was happening to my heart.

For the first time in my life, it felt light.

We did not go to DIA.

We went to a private airstrip and Knight and I got into a private jet.

We were taxiing not even five minutes after the doors were closed.

Wasting no time.

Nick was wasting no time getting me back to him.

I closed my eyes as we took off.

When we were climbing into the sky, I opened them, turning my head so I was looking out the window.

We were flying east.

We were flying into the dawn.

We were heading straight to the morning light.

I was going to Nick.

Another first in my thirty-one years of life.

I was going home.

Creed

Thirty Minutes Later

His wife's back to the wall, her ass in his hands, his cock drilling inside her, the noises of them fucking filling their hotel room, Creed felt her move her hands so they framed his face.

He lifted it out of her neck and looked to his Sylvie.

At the look in her green eyes, he stopped moving, buried deep inside her.

"I love you," she whispered.

Yeah.

Fuck yeah.

His Sylvie.

"Born to love me, baby, like I was born to love you," he whispered back.

Her eyes got soft as they dropped to his mouth. He suspected his did too, as he dropped his mouth to hers.

Creed kissed her, moving her from the wall. Still inside her, he walked her to the bed and put them both into it.

There, they stopped fucking.

They finished making love.

His Sylvie had wanted four kids.

She wanted it, Creed gave it to her.

But that night, Creed gave her number five.

⸻

Raid

Thirty Minutes Later

RAID WALKED ACROSS the porch with its now-empty porch swing to the door, through it and into the farmhouse.

A light was on, shining dim from the living room to his left.

He walked that way and saw her there, on the flowered sofa, curled up in an afghan, head to the arm of the couch, asleep.

Waiting up for her man, she'd conked out.

Pregnant women, he'd learned (repeatedly) did that shit.

He moved to her and sat in the area open at the curve of her lap, a small area considering the size of her belly.

He had a hand lifted to pull her blonde hair away from her face even as her head turned and her big blue eyes opened.

Blinking, she focused on him.

"Hey," she whispered. "It go okay?"

"Nothing sweeter," he answered.

Her head slightly twitched as she lifted it up from the couch.

"Sorry?"

"Years, my two boys, my baby girl you got in you, countless hot fudge sundaes, all that you gave me, and there's nothin' sweeter."

She was getting him, he knew it when he saw her face grow soft.

"Raiden."

His name was hushed, reverent.

Fuck, but she loved him.

Nothing sweeter.

He bent to her, his mouth a breath away from hers, he murmured, "Nothin' sweeter, honey, than the love you give to me."

He watched from close as his wife's eyes got wet.

"It went okay," she said softly.

"Absolutely," he replied.

He watched her shining pretty blue eyes smile.

Then he kissed her.

Deacon

An Hour and a Half Later

HE WASN'T EVEN to the steps of the porch before the front door opened and the dogs came bounding out.

He stopped and bent to his pups. Running his fingers through the soft fur of Boss Lady's and Priest's heads, he did it with his head tipped back, his eyes on his wife standing with her shoulder leaned against the jamb of the door, one arm out, holding the storm open. She had on one of his T-shirts, her dark hair was all over the place, her eyes tired, and she was so fucking beautiful, she looked ready for a photo shoot.

He felt his mouth curl up as he straightened. Clicking his tongue to call the dogs, they trotted beside him as he moved to the front steps and up them.

"Did you eat?" she asked before he even made it to her.

"Nope," he answered.

She raised her eyes skyward.

His lips curled up farther.

She didn't move from the door so he stopped in front of her. Boss Lady shoved into the house. Priest sat his ass down on the porch by his daddy.

Cassidy's eyes moved over her husband's face.

They ended their journey looking into his.

"It all go okay?" she asked.

"Girls asleep?" he asked back.

"For about two more seconds," she replied.

Deacon grinned again. "Call Milagros," he ordered.

"And I'm doing that…why?" she sassed.

"She's lookin' after our babies tonight. We're spendin' the night in cabin eleven."

Her eyes changed. They went soft, and with that look, she reminded him what she made him feel, always, even when he wasn't conscious of feeling it. Something he never thought he'd feel again, not in his life, not until she gave it to him. Something he now felt every fucking second of every fucking day he woke up by her side knowing he'd end that day going to sleep the same place.

Warm.

Safe.

Loved.

And *happy*.

⸻

Nick

One and a Half Hours Later

NICK STOOD ON the tarmac leaning against the beat-up old Defender he'd bought, watching the plane taxi toward him.

It stopped well away.

He didn't move.

He just watched.

The door slowly folded open.

The stairs barely hit the concrete before she came out, quickly and awkwardly, walking sideways down the narrow steps, holding on to the railing, her eyes aimed his way.

Suddenly, after months, Nick could breathe.

She was in pants. A blouse.

They didn't match.

Suddenly, after months, Nick almost smiled.

And she had on spike heels.

That didn't stop her.

He finally pushed away from the truck when he saw her begin running.

He started toward her swiftly but had to stop as she picked up speed.

He braced for impact, which was good since, when she hit him, she nearly knocked him off his feet.

Her hands were wrapped around the back of his skull, her head tipped back, her hair streaming down the arms he'd curled around her, he got one look into her shining green eyes. A look that obliterated the cold dead he'd last seen in them, which was a look that had tortured him for months. A look that was so gone, he got half a second to wonder if he'd actually seen it before she was up on her toes and her mouth was pressed to his.

He had words he wanted to say.

He'd take the kiss.

So he took it.

The sob that tore from her forced its way down his throat as she ripped her lips from his and buried her face in his neck.

He liked that, that emotion from his Livvie, fucking loved it.

But he wasn't going to give her time. Maybe later.

Now he had to know.

He dipped his head and put his lips to her ear.

"Do you believe, Livvie?"

She nodded immediately, her face moving in his neck, her body trembling in his arms, her fingers digging into his scalp.

"Say it."

He felt her swallow. He knew by the feel it was painful.

But she did it.

Her head dropped back and her shining eyes came again to his.

"I believe, Nicky."

Nicky.

Yeah, finally, he could breathe.

Before, she'd kissed him.

Right then, he kissed her.

When he broke it off, it was Nick who tucked her face back in his neck.

Her sobs were gone. Now her tears were quiet and through them she held on.

He lifted his gaze to his brother standing at the bottom of the steps to the plane.

Knight had his arms crossed on his chest, but even if he wasn't close, Nick could see his brother's smile.

Nick held tight to his girl and smiled back.

∗∗∗

Anya

Five Hours Later

I OPENED THE door to our condo, peeved.

Knight had gotten home twenty minutes ago, or so his text told me.

His *text*.

The man was exasperating.

He'd not said how things went with Nick. He just said he "had the girls" and he'd "see you at home, babe."

That's it.

Of course, I left the salon immediately after my return text of, "How did it go?" went unanswered, as did my three calls.

I threw my keys and clutch on the table by the door and my heels declared how pissed off I was as they struck the floors on the way down the hall.

When I made it to the end, at a glance, I could see that Kasha was totally bossing whatever was happening in our sunken living room. In this glance, I also saw my man on his ass on the rug by the coffee table, Kat on hers next to and slouched into him. Kasha was on her feet, bossing (of course) but also leaning her front into the other side of her dad, the side that Kat wasn't occupying.

Of course, the vision of this made me no longer pissed off which in turn immediately pissed me off again because just seeing my man with our girls made me melt and that was tremendously annoying.

I stopped at the top of the steps, looking down, my eyes pinned to Knight.

"Well?" I asked.

His mouth twitched like he was amused.

Oh yeah.

The man was exasperating.

"Babe, been gone hours. It didn't go good, I would not have been gone hours," he stated as a belated explanation.

"What went good?" Kasha demanded to know.

"Nothing, baby," Knight muttered to his baby girl.

"Can we speak in our bedroom?" I asked, starting to move that way.

"You gonna give me shit, I go with you to our bedroom?" Knight asked, making me stop dead and whirl his way again.

"Do not say shit in front of the girls!" I snapped.

"You said shit too, Momma," Kasha pointed out. "Just now."

Knight burst out laughing.

I looked to the ceiling, making a frustrated noise.

"No need to go to the bedroom."

At his words, I rolled my eyes back to my man.

"You remember what I said to you in that kitchen the first time you were in this space?" he asked, tilting his head toward our kitchen.

My heart skipped as I pressed my lips tight.

I remembered. I remembered every word.

He'd held my face in his hands and said, *Wars fought over a face like this. A man would work himself into the ground for it, go down to his knees to beg to keep it, endure torture to protect it, take a bullet for it, poison his brother to possess a face like this.*

"My brother found that face," Knight finished.

Nick hadn't found that face.

He'd found that woman.

Suffice it to say, I was getting it that all went *really* well with Nick and his girl.

"Good," I whispered and watched Knight's face grow soft.

"What face?" Kasha demanded to know.

"Later, baby," Knight muttered.

"Is Uncle Nick okay, Daddy?" Kat asked quietly.

"Yeah, beautiful girl, he absolutely is," Knight answered.

Kat smiled at her father.

"Momma, we're playin' Uno! Get down here and play with us," Kasha bossed.

"We're not playin' Uno," Kat contradicted. "Daddy and I wanna play Operation."

"Operation is stupid!" Kasha, whose little fingers weren't as coordinated so the patient's nose was always glowing red, snapped.

I watched this go down, no longer shocked the intensely masculine, slightly scary, totally badass Knight Sebring was completely cool with playing Uno (but he preferred Operation).

Instead, I watched it remembering that I'd been tormented by bad dreams since my parents died when I was a little girl.

But when Knight entered my life and made me his in a way he told me was forever, then proved that true, I'd not had one dream.

No, in sleep, I never dreamed.

Now, watching my man with our girls, knowing Nick was somewhere safe and happy...

Life was another story.

Olivia

Fifteen Hours Later

"LIVVIE."

I was dreaming.

I felt soft breath on my neck as a gentle finger slid over my shoulder.

"Baby."

Happy dreaming.

A hand cupped my jaw, a thumb sliding across my cheek, my ear, into my hair.

And a whisper from close.

"Dawn is coming, honey. Open your eyes."

I was scared.

Terrified.

If I woke up, like so many mornings before, a lifetime of them, it might be gone.

But the promise was too beautiful.

And now, I believed.

I opened my eyes.

And there it was, an inch away.

Swimming in an ocean of blue, a new day dawning.

And me?

I woke up from my dream to a living dream.

Complete, happy...

And loved.

Epilogue

PERFECT WORLD

Nick

Three Days Later

NICK OPENED HIS eyes and saw the bed empty.

Three days he'd had his Livvie there with him in Tennessee and each morning he'd had to wake her up.

Now she was gone.

He threw back the covers, knifed out of bed and saw the door to the bathroom open. Seeing that, he prowled through the house but stopped when he saw her out in one of the Adirondack chairs on the back deck.

She was sipping coffee and staring at the mountain view.

He drew in breath, let it out, retraced his steps, took a piss, washed his hands, brushed his teeth and headed back out, straight to the coffeepot.

He got his cup and kept his gaze on his girl as he moved out the back door to join her.

She looked over her shoulder at him, her face soft, untroubled, and Nick relaxed more.

Approaching her at the back, he stopped behind her, bent, and kissed the top of her head.

She gave him a small smile as he straightened and she turned back to facing the mountains as he moved to the chair situated close beside her.

He settled.

They sipped.

No words were said.

But she'd been there days and they hadn't talked much. There were other things to do. Show her the house. The town. Familiarize her with the area. She'd unpacked the surprisingly little she'd brought. They got groceries. They cooked. They slept. They fucked.

Now there were things she had to know.

"We're covered, baby," he said to the rim of his cup. "You know I owned that building where my place was. Sold my place and the building. Knight bought out my stake of the club. Hawk Delgado is lookin' after my boys. He gets a cut, I get my take. And I got healthy investments. We got no worries here. We're good."

She held her cup close to her mouth, eyes to the view, and didn't respond.

"We gotta get you a car," he continued. "Go into Nashville, get you some more clothes—"

"Stop," she said in her delicate voice.

Nick stopped.

She didn't start, she just stared at the view.

"Liv—"

Still in that voice, she cut him off, "My job to make it worth it."

Nick didn't like that.

"That's not how it works," he stated.

Finally, she turned to face him.

"You're wrong. It is. I get it now. It was your job to do all that. Now it's my job to make it worth it."

"Babe, this is just our life how we gotta live it."

"Yes," she agreed. "It's our life. It's your purpose in this life to take care of me. And it's my purpose to give that back."

He tried to read her, thought he got a bead, and said, "You don't gotta make any grand gestures."

But he'd read her wrong.

"You're right, I don't. You love me and I have one simple task. To make that worth it."

"That's not gonna be hard, baby, you do that by breathing."

Wet welled in her eyes as she held his.

Then she leaned his way. Dropping her cup to the arm of the chair, she reached her other hand out to slide the tips of her fingers along the stubble at his cheek. Up, she smoothed the hair over his forehead. Back down, she cupped his jaw.

"I think, if you don't mind, sweetheart, I'll put a little more effort into it," she murmured.

Fuck, he loved her.

"Knock yourself out," he murmured back.

Her glistening eyes smiled and she slid her thumb over his cheekbone, his lips, before she took her hand away and settled back in with Nick and their view.

"One regret," she said quietly.

Fuck.

He looked to her profile.

It was still untroubled.

"What?" he asked when she spoke no more.

She turned to him. "I never got a ride in your Jag."

He bit back laughter.

"No worries, Livvie. It's in storage. We'll get it back."

Her green eyes smiled, this time bright and carefree, and she turned back to the view.

Nick did too.

He gave her time. He gave himself time. When the peace settled deep, it was time for something else.

"You want breakfast?" he asked.

She turned to look at him again and when she did, her eyes had a different look. A look he felt in his cock.

"French toast," she answered.

That was when Nick's eyes smiled.

Five Weeks Later

HE KNEW IT the minute his stomach clutched, pushing bile up his throat so severe, in reaction to it his body convulsed right off the commissary stool.

"*Clear! Clear!*"

It was a bellow but it sounded far away.

His frame spasmed violently, pain raking his body as the foam filled his mouth.

A shadow crossed over his closed eyes.

He opened them to see the prison guard leaning near.

He bent closer. So close, he disappeared.

The foam slid from his lips.

The whisper came in his ear.

"Sebring's got a message. He wants you to know you shouldn't worry. He's gonna do what you didn't. He's gonna take care of Livvie." The guard pulled away, doing it shaking his head. "You shouldn't have hit her, man," he went on. "This woulda gone a lot different if you hadn't."

Foam and spittle bubbled out of his mouth.

"For that, you pay," the guard continued and again got close, "For Hettie, you burn in hell."

The guard again pulled back but stayed kneeling beside him, staring in his eyes.

So he was the last thing he saw before Vincent Shade died.

———

Nine Weeks Later

THE DAY HAD been long. All they'd seen was hard, cold road the length of it.

They hadn't even stopped to eat.

After they checked in, she demanded they eat.

So they ate.

Now they were back at the motel in the middle of nowhere that was so in the middle of nowhere and so *nothing* it cost only twenty bucks a night.

Not what she'd worked her ass off her *whole goddamned life* to have.

He opened the door.

It didn't happen until they were both through.

When the light came on, with the amount of guns on them, they didn't move as the door swung shut behind them.

Her eyes were pinned to the man sitting on the edge of the bed, a woman standing next to him, her hand on his shoulder.

Benito Valenzuela and his woman, Camilla Turnbull.

Fuck.

Her man made a move at her side.

Stupid. So fucking stupid.

But he loved her.

There it was. Proof.

Love made you stupid.

And in Gill's case, dead.

The shot only gave a sharp buzz. She felt the spatter hit her face but all she allowed herself was a flinch as he fell to the floor at her side.

Gone, now.

Everything.

Gone.

Her heart shriveled inside her.

Fucking shit, maybe in all her bitching, Liv had been right.

"You *were* simply affecting profit margins," Valenzuela noted like a member of his crew had not just shot the man she loved in the face. "Which was annoying and needed to be dealt with." He shook his head. "This business after what happened with your sister. Quite the nuisance."

He said no more, just continued to shake his head.

"You burned her in her bed," Georgia hissed.

"For many years, you haven't been stupid. What's turned you stupid now, Georgia?" Valenzuela asked.

"We have one enemy," she returned. "You."

"And as that enemy, you know me. You know it's bad business to eliminate something that's not a threat." He tipped his head sharply to the side. "Worse business if eliminating that non-threat suddenly makes me the enemy of someone who gives not one shit about me and," he leaned slightly forward, "*I don't want them to.*"

"You don't know your enemy either, obviously, since I gave a shit about you," she snapped. "We could have made a deal."

His eyes turned shrewd. "I was talking about Sebring."

"Knight has dick to do with this," she retorted.

"That's not the Sebring I mean."

All over her body, her skin got tight.

"Nick's unhappy," Valenzuela said softly.

"I don't give a fuck about Nick," she shot back.

But it was a lie and they both knew it.

"That's your mistake," he whispered, standing. "Pretending that's true, that's been your mistake for years."

She felt her lip curl. "He'll be taken care of."

"Such bravado," Valenzuela muttered.

That was when every inch of her skin got cold.

"You've blown up all my labs, taken out or turned all our boys, Leary's running one of your fucking *crews*." Saliva filling her mouth, she swung an arm down to the body prone on the floor at her side, indicating a termination of her resources, the finality of which Valenzuela was sure not to have missed. "You don't eliminate something that's not a threat," she reminded him.

Valenzuela settled in like he was about to tell a tale and spoke again.

"You see, Georgia, I have a rather tenacious adversary. I'll need patience in dealing with them, and in the meantime, I need nothing further to take my attention. I also need not to damage relations with those who keep out of my way. I'm afraid, for you, it's important for me to keep the Sebring brothers happy."

"So you're telling me, Nick playing my sister…what? He's got some guilt and he wants me dead because pissing you off got *her* dead? So to make him happy you're gonna take me out even though because of you I've got nothing?"

He shook his head. "Nick doesn't want you dead. He wants you neutralized."

So the invisible Nick Sebring was communicating his wishes.

Fucking fucker.

She should have taken care of him first. Unfortunately that had not been a viable option, considering at the time the House of Shade wasn't strong enough to withstand the onslaught from Knight Sebring and Marcus Sloan if she had.

Then he played her sister and when shit got hot for him, he disappeared.

Months…nothing.

Now…

Fuck.

She leaned back slightly and crossed her arms on her chest, drawling acidly, "Congratulations. Job done."

"It's *me* who wants you dead," Valenzuela stated.

Georgia Shade froze solid.

"You've cost me money. You've cost me time. You've cost me assets. All of that has value. I don't like losing things I value, Georgia," Valenzuela went on.

She stared at him, giving all she had to keeping her breathing even. She'd lost everything to this motherfucker. She was goddamned going to keep her dignity.

"But because he loves your sister, Sebring wants you neutralized, which means breathing," Valenzuela continued.

She let out a heavy breath, saying, "He didn't love my sister. He *played* my sister."

"He seems to be going far out of his way for a woman he's playing with."

"Then he's going in the wrong direction since, because of you, there's no sister to love."

Valenzuela's knowing smile sliced through her sternum all the way up her gullet.

A knowing smile.

What did he know?

He loves your sister.

Loves.

Goddamned *loves*.

In her current situation, the only thing that could keep her alive was the wishes of Marcus Sloan.

Or a Sebring.

No. Not the wishes of a Sebring.

The wishes of Olivia who would never want her dead.

Fuck, Liv was alive.

This was Sebring.

She looked down at Gill and felt the dry sting her eyes.

It was all Sebring.

She looked back to Valenzuela to see his smile had died.

"Unfortunately," he kept going, "that doesn't work for me."

One of his men started moving toward her. She felt another approaching from behind.

She opened her mouth to shout.

She got not a sound out.

Fifteen minutes later, beaten bloody and bullet-ridden, Georgia Shade bled out five feet away from Gill Harkin's body.

She was found with the gun that murdered her man in her hand, powder residue on her fingers. His fingers were curled around the gun that had the clip that had been emptied into her body.

It looked like a lovers' spat gone terribly wrong in a ratty twenty-dollar-a-night motel in the middle of nowhere between two criminals desperate and on the run.

And the House of Shade was no more.

***

Eric

ERIC TURNER PROWLED out of the motel room, phone to his ear.

He heard the connect and got the clipped greeting, "This number is only for emergencies. Please, fuck, do not tell me you're calling with the score of the goddamned Broncos game like last time. I'm in Tennessee, not on the moon, and we got fuckin' DIRECTV with Sunday Ticket. I get the scores same as you do."

"I'm not callin' 'cause a' that. I'm callin', askin' you to please tell me that bloodbath is not you," he clipped back.

There was a beat of silence before Nick asked, "What bloodbath?"

Turner gave him short, curt details.

"Fuck," Nick muttered.

Turner relaxed.

It wasn't Nick.

"Well, the good news is, Denver is gonna be a lot more quiet, Valenzuela won his war against the House of Shade. No more explosions. No more dead bodies," Eric noted.

"No more war," Nick concurred.

They were both silent.

Turner drew in breath.

"She's resting easy now, man," he said quietly.

For another beat, Nick didn't answer.

And the one word was weighty with meaning when he finally said it.

"Yeah."

Hettie was avenged. The bad guys got their due. Not how Turner would have played it, but that didn't mean it didn't happen all the same.

Moving them out of that heavy, he observed, "Now all we gotta do is sit and wait to see how Kane Allen and his Chaos crew deal with Valenzuela's shit."

"That MC is solid, Turner, so I hope there are no more bodies. Least not ones from the wrong side," Nick replied.

"I hope that too. Though I'll have to get it through the grapevine." He glanced back at the open door to the motel room, now teeming with local cops and not-local Feds, feeling the twist of disgust pull at his mouth. "Done with this shit."

Nick sounded stunned. "You retiring early?"

"Job offer. Better money. And what I'm gonna be doing, likely not gonna end up in some tatty motel miles from home starin' at a man with no face."

"Christ," Nick muttered.

"Not to mention, I got unfinished business I can't take care of inside. That snake's still in the garden, Nick, and I gotta get hold of the resources I need to deal with it. Those resources not bein' in the FBI. One of my team got dead because of that. Nearly two. She's avenged. But the job isn't done."

Even with Tucker and Sylvie Creed's best efforts, they still didn't know who'd turned on his team.

Eric Turner intended to find out.

"You need anything, you obviously got my number," Nick offered.

In the new world where he'd be dwelling, that would be a number Eric could use for a variety of reasons.

And he would.

"Headed to LA," Turner shared.

There was another beat of silence before he heard Nick Sebring bust a gut laughing.

That pissed Eric off.

So he said not a word and hung up.

Half an hour later, free to do it now, Nick called him back from his old cell.

And the asshole was still laughing.

Olivia

HANDS TO THE deck railing, I stared at the trees.

"That wasn't what I wanted to happen, Livvie," Nick whispered in my ear, his front to my back, his hands at the railing beside mine moving to cover them, instantly warming them against the cold.

"I know," I replied to the trees.

"Valenzuela dismantled her operations. She was expanding too fast. Getting cocky. Making deals. She owed people money. She was screwing with Valenzuela every chance she could get. They were on the run. I communicated I wanted her shut down. Way the scene read, Harkin turned on her. Witnesses say—"

I shifted a hand and laced my fingers through his.

Nick quit talking.

"Valenzuela would have eventually made his moves. He was stronger. She had no chance." I was still talking to the trees.

"What I pulled expedited—"

I twisted my neck to look at him. He lifted his head and caught my eyes.

"She made her decisions," I said, soft but firm. "You made yours. I made mine. I knew precisely what would happen if I got on that plane, Nick. I knew. It came faster than I expected, but I knew. I made my decision and got on that plane. It still doesn't make what happened my fault. It also isn't yours. It's the life she chose. Neither of us should feel guilt because my sister decided to resurrect the family business not with sound investments but by building drug labs."

"You make a lot of sense, baby," he replied, but he did it watching me carefully, and I knew he thought I was making sense just to make him feel better.

So I decided to give him what he needed actually to make him feel better.

"Do I miss the sister I thought I had?" I asked. "Yes, but I'd been missing her a lot longer than this." I turned in his arms, curled my lips slightly and put my hands on either side of his neck. "I missed her even longer than it's been since you faked my death."

At my words, his lips quirked and he took his hands from the railing to wrap his arms around me. Closing in, he pinned me against the deck and held me tight and warm in the cold mountain evening air.

"Have I told you you have a flair for drama, body bags, burning mansions?" I teased in a further effort to lighten the mood.

He bent his head closer to me but said nothing.

"One day," I murmured, "you'll have to explain how you pulled that off."

"Coroner owed me a favor so the ID swung our way. And Baldy has certain access and assured me that particular…specimen would, in the end, do a single good deed in her life, making you safe in yours," he explained immediately.

My eyes slid away. "Okay. Maybe I didn't want to know."

"Though, he was so willing to help, I wasn't likin' that much," Nick stated and my eyes slid back.

"Dr. Baldwin has a soft spot for me."

He gave me a squeeze. "Yeah, caught that. That'd be the part I wasn't likin' that much."

"I wouldn't allow a man to fake my death and then get on a plane, leaving everything behind, knowing my shoes and handbags were all going up in smoke, if that man was Dr. Baldwin." I squeezed him back. "I did it for the man I love. I did it for *you*."

Again, Nick said nothing.

Weirdly, he did this for a long time. So long, it concerned me.

"Nick?" I called on another squeeze.

Finally, he spoke.

"The man you love."

"Yes," I confirmed rather unnecessarily.

"The man you love," he repeated.

"Yes," I repeated as well, getting annoyed because I was getting confused.

He stared at me again.

When I was about to open my mouth, he gave me a shake and declared, "Babe, you've never said that to me."

I stilled.

Hadn't I?

Months in the mountains with my man and I hadn't told him I loved him?

"I...well..." I stammered as it hit me.

I actually hadn't.

How on earth had I not done that?

"Well, I allowed you to fake my death," I pointed out lamely.

Nick stared at me yet again.

Then he scowled at me.

"That's it?" he asked.

"Nick, I *allowed you to fake my death*," I repeated with emphasis.

In normal people world, that would be a big thing.

In our world, it was lame.

Totally lame.

And he *so totally* knew it.

"Liv," he growled.

I shifted my hands from his neck to his stubbled cheeks and rolled up on my toes.

When I got close, I pressed my fingers in and whispered fiercely, "I love you, Nicky. You've made me safe. You've made me free. You've made me happy. But I don't love you because you did all that. I love you because you're Nicky."

I might have said more.

I didn't get the chance because Nick was kissing me.

He was also done with the cold mountain evening and I knew this because he picked me up and took us inside. Right through the big living room with its stone fireplace, the picture I gave him hanging over the mantel. Right down the narrow hall. Right to our warm bed.

And there I was safe.

There I was free, complete, happy.

Because I was with Nicky.

Nick

LATE THAT NIGHT, he held Liv's naked body close to his under the warm covers in the dark.

She was restful, her weight pressing in to him, and he thought she was asleep.

He would find she wasn't when she whispered, "Tell me about her."

Nick felt his body get tight.

She slid a hand up his chest to his neck where she used her thumb to stroke his jaw soothingly. Otherwise, she didn't move.

"You've let her go," she noted softly. "In that way, you've let her go. I know you have with the way you are with me. But now it's done, sweetheart. It's time to get her back. She was a part of your life. You're all of my life. If you want to do it, I want you to know you can give her to me."

In the drama they'd had, he often forgot how fucking wise she was.

And she was wise because, that day, when he could finally lay Hettie to rest, he needed to give her to somebody. Keep her alive. Even in the dark in the mountains in Tennessee, Nick with the woman he found who was not Hettie, but who was beyond a dream.

He turned into Olivia's arms.

She tucked herself closer.

Safe in her hold in the dark in their bed, Nick Sebring gave his Livvie the last thing of his he had to give.

He gave her Hettie.

"Her name was Hettie and she couldn't fry an egg to save her life."

She relaxed against him and rubbed her nose along his throat.

Nick kept talking.

Liv kept listening.

He ended with, "She'd like you for me."

Liv emitted a dubious sound before she said, "That's sweet, honey, but it's hard to believe."

"She would."

"Right."

She didn't believe him.

"She would, Liv," he asserted on a squeeze of his arms.

"Okay, Nick."

She totally didn't believe him.

He lifted a hand and hooked a finger under her chin, forcing it up.

He caught her eyes in the moonlight.

"She would, Livvie, because you make me happy."

She melted into him.

"Now that," she said in that voice of hers, "I can believe."

He bent his head and kissed her soft.

When he released her mouth, she snuggled close.

He was nearly asleep when her drowsy voice came again to him.

"You're good at what you do."

He had no clue where that came from.

"What?" he asked, sounding just as drowsy because he was.

"Taking care of us, the women you love, making us free in all the ways we can be."

Suddenly, Nick was wide awake.

Just as suddenly, Liv was sleeping.

Nick held her close and turned his eyes to the paned window where moonlight shone in.

"I hope you're free, Hettie," he murmured to the quiet night.

Hettie did not reply.

For Hettie had long since been free.

Two Days Later

SHE WAS IN the kitchen making dinner, an alarming prospect, when the commotion that was him and what he'd picked up in town came through the door to the garage.

She whirled and stared down at the floor in horror as the commotion swept through the room, headed straight her way, taking the braided rugs strewn around with it.

But Nick stared at her face.

Fuck.

He thought she'd freak at his surprise, but in a good way.

"You don't like dogs?" he asked.

With visible effort, she tore her eyes away from the puppy now attempting to climb up her leg. Her hands were held up in the air, covered in something that looked slimy, a quick glance at the counter telling him she was doing something with hamburger.

If she had the time, she could use hamburger to wipe out an entire army in a way they did not mind dying.

Fuck again.

"What's that?" she asked, unmoving, her eyes didn't even drop down to the dog.

He walked into the room. Crouching close to her, he swept up the puppy.

It started licking his jaw at the same time trying to chew his ear and climb on his shoulders.

"Pet store next to the hardware store. It's adoption day. I went in," he explained, watching her closely. "I couldn't leave without taking him with me."

"What's that?" she repeated.

Nick didn't reply as he tried to read her.

"What is *that*?" she enunciated each word clearly as he continued to try to contain the pup at the same time figure out what was going on behind her blank green eyes. "The breed," she finished.

"Mutt, but they say mostly Labrador."

He watched her green eyes instantly round huge.

Then they squeezed tightly shut as she burst out laughing.

He stared stunned as she clapped her slimy hands, catching the pup's attention, his ears flying out as he looked to Liv, and she stumbled—actually fucking *stumbled*—gracelessly to the sink.

She did a shit job washing her hands and they were still half-wet when she came back to him, still laughing, eyes on the puppy, hands up.

She tore the dog right from his grip, cooing, "Come to Momma, baby. That's it," she stretched her neck as the dog bathed it with her tongue, "give Momma kisses."

Nick stood still as she wandered away, a princess with shining black hair in designer jeans and high heeled boots in a rustic, old house in the mountains of Tennessee being lavished by dog spit, still cooing and doing it nonsensically as she walked out of the kitchen into the living room

"At least he didn't take us to a trendy country setting that's really a suburb. We are firmly in a *country setting* that is *not trendy*," she assured the dog absurdly. "But there are no horses to be raised in *sight*."

Nick still didn't move as she disappeared into the living room but he heard her go on.

"Ooo, you're a boy. We need to name you." Her voice rose. "Nicky! We need to name him. Come in here and *do not touch the food*. I'm cooking dinner and I'm not taking your shit."

Nick continued to stand still until, slowly, he turned his head to look to the door to the garage. He then turned back to look into the kitchen.

"Whiz." He heard her say. "You move like lightning. No, Punk." He heard the dog whine. "You don't like Punk? Okay, but you can't be Spot, you're not spotted."

He looked back to the garage door.

"Nick!" she called.

He stared at the threshold at the bottom.

Fuck, he hadn't noticed.

"Sweetheart." He heard her again and knew she was back in the kitchen. "Our dog needs a name."

He looked to her to see she was bent over, ass in the air looking fine in her jeans, putting their new puppy on the floor.

It jumped back in her arms.

Now, he noticed.

There he was.

He'd made it.

He'd fucking *made it*. With his own hands, sweat, balls, gut and brains.

He'd made it and he'd earned it and there he was...

Living it.

His perfect world.

The Next Day

HE DIDN'T GAG her. He wouldn't ever gag her. He liked the noises she made too much.

But he did blindfold her.

And he strung her up.

She took it all, his Livvie. Even if he'd intended to break her in slowly, she writhed against the leather straps around her wrists hung from the hook on the wall, her naked body arching, seeking, inviting, the noises she made telling him where she was.

That being that she wanted more.

And more.

And more.

He gave it to her, his cock pulsing with each fall of the crop, his balls tightening with each red welt that rose against the beautiful skin of her ass and thighs.

She even rode the handle of the crop like he ordered.

His princess at his command.

He watched her work the crop in and out of her wet cunt, her teeth sunk into her lower lip, her tits bouncing, the nipples he'd worked first, taking his time doing it, hard and straining.

So fucking pretty.

She gave him that, he gave her what she'd needed and never been able to have, he'd give it to her again.

Now, enough was enough.

So he pulled the crop out of her, tossed it aside, wrapped an arm around her belly, cupping her pubis with his other hand to tip her back for him, and he drove his cock home.

Her held fell back against his shoulder, her lips whimpering, "Nicky," she came for him the instant he filled her.

He fucked her strung up, holding her tight to take it, after she came down going after her clit to make her come for him again.

She did.

Then he did.

He didn't move, stayed buried, his arms wrapped around her as she hung for him, filled with him, her head still back, turned, her forehead in the side of his neck.

"You good?" he murmured.

"Yes, Nicky," she murmured back.

"Good they had a decent hook at the hardware store," he teased.

He felt her smile against his skin but she only replied, "Mmm."

He slid a hand up to her breast and cupped it.

"Who do you belong to, Livvie?" he asked.

"You, Nicky," she whispered, pressing her forehead in harder.

"Who do you love?" he asked.

More of her whisper, "You, sweetheart."

"Whose heart do you own?"

She shifted her head back and he tipped his chin down, lifting his hand from her breast to pull the blindfold away so he could catch her eyes.

Her beautiful voice wrapped sweet around the word, "Yours."

That was when he kissed her, slow and wet.

He'd barely broken their kiss, his lips still to hers, when she murmured, "You forgot my plug, master."

Nick caught her eyes.

Olivia, naked, strung up, red-assed from his crop, still full of his cock, he couldn't hold back.

He burst out laughing.

Pressing her face into his neck, he heard it and felt it when his girl did the same.

———

Four Days Later

NICK WAS TOSSING a log into the fireplace when he saw movement in his peripheral vision.

He looked that way and caught it as Whiz entered, doing it galloping, puppy ears flopping.

Not long after, Olivia came in holding a shoe.

"You are correct," she announced haughtily. "He's fast. The name Whiz suits him." She shoved the shoe toward him, a shoe he now saw was chewed to shit. "I'm also correct. He's also a *punk*."

Whiz made a whining sound.

"He doesn't like Punk, baby," Nick told Liv something she knew because the dog spoke fucking English and whined every time that word was uttered in reference to him.

"Then he should stop being a punk, sweetheart," Liv shot back.

Another whine from Whiz.

"He's not a punk, he's a pup," Nick pointed out.

"The closet door was closed," she returned. "He's not only a puppy punk. He's a puppy *magician* punk."

Fuck.

He'd gone in to get a flannel to wear when he brought in wood and hadn't closed the closet door.

Liv read him and her hand dropped to her side as her eyes went to the ceiling.

"Nick," she snapped at the ceiling.

"I'll buy you another shoe." He grinned. "Two of them, if you're a good girl."

She returned her gaze to him. "You'll need to. This shoe," she shook it at him again, "isn't suitable to country living. But when we're back in Denver, I'll need it and the meager other selection I brought with me that didn't go up in smoke."

Taking in the strappy sandal that was minus a number of straps, some of a spike heel and a good deal of its sole, he mentally considered a visit to the vet as he advised, "Best to stock up for country living. Time we're in Denver, you won't need that many of those type of shoes."

"Sorry?"

He looked to her. "Does Whiz have half your shoe in his belly?"

"No, *Punk* decorated our bedroom floor with half this shoe so it's now in the garbage."

Thank Christ for that.

Whiz whined.

"Nick," she called.

He turned his attention back to her, straightening from the fireplace to take his feet.

"The time we're in Denver?" she asked.

"Yeah. We should think about when we can go back. A visit. Knight's gettin' impatient and Kasha's *definitely*—"

Her head tipped sharply to the side. "A visit?"

"A visit," he confirmed. "Maybe a week. But we gotta think of Whiz. Whether he comes with us, which means drivin' with a puppy, which might be the seventh circle of hell. Or he stays, which means we don't have him for very long and then we take off on him. I don't think that'd be cool. So we should wait a few weeks, a month, long as I can push it with Knight and Kash, and then not be gone too long."

She stared at him so long it was his turn to call, "Liv?"

"A visit," she said.

"Yeah, a visit," he reiterated. "What the fuck?" he asked when she kept staring at him.

"What about your Jag?" she asked.

"Jed is gonna drive it out. He's lookin' forward to it. He'll fly back. We got you your Lexus, so we don't need it. He can do it in the spring."

She didn't move and began again to stare at him.

"Jesus, Liv, what the fuck?" he asked.

When she spoke, her voice had changed. There was something in it he couldn't read.

"We're not moving back, are we?" she asked.

She thought they were moving back?

He'd bought that house, she knew that.

Her painting was there.

Whiz was there.

Liv was there and she loved it there.

"You wanted the mountains," he reminded her. "You wanted to be away from it all." He swung an arm out. "So we're here."

"Your business is in Denver. Your life is there. Your family—"

He cut her off. "You're here."

She snapped her mouth shut.

Whiz attacked the rug under the coffee table.

Nick went to his woman and wound his arms around her.

"You like it here?" he asked.

"I love it here," she answered.

"So we're stayin'."

"But—"

"We're stayin'."

"Nicky—"

He squeezed her.

She shut up.

"You get the perfect world, you don't leave it. You love it here. I love you. We live here."

She pressed her lips together but that didn't stop her eyes from getting bright with wet.

She unpressed them to ask, "What are you gonna do here?"

"We'll figure it out."

"What am *I* gonna do here?"

"We'll figure that out too."

"Your family—" she tried again.

"Livvie, we're in Tennessee, not Timbuktu."

She shut up again.

Then she quit shutting up. "I love you, Sebring."

He grinned.

"Back at you, Shade."

She smiled.

Then she stated, "I'm still calling our dog Punk."

Whiz whined.

Liv pressed into him and giggled.

Nick listened to her giggle, feeling her body moving against his.

Oh yeah.

They were staying here. He'd die a slow death by hamburger recipes, copious use of salad dressing and Olivia's driving need to add crumbled Reese's cups to every dessert she made here. He'd be anywhere and do anything that made Liv giggle, openly happy.

That said, he was not calling his dog Punk.

Livvie

I SAT ON Nick's knee.

"One, two, three…" I whispered into his ear, watching surreptitiously.

"It's still five, babe," Nick stated, sounding like he was smiling.

Five.

Yowsa.

Little Sylvie pushing that many out.

I watched her with the swaddle in her arms, holding it second nature, sitting and gabbing with Anya.

I turned my eyes back to the mayhem of our yard. Adults, but mostly kids, everywhere. Kids going crazy because their wedding gift from Nick and me were Nerf guns. Kids going crazy because it was way early and they'd had donuts for breakfast. Kids going crazy because Whiz liked kids (and showed it) but Whiz might like Nerf darts better (and showed that by trying to eat them, something Kat was in charge of making sure he did not do, a job she took very seriously if her stern eyes on our prancing puppy were anything to go by).

"Hanna and Raid gonna stop at three?" I asked.

"According to Hanna, yeah. Raid wants another baby girl," Nick answered.

"Cassidy and Deacon just the two?" I went on.

"Just the two girls. Like Knight and Anya, gonna stay that way, if you ask Deacon. Though Cassidy wants a boy. I had to guess, she'll be knocked up soon. Deacon doesn't say no to his woman very often."

I knew how that went.

I watched the mayhem, feeling a little bit guilty (but only a little bit) because I'd caused that mayhem, forcing these families to get up early, buying the kids' everlasting love through Nerf guns and unlimited access to a Labrador mutt puppy, all so I could marry Nick at dawn.

My eyes went back to Sylvie.

One day.

One day it'd be second nature to me too.

I sat in my simple (but elegant) strapless, chiffon wedding gown on Nick's knee, wondering—even if I'd lived through every second—how I got there.

How I found my way to happy.

It hit me.

I'd gone to a sex club and essentially jumped Nick.

On that thought, it started slow, just with my body shaking, but I didn't try to hold it back.

I didn't hold anything back anymore.

I didn't have to control it.

I was free to be me.

It built to chuckles, sitting on my husband's lap in my wedding gown on our wedding morning, laughter bubbling inside me.

"Shade," he called.

I didn't answer.

"Shade," he called again, this time on a squeeze.

I kept my gaze to the mayhem and again didn't answer.

"Baby," he called, lifting a hand to my chin and turning me to face him.

The instant my eyes hit blue, I corrected, "Sebring."

That blue lit like the ocean on a cloudless day, bright and sparkling.

And his voice rumbled through me, echoing how I felt at that moment, a way I'd feel for eternity—proud and happy—when he replied.

"Sebring."

This concludes The Unfinished Heroes series.
Thank you for reading.

ORLAND PARK PUBLIC LIBRARY

CPSIA information can be obtained at www.ICGtesting.com
Printed in the USA
LVOW12s1712260116

472354LV00003B/517/P